THE VICAR'S PASSION

HORACE DE SAINT-AUBIN
(HONORÉ DE BALZAC)

THE VICAR'S PASSION

*Translated from the French
by Ed Ford*

GREEN INTEGER

KØBENHAVN & LOS ANGELES

2006

GREEN INTEGER BOOKS
Edited by Per Bregne
København / Los Angeles

Distributed in the United States by Consortium Book
Sales and Distribution, 1045 Westgate Drive, Suite 90
Saint Paul, Minnesota 55114-1065
Distributed in England and Europe by
Turnaround Publisher Services
Unit 3, Olympia Trading Estate
Coburg Road, Wood Green, London N22 6TZ
44 (0)20 88293009

(323) 857-1115 / http://www.greeninteger.com
Green Integer
6022 Wilshire Boulevard, Suite 200A
Los Angeles, California 90036 USA

First Green Integer Edition 2006
This book was first published as *Le Vicaire des Ardennes*
by Horace de Saint-Aubin in 1822
English language edition copyright ©2006 by Ed Ford
Back cover copy ©2006 by Green Integer
All rights reserved

Design: Per Bregne
Typography: Kim Silva
Cover photograph: Drawing of Honoré de Balzac

LIBRARY OF CONGRESS CATALOGING IN PUBLICATION DATA
Honoré de Balzac [1799-1850]
The Vicar's Passion
ISBN: 1-933382-47-6
p. cm — Green Integer 150
I. Title II. Series III. Translator

Green Integer books are published for Douglas Messerli
Printed in the United States on acid-free paper.

Translator's Preface:
A Forgotten Classic

Balzac's *The Vicar's Passion,* first published in 1822 under the title *Le Vicaire des Ardennes* and the pseudonym Horace de Saint-Aubin, is a book whose time has finally arrived. At last, after all of these years, we can appreciate it as an important plea for free speech in an age of censorship, as an important step in the career of one of the greatest writers of all time, and as an important fictional achievement in its own right. It has suspense, humor, vividly drawn characters, exotic locales, and a controversial subject matter which caused it to be banned shortly after its initial publication.

Today we are used to seeing headlines about priest sex scandals, and we like to applaud ourselves for being open and frank in dealing with them; however, it is hard to imagine just how far ahead of its time this vigorous tale was. Literary critic Raymond

Trousson commented that "in this novel, it was not only the speeches, but the situations, which must have annoyed people with orthodox tastes" (*Balzac: disciple et juge de Jean-Jacques Rousseau*. Geneva: Droz, 1983. 80). Everything about the novel would have been offensive to the Catholic Church which would remain the official state church of France until 1905. Critic Arlette Michel observed that the *Vicar* is "a novel of crimes and of the horrors of love" (*Le Mariage et l'amour dans l'oeuvre romanesque d'Honoré de Balzac*. Lille-Paris: Champion, 1975. I, 77).

The standard view of Balzac's early fiction is that it is dreadfully bad. This opinion is so wide-spread that it is taken for a fact by people who have never opened one of his early books to judge for themselves. However, the eminent authority on French nineteenth-century literature and Balzac biographer Graham Robb did read the novel and was impressed. He commented that this book is "the real basis of Balzac's fortune" *(Balzac.* New York: W.W. Norton, 1994. 104). By causing a scandal Balzac scored a *success d'estime* which got his name publicized and caused an eager public to buy up the sequel that was published shortly thereafter. Graham Robb goes on to comment that the *Vicar* "for a few memorable pages, introduced an entirely new tone into the French novel" (105). Written with a warm love for humanity, a fine sense of dramatic timing, and a great deal of humor, this book is a major achievement that does not deserve to remain neglected.

Tucked away in his Parisian garret Balzac was determined to keep writing until he made a success of himself. In November 1819 he sent a despairing, but characteristically energetic, letter to his sister Laure: "Ah Laure my sister! How I have trials and tribulations, I am a martyr and I am petitioning the Pope for the first available pedestal that needs a saint on it" (Balzac, Honoré de. *Correspondance*. I. Paris: Garnier, 1960. 58). In the years that followed his sister married and became Laure Surville while Balzac made his first publications under an improbable pseudonym. At the end of January or early February 1822 his spirits were looking up as he thought of all of the writing that he planned to do that year. He wrote:

In just a little, Lord R'Hoone will be the man of

the times, the most fertile author, the most lovable man, the women will love him like the apple of their eyes and all that stuff, and then the little hound named Honoré will arrive in style, his head high, his eyes proud, his wallet full. At his approach they will murmur with that flattering murmur, and they will say that he is the brother of Madame Surville!... Then, the men, women, children, and prenatal babies will kick up their heels, and I will have a host of good fortune. (Corr. 133).

On August 11, 1822, Balzac signed a double contract for *Le Centenaire* formerly known as *Le Savant,* and for *The Vicar's Passion.* The contract stipulated that he was to receive 2,000 francs for *Le Centenaire* once it was submitted, and to submit the *Vicar* by November first when he would get the first installment of 300 francs. This contract helped to alleviate Balzac's debts, but there was one problem. He had not written the *Vicar* yet.

He had been planning to co-author with his sister.

Balzac's correspondence contains an impassioned plea written on August 14, 1822 to his sister: "Send me *The Vicar of the Ardennes!*" (199) He goes on to state that he has a contract for two novels by the "First of October. The first is *Le Savant,* the second, the *Vicar*" (199). Apparently when writing to his sister he advanced the date that the *Vicar* was due at the publishers by a month in the hope that his sister would send what she had written soon and give him more time to work on it. He was also in a rush because his sometime collaborator Auguste Lepoitevin had told him that he was also planning on writing a novel about a vicar which he had not started yet.

Even though Balzac asked his sister to mail him the novel, he states that he will "redo" the entire work:

> So we have the month of September to do the *Vicar.* I think that it will be impossible for you to write two chapters a day so that I can have the *Vicar* by the 15th of September, which would only leave me 15 days to reformulate it. What do

you think?... I hope that you, Laure and Surville, that you see the infernal need of money that made me sacrifice our idea of doing the *Vicar* together. But on that score, I did something advantageous in that you are sure to sell your novels to Pollet. As soon I have received the manuscripts of the *Vicar,* I will send you the outline of the novel explained clearly, and I think that it will be on the generative idea that Laure had about the Bookseller. (…) This awful work is impossible for you Laure. I do not think that you can write 60 pages of a novel per day. What is more, if you could, if you respond that you will send me the novel by the 15th of September, do it, but understand that the if on the 17th of September I do not have the manuscript, I will start work on it, and you know that for Pollet one can write a novel in a month (200-1).

This letter shows that he intends to revise what his sister sends him, and that if necessary he will write the whole thing himself. It also alludes to his sister's ambitions for writing her own novels. If the opening of the *Vicar* is any indication of her work, then she was a woman of some talent. A mere six days later he wrote to her on August 20, 1822:

> Earth, sky, sea! Dear sister, you are putting me in a terrible situation, Auguste is writing a *Vicar*, mine has been sold, Pollet is awaiting its arrival, because he needs to bring to press the part that is written; I will write it as they are printing it (203).

He begs her to "place the manuscripts in two or three pieces of grey paper," (203) and states "I am coming back during the month of September to turn in the end of the *Ardennes* and the *Centenaire* and claim my money" (204). Even though Laure has written the start of the novel, he is revising the whole thing. He states: "I will have to do the *Vicar* while they print it and correct the *Savant* on the galleys" (204).

Apparently what Laure sent him was just the first of the four parts which was all that she had time to write for he states:

> The *Vicar!* The *Vicar!* The *Vicar!* The *Vicar!* by return mail. Because I am going to work on it. I will start the second volume. Goodbye. Your hand in mine, no one is listening, we are two friends, send me the *Vicar* (205).

This passage would seem to indicate that he wants to keep Laure's participation in the project a secret, but it is a secret no longer, and we can now recognize his sister as a fine woman author. Despite Laure's contribution to the novel, when their mother wrote to her on August 30, 1822, she referred to it as Balzac's work and not hers: "His *Vicar* is positively his best work, you will be, I think, quite happy" (206). That his mother had read some or all of the manuscript shows that the launching of Balzac's career was a family affair for which he took credit, only fair since he did most of the work. There is no abrupt stylistic change after the first volume, so we may assume that Balzac successfully incorporated his sister's chapters into his larger work.

I was first told of the existence of neglected Balzac by a now retired artist's representative in San Francisco in 1999. Aware of the bad reputation of the early Balzac, I was hesitant to bother reading any of it at all. Just finding a copy of the book was hard enough. However, he encouraged me to give it a try and repeated his exhortations for the next two years, and when I finally did read the *Vicar* I was charmed. I enjoyed the masterful descriptions and the humor of the first two volumes, but from the moment the pirate Argow appeared, I was hooked. It took me two years to translate the book since I was working on other projects at the same time, and then I began circulating it to publishers. A New York press that passed on it recommended that I try Green Integer in Los Angeles. I followed up the lead, the book was accepted, and the 2006 publication of the first translation of this important, witty, dramatic, adventurous, and controversial work of creative fiction became a reality. *Le Vicaire des Ardennes,* translated under the title *The Vicar's Passion,* is now readily available for the first time in its history, which lets us put another feather in Balzac's already bountiful cap as we enjoy a lost classic whose day in the sun has finally arrived.

EDWARD FORD
Lexington, Massachusetts
May 2005

The Vicar's Passion

PREFACE
which you should read if you can.

Because people may criticize this work, and because people surely will criticize it, I declare that I am young, without experience, and without any knowledge of the French language, even though I have a bachelor of arts...Perhaps my critics will not be wrong in saying that this work shows ability along with the aberrations of a twenty year-old imagination and despite the stylistic flaws which are found in it... But I have reserved for these critics a blow which they were not expecting, namely, that this work is not by me. In truth, if I were the author of this work, then I would have taken care not to have attached a preface to it, for I have too much self-respect to write even a single word knowing that it will not be read.

With the petty critics put off by my frank confession, I address myself to the reasonable segment of the public, that is to say, to those who have the good sense to read me, to those whom the delirium of politics has not seized, and who, devouring good novels with joy, escape from life and cast themselves into the ideal world that has been created by a capable author, and who in so doing alleviate their sorrows by living only with imaginary beings who please them, or who sometimes annoy them, because no one is perfect, even in the world of novels.

It is to this *class* (notice the word) of readers that I address myself, and I have reserved the explanation of the enigma that was contained in the first lines of this preface for them. I will be sincere, I will have the courage to confess all of my wrongs and to appear at the censor's court which corrects the opinion of the readers of novels by asking for their indulgence when they are speaking of me…But, as we will be knowing each other for quite a while, since I have thirty more books to publish, I think that we can say our truths to one another without fear.

I am sad and subject to nervous conditions. A doctor friend of mine assures me that I am a very big hypochondriac…You will cry out and say that it is conceited to instruct the public about what I do or do not have...Are you a great enough man that your maladies are of interest? It is amusing that at the age of twenty an unknown author has come to usurp the rights that a genius only is granted at his death... Patience? The scope of my fears will explain to you how I cannot live with anybody, how I find everybody low, corrupt, how none of the government ministers suit me, and how each one seems to be irritating, mean, and sorrowful. I have friends who pretend that people avoid me because I have all the faults that I assign to others; but this is surely untrue, because I am the most accessible and accommodating of men. I am not envious, even though a man of letters; I am poor and do not wish for anything, except for a little glory and a little money.

All this explains how, in the end, I was hidden away in Père Lachaise Cemetery, led by my fears, according to my doctor, and out of disgust with humanity, according to myself. In Père Lachaise I hoped to find virtuous men of loveable ways!...I found something quite different!...

At first I only saw creatures with all sorts of accomplishments. On the tombstones the world seemed turned upside down: each wife was faithful; all the mothers adored; all the children born of their lawful fathers; and the most ceremonious superlatives were given to butchers, merchants, bakers, tailors, masons, etc...so that for the men that France admires most one could not put on the marble anything but *Masséna! Jacques Delille! Evariste Parny! Méhul!* The masons have taken all these people in. In the end, each piece of earth covers a celestial flower, or encloses a phoenix which, happily for its heirs, cannot be reborn; no woman is bitter or flighty; men are excellent and furnished with excellent certificates of good morals. It is another world entirely; one in which a peace, a calm and admirable decency reigns supreme. In praise of human nature I declare that after a demanding inquiry, I saw only one doubtful epitaph. It reminded me of what happened to the Duc d'Ossone when he visited the galleys and interviewed all of the oarsmen who each told him their stories in such a manner that in each of their cases justice had commited a gross error. He saw only one man who abashedly confessed his sin.

"Have them take away this rogue before he corrupts these honest men!..." the duke cried.

I noticed big footmen with sad expressions who, by the orders of their sensible mistresses, brought the widows' offerings, and set down the branches of the Immortals by proxy; I do not know if they also cried by proxy or *on command*.

In the end, I walked with a true pleasure amid those archives of death, and I found all the tranquility and freedom that makes life lovable. I did not quarrel with anyone, they all took my remarks well; none of them rose up from their tombs to reproach my innocent sarcasms; and, except for a few statues which the sculptor had arranged so that they were looking crosswise at me, I was going to leave convinced of the kindness of my hosts, then I saw a young man not far from Héloïse's tomb. As I had gone without human company for about three days, I frankly confess that I examined this Christian with the attention which one gives to the sample of cloth which one is going to be forced to wear.

Here my crime begins; now you will see all the

curiosity that caused the fall of our mother Eve unfold itself in one of her children with a truly diabolical strength; and yet, you yourself who read *this* present piece of prose should confess that you also wish to get to know this young man: and this is the first reason why I am absolved.

I stole up to him lightly, and I saw that he was sitting on one of those portable stools that are made with a walking stick. I concluded that he liked to sit, and I presumed that his pain was not deep. Soon I noticed that he had a considerable mass of papers on his knees and that he was hastily rummaging through them.

When I saw this, I thought that he was one of our artists sketching our monuments and contemplating death. Emboldened by this idea, I quickly drew forward...People have always said that my face is lacking grace and even my most intimate friends claim that if they met me at the corner of the woods, they would flee: I confess that if I met myself I might do the same thing; but, whatever the case may be, the result of my hastened movement and the friendly laugh that I had prepared was that they caused the honest young man suddenly to retreat.

Taking command of the locale, I looked around. I saw a little, marble column on which was written "*soon.*" This inscription completely changed my thinking. The earth around the modest tomb did not have that freshness which is a sign of the worship that we lavish on sepulchres. It was trampled, there were no flowers on this last resting place, the small, obligatory fence did not go around it...No, everything indicated a wild grief, without luxury, without affectation, whose sorrow bore no disguise. Then, I thought that perhaps this young man was promising more than he could deliver.

As I drew back, I saw him return, quite disturbed by my visit, he leaned on the marble, raked a hand through his hair and began writing. What astonished me the most was that he was not sighing, nor crying, nor biting his nails; only he glanced at me every now and then and finally grew accustomed to my presence. I made use of the times when he was writing to draw closer to him, and, little by little, I succeeded in getting just three steps away from him. I sat on the grass, and I resolved to insinuate myself into his confidence in order to learn what he was writing, because all of this seemed strangely novelesque to me. Then, I advanced by an imperceptible movement of my buttocks, so well that without his saying a single word, we found ourselves side by side.

No sooner had the unknown man noticed me, than he got up and fled for a second time. Judging that I had done enough for a first try, I left, but I was resolved to return.

The next day I went back to the cemetery, where I alone went in. I ran!…You can imagine my astonishment when, arriving at the tomb from the day before, I found the young man still writing with the same rapidity, but pale, his eyes downcast, and his hair wet with dew. Had he spent the night here? How? Why?…

It became evident to me that his story must surely be quite interesting, I did not try to understand the strangeness of such a fact, but, by a lucky guess, I judged that I had before me an unhappy man. A most vivid compassion took hold of my heart, and I will have the frankness to admit that in this compassion was contained the desire to read his manuscript.

Taking up the most anodyne sound for my voice, I said to the stranger, "Monsieur, you seem deeply moved?...May I be of service in some way? I have a bachelor's degree in literature."

"No."

This *"no"* was slightly flattering, despite the severe tone with which it was pronounced, because at least the young man had spoken to me. At this moment, the stranger's feather pen fell to earth, I picked it up, and gave it back to him with all the grace that nature provided me with, and I succeeded in getting a rather friendly movement of the head.

Reduced to a passive role, I contented myself with it, and, like those dogs which follow the morsel that their master holds on his fork with their eyes so that they escort it with their sparkling gaze until it has disappeared, so I followed the hand of the young man as it moved from one end of the page to the other, or when it dipped for ink. I tried to understand what strange story could cause a man to write out in the open, rather than in his warm room on a convenient table, when suddenly the young man drew a rather strong line at the end of the page which he clutched; then he rolled the entire thing up in a sheet of paper. Once this was done, he got off his stool, sat on the ground, and leaning his head against the marble and crossing his hands, he closed his eyes and did not move. He had a handsome face, and his noble pose was a pleasure to look at.

But all of his actions had an original style to them that was too similar to madness, too similar to the ways of the men whom France has honored for the last ten years for me to remain idle. I said to him warmly:

"Young man, will you listen? There are times when the battered and weakened soul draws back from the weight of human misery; at times the flower of life loses its delicious smell; it suffices for a few cold reflections to knock us from atop that ideal throne that has been constructed by a brilliant imagination; but, night fathers day, pain fathers pleasure, winter makes the spring more enjoyable, so come out of your affliction, cast it off like a coat that is too heavy…"

At the sound of these harmonious tropes, he raised his eyelids and responded to me, "By grace, Monsieur the Bachelor, do not stifle me, and let me die in peace."

"Die!" I cried casting myself upon him, and seizing him by the pocket in which the manuscript was contained, "Die, my dear sir, what are you thinking?…"

"How do you expect me to live, when my soul is there!" and he indicated the marble against which he was leaning. Joyfully I noticed that this movement caused the manuscript to slip out of his pocket.

"Oh, Monsieur, live without your soul, there are so many people who do not have one, you can be like them!…"

"*My friend,*" he continued just as I put my hand on his papers, "death is gentle to the unhappy."

"*Monsieur, my friend,* though such unhappiness may be! It is very nice to live: existence is a weight, so be it! But it is very nice to carry it, and without the humans who attack from both sides, it would be even more…"

"Water, water!…"

The manuscript fell to the ground.

"What is wrong?…" I asked him as I took up the roll of paper.

"I am dying of hunger…and…I want, I want to die. Goodbye Melanie, goodbye mother!…"

Without hesitating any longer, I took the manuscript and went to get the help that would arrive too late. When I came back I found the unhappy young man dead, his mouth was full of the grass that he had tried to suck in vain, his fingernails were dug into the earth, his positioning betrayed a violent convulsion and his mouth was stuck to a woman's portait. I quickly took this charming miniature painting, not the watch and chain which were of pure gold, but because I presumed that this portrait was of some importance to this handsome young man's story. His death struck me strangely: what consoled me was that he absolutely wanted to die, and that, even if I had arrived earlier, he would have refused everything.

Drawing away, I saw a two horse carriage arriving at a great gallop. This carriage had the heraldic of a marquis on the side. A woman rushed out crying, "Save my son!…Save my son!…"

I did not think that it was wise for me to be present at this meeting.

So the young man had a mother!…Perhaps, on this pretext, some censor might contest the legacy that I had just appropriated. I will have him notice that:

First, this young man had called me his friend.

Secondly, this benevolence indicated his intention of willing me the manuscript, because this sort of manuscript is only confided to friends.

Third, intention is reputed to be fact. And finally, how would his mother have acted? She would have destroyed the portrait, she would have torn up the manuscript, since she would not have spared anything in her pain, and all of France would be bereft of this literary production.

I read the manuscript. I recognized that never before had such an interesting story been published. So I showed it to a very honest publisher in my section of Paris. The amount that he offered me was seductive, but he warned me that he could not publish the manuscript unless a man of letters put his hand to it; so, looking at him with the noble pride that accompanies a modest talent, I told him, "I have a bachelor's degree in literature."

Well, you can imagine how this fact was indispensible. It means that what you are about to read is only too true, and that it is a diamond in the rough which I have polished, mounted, and allowed to shine. The bad things that you are going to find in it must be ascribed to the account of the dead man, and if there is any good in it, then please attribute it, I beg you, to this young holder of a bachelor of arts degree.

You will notice how much effort is needed to guess, merely by the strength of one's imagination, all that the young man's manuscript does not say, and to make use of his story in such a way as to form a dramatic work of its plot, characters, etc.

It is true that fate willed it that I still had, at that time, some money, because the pockets of bachelors of arts are often empty, and I employed my little nest egg to go on foot to Aulnay-le-Vicomte. There, I informed myself of the circumstances which the young man omitted, and I set his work in a frame that, without wanting to praise myself, I do not doubt that you will be able to appreciate.

It is understood that the publisher did not reimburse me for my traveling expenses although the trip was taken in everyone's interest, so I beg you who will have the goodness to read me, to set this work on the flattering road to a second edition: that is the only way to prevent the complete financial ruin of a poor holder of a bachelor of arts degree who is making his first attempts at commercial literature.

In closing this friendly interview with my judges, I beg you to forgive me for having introduced you to my own personal undertakings, and I recommend one last time that you have courage, patience, and above all that you give me your friendship; and as for my friendship? You will be sure to have it upon the publication of the second edition; and if you wonder how I will express my literary affection for you, then you only need to try to do so yourself!...And then, in response, I will publish: *Le Traversin ou Mémoires se-crets d'un Ménage; le Fiancé de la Mort; Mon Cousin Vieux-Pont; Le Bâtard; les Conspirateurs;* and *les Gondoliers de Venise.*

H. SAINT-AUBIN

BACHELOR OF ARTS OF THE ROYAL

UNIVERSITY OF FRANCE

ILE-SAINT-LOUIS, SEPTEMBER 30, 1822

CHAPTER ONE

Everything was in motion in the village of Aulnay which was situated beside the Ardennes forest: the bell resounded with mighty strokes which were of such strength and rapidity that they spoke honorably of the beadle's arm. Most of the village men leaned against the doors of their huts, looking, without saying anything, towards the entrance of the hamlet, while the women who were talking to each other, either from one side of the road to the other or from their windows, would have made even the most feelingless stoic curious. Their conversations revolved around the youth, spirit, height, and conduct of the expected person. In the end, numerous groups of peasants seemed to be discussing something important, and each, better dressed than they would usually be for a simple Sunday service, waited for the last moment of the mass so as not to miss being witness to the installation of the young vicar sent by the bishop of A...y.

The most knowledgeable, that is to say those who read well, proudly carried hereditary prayer books with worn and dirty edges.

Nothing could be easier than justifying the murmur of the conversations, the thick laughter of the peasants, and the expectant air imprinted on all the faces on the occasion of an event which at first might appear to be very simple.

In truth, the commune of Aulnay-le-Vicomte, although the regional capitol, was self-contained, and well separated from the neighboring villages by three uninhabited leagues of land; but, I leave it to your imagination to see if these eight hundred good souls confined in their solitary valley did not have good reason to torment one another because someone else was arriving; and, above all, because this person arrived provided with an authority that was difficult to place in the hierarchy of rustic powers. Also, the ministerial body of the place had assembled spontaneously in the church square so as to be able to comment on the bishop's decision that had been so unexpected and so remarkable in the annals of the commune.

To give an idea of the effect that was produced in the village by this decree of episcopal power, we shall introduce the reader into the center of this crowd of the strongest willed people of the region. The most imposing character was the mayor, M. Gradavel, who was also the village grocer who had been elevated in 1814 to his lofty position. He fondly caressed the remains of an old, white, Florentine robe from which he had created a sash; all of Madame Gravadel's imagination had been needed to make this rag respectable, although one might think that this rag could be an ornament or a sign of decrepitude. The entire village had seen the remains of the robe, in M. Gradaval's window, the day that the king returned. The dull face of this functionary of Aulnay announced its morality like the sugar breads which were the trademark of his store and which indicated his profession. Around him were found the satellites of municipal power, that is to say the forest warden adorned by his badge and his clean clothes, and the postman of the small post office in his big costume.

Not far from this administrative trio was M. Engerbee, the fattest farmer in the village, and Marcus

Tullius Leseq, the schoolmaster and teacher of the farmer's son, and they seemed to be leaning against each other. In the middle was found M. Lecorneur, the tax collector, who had intertwined his fingers over his big belly, and was talking with an adjunct who had been mayor in 1815; while the judge, wearing his robe and with his head covered with his checked hat, walked around the group trying not to be on the right, on the left, or in the center.

At last, a few members of the commune walked around as if to discover what the haphazard council was talking about and catch a few snatches of conversation which would determine their politics.

"Yes, Messieurs, I maintain," cried out Marcus Tullius Leseq, in a voice which he tried in vain to soften as he larded his sentences with Latin which created an unintended comic effect, "the Monseigneur only sent us a vicar because Monsieur Gausse does not know Latin: no matter what they say, I was the one who informed Monseigneur the Bishop; the fact is too well known to need to be told. Just the other day, *olim,* for a marriage, *pro matrimonio,* he would have begun the libera which means 'take it away!' because it is in the imperative, if I had not stopped him!...If you want me to say *libentur* to you, that is to say, my heart in my hand, I believe that he was drunk, not *forte* but *piano*, lightly, as Cicero says."

In pronouncing the name of Cicero, the schoolmaster took off his worn hat and bowed. (Despite the disfavor which might result for the schoolmaster, we will have the courage to attest that Leseq, who before the Revolution was named Jean-Baptiste, profited from that period of anarchy to change his last name from Welches and to take on the glorious first names of the Roman orator Marcus Tullius Cicero.)

"From that," he continued, "you can tell that Monseigneur the Bishop had to give Monsieur Gausse, a vicar, more to watch over his conduct than to help him, because the priesthood, *summus pontifex,* is not such a heavy burden..."

"What the devil, M. Marcus Tullius, you have to be of good faith," replied M. Lecorneur, who dined quite often with M. Gausse, the curate; "Monsieur Gausse does not merit such an affront; he does his job quite well; his morals are irreproachable, and for the thirty years that I have been here, the curate has never allowed a single mention of his contributions to be made. Have you ever seen him look a woman in the face? And isn't Marguerite at a ripe age?...You should know full well that Latin does not make one a genius."

"No more than Barême!..." replied Leseq, the schoolmaster.

"At least I have never bragged about my knowledge!...You cannot reproach me for that," replied M. Lecorneur, "Even though I know the *measures,* I have never bragged about it! But, to get back to the curate, the pieces of Latin which you fatten your sentences with are certainly not worth the excellent proverbs that he gives us in good old French. They are wise; everyone understands them, and they often take the place of sermons. To finish, and to respond to the charge that the priesthood is not such a heavy burden, M. Tullius, I will point out to you that we have here eight hundred people to baptize, confess, marry, and bury; that M. Gausse is seventy, that he is infirm, that he asked for the helper; and so, if, in the end, they sent him one, what is so extraordinary about that? This vicar is young, that is understand-able. They do not send an old man to help out an old man!…"

"All of that is fine and dandy," said the mayor in a doctoral tone; "but you are mistaken in your *conjectures.* If they sent us a vicar, it is for the sake of M. Gausse who gave an oath, and…"

At these words the postman and the forest warden made approving motions with their heads which seemed to say, "I was there."

M. Lecorneur, overcome by the weight of this highly political reasoning, remained mute.

Marcus Tullius Leseq, the curate's enemy, tried to carry off a final blow, "If M. Gausse's words are pure, then it is not his fault; it is *invitus,* as Cicero says, and we know why! And for the rest, he does himself ill with his love of food, *vino et inter pocula!*"

The judge threw oil on the fire by adding, "It is truly a shame that we have an incapable curate, be-cause a vicar is a burden to the community, and my poor clerk may well be lost. If the coming news is taken up by the councilor, he will extinguish the just arguments and sacrifice his legitimate rights to everyone so as not to complain, which is evidently against the standard format and the spirit of justice which wants everyone to have their due."

"*Cui que tribuere suum jus,*" added Tullius.

The adjunct, who was stripped of his position as mayor in 1815, took up the thread, "So what are you complaining about?...The community, isn't it rich enough to pay for a vicar? Unless its revenues have gone up," he said (casting a glance at his successor). "But all that has not been said very well. I see what it is about, you are ambitious and greedy for power. What of it! Just because M. Gausse is richer than you, is that a reason to denounce him? He eats and drinks well, you say. By God, everyone has his job; has he ever buried a living person instead of a dead one?... Has he refused to come to a baptismal meal or to bless our marriages even if they are a little late?...But he is welcomed at the castle and you are not..."

"What do you mean?" cried out the mayor-grocer, "hasn't Madame the Marquise already invited me a couple of times?"

"Yes, to ask you to repair the road leading to the

castle," replied the adjunct bitterly.

"And a third time for Saint-Louis' day, and we ate there, my wife and I," replied the mayor.

"Whatever, your thinking about the young vicar's arrival does not show any common sense; the Bishop refused one six years ago when I was mayor, and more recently still, M. Gausse reiterated his demand, which was no longer heard: that all goes to prove that there are other, secret causes, important and political ones perhaps, since they say that the Jesuits are coming back. Read the papers, and you will see the state of European politics..."

M. Lecorneur seeing that he had support, defended the curate once again; he addressed the mayor, astonished by the fate of his vindictive predecessor, saying, "In the end, Monsieur the Mayor, isn't M. Gausse the one who buys the most coffee, sugar, and chocolate from you?..."

"That is true," responded the mayor-grocer.

"Doesn't Marguerite buy two dresses a year?..."

"Yes."

"Don't you furnish the cloth and the fabric of the curate's soutanes?..."

"That is also true."

"His noodles, pepper, olives, Saint-Vincent, oil, candles; don't you alone sell them all to him?..."

"And I dare say that there is no reason to repent, since I have never deceived him, either in weight, or in quality of merchandise; *because,* even though in the decimal system there is no longer a half pound since the division has been arranged otherwise, so that...you see...there are about five quarters to the pound, and..."

The mayor's mind never allowed him to complete a long sentence or explain things clearly; he looked at Tullius, who in turn, used to such signs of distress, provided the conclusion.

"And M. Gravadel would have considerably lost in his negotiations, *négotia,* if the five decagrams had not evenly replaced the four quarters of the old system."

"That's what I meant," said the mayor, "We did not gain by it."

Leseq the teacher ended this trivial digression, by crying out, "It is as if our five cents could only buy us yesterday's sun!" And, seizing M. Gravadel by the loosest button on his coat, made him doubly distressed by saying, "Isn't it true, to get back to M. Gausse, that he could have shopped at the new grocer in town?"...

"Never, Monsieur Teacher, because James Stilder is not well supplied. He makes poor liqueurs, wets his salt, bloats his rice, and mixes chickory in with his ground coffee; I know that for a fact, I know the factory where he gets it..."

"That may be," replied Lecorneur, "and M. Gausse only does what he needs to in shopping at your place, but you will admit that, on the other hand, he scarcely gives a dinner to which you are not invited."

"That is true."

"Even today, aren't we all supposed to go to the vicar's installation dinner?..."

"They left me out," said Marcus Tullius Leseq with disdain.

"There are good reasons for that," replied the tax collector.

"Yes," added the Mayor, well aware of his bias against the curate; "you Tullius, the subordinate of M. Gausse, you..."

"You have no affection for him," said Lecorneur; "you burden him with the weight of your erudition, with your Latin."

"That is true," continued the mayor-grocer, "but your pride could be lowered; the sub-prefect, on his last visit, said that usury was forbidden."

"But," Lecorneur added, "you are the mayor's secretary, schoolmaster, first bard, market collector, and…"

"That makes four jobs, if I count correctly," M. Gradavel, the mayor, continued, "and if you do not watch out for your bosses, you could well…"

"Lose them," said the teacher.

At these words, and to the fright of Tullius, M. Gradavel, calming down, added, "I know that you are very useful to me for writing, but just because of that you need not think that you are an eagle; I would have preferred to see you with your Latin repairing the local roads."

"Ah! Do tell!" said the farmer who up until then had not said a word; "you used the thousand francs so well that my gray horse almost stayed stuck in a badly filled marl pit."

Tullius had too much to be careful about with the mayor and M. Engerbé to say another word; he remained impassive.

"The fact is that they could have repaired them better," cried out the former mayor rising up onto the tips of his toes and stroking his chin.

The mayor-grocer's sparkling eyes showed storm, but the good teacher deflected them. Then, Lecorneur said to Leseq, "I would also have like to see what good Cicero would have done with the accounts of the forced lending when the allies went through!"

M. Engerbé, seeing the teacher of his son vexed by these sarcasms, replied, "It is true that you made out very well for yourself, Monsieur Lecorneur, at that time, or about then, that your income grew, and that you bought your house, but that is not a reproach, each to his own task!"

"Yes," said Leseq, *cui que suae clitellae,* to each his own clientele."

"But where is this young vicar going to live?" asked the judge.

"In the presbytery," responded Gravadel.

"They could take his lodgings out of the discretionary fund," the tax collector observed.

"We have a big enough burden," cried the farmer.

"Messieurs," said Marcus Tullius, strutting into the middle of the group, "do you want me to uncover the real reason why our fine young vicar is arriving?"

"Very well?" the mayor, the adjunct, the tax collector, and the farmer asked all at once.

"Very well," said Leseq, "can't you see that Madame the Marquise de Rosann has succeeded in placing one of her protégés; she does not often have company when she is so far from Paris, you see!... And we all know that M. Gausse does not know the game well enough to take part!..."

Marcus Tullius was never so happy as when he said something mean; he would have given anything for a nice jab; poor and expecting the world from his superiors, he immolated them, without pity, under the blows of his tongue, but his meanness never went beyond words.

While the good men of Aulnay-le-Vicomte spoke like this, M. Gausse the curate was quite embarrassed. A simple letter on the part of the bishopric of

A…y had told him that the fourth of May, M. Joseph, a young, newly ordained seminarian, would come and help him by assuming the august functions that the title of vicar implied, and that they should install him with pomp and dignity. The bishop regretted that the dangerous situation in which he found himself kept him from presiding at the ceremony for which he named three curates from the region to replace him.

The curate felt that the term *"young seminarian"* had been sown throughout the village by his servant, Marguerite, who did not fail to frame this epithet with a wide margin of comments and conjectures which piqued their curiosity.

In the end, for two days, Marguerite, assisted by the oldest of the choir boys, had swept and cleaned the presbytery with the greatest care: the dust which had seemed like a veritable decoration was fought with such tenacity that it flew off of places which were previously thought to be inaccessible. Everything became shining like gold. The servant whirled about the kitchen before the five lighted fires. Food arrived and each person, in bringing some, cast an eye on Marguerite's preparations; after the glance they gave a word of advice, and this advice led to a chat in which the good Marguerite never declined to take her part.

The curate, since the morning, had taken a half-hour to come down to his only library, the one in the basement, to search out and select his best wine and liqueurs.

Once these preparations were finished, calm reigned in the presbytery for an hour while Marguerite, sitting in the kitchen by the chimney, rested on her laurels.

"Marguerite?" cried the curate from the back of his room, in which the windows were garnished with old curtains of red lampas, "Marguerite?"

"Here I am!…"

"Are the decorations ready?"

"Yes, Monsieur."

"Show me, my child; so that I can see this joyous spectacle."

The good old man, having just reached the rotundity of a lectern prelate in his old shepherd's cloak of red Utrecht velour needed the help of the plump hands of his fat and fresh servant in order to get up. Marguerite led him towards the dining room that was decorated with old paper with green floral designs on it.

The curate's vest of black velour never reached down to his wide pants, so his shirt, revealing itself in this little interval, broke his uniformity of color. This little observation gives you an idea of the neglect of his attire. M. Gausse's face was in harmony with this negligence: without being too red, it had an honorable color; his blue eyes, filled with angelic gentleness, were the sure sign of an excellent heart, and the limpidity of their crystals never allowed him to disguise a single one of his candid soul's many thoughts.

The goodness displayed on his face was tempered by a shade of joy and satisfaction which proved that the curate had nothing to reproach himself for, and that he was a man *according to the heart of God* who did not worry at all about the why or the how of life, nor of everybody else's mysteries; having chosen the good side of existence and not bothering anyone.

His features became animated, and his lips drew back a little towards his nose at the sight of the fine white linen which covered the table set with a thick paté, cold fowl, etc…but, noticing the array of bottles that Marguerite had placed on a small serving stand beside his place at the table, his laugh became more pronounced, his eyes happier, and looking at Marguerite with a gaze of approbation, he passed his hand under her chin, which in turn made her smile, be it from a memory, or from happiness.

"Ah! Ah! My child, don't you think that it looks nice?"

"Very nice, Monsieur!"

"The coffee, Marguerite, is it ready?"

"It is ground, pressed, and dripping."

"You set the vicar's place beside mine?"

"Yes, Monsieur: it is right here."

"Aie, aie!" This exclamation was caused by a sciatic pain which afflicted the curate. "Ah! Marguerite," he said, "the pitcher goes into water so often that it ends up breaking!…I am not well, but he who knows how to live, knows how to die."

"Ah! What do you have that is so bad that it gives you a right to complain?"

"Ah! My daughter, I have too many years behind

me," he continued with a hearty smile, "Like those moments of sun that shine in winter; you see my white hair, Marguerite; it is true that a crazy man's head never whitens, and like a good grip is worth two that you might have, I would rather be at the end of my career than have to begin it all over again: into the bottom of the well I am falling!..."

"Monsieur," said Marguerite, "don't talk about all that, it makes me sad, and I would rather not think that you are going to die..."

"Marguerite, you cannot say to the fountain: 'I will not drink your water;' time passes and death comes. I like sleeping well enough, and after all, maybe death is just a dreamless sleep...Why be afraid?...The Indians say: 'It is better to be sitting than standing, lying than sitting, but it is better to be dead than anything else!...'"

"You can laugh now, Monsieur, but when one dies, one would still like to live a little!..."

"Habit is a second nature," said the curate, "but, in the end, as long as I die among friends, so long as I smell the bouquet of a good wine from *Nights,* and Marguerite closes my eyes, I will give my soul to

God, such as he gave it to me, not more or less; he will send it where he will, and what he does will be well done…"

There was a moment of silence: Marguerite looked at the old man with tender eyes as he contemplated heaven with a sublime expression of good nature and simplicity.

"Listen, Marguerite," said the curate in a low voice, "I did not ask Marcus Tullius to come, because he always criticizes me, and I must keep a certain decorum in front of my vicar; but he is poor!…Well my child, tonight, without anyone seeing, you will bring him a big slice of paté, a bottle of good wine, and whatever is still presentable of the fowl."

"Poor dear man! Always the same!…" cried Marguerite, while her master went from chair to chair, to cork a bottle whose cork had popped off.

"Marguerite, does anyone in town know the young vicar?"

"No Monsieur."

"Alas! my child, we will have to hope that he is a good young man; because if he were otherwise, he might criticize the poor people for their dancing, and the little faults that are bound up with their nature. If he is too rigid, then I will be in trouble!..."

"Monsieur, if he is young, then you can teach him."

"That is true, Marguerite, hot wax is easily imprinted."

"And then, if he is young!..." with these words Marguerite looked at herself in the mirror, neatened her hair and a sudden redness suffused her face while the curate looked at her, because the naive tone in which she had uttered these words of hope, did not cause M. Gausse to doubt for a moment, and even if he had doubted, the sum total of the flirtatiousness which governed Marguerite's attitude would have warned him.

The curate eyes did not express disapproval, his face did not hold any severity, only he said in a paternal tone, "You waste your time in whitening black."

"But, Monsieur, I am only thirty-seven and a half years-old, and I would like to get married."

"There is no pot so bad that it will not find its cover."

This epigram was the curate's only vengeance.

Marguerite looked at him with an angry eye; the good old man could not withstand it, he drew nearer to his servant, took her arm which she let him take, and the curate, following the cheek that she turned slowly away from him, kissed her, and said to her in a tone which would have moved the heart of an enemy, "Marguerite, I did not mean to hurt you!...Go, my child, do as you like, I will not reproach you, just as long as you save a little love for your master!.."

Marguerite, a tear in her eye, gripped M. Gausse's arm, and at this moment, as the principal characters whom we saw in the village square arrived and rang the bell. The servant ran to open the door...

CHAPTER 2

M. Gausse went into his living room to receive his guests, who were soon followed by his colleagues: the latter declared that they had waited in vain to meet the expected young vicar out on the road. Ten o'clock rang out, they began to grow impatient, when, after a quarter of an hour, they heard, outside, the sound of the footsteps of a silent multitude, Marguerite entered nervously, she drew near the curate's ear and said to him, "Monsieur, here is your vicar!..."

"It is better late than never," responded Jerome Gausse; and, leaning on Marguerite's arm, he went towards the hall to receive the young priest.

On seeing him, the good man shivered, and held back the kindly and proverbial word that he had prepared, as a sort of fear slipped into his soul. The young man, seeing that his presence was disturbing, said to the curate in a serious tone, "Monsieur, I am Monsieur Joseph, the vicar that Monseigneur the Bishop of A...y told you was coming. For a few days now I have been anxious to follow his orders and to assure you of my respect."

In pronouncing these words, the young priest tried in vain to spread a little pleasantness over his face, but this lying contraction produced exactly the opposite effect.

The curate trembled again and could not respond since he was so surprised. In fact, through the sun-tanned color of an Indian, he noticed a livid paleness, almost mortal, spread over the young man's face: colorless lips, his gloomy attitude seemed to display the practice of the most rigorous laws of an ascetic life, his black hair, cut in front but falling in big curls on his shoulders, gave his face an inspired look, whose vivacity was even more strengthened by black eyes that pierced one's soul and were filled with a dark energy.

Here is a man who will only drink water, the pastor mumbled sadly, they have sent me some young fanatic!...

Then, casting a glance at the desolate Marguerite in which all of his thoughts could be read, the curate took the priest by the hand and lead him into the living room, saying in a bleating voice, "Messieurs, I present you Monsieur Joseph, the vicar whom Monseigneur the Bishop of A...y had the goodness to send me, to help me in the practice of the priesthood."

Everyone stood; M. Joseph greeted them with a nobility and an ease which astonished those present, since they had not expected to find such manners in a country vicar; but all of them, as well as the curate, felt an involuntary fright when the young stranger let his striking glance fall on them, like the eyes of an eagle. The look of crime or remorse incarnate could not have been more eloquent; still, that of the vicar had a terrible expression which froze the soul and was piercing just as one sees a ray of sunlight though the clouds. This priest seemed to contain death in his chest, or to be crying inside for a crime that an entire life of penitence would not be able to atone for.

The young priest sat down, the conversation ceased, and a great silence ensued. M. Joseph did nothing to break it, and his presence produced an effect that was as magical as that of the famous Gorgon's head: fear and dizziness seemed to accompany the vicar, or rather the sense which causes us to keep quiet before great pains, great wrongs, great virtues, was acting in full force.

Still, to look closely at M. Joseph's face, one would recognize something gracious and knightlike, but they were only light vestiges that were almost effaced, be it by a strong passion or by memories, until at last, just as there are people whose ways welcome you immediately into their souls, whose lovable frankness and naive frolicking causes all barriers to fall before them; so there are others in whom a gesture, an expression, a look, a word, contain all that is great, severe, noble, and respectful, who force one to think, to be quiet, and to admire or fear.

The vicar was a striking example of this second category of faces, and one could not keep oneself, on seeing him, from having a high idea of his waywardness or of his virtue.

At last the mayor, who did not suspect anything, risked breaking the silence by questioning this extraordinary character.

"Monsieur," he said, "have you found our town to be imposing?"

"Yes, Monsieur," responded the vicar, and a sardonic smile blossomed on his colorless lip.

"It seems," the mayor continued, "that this town is well situated, because strangers sometimes come to visit it, which would make you think that the countryside and its surroundings...the plain...the woods... of course the village...have..."

Here the mayor-grocer confounded by M. Joseph's icy and severe air, stopped suddenly, and looked for help from his faithful aide-de-camp Leseq, who, not being there, this time could not complete the sentence.

Curate Gausse took up the thread and said with a jocularity which should have intrigued the vicar, "M. the mayor meant to say that our countryside is delightful: in truth, the vast forest of the Ardennes crowns our mountains on all sides, and its trees seem like a crowd assembled in an amphitheatre enjoying the spectacle of our lovely valley. The little river which snakes through it animates the place with its turns; its thatched huts set here and there; the gothic bell tower which dominates them, the castle at the end of the village, its fine park, the ruins by the lake;

everything here is enchanting, and one would be happy, Monsieur, in this hamlet, if ambition did not torment people, but everyone wants to climb higher than his ladder, and ambition is sometimes the cause of the little torments of our villagers, even though I often repeat: to each his own task, the cows are well guarded!...But, in sum, people are good here, and you will want to die here, my dear Vicar, when you have seen the charming spectacle that nature presents when one does not oppose it!..."

In saying these final words, the good curate looked for the vicar to raise an eyebrow; but the young priest, while seeming to be paying attention, veiled, by his modest pose, a perfect indifference, and his gaze, fixed on the mantlepiece above the fireplace, seemed to see something other than the cold marble. The fat farmer twiddled his thumbs probably thinking of nothing; the mayor-grocer opened his eyes wide when he realized that his shop did not carry any linen that was as fine as what M. Joseph was wearing, while M. Lecorneur was already itemizing the tax on the newcomer, and the three colleagues of

Curate Gausse remarked that the young man's shoes were not dusty.

"What more could one want?" the curate continued, "than a charming valley and a friendly, good townspeople whom one encourages, without stopping their innocent pleasures: they have enough trouble, good God!.. As for me, I respond that my tomb will be among theirs!...."

"And mine too!" replied the vicar with a deep, melancholic tone.

At this word, silence reigned once more in the living room. After a few minutes, the three curates drew the young man into the opening of the two windows, and one of them asked him if he had prepared his installation homily.

"No, Monsieur, do you think that that is necessary?"

"What do you mean? Like a bottle needs a cork," cried Curate Gausse, coming over unexpectedly.

"If you wish," said one of the other curates who took the expression on M. Joseph's face for embarrassment, "I can give you one of mine."

"Thank you," replied the vicar, "but a few sentences dictated by the deep feeling that inspires the sublime duty of the priesthood should suffice and will be more moving for the hearts of the countryfolk than the thoughts of a stranger which were not dictated by the circumstance in which I now find myself when he wrote them."

The vicar pronounced these words in a solemn tone which struck the curates. At this moment, the bells rang with a fury that was without precedent, a small wretch in a white robe that was too short so that his torn pants and ripped stockings were visible, entered while holding in his hand a little skullcap of red cloth, made with the remains of one of Marguerite's old blouses. He announced that everything was ready in the church, and that the last strokes were now ringing.

The members of the municipal body went to the church, and the priests to the sacristy through a hallway that connected it with the presbytery.

The church of Aulnay was one of those original creations that Gothic architecture had sown throughout France. Its foundation went back to very ancient times, and on this church an abbey once depended although there were no longer any vestiges of it. The bell of the church had a happy heartiness, and the eye was pleased by the adornments which accompanied its pyramidal needle. The walls, blackened by time and ruined in a few places, inspired that melancholy which rises up in our souls, at the sight of the slow and successive destruction which the works of men cannot escape. The door was rather wide, the vault of the nave was broad and sonorous; the pillars, composed of little assembled columns and decorated by a sort of trefoil, were graceful. For the rest, the edifice was not disfigured by any foreign ornament. The pulpit was simple, and the marble main altar surmounted by a cross garnished with six candles shone in all its church beauty, that is to say in all the majesty of the person who stood there!...

The nave contained very clean benches, and the entire population of Aulnay was assembled. The sun passed through the stained glass windows set in their lead, though it was dark and cast a tint such as was not found in basilicas, and this half light was pleasing since it inspired meditation.

This crowd, which was once noisy and agitated by as many passions as the people who made it up, had become suddenly silent. Meanwhile, it was presumable that M. Joseph was largely the cause of this silence, because everyone, his eyes fixed on the sacristy, was impatiently awaiting his appearance. A murmuring that was hardly catholic was raised in the assembly when he appeared, followed by four curates and the country clergy from around Aulnay, but soon a great calm followed this agitation, and the calm was not broken thereafter.

The mass was given by the young vicar, with an air of conviction which seized the multitude; a sort of inspiration which governed the priest's manners, passed into the souls of the watchers, and this august sacrifice, made with such sanctity and contemplated with such fervor, became a sublime spectacle. This simple soul was drawn by a similar feeling towards the divinity. His glances, at times towards the vaulted ceiling, at times lowered to the earth; his unity of action, his religious silence, and all of the attention directed on a single being who was placed as intermediary between the human and the divine, between the earth and sky, asking the creator, for mercy for the guilty, strength for the afflicted, and the entire treasure of his graces, completely filled with admiration, and that will form for all ages a poetic portrait; but if one thinks that the victim of the sacrifice is a god, then one will recognize that Christianity has gone farther than the religions that preceeded it.

Soon the young vicar came to the point which Curate Gausse regarded as the most frightening: it was time for the homily. At first it did not enter into the curate's head, nor I believe into any of the country parsons' heads, that if he spoke off the cuff, then his vicar was necessarily going to make a profession of faith, and Gausse, looking at the eloquent and melancholy eyes of the priest, mistaking this expression, which he took for the sign of severity, confirmed in his conjectures, by the dignity and exaultation of the young priest, the curate thought, that M. Joseph would be a scrupulous observer of the minute practices of the religion.

On the other hand, everyone wanted to hear this priest who officiated with so much eloquence, above all the women who had waited for this moment so that they could see beyond the face which they only saw when M. Joseph turned around, and know the voice, the feelings, the young priest's form, etc…

The good curate, happy to find himself forever rid of having to do homilies and sermons, which for him had been the most difficult and tiring tasks, spoke with his habitual goodnaturedness the last homily that he had composed. I transcribe it, because of its originality though it was unintentionally comic in its overuse of proverbs, "My children, to be properly blessed, all that is needed is a word to clear one's conscience, but, naked one comes, and naked one goes; think of that, and you will see that you should only bring to heaven a soul that is without remorse, without that you would be received like dogs in a game of quilles, but, one does not chase two rabbits at a time, one does not please God while amassing a fortune; it is easier to pass a rich man through a needle than get him into heaven; honors change one's morals, and a golden bit does not make the horse better. Alas! The road to heaven is narrow, and the way to hell is broad; therefore keep a pear for thirst, by conducting yourselves well; don't be half fig and half grape, and without looking for noon at two o'-clock, go your way and you will arrive. I know full well that they will tell you that you have to howl with the wolves, but remember that advisors are not customers, and that whoever breaks the glass will pay for it; go, think of your salvation, and for that two certainties are better than one, because Saint Peter will not let cats pass for hares. It is true that no horse is so good that it does not stumble, and not everyone is able to go to Corinth, even though I do not know where Corinth is, because for little thanks you get little bread. I can assure you, that the Lord is good, and without being between shell and the zest, often check your accounts with him, so that you do not die guilty, since good accounts make for good friends. I leave you, my children, because there is no company that is so good that they do not have to leave. Therefore allow me to repeat one last time that each of us is the child of his works, and a good piece of advice is worth an eye in your hand: but, he who knows how to live, that is to say, live well, knows how to die. I know full well that there is no rose without a thorn, and that life is difficult, but recall that with time and patience, the leaf of the mulberry tree becomes satin; for the rest, if the devil is fine, then we are like the awakened people of Poissy, and to the trickster comes the trickster once over. I respond that he will lose his Latin, because end to end, there is no doubling. In addition, do we not have the hope of paradise? But, he who has land has wars; protect us from the demon; to the good cat goes the good rat; and remember to the sheared lamb, God measures the wind; he will help you, my children, a father is always a father.

"You see that today, as always, I have not sought to cast dust in your eyes. I tell you things without the flower of rhetoric. Goodbye my children, the monk responds to the abbot's chant; I hope that my successor will lead you even better than I have done! Nevertheless, I believe that you will not forget your old pastor who wishes you the beatitude of angels."

Hardly had M. Gausse finished when the young priest, preceded by the beadle, went up to the pulpit of truth. A great silence reimposed itself, the clergy gathered around the entrance to the choir, M. Joseph placed himself in the pulpit, and looking, by turns up at the ancient vault and down at the parishoners, said to them in a tone of voice that was slow, serious, and paternal, "My brothers, it is here, in this humble countryside, that I will preach the divine word, the bread of life; it is in your simple hearts which are free from great passions, that I will always address myself, because I always want to stay with you; it is in this valley that I have chosen my home.

"My children, I give you this name, because I am adopting you and want to be for you a veritable spiritual father; I will do all that I can to win your love. I will be happy if I succeed! I will be happy to lead you down the good path, after having led the fathers, I will console them with the notion that they will have left sons who are worthy of them. We will try to ward off the storms which could threaten our valley, and we will burn it in such a way as to purify it, so that only happiness will grow, that plant which is so rare and which has such a soft scent!

"My children, never expect eloquent discourses from me, nor severity, nor unreasonableness: the minster of God says: 'let the children approach me,' I will only speak to your hearts; Jesus pardoned a

Samaritan: Jesus was happy with little, I will try to imitate this divine master. I will only preach to you what he preached, gentleness, charity, and...love, this last notion contains them all."

A tear escaped the vicar's eye as he said this last phrase, and his emotion was noticed by all.

"Especially," he said, "we will protect you as best we can from those great passions, those evils that afflict the sensible man, and if we cannot succeed in warding them off, we will offer you consolation: in the end, we will cry with the unhappy, help the poor, let the dying see the goodness and not the vengeance of God. Always blessing, recompensing and conciliating ceaselessly, we will hope that our death will be seen by you as an affliction, and that often in your afflications you will say: 'that is the only funeral hymn, the only praise that we desire after having been forced to sow flowers along your paths in this life of pain. Always consider how it is up there" (and he pointed his hand and raised his gaze to the vault of the heavens) "that we shall all meet, and enjoy eternal happiness!"

It seemed that this gentle voice made the divine

music of angels resonate in their hearts. A general softening was for the young vicar a triumph that could not have been better.

"He did not say a single word of Latin," said Marcus Tullius Leseq to one of the curates, "besides that his speech was not half bad."

When the young man came back to the choir, M. Gausse took his hand and shook it with an admirable expression of thanks and compassion, because the good curate had cried when M. Joseph had spoken of his coming demise.

The mass was completed with the same compunction; the hearts of all of those attending had been moved; and in the assembly there was a young lady who cried bitterly when the vicar spoke of the evils caused by passions. This was the daughter of Marie who was the concierge at the castle of Aulnay. Before the end of the mass she found that she was so ill that her brother Michael had to take her in his arms and carry her back home. Poor girl! Soon she would have to come back into this church, for the last time, and again carried by her companions!

Leaving the mass, people spoke for a long time

about the vicar, the homily, the young lady, and each had their own comments to make which we shall avoid repeating.

The good curate, followed by his vicar and his three colleagues, returned to that dining room where guests were already to be found, and soon they gave themselves over to the joy of the celebration. This joy was slightly contained by the melancholy stamped on all the manners and words of the young priest; M. Gausse, who was already complaining of the malady which he did not know about, seemed less happy than was his custom. He adopted a gentle and cautionary affability towards his young substitute which no one had the power to reject, at least no one except those who have in the place of a heart, only those veins and arteries destined to receive and expel blood.

The conversation was too banal for us to include it. M. Joseph did not provide anything but an ample collection of the following formulas: yes, no, I beg you, thank you, I thank you very much, I will have that honor, etc...etc...

When the attending curates had left along with

Aulnay's high society, when M. Gausse and M. Joseph found themselves alone in the living room lit up by candles on the mantlepiece and on the table where they had sampled everything like flies, the good curate examined the vicar who, thoughtful, his head cocked, did not say a word; he was alone with him, and taking his hand, "My young friend, you will stay here and nowhere else; your apartment is all prepared; it is decorated with the luxury and the friendship and the kindheartedness which an old man like myself should have for attributes.

"Marguerite has her room not far from yours, so that if something happens to you, she will be there; she used to be on the ground floor so as to be closer to me, when my attacks of gout made me make requests that were not very respectful. To perfectly understand what is half-said, I know what they signify; but several days ago Marguerite explained to me that a bell beside my bed was much more trustworthy; she gave me good reasons, one can always ring and sometimes it is hard to get up and call; so," added the curate and, noticing that the young man was going to speak, "do not worry about me."

In this good curate's manners there was a frankness which set one at ease and which made the intervals of time and age disappear. In the end, he was already the young man's friend, and Joseph felt, despite his dark misanthropy, a secret liking for this likeable old man. So the vicar accepted, but in accepting he made the curate understand that he was sacrificing a lot for him—most notably his freedom.

"Ah! My friend, there are no beautiful prisons or ugly love affairs, so consider that in this house you will be at your utmost liberty; no trouble, do as you like, act as you please, each of us is the child of his works. Take care of Marguerite!...As for the rest, it is all yours: gardens, house, hearts, in sum everything; and as they say: free vinegar is better than purchased honey...Not that I mean to put a price on this service which should be rendered worthy by frankness and friendship."

What could he say to that? The vicar shook his host's hand and thanked him warmly with expressions which showed that his exterior calm was like ice covering a volcano.

"Young man," said Gausse with a conciliatory tone, at the moment when they were going to say goodnight, "remember that with time and patience the mulberry leaf becomes satin."

This proverb seemed to have an effect upon Joseph who went thoughtfully up to his room.

For the first time in a long time, the curate began to reflect as he got ready for bed with Marguerite's help. The servant was astonished by the tactiturnity of her master; still, when he was in bed, he said, "Marguerite, there is something wrong with this young man!..."

"Oh! Monsieur, certainly, there is a snake in the grass..."

"Goodbye Marguerite!" stopped the outpouring which was going to follow this response. Then the servant, retaining her words, went to rest from her labors not far from the place where the handsome vicar was sleeping...

CHAPTER 3

Yes, of all the servants, and I do not even except the chambermaids of great ladies who often wait secretly on the stairs; I maintain that the servant who shows the greatest amount of creativity is the servant of a curate. Making this assertion does not bother me; since it was pronounced between one and two o'-clock in the morning by Marguerite herself who was not sleeping and whom I will let prove it by what she says.

"Ah, great God!" she thought, "how we have a sorry lot!.. What schemes, what skill, what wisdom we must display from the moment we enter into a curate's service, until the time when we become the absolute mistress!...And what prudence after that, so that our control is not overly felt so as to cause repentance. Must we, in addition, be content with our master's virtue? Because a curate's servant cannot give herself over to the secular virtues of the village, she must add a gloss of sanctity and compunction which astonishes the honorable people and quiets the insolent ones. It is not that…" (Here the servant's ideas became too complicated for her to dare to enter into the labyrinth.)

"But," she began again, "I have accomplished everything, and now I see that it is back to square one!…The true *chef-d'oeuvre* is, if a vicar comes, and he is young, to have him live with the curate, just a few feet from me, and if the curate is old…one has to know how to make the goat live with the cabbage, as M. Gausse would say, poor, dear man!…But is he almost seventy years old, and since Saint Jerôme's day of the year 18…" Here Marguerite completely lost herself in her calculations.

"The good man will not get mad at me," she added after many reflections; "and, in truth, why did this vicar come? To succeed him in his post, in his perogatives, in his perquisites, in everything…in sum in everything!…" Marguerite caressed this idea, and after a moment of silence, she added: "what wrong would there be then, if, as of now, I tried to captivate…"

A "yes" and sleep ended the discussion.

Certainly the reader will notice a relationship, a

coincidence between this monologue and Marguerite's armoire...Very well, it is not less true that it was a monologue that caused the servant to get up earlier than usual in order to take stock of what her finery could offer in the way of coquettishness and seductivity. She consented to subject herself to the punishment imposed by a pair of shoes which made her feet look small; she curled her hair, arranged her sheer linen handkerchief in a way so as to show her cleavage, which I will freely call her *killers,* since they were supposed to do the vicar harm. In the end, Marguerite tucked in her belly and put on a blouse with short sleeves, and resolved to live with the expenses caused by this outfit of a military undertaking until M. Joseph's heart was engaged, invaded, captured, and submissive.

The young vicar came down to say his mass and returned for lunch, he greeted the curate, but the rest of the time he did not say a word, and his chaste eye did not even fall even once on Marguerite, whose ruses were to no avail. In vain she brought the coffee and entended her beautiful white and plump arm over the black sleeve of the priest, in vain she tried to question the young man about his tastes, in vain she tried deliberately forgetting the bread in order to get a glance, the vicar remained impassive like the marble of a statue, and M. Gausse imitated his silence although all the while taking notice of Marguerite's doings and the severe attitude of the young man.

"Marguerite," said M. Gausse at last, "he who has drunk will drink, and I know well that where the goat is tethered he must eat, but the grapes are too green, my child, man proposes and God disposes, you see. Believe me Marguerite, for lack of a monk the abbey is not without anything to do, and in chasing two rabbits at once one loses one's dinner..."

Marguerite was startled and unnerved by this tirade of proverbs; she quickly disappeared since she could not respond, but she still cast a glance on the young priest, who, for his part, raised his eyes to M. Gausse and seemed to ask for an explanation.

"She is a good woman," added M. Gausse, "but you know, my young friend, that the barrel always smells like herring, and women are creatures of habit; let it be, do you want to take a trip around the valley?... My sciatic nerve is good, there won't be anybody, and I have not taken a walk in a long time."

The young vicar took his hat, went to get the curate's, and, offering him his arm, they went out to contemplate the beautiful setting of Aulnay.

Joseph seemed to grow animated at the sight of this delicious valley that he had chosen for his retreat, and he was prey to the most vivid emotions seeing the appearance of this admirable setting, he seemed to know these good places, and he had a vague knowledge of them in his soul, as if his dreams had shown him this place, or as if the first days of his childhood were spent there. He unveiled these sentiments and his astonishment to the curate.

Nevertheless, after a half an hour of silence: "One should be happy here!" he said with a sigh! But this reflection caused him to fall back into his reveries, and his face alternately expressed, either deep pain or bitter resignation. This preoccupation did not allow him to hear the curate's long discourse made up of proverbs; they came slowly back to the house, and M. Gausse, believing that he had been listened to given the young man's silence, continued his discourse which he ended like this, "Yes, my friend, to measure one's wine when the barrel is almost empty is to act too late; I am sure that you have sadness, I do not want to ask the cause; each of us is the master of his own secret, and confidence is given but not taken; but listen, my friend, a good piece of advice is worth an eye in the hand, do not wear out your soul, it seems to me to be of fine stuff, live for others if you do not live for yourself, and do not imitate that young person who is dying of sadness: even though for sheared lambs God measures the wind. The poor girl was too much in love and she could not bear the news of the loss of her soldier."

"That is true, Monsieur," added Marguerite who found herself on the doorstep, "since yesterday when she was carried out of the church, has she grown worse?"

These words germinated in the soul of the young priest, and redoubled the dark veils of his forehead, so well that in sitting at the table, his pallor was so frightening that Marguerite cried, "M. Joseph, you are ill!..."

"My child, what is wrong with you?" said the good curate. "Marguerite, pour a glass of Malaga wine and give it to him…"

"No, thank you," he responded, "you said that a young lady was dying?…"

"The poor child! She might be dead!…" cried Marguerite.

At this the vicar looked at the servant who blushed and lowered her eyes.

"Where is she? Where does she live?" Joseph continued…"I must go and see her and console her. Poor wretch! How I pity the way that she is suffering!…"

"There is no hope," said the curate, "they got the news that Robert died in Russia: a rolling stone gathers no moss."

Tears began streaking down the young priest's pale face at the words "no hope," and he could not eat.

Leaving the table he was told the way to the castle where he went to the concierge's house. The vicar arrived, entered, saw the young lady on her bed of pain. He sat on the bedside and took her burning hand. Her words expired on her lips, he stared at this victim of love, and thick tears fell from his eyes!…The elderly mother, the brother, and a woman gardener who found themselves in the room, stood stupefied at this scene; silence reigned, and the vicar could only look at Laurette and repeat, "Poor child!...What could you do on this earth when your heart is broken, poor child!..."

After an hour, the overwhelmed vicar left; and in shaking the hand of the elderly mother he said, "I will be back!..."

One could easily see that the young man had taken part in the suffering, much more than he should have, and the desolate family remained struck for a long time by this visit that was eloquent with pain.

A few days later, the curate, seeing that on the whole his vicar was not as much the devil as he appeared to be black (that was his expression), and the vicar's first homily kept coming back to him since there had been no fanaticism in it, nor hypocrisy. So, as they were sitting side by side in the living room, on a Saturday night after supper, he began a conversation by risking the following propositions, "Listen, M. Joseph, now we must share our task. Good accounts make for good friends, as you know. So I will say to you, that, being infirm, I hope that you would indeed take over the shopping in the village, the giving of alms to the poor, the giving of consolations, the helping of the sick?..."

"Monsieur," responded the young man, "these are the most beautiful privileges of the ministers of the Lord, and if you cede them to me, then I will be obliged to you."

The curate, enchanted by the docility of M. Joseph, continued like this, "He who speaks well cannot speak too much! My dear vicar, your *unprepared* homily seduced me all the more since it had an effect on my flock, and, since you have a great facility, I see no problem in also burdening you with the sermon..."

Now he looked at the vicar with a sort of anxiety.

"Monsieur the Curate, your parishoners will regret no longer hearing the voice of their dignified pastor, but I can tell you that they will find in me your zeal to make them avoid the evils which vices lead to."

"My young friend," responded M. Gausse hesitating visibly, "I have one last thing to ask you: I am getting old! Be it weakness, be it sorrow of seeing the poor people whom I love die, the ones with whom I have lived so long, burials are hard for me. Do not suppose, my friend, that finding myself close to death, that I prefer to lie back to back with it rather than face to face, no, with God as my witness, I am resigned! Besides since I was born, don't I have to die?...But baptisms, births, are better for me, my meals don't suffer at all, and you are young, brave, you do not know anyone here, so..."

"Yes, monsieur, burials suit me, death pleases me more than life, a birth, a marriage, sadden me, and I smile at the tomb. Who are you M. Gausse? What is death in comparison with life?...To live is to suffer!...But..."

"But reality is worth more than hope," the curate broke in with a lively, happy tone since he wanted to turn aside the young man's flow of sad ideas. "My friend," he added, "try to be happy with an old man who cares for you, and remember that time is a great master"(these words were affectionate and he sought the vicar's hand).

The good curate's tone went to Joseph's heart, and his fiery soul warmly expressed his appreciation for the tender interest that M. Gausse took in him.

So ended the conversation in which the curate made his vicar accept the duties which he was so happily rid of.

The day after the one following these arrangements, several carriages of furniture arrived in Aulnay for M. Joseph; the simple, noble elegance of all that belonged to him was noticed by Marguerite. The vicar paid the moving men who set up his room lavishly, and the curious servant profited from this circumstance to examine all that composed the young ecclesiastic's furnishings. She saw many things which she did not know the use of and which provided her with material for ample commentaries.

When everything was in its place, so that M. Joseph's bedroom and two chambers were furnished with a refinement that passed for sumptuosity in Marguerite's eyes, she was quite surprised to hear the vicar calling her; she went into his room. It would be impossible to get on paper all of the reflections, hopes, and fears which crowded Margeurite's soul; she went forward, red, trembling, timid, and asked in a voice that was gentle, tender, and halting, "Monsieur, what do you want?..."

"Marguerite," said the vicar like M. Gausse would do, "I see that it would be impossible for me to make him be reasonable on certain issues..."

The servant went up to the priest and responded with a "so?.." whose loving expression would have enlightened anyone but the chaste Joseph.

"So, Marguerite, we have to arrange things among ourselves...and..."

"Monsieur," the coquettish Marguerite interrupted, "I did not think that you would have thought of such things so soon!..."

As a faithful historian, I must say that the servant, in pronouncing these words, cast a rapid glance at the cabinet, and, only seeing it furnished with books, a wide bureau, and a single chair in which the young man was sitting, a very feminine reflection slipped into her soul. A painter's easel excited her wayward imagination, and she said to herself: "What in the devil, could that be used for?..."

"Why, Marguerite, it was the first thought that I had, when M. Gausse offered me his house..."

"Really, Monsieur?" and the servant moved even

closer to the vicar, whom she regarded with a thoroughly jesuitical air.

Poor Marguerite! Now she will lose her illusions.

"So," replied Joseph, "I myself got together the money..."

"Ah! Monsieur, you must have a poor opinion of me, a curate's servant may be lovable..."

At this tone, and at these words, the vicar raised his head, just as Marguerite lowered her eyes modestly, leaving the young man puzzled. The second of silence which followed was still a moment of intoxication for the servant. And, I will observe, that after fifteen days of reflections, moods, and desires, had certainly sufficed to fill the cup of hope which Marguerite drank from in long draughts. How can we comprehend her surprise, her despair, when the following words knocked her off the throne that she was occupying.

"I thought, Marguerite," continued M. Joseph, in a voice which seemed severe to the poor servant; "I thought that a sum of two thousand francs would be a sufficient sum to cover the expenses that my lodging here will cause M. Gausse, my food, etc...Here,

Marguerite, is the money, because M. Gausse would not want to hear of it..."

The two thousand francs that the vicar placed on his desk, did not seem to be worth fifteen cents to the servant, and despite her interest in the money, a bigger sum would have meant nothing to her at that moment.

"But," added M. Joseph, "I would ask one thing of you, Marguerite, that is to never speak to me or interrupt me during my thoughts. I know what time lunch and dinner are, I will be there only occasionally, so, for no reason should you come into my room, and do not bother me...Otherwise I will be forced to leave this house. In the morning you can make my bed. That is all that I ask of you; can you go now?..."

Marguerite went out astonished, with tears in her eyes. Ordinarily a woman changes to a marked hatred when her batteries have not conquered the enemy; but the vicar could not inspire Marguerite's hatred...He seemed so unhappy!

Cruelly *disappointed,* she ran to pour her pain onto M. Gausse's breast, and told him about the strange conduct and strange requests of his vicar. M. Gausse, formed of the softest and rarest clay in the world, was sympathetic to all her troubles, but he sympathized in proverbs; so that, when Marguerite had finished her long litany, the good curate told her, while turning off the light:

"It is not permitted for everybody to go to Corinth; on the whole, Marguerite, it is just powder shot off at sparrows, and happily you only have one string in your bow."

It became obvious that the vicar was not an ordinary man: for several days, the servant was sad, morose, but in the end, she was resolved to her task and stopped regarding the vicar except as a superior being who had no relations with the curate's servant. All of her thwarted love converted itself into a curiosity, but what a curiosity!...A thousand times more *appled* than Eve's apple, if it is permitted for a bachelor of arts to use such a risky expression.

The vicar did not deviate from what he had said: he was in the house without being part of it, and attended to his sacerdotal occupations, with the punctuality of the shadow that marks the sundial, Curate Gausse grew accustomed to this mysterious character, so that he did not change his habits, and acted as he ordinarily would have, and so the vicar took up, as we have mentioned, all of the obligations which bothered the good curate.

Meanwhile, the vicar was still the subject of conversations in the village, which began with Marguerite who, talkative by nature, chatted with anyone that she could corner.

"I always get back to thinking," she said to M. Gravadel, "that a young man who does not eat, or speak, or..." (Here Marguerite lowered her eyes confusedly, be it from her uncontrolled tongue, or her disappointed expectations), "is not a *normal young man*," she added.

The poor mayor would never have understood these misgivings, even if Marguerite had expressed them more clearly, because never was there a more tranquil spirit than that of M. Gravadel.

All of this cackling was done on the sly since the curate did not like external talk, which disturbed him; talking too much at night is like scraping what you are cooking too much, he often said to Marguerite; also the latter had to take care that everything happened as ordinary, so that her master did not notice anything. Despite all of the care that she took, and the words that she said, Marguerite still had time to think; this girl Marguerite was certainly singular! To prove this proposition, she dreamed of a reconciliation with Marcus Tullius Leseq, whose intelligence she predicted would be useful in uncovering the vicar's secrets since she said to herself:

"All of this has to have a cause."

To this end, she undertook the first negotiations which consisted in greeting the schoolmaster with more care, and asking him news about his health.

The good Curate Gausse always following the lead given by his servant, prepared, without a doubt, to look on Leseq more favorably: meanwhile, while taking good care of his existence, this good man was more dreamy than usual, the rarity of his proverbs made Marguerite notice that her master was greatly given over to thought (an unheard of thing!)

M. Joseph, faithful to his promises, went throughout the village caring for the unhappy, and went back to see young Laurette who was in such a feeble state that she would not live much longer. Eventually the young vicar was regarded in the village like a second Providence. He attended the curate's meal hours; sometimes he spent the evening with him; but an indifference to life was still visible in his slightest actions, in his least gestures; a smile never blossomed on his lips; his eyes only expressed misfortune; his voice was dark, the most innocent words often made him shiver, but no complaint ever came out of his mouth, and this resignation pierced the soul of the good curate, who saw himself forced to remain silent, rather than console the young man.

"He who walks carefully, almost always stumbles," concluded the good man who, as he needed, invented proverbs; "so as long as he does not mention his troubles, we must not try to alleviate them."

A new incident raised the curiosity and talk about M. Joseph to new heights: this incident even cast a glow on his conduct which gave rise to the most serious reflections as we shall soon see.

Marguerite discovered, *seemingly by chance,* that, even though M. Joseph spent entire days shut up in his room, he was often awake much of the night. One evening, Marguerite, unable to resist her curiosity, set up a ladder beside the window to his room, and, looking through the slats in the Venetian blind, she had the wherewithal to observe M. Joseph in all of his movements. She saw him sitting on his chair, his eyes fixed on an object which she could not make out, to her great displeasure: the servant, astonished by his maintaining such an attitude, grew tired of hers and was obliged to come down off her ladder every quarter of an hour. She kept climbing back up with a truly heroic tenacity, if we consider the perilous position of a fat servant on a weak ladder. The vicar was always immobile like a statue. At last, on the fourth trip she shivered when she perceived the young man raise his arms and his eyes to the sky, approach the table, and begin writing with an incredible swiftness. He spoke…Marguerite risked a fall in trying to press her ear against the glass, but the effort was in vain, the window was too firmly shut for her to be able to hear anything. The young man seemed to be oppressed, tears fell from his eyes, soon he got up, tried to read, tried to pray, but an invincible charm always brought him back to his initial contemplations. Marguerite finally raised her siege, that is to say she took her ladder away. It was one o'clock in the morning, and the vicar did not seem willing to go to sleep yet.

Marguerite, the next day, began by telling M. Gausse of this significant occurence. M. Guasse and she spoke about it all day long, and M. Gausse ended up concluding that each is the product of his own works. Marguerite, seeing that in the course of the day everything had become so serious with her master and that it was impossible to speak about it again the next day, decided that the village's curiosity would at least give her the pleasure of repetition: so she went, under false pretext, to Madame Gravadel's house, and her air of mystery attracted the attention of a few regular members of the circle who saw that Marguerite had carried off a kind of treasure.

"In the end, yes," she said, striking the counter with her key, "it is not that I am mad at him, not in the least, but I say, I maintain, I repeat, and you will agree with me, that this young man's life is dominated by something very deplorable, very interesting, or perhaps even criminal!…" And she pronounced these last words slowly in a low voice!…

"Ah!" responded Tullius, who risked setting a hand on Marguerite's arm which made one presume that negotiations between them were still going on; "the person who does not know Latin always has something to reproach himself for!..."

"You like to say that," Gravadel interrupted, "but as for me who does not know a word of it, that does not keep me from being an honorable man, just as much as you are an honorable woman Mademoiselle Marguerite..."

"Go on, M. Gravadel, I would rather believe you than have to prove it. *Lis sub judice adhuc est.*"

"What does that mean?" cried Gravadel with anger.

"That it does not need to be proven," replied the schoolmaster promptly; "that does not mean that if I were a mayor or judge, I would know if some culpability were causing his sadness..."

"Because a man is serious," replied the mayor, "is that a reason for us to hang the wretch? If he is up at night, he needs candles, that is all that I see. He knew quite well how to speak to me about it the other day, when he asked me to pay off the debts of all the unfortunate in the village, because he reimbursed me for more than thirty articles, among which there were some that were rather considerable, by faith, I really thought that I was going to lose them, and, you see, a priest who has humanity, who does not make you lose anything, the business, charity, benevolence...You see...So...It is clear..."

"I am of exactly the same opinion as Monsieur the Mayor," said Leseq, "so amen! Because if the vicar is rich, if he does well, *errare humanum est,* unless I am mistaken."

Marguerite tried in vain to reanimate the conversation, to which Leseq's "amen" had given the extreme unction, she had the pain of seeing that the amen succeeded. In effect, the session came to an end when all of the members who had made it up left; she took the path back to the house, meditating on the shortness of the words and the length of the silence.

While waiting for the researches that Leseq proposed, and, as nothing else fed the village's curiosity, she always kept an eye on the vicar. His beautifully curled hair, his eyes that were so black, whose fire was often tempered by pain, his noble bearing, his gracious movements, are qualities which cause interest, even in the village, and made people notice him. Each time he went out, the women came to their door warning the others by saying:

"There's the vicar, there's the vicar!..." and everyone came on the run and watched the melancholy young man go by!...

Chapter 4

While these little events occupied everyone's mind, and were, for the village, things of the highest importance, an elegant carriage drawn by two handsome horses rolled down the road from A...y to Aulnay-le-Vicomte carrying Josephine de Vaucelles, who was now known as the Marquise de Rosann, to her castle.

As she is only a league away, it is urgent that we give an idea of her and her husband's character.

Madame de Rosann was a woman of thirty-eight, but in seeing her svelte shape, her still seductive face, her black hair and her white coloring, men and even women mistake her age. At all times her spirit, her goodness, make people forget that she is beautiful. Madame de Rosann carried on her face a good expression, her lips formed a fine smile, her eyes had an eloquence which announced a tender soul, an excellent soul, containing that mobility of thought and that exquisite warmth of feeling which are sometimes the source of much trouble! Without being lively, flighty or light-headed, she was drawn to people with brilliant qualities. She complied with the enthusiasm that they inspired; in the end the irresistable inclination that nature imprints upon women, this admirable desire to please, to make happy, this touching sensibility deployed itself to the utmost degree with her; and, if since her marriage she knew how to tame this tendency of her heart, it was from the esteem in which she held her husband or because she had not met any other men who were susceptible to respond to the *ideal* that she had formed of masculine beauty.

So she arrived, young at heart, almost forty years-old; that is to say, the age when women's passions achieve their last degree of intensity. She liked to be meditative, and the tears that she sometimes shed in secret gave her a lot to think about. Her childhood had been hard as she had become an orphan at birth, her mother, already a widow, died in bringing her to daylight, and the aunt who cared for her during childhood had a cold character, contrary and meticulous, which was in singular contrast to her young niece's temperment. So one can easily believe that the Marquise's qualities were, in short, the consequence of a sort of monastic rigor which the aunt employed in her education; for it is quite certain that children never take on the faults of those who raise them.

This aunt, Mademoiselle Ursule de Karadeuc, was an extreme Jansenist who did not see clearly despite the glasses which helped her read books about grace, while her tender charge, who was then named Josephine de Vaucelles, sometimes read things that were entirely different from Father Quesnel or the works of Arnauld.

A devout lady is not required to know the details which pertain to the birth of a child; also, when she found herself charged with her niece, she confided her to a wet nurse and only took her back when the poor little thing was in a state so that she could keep still on a chair.

So the only pleasure for this unhappy child consisted socially of church ceremonies, and inside the house in the care that she took not to embarrass Mademoiselle Ursule de Karadeuc. It was a crime to disturb the inviolable disposition of her rosary, her books, her snuffbox, and in general all the furniture in her room. She had to flatter the lady bulldog so as not to contradict her; she had to quietly leave the apartment of Mademoiselle Karadeuc as soon as certain ecclesiastics entered: she learned this when she saw the bad mood which overwhelmed her when she stayed the first few times. She also had to listen in silence, and never risk attracting the attention of the abbots, be it in playing with their cane or their hat; but above all, she was not allowed to move the sugar bowls, the marzipan, and the jellies which were intended for them; this last crime could only have been surpassed by the capital crime of looking through keyholes.

In the middle of all of this constraint, the poor Josephine, passive and reserved, contracted an angelic gentleness which covered a heart of fire. In this solitude and ignorance, the beautiful qualities of her heart developed as did her faults, and the meditations of her naive soul were not directed by anyone. In the end, this lovely child was not understood by her aunt, nor by those who, accustomed to her timid silence, took her for a vacuous spirit; she would have been surprised and happy when a lovable creature, guessing her merit, knew how to instruct her well!...From there came the evils which, in such cases, never fail to fall on young people left to themselves.

The severity of her aunt made Josephine's poor nanny in Aulnay dear to her, since the nanny loved her like a mother, and took great care of her; and in return Josephine was very thankful. It was always a great party for her when her aunt, won over by her exemplary conduct, permitted her to go spend some time at the nanny's thatch hut. Mademoiselle de Karadeuc often having such ecstasies granted her this permission increasingly often as she grew older.

So all of the Marquise's memories of youth were attached to the village of Aulnay-le-Vicomte which made it dear to her; also, when her aunt's death allowed her to marry, rather than go reign in a German convent where the intrigues of Mlle. de Karadeuc would have sent her, Josephine de Vaucelles felt a great joy in becoming, at the age of twenty, mistress of the estate at Aulnay which was one of her husband's possessions.

For his part, her husband the Marquis de Rosann

had gone into the service at age twenty, and obtained the remainder of his father's regiment. The state of peace in which France found itself permitted him to follow the whirlwind of the court: he gambled, had mistresses, acquired debts, beat off his creditors, worked his horses to death, drove and wrecked carriages, followed all of the intrigues, in a word, realized all of the things that one can imagine a young French marquis doing. Through the vices of the times, the young Marquis de Rosann had courage, honor, and this passion for the *knightly* which constitutes the character of the French nation. In short, emigrating stylishly, returning to France out of bravado, at forty he found, having traversed the storms of life and politics, and, become wise, he now understood what happiness was.

Through the events which gave Leseq the ability to take the glorious name of Tullius, the Marquis, once Lord of Aulnay, was now only its protector; it was in this land that the Marquis de Rosann whom we are considering, happy to have preserved his fortune in the great shipwreck of the nobility, retired to reflect on his future life. Then, he cast his eyes about him to find a wife who, while not lessening his dignity, would have solid enough qualities of gentleness and aimiability to assure the happiness of the second half of his life.

At this moment, Josephine de Vaucelles, having lost her aunt, and leaving the administration of her wealth to a business man, withdrew to her nanny's, whose thatch hut promised her refuge from persecution. M. de Rosann saw this young orphan: she had a melancholic expression on her face which the Marquis attributed to the way in which she had been brought up, and he thought, from that moment on, to make up for the privations of Josephine's youth by a continuous happiness whose charms they would enjoy together. To the Marquis the young lady seemed to be decorated by all the lustre of virtue, and no one could destroy this idea by revealing Josephine's fault, because no one knew about it, and no one, on seeing her, would have believed that at fifteen she had believed herself to be in love, and that she had been taken in by this first awakening of her senses.

Josephine was only happy with her former nanny; and, by the way in which Marie sympathized with the former nursling's pains, one would have said that she knew about the important secret which caused the young lady's tears. Whatever the case, Josephine's beauty, and above all, her fortunate character seduced M. de Rosann: he spared no expense in the hommages that he offered her; at first his attentions were greeted with indifference, then with the smile of friendship. At last, recognizing in the Marquis some of the qualities that she admired, Josephine consented to marry him, but only by viewing him as a true friend. One saw that this young lady's heart having already been won and misused, she considered this union as a port of refuge for a soul that had not yet met and who despaired of ever finding the person that would please her. They were married in secret, and this touching ceremony, celebrated in the middle of the night in the ruined chapel of the castle, caused the young lady to cry many tears: but since her marriage her melancholy was moderated by degrees, and only reappeared at times, and she ended up taking great care to make the Marquis de Rosann happy.

Marie, having steadfastly refused to follow the Marquise to Paris, had no other ambition than to become the concierge at Aulnay castle, where she wanted to die in the service of her former nursling.

The castle was ten minutes down the road from Aulnay-le-Vicomte. There was a lovely avenue of four rows of trees leading to an enormous iron gate, on each side of which were two pretty brick buildings: one was Marie's quarters, the other the gardeners' quarters.

A long field began at the gate which ended at the castle and its view encompassed the entire village. On the back side, they enjoyed English gardens, a park, the forest of the estate, and the romantic ruins of the old castle situated on a little lake. All of these surroundings served to make a stay there pleasant. The modern castle had been built by the marquis' father: it was big enough so that they could entertain friends there, yet not so big that it became sad in its solitude.

As I have already said, this estate recalled the Marquise's memories only too well for her to fail to occupy it in the summertime; as for the Marquis, he went there when his work allowed it.

Five o'clock sounded on the parish clock: at this

time, Marie was sitting at the foot of her daughter's bed. Cares, even more than time, aged this poor nurse; her hair was all white, and numerous wrinkles furrowed her face. With her glasses on her nose, she tried to knit blue socks with a wide, white border which she held in her hands, but every minute, her eyes rose to her daughter, she sighed, and large tears fell down on her work. Although Laurette's fever had just diminished, a trace of delirium still wandered through her weakened mind. She thought that she was seeing the man she loved, her eyes became lively with a rejuvenated flame and she said, "Robert, wait for me, we will go together to pick flowers for my mother…"

Then she was silent, but soon falling back into other memories, she turned her head towards her mother:

"Do you see," she began again raising her arms towards the window, "do you see mother?… He is going!…He made his last wave to me! His eyes tell me that he loves me…that he will not forget me…poor Robert! When will I see you again?…"

"Him! Always him!" murmured Marie while looking at the trunks of the legs of the worm-eaten table.

"Mother, tell me that he isn't dead?" cried the young lady in a heartrending tone of voice; or worse, she added in a tone that was even more heartrending: "yes, it's true!…I am going to join you Robert!"

The old mother shivered, grew pale, looked around her with fear.

"Michel is not back from the castle?" and she pronounced these words in a bleating voice which showed how much she disliked being alone with her dying daughter.

Laurette, falling back in her bed, seemed overwhelmed by a great weight; suddenly the whinneying of a horse, the rolling of carriage wheels, a coachman's cries were heard interrupting the silence of the avenue. Marie recognized the Marquise's horses, she descended the three steps in front of her house, with a thin and trembling hand she opened the gate, after long efforts, she painfully pulled aside each wing of the heavy gate which squeaks on its hinges; her face grew animated at the sight of her mistress, she tried to smile, but one could guess that sadness is the normal expression on her face.

The Marquise, noticing Marie's sadness, made a sign for the coachman to stop.

"Good nurse," she said, "how is your daughter?"

Marie's tears were her only response.

The Marquise grew tender, feared to ask a second question, and looked worriedly at Michel, her nurse's son, who came on the run at the sound of the carriages; understanding when he made a head motion that it meant that his sister was still alive, but his eyes were raised to the sky which indicated at the same time that now only heaven could help her.

"Go ahead, good Marie, tell me your troubles, go on," said the Marquise.

"Alas! My dear mistress, I cannot, my poor daughter is dying, and, up until her last second I have to see her smiles and her tears! I have to hear her words and even her sighs!…Dying at twenty," added the sad mother, "and dying of sorrow for the one she loved too well. O Laurette!…" And, pulling her apron up to her eyes, she could not hold back the sobs which choked her, Marie, her back hunched, her head to one side, went back up the steps of her house and disappeared.

"How painful it is to see a mother cry," said the Marquise; "Michel, come over tonight so that I at least hear some news of Marie," and the team of horses drew away with Madame de Rosann whom this scene had moved violently.

Upon entering her rooms she grew tender on seeing the fresh flowers which decorated the flower-stands: the ones that she prefered had been set in her room. Everywhere, and in the smallest details, they had studied her tastes, so that Marie's will had directed Michel's work. "Who will love me like my nurse when she is no longer alive?" she asked herself.

The air was so calm that it could not move the lightest curtains, day was drawing to an end, the bell which rang the evening prayer, the dying young lady, everything pointed her towards melancholy and the marquise let herself succumb.

Sitting before the window, she was contemplating the sky, when Michel arrived in the room. Madame de Rosann smiled at him with a touching expression in which Marie's sorrow was depicted, and with a finger she indicated a chair to him.

Michel gave Madame de Rosann all of the details that she desired about the events which had so suddenly worsened Laurette's sufferings.

"Ah! Madame, Robert in the depths of that Siberia must have often longed for the flowers and the lovely fruitwalls of Aulnay."

"So he is dead?" cried the Marquise.

"Alas! Yes, Madame, we learned about it suddenly in a letter from the Secretary of War. Robert's elderly mother, believing that it was good news, had hastened to give it to poor Laurette to read. It was just the day before the arrival of our vicar. It was a deadly blow to my poor sister. We all agreed that Robert was so lovable! He was your best gardener, by God! Well, he died without seeing his Laurette again!…"

"So it is true," said the Marquise, "that hardship strikes all classes, and passion strikes all hearts." Tears flowed in her eyes, and these tears seemed to have two sources: Laurette and herself. "But Michel, you mentioned a vicar, is the good Curate Gausse gravely ill?"

"No Madame, but…"

As Michel was going to explain, he heard a call from the end of the field: fearing that his mother might need him, he made, with an embarrassed expression, a few reverences that seemed very awkward to the Marquise, bumped into the door while backing up, and left the room.

What Michel had just said about the vicar had awakened Madame de Rosann's interest, for it seemed that fate wanted for this creature to excite the same feeling of curiosity and interest in everyone who heard about him. She tried to explain to herself why a vicar had come, since M. Gausse was healthy, since she did not know either M. Gausse's wishes nor the needs of the village: but, as a vicar, and especially a country vicar was hardly important to her, according to the admirable ways of her sex, she did not think about him very long and ten minutes later she was not thinking about him anymore. What disturbed her even more was poor Laurette, whose fate touched her soul; she had watched her be born, raised, she had followed the progress of her beauty each year, along with the development of her mind and heart. Meetings that were often repeated, confidences which the Marquise's affability had solicited and encouraged, all attached Madame de Rosann to her nurse's only daughter.

The Marquise, after having arranged Laurette and Robert's marriage, was to have given Laurette a dowry, and the wedding was to be have been held at the castle. Again she was the one who had taken the steps to try to exempt Robert before his enlisting in the army; but, as the name of Rosann did not hold much value under Bonaparte, and as Robert had no good excuse to give in order to be exempted to serve since he was big, handsome, and well built; if Madame de Rosann did not succeed in this attempt at least she consoled Laurette on the departure of her loved one and often led her to have hopes which, as a result, became quite baleful to the young lady.

As Madame de Rosann recalled everything that had happened, she feared that Michel's leaving was because of something serious; so after resting a few hours from the tiredness of traveling, she did not want to go to sleep until she had seen the young lady, for even if this visit was going to be painful for her, she imagined that it would bring pleasure to her nurse and perhaps to Laurette. So she walked towards the field which separated her castle from Marie's lodging.

Even though the moon lighted the landscape with a blue light, thick black clouds collected themselves on the horizon and announced a coming storm, so she felt a terrible heat even though the evening was already advanced.

"Perhaps the coming storm will put an end to Laurette?" thought Mme. de Rosann: this presentiment filled her with fear, she drew near, she arrived, she did not hear anything: this fatal silence multiplied her fright; the door was open, she went up slowly, her breathing was intermittent, one could say that she feared to break the silence which she believed to be the silence of death. Her steps did not make any sound, she was in the funeral chamber, no one had seen or heard her arrive.

The elderly mother, her face in her hands, did not dare look at her dear daughter, Michel cried, the dying girl clung to life by still trying to make a few movements. The Marquise had barely seen all of this, since she was entirely given over to the contemplation of a being who, by his touching, harmonious voice, tried to alleviate the pain of such a moment!...

Laurette's faint eyesight could only stand the glow of a lamp set on the table behind her bed; but the moonbeams arrived through the windowpanes, and this pale tint combined with that of the ruddy lamp lugubriously lit up the room and imprinted a sinister expression on everyone and everything that is there.

Beside the desolate mother, the immobile brother, and the dying girl, was a man of handsome stature, he was wrapped in a black soutane which added to his imposing attitude the sort of majesty which results from wide and simple clothing; the young man, to be exact M. Joseph, his face turned towards Laurette, and, on this face, the gentle compassion, the human pleading, the divine consolation appear and make him shine, in the middle of this group of pain this man seemed a celestial envoy who both suffered from the spectacle and brought hope.

This was the scene that the vicar was a part of which kept the Marquise immobile and almost stupefied at the top of the stairs.

Noticing this exhalted figure, noble, and gentle

and which kept the mark of a deep melancholy, the Marquise felt her heart beat, her eyes experienced the sensation of a lightning stoke, and, a sympathetic power, an invisible attraction caused her to forget the dying Laurette, so that she was only concerned with this creature who overwhelmed her entire being. She could not form any idea of how she felt, her soul seemed to have left her body, it wandered around the vicar, and Madame de Rosann listened greedily to the gentle murmur of the consoling words of this young man whom she did not know.

"Yes, my daughter," he said, "the divine concert of angels is ready for you, your reception at the celestial palace will be shining, leave this earth, beautiful virgin...Yes, beautiful with all that is virtue and with all that is human beauty, leave this earth, for you will not find here the fragile happiness of the children of Adam, and since you are going to be happy up there with the felicity of the angels! Your beloved is waiting for you, he has made a place for you!..."

"So he will be there?"...Laurette murmured feebly, still trying to raise her heavy eyelids.

Madame de Rosann was even more astonished by

the young priest's language: his words bespoke of a
fine education, she tried to examine it more carefully, but this attention started a strong commotion in
her soul, and, despite the solemnity of the moment,
despite her will which wanted to direct all her
thoughts, all her affections towards Laurette, she still
felt drawn to the vicar, she was forced to contemplate him and to notice his smallest gestures!...

"Are you suffering my daughter?" asked the
priest.

"Mother, I can feel that I am dying!" said Laurette
in a plaintive tone, while trying to seize the young
man's hand.

At this moment, her eyes fought against the night
of the tomb, she still wanted to see, but the pulsa-
tions of her heart stopped unnoticeably, her blood
grew icy, the girl suffered in silence, a slight contraction wrinkled her face and her last breath escaped
her.

What silence!...The Marquise had not noticed it,
but all human activity had ceased: soon, Laurette's
face was embellished with a celestial freshness. It
seemed, that in entering the grave, she had a sublime

vision of sublime eternity and that the magic of the heavens was reflected in her face; on her white and pure forehead death had engraved the mark of immortality: the secrets of the other life.

It was at this moment that the priest, deeply moved, cried out, "Pure and dear soul, your time on this earth has been the time of a flower! Like a flower, a storm has caused your death!"

"My girl, my dear girl," cried out Marie in a heartrending tone; "she is asleep," she added with a distracted air.

The vicar got up, leaned respectfully over Laurette's body, and seeing the beauty of her features, "Angel of the sky," he said, "watch over us!...Be brave, poor mother," he added, "She has heard us...Goodbye...Tomorrow I will come back and pray."

At the same time he looked at the Marquise, and with his finger pointed to the young lady's mother. This look said everything, the Marquise obeyed like she would a master, she led away Marie whose eyes were dry and who did not seem to see anything nor hear anything. Nature seemed to take its part in this moment of horror. The clouds which concealed the moon seemed like a funeral shroud spread out over the sky, to announce the death of an innocent, and the winds, gathering for a storm, blew from afar and caused the village bell to ring out uneven notes...

The next morning, her friends and the other village inhabitants awoke to the story of the young lady's death. Everybody cried and the curate was not the one least moved by it. The vicar, whom religious enthusiasm no longer sustained, was in a distress that is difficult to describe. Marguerite was desolate and did not fail to recount all of the circumstances of Laurette's life, from her birth to her death. Leseq announced that there would be no class; but the children, who still did not understand what human sympathy was, only saw it as a day off, and were glad. Madame de Rosann took care of her nurse whose anguish tore at her heart. Michel watched over Laurette's body, the vicar came to pray beside her. He had a meal at the castle; Madame de Rosann became disturbed when she saw him, when she heard him; and, trying to understand her own heart, she asked herself if it was the young lady's death or the vicar's words which troubled her more.

The time came to make the last ministrations over Laurette's body. The vicar, having put on his sacerdotal trappings, came preceded by the silent retinue which was going to escort the young lady's body. They began walking, passed through the iron gate, and crossed the long avenue, which was the scene of parties and dances at which Laurette had been so lovely!…They passed over the lawn where she had learned to walk; before the thick oak where she had pronounced testimonials of love; farther on, a young tree had received in its bark Robert and Laurette's tender initials; here she had sat beside him, and they had spoken of their future happiness.

Ah just as before when, throbbing with hope, she had run down this avenue asking the soldiers who by chance passed through the village if they had any news of her Robert! Now her beauty, her love, everything was dead, and the ground of the avenue was supporting her body for the last time. The trembling, desolate young ladies lowered their eyes, they seemed to dread the sight of the avenue that was fertile with memories.

The lugubrious songs of the mourners and the cheerful bird songs made for a grievous contrast, their footsteps echoed down the avenue, the moments of silence, the rustling of the leaves which the wind gently shook, the white clothes of the young ladies, the coffin and its white crown, all together they produced a sublime picture of pain...

CHAPTER 5

The monotony of the fifteen days which followed the young lady's death cause me to pass rapidly over them. Marie fell dangerously ill, and the vicar often came to console this mother in her desperation; while, for her part, the Marquise cared for her nurse, and kept meeting up with M. Joseph, because, having noted the times when the vicar came to see Marie, she took care to be there too.

Joseph's presence produced shiverings in the Marquise's soul which she was not able to repress. This invincible movement, something like fear in the violence of the emotion that it caused, was, in the Marquise's case, the debt that one pays in seeing for the first time a superior man, one of those beings who possess the gift of astonishing just by their looks. In truth, this impression was renewed each time Madame de Rosann heard the vicar's steps, and each time it acquired a greater degree of strength. She trembled when she looked at him, but in the way that one likes to tremble; seated in a corner of the room, she remained for a long time with her eyes attached to this imposing young creature, and she forgot the sufferings of her nurse since her soul was so filled with other emotions that she did not want to deal with. The impassive vicar did not notice anything as he consoled Laurette's poor mother with angelic language which drew tears from the marquise.

In the end, even when the vicar was absent, all of Josephine's thoughts revolved around the young priest whose suntanned face, his deep gaze, and his concentrated pain made her heart beat faster although she would not have noticed it without the help of her imagination.

Marie was doing better, she was out of danger and convalescing; the vicar was to come to see her for the last time. Madame de Rosann waited impatiently for the time at which M. Joseph would ordinarily arrive at the little brick house which seemed a temple to her.

Josephine, sitting opposite the nurse's antique chair, thought deeply, and Marie, in turning around, noticed tears flowing down her mistress' cheeks.

"Alas! What is the matter, Madam?..."

"What I have, Marie...don't you know?" ·

At this word tears inundated Marie's wrinkled cheeks.

"As you say Madam, I have just learned it!...Before I only felt half sorry for you! Now I know all of your pain!...Your poor child!..." added Marie in a low voice, "he would have been the same age as our vicar...Ah! Madame, what an anticipation of death to see your child die! At least you have not seen that happen!"

"Marie," cried the Marquise, "you have enlightened me: if this young man is so pleasing for me to look at, it is because he represents my son to me!..."

"Madam, he is named Joseph!..." said the nurse with an air of mystery.

At this name, the Marquise paled, she raised a frightened eye towards the nurse, and, placing a finger on her mouth, she said to her: "Marie let your lips be like the marble of a tomb which would have enveloped this name and this secret, to which the honor, and almost the lives of three people are attached…"

Scarcely had the Marquise finished these words, when the vicar entered.

Josephine looked at his face, something took hold of his countenance that made it seem like the incarnation of a pomegranate, and she felt her heart become troubled at the sight of the young man's severe forehead.

"Very well! Marie, I see you are better…" said M. Joseph after having respectfully greeted the Marquise.

"She is saved," responded Madame de Rosann, "and you too have certainly helped make her so by your cares."

The vicar bowed as he said, "Madame, I am only doing my duty."

"Monsieur the Vicar," responded the Marquise smiling, "you must know how curious we are, and I am going to give you clear proof of it by asking your age."

"I am twenty-two, madame."

At this laconic response, Marie cast a look on

Josephine at the moment when she secretly stared at her nurse, and, with this rapid glance, they exchanged a multitude of thoughts.

"And where are you from?..." asked the happy nurse.

"From Martinique!..." responded the priest drily, and by his unconscious movement he let it be known that these questions displeased him.

As soon as Joseph had responded, the Marquise's eyes, which had glowed with hope and happiness, went to an extreme sadness. She looked at Marie in a lamentable way, as if she would have said: "it is not he!"

"What a useless search!" said the nurse in a low voice; "didn't he tell you that your Joseph was dead!..."

Tears filled the Marquise's eyes, she grew silent, drew her chair away, in a way so as to be able to contemplate the young man at her leisure, and her radiant face showed just how much she liked to look at him.

"You are still very sad," said Marie to the thoughtful priest.

The vicar did not respond, silence reigned, and soon M. Joseph left after having taken his leave of the Marquise and said goodbye to the convalescent nurse.

"Very well Marie!..." cried the Marquise in a sadly affected voice, "is he a son?..."

"Oh no!..." responded Marie.

Meanwhile, as soon as the young man had disappeared, it seemed to Josephine that her nurse's room was empty, it seemed that her life had just been taken away.

The vicar's visit had been preceeded by a host of memories that had been evoked by Marie's words, and these memories plunged the Marquise into an inconceivable state, augmented by Joseph's presence, everything contributed to making this scene an almost magical moment. Josephine believed that she had had a dream, for her the young man's departure was an awakening.

She trembled with the confused feelings that were fighting in her soul, she suddenly left Marie, and took refuge in her room, as if to avoid a being whose memory pursued her in too lively a manner in

Marie's room, in that place where she had contemplated him for the first time, where for the first time she started at the sight of him. She lay on her sofa, but if that was where she thought that she could forget M. Joseph, it was in vain; because for a fortnight all of her thoughts went in one direction: to the presbytery where the young man lived.

The Marquise had not yet come to the point where she would admit to herself what she felt. In examining what was happening in her heart she was like a young forest creature who, for the first time is pierced by an arrow and runs through the woods without worrying about the mortal wound, and only after much running, settles under an old tree and contemplates its wound and tries to take out the arrow which perhaps it will remove.

So Josephine, alternately noisy and silent, often wandering through the park, and sitting on a height from which, contemplating a fugitive cloud, she liked to hear the sound of rain, the power of the wind, and to see nature's fright at the approach of a storm; or even, she admired the blue scarf of the sky without clouds, and all of these actions were accompanied by a deluge of vague thoughts, which plunged her heart into a delirium that was full of charm, for she forgot her age when she was only thinking about her soul. Then she had her horses attached to her carriage, ordered it to go at full speed and, pleased at being carried along at such a velocity, tried to get some distance from her thoughts so as to reveal them to herself. In the end, one saw her sitting in her boudoir, eyes fixed on an ecclesiastical portrait which was always on her chimney; and there, immobile, she spent whole days entirely, without saying a word, sighing at times, and crying often: her husband's letters were received with indifference, and sometimes at the table, the people serving her were afraid of her pallor and her distractability.

For eight days the vicar had not come to the castle, Marie was doing quite well, and the Marquise did not hope to see M. Joseph again. The week seemed like a century to her.

One evening the curate and his vicar were talking together when the curate admitted to his assistant how astonished he was about not hearing of any more misery in the village, and in doing so he let M. Joseph know that he was not unaware of his good works. The young man, full of modesty, was going to respond, when the door to the curate's room opened and the Marquise appeared.

"Ah Madame!" cried M. Gausse getting up suddenly, and offering her his shepherd's cloak of red Utrecht velour, what an honor you are giving your pastor!..."

"He well merits it," responded the Marquise trembling and looking at M. Joseph, who greeted her with a blush.

The unusual redness of M. Joseph caused a feeling of hope to be born in the Marquise's soul which it was impossible for her to explain or express. "He has thought of me!" she said to herself, but also quickly thinking that even though he had not visited Marie or the castle, his will had commanded him, she experienced a movement of pain which caused her face to fade.

"I felt, Monsieur Gausse," she said in trying not to look at the curate, "I felt that if you had not come to the castle it was because your infirmities kept you in; and, then not wanting our dear poor people to suffer,

I came to find out about you myself and to bring you a little sum that I remit to you every year to help the indigent."

"Madam, we don't have indigents any more, Monsieur Joseph has taken over our pleasure of making people happy!"

"That's too bad, Monsieur," said the Marquise, turning towards the young man and looking at him with a pleasure that she could not dissimulate.

"Just so, Madame, I was giving him a lively reproach just when you came in."

From the Marquise's attitude an capable observer would have judged that her visit to the curate was a step that she had considered for a long time and the object of a long internal conflict. Josephine, embarrassed, tried to attach her gaze to something else besides the vicar, and yet an invincible moral force constrained her to keep bringing her eyes at each instant to the sight of the being who had become the entire universe to her!

"Well," replied Josephine after a moment of silence, "I will beg Monsieur the Vicar to accept my little sum so that I may participate in his secret works of charity." And, without waiting for a response, Madame de Rosann pulled out a purse filled with gold and held it out to M. Joseph. The latter could not do other than take it, and the Marquise took this occasion lightly to brush the vicar's hand. This fugitive feeling, this moment's sensation made such an impression on Madame de Rosann that she felt something like pain. Joseph, astonished, looked at her, she lowered her eyes and blushed as if she had committed a crime.

M. Gausse, looking alternately at the Marquise and the vicar, began to understand that this visit, the first that the Marquise had ever paid him, might well not be for his sake. For her part, Marguerite, her eyes glued to one of the cracks in the door, did not miss a word nor a glance as she held her breath.

"One can only praise you for having obtained for a vicar a man such as him, Monsieur," the Marquise continued, "and, since you are quite willing to accept my offering, I no longer have any complaint with you. M. Gausse, you must be quite satisfied, talents, virtues, everything is united in your assistant."

"Madame," cried the curate, "I thank God every day for him."

The cold, impassiblity of the young priest's countenance froze Madame de Rosann's tender soul. For a few moments she contemplated M. Joseph's handsome and noble face, and withdrew grieved, her chest swollen with the sighs that she had retained.

This visit, commented on by Marguerite as she recounted it, reawoke the village's curiosity and the vicar became once more the subject of conversations, because Laurette's death had caused the vicar to disappear for a long time as the principal object of discussion. But other people's misfortunes only give people fleeting emotions which promptly give way to the insouciance named happiness. They finished by forgetting Laurette and began speaking of the vicar as before, but added to what they said about him the account of Madame de Rosann's visit to him rather than to M. Gausse. Marguerite did not forget the icy air that M. Joseph had affected in listening to Madame the Marquise, and a certain satisfaction shone after that in Maguerite's conversation for she thought that she was not going to be the only one to be humiliated. The sort of disdain that M. Joseph showed the Marquise succeeded in raising her curiosity to the utmost degree, and this circumstance overturned all of Leseq's conjectures. Who could not imagine that one would not bow one's head before power?

After the coldness that the vicar had manifested itself, the unhappy Marquise judged that the priest would never address her a word of friendship, and that the internal fanaticism which devoured him would form an aegis which would cast off all human feelings. She groaned and resolved to content herself with the simple and naive happiness of seeing him, but she resolved to have this happiness often, because it was the only one which she could enjoy. If the Marquise had been in a state that would let her think for even ten minutes, she would have perceived that the feeling that she had for this young man, this sympathetic feeling that was born in an instant, and was rapid in its development and strength, was love: so frightened, she would have fled and never seen Aulnay-le-Vicomte and its vicar; but, I repeat, for a month her life had been a delicious dream, a true dream, a delirium, an enchantment! Not being herself any more, she became young again and rediscovered all the richness of a new and unsuspected feeling. She lived without living, and threw herself beyond creation, finding for the first time in her life a being who responded to all the ideas that she had formed of the one whom she would always love. In the end, she had encountered the man of her dreams, the man of her choice, the man whose exterior and moral qualities would always please her. Unfortunately she had met him too late!

This will explain why M. Gausse and his vicar received an invitation to go dine at the castle. The curate responded, without telling M. Joseph, and on the indicated day the curate brought him along.

This method had been the subject of a long meditation by the good curate, who did not even speak to Marguerite about it. "A scalded cat fears cold water," he said to himself, "if my vicar is unhappy, it is because of some passion, and he avoids occasions to fall back into his first misfortune: that is quite good! But, if the fox knows a lot, the woman in love knows more; and, if Madame the Marquise wants this young man's welfare, he must not miss his path because of a false weakness: he could become bishop. And Jerome Gausse must beat the iron while it was hot. If the young man does not beat the iron himself, the monk must respond as the abbot sang, also, could she do so well that he will notice Madame the Marquise despite himself, more than he did on the day of her first visit? Alas, the abbots of my time were quite different from M. Joseph. In the end, I will set him on the road: to properly receive a blessing, to the good player the ball comes."

It was with this intention that the good curate brought M. Joseph to the castle.

Since the morning, since the night before, the Marquise thought that she was going to see M. the Vicar, and to see him for the better part of a day. She dressed with a noticeable simplicity, for the greatest amount of effort and all the art of make up had governed her finery. In the end, seated in a room that looked out over the courtyard and the avenue, she waited for her two guests impatiently, and afforded herself the pleasure of watching them without being seen. Five o'clock rang, she heard the gate's bell ring, and she noticed M. Joseph supporting the respectable curate. She admired the careful attention and the efforts which the vicar used towards the old man; for an instant she wished that she were M. Gausse, to be helped, protected, and leaned against by this young man, with his creole color, and his silent behavior.

"How passionate he must be," she said to herself, "what a noble forehead! what distinguished manners! That is not an ordinary man, the son of a peasant. What is the mystery that surrounds him?…" And while thinking this she was content to watch the vicar walking. This philosophical pairing of youth protecting a frail old man did not strike her; she could only see the exterior qualities which adorned M. Joseph, qualities which seemed to her the sign of moral perfections which she still desired.

In the end, Mme. de Rosann was at table, she was between the two ecclesiastics, and she felt at her side the man who made her heart strings vibrate.

"I hope Monsieur," she said to M. Gausse, "that we will take up our old habits of preceeding years, and that, now that you have a young arm, gout and sciatica will no longer prevent you from coming to dine at the castle at least once a week."

"Madame," responded the curate, "if I were young, I would not think that that was enough. I would want to be your companion more often, but Monsieur Joseph will help me!...I give him over to you, Madame," said the curate with a wise smile; "it is to beautiful women that I confide the care of dissipating his deep melancholy and dark sadness. The health of the body is the poppy of the soul, so, Madame, seeing how afflicted he is! You can judge how his soul is affected and burns with a devouring fire."

"Do you have sorrows?..." asked the Marquise in a trembling voice; "the clouds on your forehead, could they have gathered because of your lack of fortune, because of ambition..."

"Madame," said the young man without looking at Madame Rosann, "my ambition is satisfied with the position that I occupy, and I have more money than I could ever have hoped for."

The haughty tone which the priest adopted as he pronounced these words, his eyes lowered to his plate, surprised the curate, and broke the Marquise's heart.

"Young man," said M. Gausse, "you do not want anything?"

"Yes, Monsieur," cried Joseph, raising an exulted eye towards M. Gausse, "I desire the rest...of the tomb."

"At your age!..." the Marquise began again, "and who gave you this funeral wish?"

Two fat tears traced the cheeks of the priest, and this mute response made the marquise become quiet.

"Madame," replied the vicar, "happy are the pure souls who have no source of pain, and who can look on their entire lives without blushing and without trembling."

This innocent phrase was too easily applied to Madame de Rosann's youth for her not to be moved.

"What," she said, to change the conversation, "you are not trying to make friends for yourself when their affectionate voices could console you?"

"There are pains whose remedies are unknown, for which nature has no product that serves as a balm."

"Time is a great master," said the curate.

"Because it brings death!" replied the vicar.

"Do you know that it is not very Christian to desire it," cried the Marquise.

"So, I am not seeking it, I am waiting for it!"

Everybody was quiet. A very small occurrence aggravated the Marquise's pain. It was her pleasure, every other moment, to offer to the vicar the foods that had been brought out, and she had counted on having the joy of serving M. Joseph. The latter, very frugal, ceaselessly refused, and took only one helping that M. Gausse offered him. This small incident, in itself, was, for the Marquise, a trial. Her imagination depicted these refusals like a determination stopped by the vicar, and she accorded it with the rigidity that reigned in the words of the priest and the chastity of his eye, which did not fail a single time on Madame de Rosann.

This evening, which she believed would be a joy, was a perpetual torment, a torture: she endured all of the sufferings that one experiences at seeing oneself disdained in a cruel manner. Near the end, the tears came into her eyes, more out of sensibility than out of spite.

There are actions which wound more than real

offences. The Marquise had let her handkerchief fall, alas! naturally by inadvertence and without ulterior motive. The vicar stopped Madame de Rosann and, without picking it up as he should have done since he was behind the poor Marquise, he said to her while casting her a lightning glance, "Your handkerchief is on the ground!..."

The severe Joseph seemed to say to her, "Did you drop it so that I would pick it up?..."

Josephine bent down, took up her own handkerchief, and used it to wipe away her tears. M. Gausse saw them, his heart sympathized and broke. The Marquise was prey to a mortal pain, the idea of the mistake that she attributed to the young man stayed in her soul. Very well! Although her heart had been so cruelly tormented, when the guests withdrew, she accompanied them to the gate; and there, leaning on Marie's arm, she contemplated the young vicar's gait for a long time after having said goodbye to him with her mouth and heart. Marie did not offer a single word. The nurse and the mistress remained plunged in a mutual reverie; and Madame de Rosann came back to the hell in her soul, she did not even hear

Marie's goodbye and respectful wishes.

Sleep did not visit Josephine's bed at all, and she did not profit at all from her waking to examine her heart. She did not seek at all to know if she loved, if this involuntary passion was legitimate according to nature, if she could guarantee it. In the end, if the feeling that she felt for Joseph – "no," she cried as she ceaselessly imagined the rigid glance of the young vicar, and she moaned about the misfortunes that were presented to her mind by her broken soul.

CHAPTER 6

When the curate returned to the presbytery with M. Joseph, he scolded him gently and with a deluge of proverbs about the scandalous rigidity of his manners, the savage habits and the misanthropy of his bearing, and on the coldness of his conversation. The vicar seemed astonished. M. Gausse said to him that he had wounded the heart of the protectress of the village by his ideas and by his actions, and that the great goodness of Madame de Rosann caused her to be content to moan about it. In the end, the curate obtained a promise from M. Joseph that he would return to the castle, excuse himself, not verbally, because that would recognize that Madame de Rosann had been offended, but by conducting himself with affability, by placing grace and sociability in his manners and his conversation. What the curate said to the vicar touching the pure and candid soul of Madame de Rosann seemed to produce a great effect on M. Joseph, who retired to his apartment.

Marguerite had heard everything, because all of the doors of M. Gausse's house were organized according to the system that governed those of M. Shandy, so that the servants there were the first to know all that was said. Also Marguerite, in putting her master to bed, began a conversation which would have great results.

"Monsieur, do you doubt," she said, following the praiseworthy habit of choosing out of a thousand phrases, the longest development: "do you doubt everything that the entire village is saying about us?"

"Very well!..."

At this "very well!" Marguerite crossed her arms, sat down and cried: "Monsieur, everyone assumes that it is quite astonishing that Madame the Marquise is interested in an unknown person, because Joseph, Monsieur, is not a family name?... Your vicar, did he say who he was or where he came from? No...We know nothing about him, and you will see that we will never know anything!...You will have done well, Monsieur, it is not natural for one to keep silent when one has something good to say."

"Of course, it is not natural for you, Marguerite."

"Monsieur, there is no worse water than sleeping water."

The curate, flattered to see his proverbs prospering, just smiled at Marguerite.

"Look, Monsieur, how can you justify his staying awake?…Oh! How I would like to know what he is writing! Ah! If ever the damned door to his room were open, then I would punish him well for his lack of conversation."

"Marguerite," cried the curate severely, "everyone is his own master, and what you just said is very bad. Who looks for evil, turns out evil, so take care…about what you are going to do: one should not put one's finger between the tree and the bark…"

"Monsieur," said Marguerite proudly, "are you going to reproach me for my curiosity?…Isn't it for your sake that I am looking for some information? Aren't you compromised by your ignorance? If someone comes and asks you about him…what will you say?…You will respond…I do not know what!…"

"To every lord should go every honor, he should have said to me, to me, his superior, who he is and where he comes from…"

"Monsieur, do you want to find out?…" cried Marguerite noticing her master's gaze. The curate hesistated, then Marguerite won the last round.

"Monsieur," she said, "I went back and saw Monsieur Leseq." She blushed.

"He is a widower," murmured the curate, "and I did not imagine that you two would be at war for long: he who has drunk will drink, but take care my daughter, to promise and to keep a promise are two different things!…"

"Monsieur, if you allow it, Monsieur Leseq would come tomorrow to dine along with the mayor and the judge and the tax collector. Monsieur Leseq said that, if he was authorized, he would voluntarily go to A…y—and there get a lot of information at the seminary, at the chapter, at the bishop's, in the town, about everything that concerns Monsieur Joseph."

"I do not want to see Leseq."

"Monsieur that is regrettable, he repents at having offended you, he assured me that if you admitted him into your house, he would not say a word of Latin."

"Go ahead," replied the curate, "He spoke with me the other day while I was out walking. He is an unhappy man!…Let him come because, in sum, the dog that barks does not bite."

"So be it, Monsieur, until tomorrow," said the servant going away happy at seeing that all of the ruses that she had prepared were enjoying a full success.

The curate went to sleep thinking that at last he would know, and by legitimate means, who his vicar was.

One can tell that the intimacy that Madame de Rosann seemed to want to establish between herself and M. Joseph was of too much consequence, which overly threatened the swaying of powers of the political state of the commune, for the great men of the village not to talk about it. Also, they had held counsel, to which they had summoned Marguerite; and after long, ripe discussions, which resonated off the ceiling of the mayor's grocery, they had decided that it had become urgent to know how to deal with the taciturn vicar who was aloof like the weather, and rich without any apparent fortune; so they had to find out if his former life would furnish reasons to exclude him from the castle, or even the commune, or to learn, at last, if he was really a being before whom one should bend one's head; and if the former were true destroy him, but, if the latter were true, honor him.

"Yes," said Leseq finishing off one of the mayor's sentences, "It is important to *cognoscere aliquem ab aliquo,* to know on what foot we must step around him."

It was as a result of this authorization that Marguerite engaged M. Gausse in giving a lunch for the members of this council, for the curate's consent was necessary for Leseq to leave; and besides, they thought that this would be a master stroke, to have M. Gausse enter into their group.

The next morning, Marguerite prepared a splendid dinner; and the invited guests, alerted by the servant, came to visit M. Gausse who received them cordially.

Leseq stood straight behind the tax collector, and he was torturing the buttons on his evil black coat when M. Gausse noticed him and said, "For all sins there is mercy, my dear schoolmaster, sit down and let us become good friends."

"*Amen dico vobis.* Monsieur the Curate, as was said by Cice…no, as was said in the Bible, may I be torn apart like a heretic if I am not worthy of your goodness."

"He is a good devil," replied the mayor, "and the *subsequent argument* that you had *because of*…but you see?… He is an honorable boy who writes a pretty letter, and…"

At this moment, Marguerite came to announce that dinner was ready, and that M. Joseph was coming down. Then M. Gausse, going towards the dining room while leaning on the tax collector's arm, was followed by everybody else. The officious Leseq brought along the curate's shepherd's cushion and set it on the good man's chair, who thanked him with a wink.

"Go ahead," cried the curate, happy to see a fine spread on the table, "go ahead Marcus Tullius, tell us the benediction in Latin; that will tickle you in the place where it itches."

"One cannot say the benediction any other way

than in Latin, and that is how many people profit from Latin without…"

At this word the curate raised an eyebrow, and Leseq noticed his mistake in time.

"Send away the thoroughbred, and he comes back at a gallop," cried the good priest.

"May I be bloodied," said Tullius, *"unguibus et rostro,* at the tribunal with fingernails, if I ever mean to offend you."

At this phrase M. Joseph smiled for the first time since he had arrived in Aulnay.

"What happened to you?" asked M. Gausse.

"Fortunately," replied the vicar, "our schoolmaster is not showing off his Latin, because he would have thrown his students into great confusion, *'rostro'* means 'teeth,' it only has the meaning of 'tribunal' in the plural."

Leseq bit his lips and vowed vengeance. Everyone, but especially the mayor and the tax collector, were quick to fall upon the poor school master who saw his reputation as a Latinist destroyed by the careful observation of the vicar.

The meal finished, M. Joseph said goodbye to the

gathering and withdrew.

"It has become more important than ever to find out who he is!..." said Leseq.

"Yes, Monsieur the Curate," cried the mayor, "you can tell how important it is to know at last who your vicar is: I cede the fact that he has paid many of the poor people's debts to me, but, you see, a mayor must watch over what happens in his community; and, at every moment, he should be in a state to furnish accounts of the people he administers *so that...*" here he looked at Leseq.

"So that *est togatus magistratus,* it is as it would be said by a lender."

"No, no, I am not lending," cried the animated mayor, "I only sell for cash, with the exception of Marguerite, *because...*"

"But, Monsieur the Mayor, *togatus...*"

"No, none of that!"

"But, *magistratus* signifies a judge."

"How is that," cried the judge in turn, "there are not two in a capital...I hope?"

"I was not saying that," replied Leseq.

"Be quiet," said the mayor. "Can't you see, Monsieur, that there is a mystery in the vicar's conduct, *because*...one does not hide when one has nothing to fear...*because* a merchant for example, let us suppose a grocer, if he goes bankrupt, he closes his shop and hides, so..."

"So," continued Leseq, "we must find out at A...y who M. Joseph is."

"I am of that opinion," murmured the tax collector, "because he has not paid his taxes yet."

"I think so," added the judge, "for if justice had something to do with it, my clerk, I believe...; in the end, he should know about it, the law formally says so."

"How I would like to know!..." cried Marguerite.

"Will Monsieur permit me," said Leseq to the curate, "to go to A...y?"

"Certainly," responded M. Gausse.

"So," continued Tullius, turning towards M. Gravadel the mayor-grocer, "I will leave right away!...But to avoid being tired, and to go faster, Monsieur the Mayor, you will grant me an act of generosity by loaning me your horse."

The mayor grimaced.

"If I had one," cried Marguerite to help sway the mayor, "it would already be saddled."

"I don't have a horse!" said the judge.

"I sold mine a long time ago!…" cried the tax collector.

"Very well, Leseq," responded the mayor with a noticable anxiety, "go and get my horse, but will you be careful with it? Will you let it go at its pace? Will you be good?…You will only go on grass? You will feed him at the right times? Take care of him?… Not contradict him?"

After half an hour, Leseq left, receiving a goodbye from the director of the village committee and the last word that the mayor called out to his secretary was: "Not so fast!…Not so fast!…" But Leseq whipped the horse without listening to the mayor-grocer.

Leseq promised to return in four days, and for these four days they were expecting him with an unequaled impatience. Marguerite counted the hours, and, each morning, rather than the formula, which for ten years had served as a preface to her master's rising, rather than asking: "Has Monsieur had a good

night?" she cried: "Monsieur, tomorrow or the day after tomorrow, Monsieur Leseq should be back, and
then we will know everything."

"My child," responded the curate the day before
Leseq's return, "he who wants to know everything
loses hope, I like this poor young man, and I would
be heartbroken to learn something bad about him: he
who has done bad can do worse, one is not ennobled
in a day, nor in order to expiate a fault; and meanwhile I have to live with him, so for a little curiosity I
risk my tranquility; the best is the enemy of the
good!"

Leseq did not arrive, and the entire village was
worried about the schoolmaster. The sixth day the
Marquise, as she left mass which she attended when-
ever the vicar said it, came back to M. Gausse's residence. This visit, evidently intended for M. Joseph,
greatly disturbed the mayor who feared compromising himself in sending Leseq to A...y, and above all
he missed his horse. If Leseq was not coming back,
then it was because the horse was sick, perhaps dead!

At last, on the seventh day in the evening, the
mayor came to visit the curate. The tax collector and

the judge where already there to protest their devotion to M. Joseph, and to say that they had not dipped into Leseq's plot. M. Gravadel, seeing the faces of the two functionaries, seemed to grow troubled, because he had just heard M. Lecorneur say: "it is very strange Monsieur Gausse, that Madame the Marquise asked for a noble chair for Monsieur Joseph: my brother is a servant at the minister's office..."

At the moment when the frightened mayor began to speak they heard a sound outside and a breathless Marguerite came in crying out: "Here is Leseq!..." just as the schoolmaster appeared and sat down.

"My horse?" was the first thing that the mayor said. Leseq could not respond, for the servant, taking care of the bringer of news, dried the sweat which covered the schoolmaster's forehead with her apron, brought forward a chair for him, and brought him a glass of wine. All eyes were directed on Tullius who, sensing his superiority, drank slowly, and after he had drunk brushed his sleeves and arranged his hair.

The good curate disguised his impatience by reviewing all the pages of his breviary in one fell swoop, several times. The tax collector twiddled his thumbs, the judge opened his eyes wide, but the mayor repeated:

"And my horse?..."

"Almost nothing," responded Leseq in a way that made M. Gradavel very uneasy.

"And?..."

"She lost a shoe at Vanney."

"Ah! Is that all it was?"

"When she lost the shoe she fell."

"Ah!" cried the mayor, looking at Leseq anxiously; "and then?"

"Almost nothing!...She was slightly hurt!..."

"Oh my poor horse!..."

"Why was she poorly shod?" asked Leseq, "because she cost me a hundred cents for the bandages and the drugs that the blacksmith..."

"So what happened to her?"

"Oh!" said Leseq, "she will not die of it, only she has bad knees!...But I was careful..."

"Ah!" said the mayor.

"To make a note of what it cost me; here, with the cost of my trip, it comes to fifty francs and seventy five cents."

"Who is going to pay?" cried out the angry mayor.

"The community!..." cried out the impatient group. The mayor calmed down, while grumbling, and Leseq, having collected his wits, spoke in basically these terms.

The Trip of Marcus Tullius Leseq

"I already told you what happened to me at Vanney; the horse got hurt, it would have really been too bad if the poor thing had died of it."

"Certainly, you loan your horses..." murmured the mayor.

"Because," Leseq continued, "she would not have brought me all the way to A...y. While the blacksmith shoed my horse, *ardebat Alexim,* I was roasting in the sun, so I went into an inn to sweep the dust out of my throat, and the woman hostess, fat, fresh, pretty, in the end like Miss Marguerite," (Marguerite blushed) "came to keep me company.

"That was when, thinking about my purpose, and judging that M. Joseph must have passed through

Vanney, I asked this dignified woman if our vicar had stopped at her place the night before his arrival at Aulnay-le-Vicomte. She replied, searching for the time in her memory, *in cerebro,* that effectively the carriage of the Bishop of A…y had passed by that very day, and that they had noticed a young ecclesiastic in it."

"The bishop's carriage!" cried out the listeners.

"The very carriage of the good monseigneur," repeated Leseq, "with his coat of arms, his coachman, his clothing, everything, and it is certain that they brought Monsieur Joseph in sight of Aulnay because the men stopped at the inn on the way back and spoke with the hostess: there is something else, the monseigneur's secretary accompanied him."

"The secretary!" cried the curate, "who is this vicar?"

"*Patienza,* as Cicero says," cried Leseq while continuing: "*un de factum est,* so it is a fact that Monsieur Joseph ordered, *jussit,* that they stop a gunshot away from Aulnay, and the secretary obeyed. All of which explains already a little why his shoes were not dusty, the day that he arrived.

"With great hopes after this beginning, I explained to my hostess the object of my trip, M. Joseph's strangeness; in the end I opened my heart to her, and just like Dido, she became, *dux femina facti,* the kingpin of my undertaking: this is how:

"'I know,' she responded, 'a man who will give you all possible information, this excellent man,' she said raising her eyes to the sky, 'is Abbot Frelu, who often comes to confess me: you won't tell my husband?...He does not like him, but are you staying? I will write you a note for Monsieur the Abbot.' She spoke to me even longer, because, even though she was pretty, she liked to talk."

"I could spend days listening to M. Leseq," cried Marguerite, who drew near the schoolmaster.

"My horse was shod, but she did not seem well! I had the letter, and I set out for A...y; no, I did not leave..."

Here Leseq blushed with embarrassment; Marguerite interpreted this redness right away and drew away from Tullius, especially when he said, "It was nothing, *nihil.* I slept at the inn, especially since the husband was not back yet, and because the hostess" (at this word Marguerite examined Leseq, so as to make one tremble), "told me that Abbot Frelu might come: so I stayed, and I did well because after three days the Abbot came. He took care, in entering, to ask his penitent if her husband were away, and he seemed overjoyed when she said that he was. As I knew the manners, I left them alone and did not reappear until evening when it was time to eat.

"'My father,' I said to this abbot, 'I have been waiting for you, so that you might be able to enlighten me about a young priest named Joseph, you must know him.'

"'Yes, I know him!' cried Abbot Frelu, 'he is a big, handsome man, tanned like an African, sad, speaks little, a handsome voice, and black eyes which cast of flames.'

"'That is the one,' I responded, 'he is the vicar at Aulnay!'

"'Vicar!...The hypocrite!...responded the abbot, 'soon he will be bishop. I will tell you everything that I know, and you will go to A...y, and they will just repeat to you what I am going to tell you, because the entire village has been talking about M. Joseph for more than a fortnight. For starters, I warn you that M. de Saint-André, our bishop, has been close to death for more than six months. Notice this fact.

"'A year and a half ago, a young man, M. Joseph, arrived in a postal wagon, at A...y, and stepped down by the seminary door. He was plunged in a frenzy which is hard to describe. I learned,' Abbot Frelu said to me, 'these details from Father Aubry, the director of the seminary. M. Joseph was led at his request to the director's apartment. There, without declaring any other name than Joseph, without giving a birth certificate, he begged Father Aubry to receive him into the seminary. He even paid right away for his lodging for a year and retired into a cell that he was allowed to choose. The darkest, most distant cell was the one that pleased him the most, and there is no such thing as a more austere retreat than M. Joseph's cell. His frugality was strict, and his piety, to all appearances, sincere. Always meditating, always praying, ceaselessly given over to the most severe disciplines of ancient hermits, he came to people's attention. M. Aubry came to see him, he found him deep in the darkest reverie, his eye fixed on a very erotic painting, but with tears in his eyes, pale, beaten. He praised M. Joseph's assiduousness, and the wisdom that he showed, and the progress that he was making in theology. The young man did not interrupt his ferocious silence except to respond in a manner that was even more ferocious. All of his expressions showed a marked disdain for all of humanity, his misanthropy was severely criticized by the director, who suggested that he try some recreation, and not disdain his comrades. M. Joseph did not follow his orders, and M. Aubry told me that he overwhelmed everybody with an air of superiority which alienated many people. M. Aubry believed that he should be severe with a being who maintained such pride. M. Joseph submitted to the punishments with indifference, and did not seem to be touched by them. They tried to inflict stronger punishments on him, and he went to his superior and said: "I am an adult, I am my own master, I know no one whose will can be imposed on me, I will leave if you torment me; for I have done nothing reprehensible: I believe that I am good, virtuous, religious, I have not opposed anyone!…If someone opposes me!…I will break anyone who gets in my way: I can."

"'Astonished by such language, Father Aubry, seeing that the time for a subdeacon had arrived, hurried to warn the bishop. The bishop ignored this report and was content to say to M. Aubry: "The young man whom you are speaking about is a man of distinction who must have committed some grave sin; he is someone whom the death of a dear person would plunge into desolation, and whose vivid passions brought to us: when I advance him to subdeaconry I will speak to him."

"'The entire seminary was persuaded that M. Joseph had no other goal than to satisfy the ambition which was gnawing at him; that he would succeed in getting attention; because the ardor that he showed in his theological studies proved it, and that they would soon see his aims exposed. They already began talking about him, in town, of the extraordinary neophyte that we had, and the women, when they heard of his actions, learning that he was a handsome man, full of fire, enthusiasm, and that he distrusted everything became violently interested in him.

"'The day of the advancement to the subdeaconate arrived, the bishop's room was filled with people, especially women. M. Joseph arrived in turn in the bishop's room to respond to all of the questions that the bishop wanted to ask him and at last to proclaim his family name. I learned from the bishop's secretary the details of this interview. The secretary was at the far end of the Bishop Monseigneur de Saint-André's room. The young neophyte came forward, told his name, and the monseigneur uttered a cry which made the secretary come on the run. M. Joseph, surprised, waited for the result of the bishop's emotion. The latter took a long time to regain his senses, but, having long known the habit of disguising his passions and his secrets under a severe— and impenetrable face, he came back to himself, looked at the young man with a kindness which was extraordinary for him, and said to him: "Young man what are your intentions?"

"Monseigneur, they are to become a priest as soon as possible if you can shorten the testing time, I would be infinitely obliged to you."

"'The astonished bishop, almost stupefied, examined the neophyte's face with a strange care. He took pleasure in the reverie that this examination threw him, his face indicated that he was prey to all the charm of his memories.

"And when you are a priest," he said, "what do you want to do?"

"Obtain a modest vicarage and die peacefully."

"How old are you?"

"Twenty-two years-old."

"'At this moment the vicar sent his secretary away, and we never knew what else took place between the monseigneur and the young man. M. Joseph reappeared in the ordination room accompanied by the monseigneur. The Bishop Mgr. de Saint-André confered a subdeaconate on him and withdrew him from the seminary, he let him live in the bishop's residence, in a place that conformed to his tastes; M. Joseph led the same life there that he had led in the seminary, which astonished everyone.

"'The bishop admitted to a fondness for the young man, an extraordinary affection, one would say a paternal one. What was most astonishing is to learn that the monseigneur knew nothing of the youth's earlier life, and that he did not confide anything in M. Joseph as to the reasons why he showed him such signs of love; for love is the only word which one can use to describe it. The most absurd rumors began circulating which attacked the morals of the prelate and M. Joseph. The entire village spoke of this event, the prettiest women of the village appeared in the circle around the monseigneur so that they could see M. Joseph, but he never appeared, and when they did find him by chance, his severe moods, his icy countenance rebuffed the hommages by which they tried to shake his supposed virtue.

"'At last, the monseigneur wrote to the court at Rome to obtain a dispensation, and, three months ago, the young man was ordained a priest. When he asked for the first place that was available to him, the bishop had the paper brought to him. Nothing was available, but the secretary told the monseigneur that for a long time they had been asking for a vicar in the community at Aulnay-le-Vicomte; the young man cast himself at the bishop's knees to obtain the position.

"'The bishop reflected on the name of Aulnay-le-

Vicomte and cried out: "The wretch! There are things written in the sky."

"'Since this word, monseigneur is at death's door. Gout and sciatica have combined with a fever which has not left him. He could not resist his dear Joseph's insistings, and he gave him his carriage, his men, his secretary to take our young vicar to Aulnay. Since M. Joseph's departure, the bishop had not pronounced his name, but often his glances looked for the young man, especially when he is in his gravest need. The ecclesiastics who, like myself, knew about the ways of human passions, admired the guile of this young ambitious man, and we did not doubt the conduct that he would lead at Aulnay. Wasn't he somber, reserved, distrusting even the most elevated dignitaries, affecting the greatest piety, taciturn, do-gooder?...'

"That is so,' I said.

"I guessed it!'...responded Abbot Frelu.

"We have already talked a lot about what Monsieur Joseph has done since his arrival; and about you, Monsieur Gausse, because Monsieur the Abbot Frelu greatly encouraged me to approach you, and it was not hard for him to praise you.

"'Monsieur,' said the Abbot Frelu to me, 'in conclusion, be sure that before seven years are out this young hypocrite, who for the rest is full of talent, will be a cardinal and a minister.'

"Then I thanked Monsieur the abbot, kissed the hostess, and had the horse gallop off to A…y…"

"Gallop!…" cried the mayor raising his hands and eyes towards the sky.

"There," continued Leseq, "one of my relations who is honorably employed in keeping the school children confirmed what the abbot said to me: he gave me details that the abbot had omitted: which were the little events that have taken place since the monseigneur ordained M. Joseph.

"There were a lot of people there. The young man carried the marks of the finest pain on his face, and his appearance drew tears from your eyes. A great battle was evidently taking place inside him, his gestures did not match his ordinarily noble bearing. When the bishop appeared, he fell to his knees where he was. Tears escaped from his eyes, and he cried out sobbing:

"'My God! So the sacrifice is made!…'

"The entire time during the ceremony, he cried, and they were obliged to carry him almost dying, but our curiosity was not satisfied as to the cause of the tears. He is thought to have been heard pronouncing repeatedly a name which no one could make out through his sobs.

"I thanked my relation, I went back to Vanney; I saw the hostess again; *et dixi:* I have said it!" cried Leseq straining his voice.

Then he swallowed a glass of wine that the joyous Marguerite had brought him.

CHAPTER 7

As soon as Leseq had finished his eloquent narration, everyone looked around with an astonishment that the schoolmaster believed that he had produced by his discourse, which he would have called *pro vicario;* but soon a muted murmur was raised in the curate's room.

"We don't know anything new," cried Marguerite.

"We know enough," said the judge, "to refrain from any more research about Monsieur Joseph. If he is a favorite of the monseigneur, a favorite of Madame de Rosann, we would not be well received if we caused him some trouble."

"That's it," added M. Gravadel, the mayor, "besides if he is rich, he will pay for what he takes without haggling for less!..."

"I have nothing more to fear about his taxes," called out the tax collector, "why, Monsieur Mayor, didn't you tell me that he paid in cash?"

"And in gold," replied the mayor.

"In gold!" cried everyone in chorus.

"Heavens," cried Leseq, "what a marvel, *quantum prodigium.* What if he stole it!...Ah! Messieurs, follow Abbot Frelu's advice, this man is not hiding for nothing; unless he has committed some crime!...Let us tear with our strength and our effort. Let us tear the veil that covers him: *refert,* it is important, *communae,* to the community, et *securitati publicae,* to the public gallows, which means justice, *justitia,* to know who this man is: and, if he is a criminal, who, blessed with a seductive exterior, has tricked the monseigneur, surprised the soul and good graces of Madame the Marquise, see what happens to us in unmasking him?...You, Monsieur the Tax Collector, you will become the receiver for the whole area; you, Monsieur Mayor, you will be named sub-prefect, perhaps!...You, Monsieur the Judge who will have arrested the guilty fugitive, you will go sit on the laurels of the tribunal!...And I..."

The first three functionaries of Aulnay rested with their mouths open gasping at the hope presented them by the eloquent Leseq.

"One moment, my children," said the curate; and raising his sick leg over the end table on which it had been set, he stood up adopting an attitude that was made imposing by his air of goodness; "a moment my children, each is master of his own, and you should not inculpate Monsieur Joseph like this. I agree that there is no smoke without fire, but each to his own job, and our job is not to be spies; besides one should not put one's finger between the tree and the bark, because there is no worse water than sleeping water; and what do you know will happen to you in your research, he who looks for evil, is subject to evil; from which I conclude, that each is the child of his works, and that we should not blacken Monsieur Joseph. If he is rich? Money works wonders. You take care. He who finds a thorn should look for the rose; and one knows where one is. One does not know where one is going; man proposes, God disposes; and the conquered pay the winner; so have no plot, believe me, a piece of good advice is worth an eye in the hand."

This deluge of proverbs was not designed to placate Leseq, but seeing himself alone in his opinion, he closed his mouth and left with the knowledge that he had satisfied public curiosity, without meanwhile explaining M. Joseph's distance from all sublunary circumstances.

The honor of this discovery went to Marguerite, fate had decided that the village would never know about it, and that the servant would bring her secret with her to her grave.

She had remained alone in the room, and even though she thought of the vicar, she tried to understand how the perfidious Leseq could have stayed with a pretty hostess for four days?…She was recalling the schoolmaster's embarrassment when he arrived at this part of his narration…When the trot of a horse resounded outside, and the presbytery bell rang inside, Marguerite went to get it, a peasant came to ask with insistence for the help of the church for his mother who was dying. Marguerite went up to M. Joseph's room and told him what humanity and religion required of him. The young priest went out quickly. He ran to the church and leaped on the horse which the disconsolate son had brought him. He went fast. He flew off, despite the night, despite the rain, he was already far away!...

What joy! Marguerite paled, she was alone in the room in which, since the vicar has been in the house, no one had penetrated...The imprudent vicar had, in his zeal, left everything to go to the aid of the person in distress, and Marguerite, the curious Marguerite triumphed!...

She went through the room with an unexpressable joy; she came before the easel, and stood immobile with admiration for the expression of the most beautiful woman that it is possible to imagine. This portrait was the work of a young priest, and, noticing this celestial face, the first thought which came into her mind was to believe that this woman was an imaginary creation, in which a voluptuous soul, big and filled with poetry, had collected all the disparate traits in nature so as to create that which painters call the assembly of the *beautiful ideal*.

When Marguerite had been satisfied with this charming view, she went forward towards the bureau, saw the manuscript, opened it and read...

...

...

The good curate, not worrying about his servant's absence, having put his leg in place and leaned his head agains the enormous back of his red winged chair, allowed himself to succumb to the temptation to sleep that had been produced by Leseq's discourse. He slept…

Suddenly piercing cries awoke him from his first nap, he heard Marguerite come in all angry, with a candle in her hand.

"Ah! Monsieur, an abomination…a revolt, they are going to hang him!…Kill him!…The rogues."

"What is wrong, my child? My vicar, is he back yet? Tell me!…"

"Ah, Monsieur, what a story! A ship, pirates, the poor children, their father!…He…"

"But, Marguerite, sit down, and tell me!…"

"Monsieur your vicar went out, he left the door to his room open, I went in, I saw everything, here is his manuscript, here is his story, I have read half of it, and it's a devil's sabbath!…"

"Marguerite," said the curate severely, "take that manuscript back where you found it, close the door to my vicar's room and come back here. You will not leave me until he is back."

"What Monsieur!..." cried Marguerite, stupefied by the cold bloodedness and the unknown severity of the good curate.

"Do what I say!..." repeated the curate, silencing the desire which consumed him.

"Do you realize, Monsieur, that we will know everything, learn everything, it is possible and yet you refuse!...By my faith, Monsieur, one profits from chance. What falls into the pit is fit for the soldier."

A proverb always got to the good curate, his severity disappeared, and he began to admire the rascally, curious face of his servant. She went on, "Monsieur!...Very well, I will read it to the end."

The curate began to smile cleverly, but he responded, "No!...No, Marguerite."

"Monsieur listen," the servant began again, "I am of your opinion, we should put this manuscript back in its place, but will you permit me to observe to you that 1) I began it, 2) if M. Joseph wrote his story, it was so that it may be read; 3) that in the end no one will know about it."

"And God, Marguerite!..."

"Ah Monsieur! Is that all that is stopping you," the malicious servant began again, "keep listening to me!..."

"Ah, Satan!..." cried M. Gausse who was beginning to want to read the manuscript, "if one says about hunger that the hungry stomach has no ears, what would they say about curiosity?"

"Whatever they wish, my good master," she said, slipping into a chair beside M. Gausse; "but are you listening to me?..." and placing her hand on the curate's arm, she looked at him with a tender expression and said to him, "We are two people who are very different, and the sins that one commits have nothing to do with the other."

"What the devil are you getting at?"

"Ah well, Monsieur," the jesuitical servant continued: "I take the sin upon myself!...I was the one who took the manuscript. I am the one who is going to read it. You can listen or not listen. You can act as you see fit; but I am reading it...and in two or three days, I will confess to you, I will show myself a sincere repentant, and then you will absolve me."

"That may be," said the curate moving his head from right to left.

"But Monsieur, you will not stop me from sinning. What women want, God wants. Besides, what I submit to you, this reasoning, did you not subject me to it fifteen years ago, the day after my arrival here?"

With these words, Marguerite cast a glance at M. Gausse. The curate blushed, lowered his eyes, and the servant triumphed through the means of these powerful memories. The curate closed his mouth, and by this silence he showed that he was beaten. But I have already said that M. Gausse was frankness itself; so, having consulted his heart, he cried, "Go ahead, Marguerite, read it…"

The latter, tricky and clever like an old judge, went out suddenly, and ran to wake up a child from the choir who lived just two steps away from the presbytery. She promised him a thousand sweets, his protection and reward if he would play the sentinel at the end of the village and come back to warn them when he heard the vicar returning.

The child promised. The servant, having taken care of everything, ran to her master, set herself across from him, trimmed the candle, put on her glasses, and M. Gausse, having closed his eyes so as not to witness a sacrilege, Marguerite read out loud what follows, in a nasal voice.

CHAPTER 8

"If I write this story of my youth it is with the aim of making the people who read it think deeply: I try to shed light on the most stormy seas, hoping in this way to enlighten my brothers, and show them the dangers which are contained in the most innocent feelings, and the gentle affections which nature has placed in our hearts."

"His writing ressembles him!" cried out the curate casting a glance towards the sky; "Poor young man! He has been very unhappy, or so it seems."

"Ah, why try to fool myself," Marguerite continued, "Doesn't God know that if I write the story of my adventures it is only so that I can think about my dear Melanie! No, turning away, my conscience complains? Let us avow that I am, to myself alone, the theme of the writing that I trace with so much pleasure, because all of the memories which I am going to evoke will satisfy my bridled passion. Let us not begin a true story with a lie;...I am a priest, I must remember it...O religion! Celestial bounty, you alone maintain me! Give me the strength to finish before the death which I see rapidly approaching comes to seize me. I invoke you, and dedicate all my thoughts to you, although they all concern the soft, tender, and pure Melanie.

"Scarcely worrying about the laws of eloquence, I am going to follow the impulses of my heart. I am going to obey the influence of memories, and I write for myself alone (I dare not say for her), under the dictates of a pure heart…yes pure!…It will always be so no matter what happens. All men, in speaking of themselves, are given to dissimulation; but if I dissimulate to myself, what will I do when it comes to her?…Ah! All that I say will always be too *little*.

"There are circumstances in my life, and facts which have only recently come to my knowledge; still, rather than placing them at the true time that I learned them, I will follow the natural order of ideas in these memories, and I will arrange the facts in such a way that they will form a continuous narrative.

"I was born in France, where? I do not know; of whom? I did not know for a long time; my birth was wrapped in the most mysterious veils; for, at this very moment, I still do not have a legal, authentic, and postitive proof of my nativity; it would be impossible for me to support what I am going to suggest.

"In the end, as soon as I saw Aulnay-le-Vicomte, I had a vague memory of having been nourished here and of having spent the first two years of my life here: what gave me this suspicion is that I have always had in my memory the Aulnay landscape engraved in an ineffable manner; and at the first walk which I took with the good curate, I was stupefied by recognizing, at the end of the village, on the side by the Ardennes, the pear tree under which my nurse ordinarily set me when she went to work in the neighboring field. My nurse was a fat peasant, I have sought her hut in vain; if she were still living, I would recognize her out of a thousand faces. Her hut bespoke poverty, still its thatched roof was often visited by an ecclesiastic who took me on his knees, smiled at me, tried to make me laugh and speak, and covered me with kisses. These facts are found engraved in my mind because of the strange ways of ecclesiastics.

"I was two and a half years-old, when one morning my nurse was out laboring in the fields, and I was alone in the house, I was playing, when two men came suddenly in; I recognized the ecclesiastic who was speaking to a soldier with animation. After a long discussion, which was not at all heated because these two men seemed to be friends, the soldier took me, wrapped me in his cloak, climbed into a carriage, left the village, and after a certain period during which I have no distinct recollections, I found myself in a big city by the seaside: in the end, a few days later I was transported in a sloop, and from the sloop into a big vessel which greatly amazed me. Here, in a few words, is all that my memory can tell me about my childhood.

"This soldier, captain of a vessel, was M. the Marquis de Saint-André, my father; and as for my mother, I never saw her, never did her ineffable smile bring a shiver to my heart; so it saddens my soul that I cannot recognize any woman as being her.

The vessel in which I was placed sailed to M…and, at first, M. the Marquis de Saint-André was not very tender with me. His wife, or so they told me, had emigrated, and no longer lived in France:

they did not tell me anything else, and anytime that I questioned my father about it, he bid me to be silent. Very well, when I was older I thought: how could a mother be able to abandon her oldest child? How could she send him to a village far from her and confide him to the care of a stranger? And this mother did not try to come see me a single time! Why did she not dare to brave all dangers to come and kiss me? It always was and still is a mystery to me of which I have never been able to raise the veil: it is true that as a child of nature who was eventually initiated into the sacrilegious inventions of society I do not know the abominable combinations which the particular vices of the social state and groupings of men produce.

"My father was gifted with a great energy, passionate, severe, and even hard at times. Nevertheless, I must avow that although I suffered from his coldness, he often had a paternal goodness towards me, but this was when my moral qualities developed, and he thought that I could do him honor one day. M. de Saint-André was frank, generous, exceedingly brave, educated, doing everything to please, and never succeeding, even when he wanted to. Perhaps he let his superiority be felt a little too much, the habit of commanding, like a king at his table, had helped to fertilize the seeds of pride and haughtiness which his soul contained, and those seeds which were associated with his self love were to be esteemed, feared, even admired, but were never pleasing.

"We arrived at M..., and it was in that island that I spent the greater part of my youth. Here, I must observe that France was in the middle of a revolution, so that my father's peaceful trip was a new mystery which I cannot solve: I still do not know at this time if my father exists, and he alone can explain these contradictions to me.

"In M..., my father's first concern was to buy a small property, far from everything, and to confine me there by placing me in the hands of the wife of one of his foremen. Mme. Hamel and two blacks were the only people that I saw up until the age of nine. Mme. Hamel became almost a mother to me: she was not spiritual, but she had excellent judgement, a soul molded with gentleness, goodness and loveable virtues; from the most tender age she inspired the fear of God in me, and nourished me on the celestial precepts of the Gospel.

"M. de Saint-André did not stay very long at M…; I only saw him again at very infrequent times, but the sailor's life does not permit long visits, and he could only visit us when he found himself in the vicinity of our isles.

"So my first years were spent far from cities, far from people, far from vices; I was given over to nature, and I can call myself its child, for Mme. Hamel never contradicted me, she let me follow the penchants of my soul, judging, as she told me, that people are born good, and that in saving them from civilization, they are given, by this single and simple precaution, the most beautiful education possible. The poor woman was the very innocent cause of all of our troubles!…

"This good Mme. Hamel did not even think once of having me study the sciences; she never understood that Latin, or mathematics, etc…could be essential to the happiness of humankind. I submit as a fact that she does not know if M…where she lived for half of her life, was below the equator or in a tropic. She does not know the differences between the plants of America and those of Europe; she would not give a cent to teach me a new discovery, and she only showed me a few things that most people knew.

"The instructions which she constantly repeated to me, and which were her most gentle preoccupation, consisted of a few maxims that were more difficult to practice than to remember. 'My friend,' she said to me looking at me with a tender eye, 'be worthy of the name Joseph; render good for good; respect age and children, for you are a child and you will be old; do not make fun of anyone; do not annoy anyone whatsoever, not even the smallest of animals; prefer other people's happiness to your own; try to be selfless; admire the universe and draw your own conclusions from what it shows.'

"The good thing was that she preached by example. She would have blushed, as if from a crime, to betray the renegade blacks who came to hide out in the mountains; rather often these unfortunate fugitives came bringing fruits, curiosities, and protected me when I went shopping. Our two blacks adored this good and lovable woman. In the end all that she told me was supported by virtuous actions, accomplished with that simplicity, which must make them seem doubly valuable in the eyes of the Eternal One.

"I lived for seven years without knowing any laws but my own, or other places than the scorching mountains and the humid forests which surrounded us. From nature I received an impetuous and passionate character: this terrible energy, son of the firey climate and the volcanic land that I inhabited only deployed itself in two passions which were so to speak its refuge, for, in all the rest of its sentiments, in the practices and accidents of life, I was praised by other people for my gentleness and patience; still, I do not think that I shine by those qualities.

"The first of these two passions is a gentle fanaticism for the religion of Jesus Christ. I was Christian by my own choice, and I attribute this enthusiasm of my soul to the liberty that I enjoyed ceaselessly in the countryside, contemplating that immense American nature. I felt lofty sentiments being born in my soul, and I found that only the gospels were at the level of these marvels: you can recognize the same hand in them both. The book is like nature, vast, simple and complicated, naive and grand, varied and sublime. The mountains, the forests made me religious, mystical, and for a long time I saw the most beautiful side of the world. Until I was nine I ran through the area surrounding our home without any fixed ideas, like a young satyr playing all the time, going from amazement to amazement, climbing up bamboos poles, on rocks, on coconut trees, and was like a young monkey, curious, light, and wild.

"Often I came to the lair of the runaway slave. The poor fugitive recognized me as the child whom his comrades had designated as the son of Mme. Hamel, and the black man, bringing me a mat, told me about his troubles, his harsh treatment. I cried along with him, and he respectfully kissed my hands, *because I was white*. Oh memories of childhood, how you are gentle!…This part of my youth was like the dawn of a fine day: my pure pleasures, the freshness of my feelings, the calm, the naïveté, everything contributed to make the memory of my first strides in life enjoyable, and I could not think of the sound of the bell of our habitation, without its giving my heart a sweet festival, gentle and beautiful with all the harmonies that the sky of my island revealed to me.

"Meanwhile, in the middle of my promenades, I sometimes got to thinking; I began to feel in my heart sharp feelings, affections which sought someone that they could fix themselves on; in the end, I was lacking something. Often I went to find the old renegade black man to confide in him how much pleasure I drew from looking at a beautiful landscape, and a hanging rock which seemed destined to fall on the spring that escaped from under his feet. I wanted him to share in my discoveries, for a beautiful dawn, or a sunset did not please me as much when I saw them alone. Good Mme. Hamel never reproached me when I left her to go run off, and yet the good woman almost died of fright when I spent a night in a cave with my good friend Fimo, the old black renegade, the chief of the fugitives. Was it not the utmost goodness, to suffer so without complaining!...O Mme. Hamel!...

"I was nine years-old, and for seven years I had not seen my father. One day I came back to our house; it was almost dark; I noticed the many lights from far away; I ran to ask what was producing this extraordinary brightness. While going down the avenue that was lined by a hedge of young guava plants, avocadoes, and dammar pines, I saw that there were many soldiers in front of the house, I arrived, and I saw my father.

"I leaped up to his shoulders and kissed him. What was my surprise in turning around to see, next to Mme. Hamel, a young girl aged around five years!... Mme. Hamel held her on her knees, and when I looked at her, she cast me a glance which I have never forgotten. She was sitting on Mme. Hamel's lap with an elegance which seemed natural to her. Her little face shone with all the beauties of childhood: on her fine white skin appeared all the seeds of grace and attractiveness; it was a short version of the perfections of nature, and her childish pose, her naive smile!...Her long and thick curls of blonde hair, which fell on her fresh and little shoulders. Ah! Unhappy man! I can still see everything, just as I am writing these lines.

"'My son,' M. de Saint-André said to me, 'I have brought your sister to you.'

"At these words I kissed the charming child.

"'Do you really like her?... because she is the living portrait of Madame de Saint-André, and is *the only one that we could have.*' In saying this, my father shed several tears. 'She died!...' he continued; but he could not complete his thought.

"I took the news of my mother's death with an indifference which I am still ashamed of, for I only felt bad about the pain of my father, and, as for me, I was not affected at all: still, that morning I had bitterly wept the death of a young loxia which I had cared for along with my old black friend. How can you explain this strange attitude? Is it not because we can only love beings who are always present, whom we know, and with whom we have continual relations.

"When M. de Saint-André was alone with me, my sister and Mme. Hamel, he addressed the latter, and said to her, 'Madame, I have brought you Melanie because there is still too much danger for us in France, and I did not know of anybody else to whom I could give this dear child. As soon as we can go back to Europe I will come and get you. You know what dangers I am risking once I leave here!...Perhaps I did too much in coming here. I do not know how I am going to rejoin my ship, but my men are many and well armed.'

"After this short meeting, my father kissed me, covered Melanie with kisses, and left. I wanted absolutely to accompany him all the way to the shore and to follow him in order to participate in the dangers that he would undergo. He ordered me to stay with an imperative gesture and a stern glance whose authority it was impossible to escape.

"I went into the house and all evening my eyes were attached to the little Melanie. A crowd of reflections assailed me, and I felt an attachment being born inside me that I did not understand. The emotion that I felt at the sight of this young child was undefinable, and I saw with joy that she shared it in all of its depth. We slept in the same bedroom not far from Madame Hamel, for I wanted at all costs to take care of my sister.

"From that moment on an entirely new way of life opened up before me. I did not lack for anything and the most terrible passion mutely set its foundations in my soul. All of my sister's smiles belonged to me, so that I no longer did anything except in her name or for her. I brought her along in my wanderings which I tailored to her little legs, and each lovely flower that I encountered was offered to her as a toy, each lovely fruit, each bird's nest, arrived in her lovely hands before she even had the chance to desire them. Where Melanie was seen, I was sure to be found also, for the one of us never went off without the other. A quarter of an hour's absence became a trial for both of us, and our only intention was to please each other, to seek to make one another happy. Proud of my age and of my strength, I rendered Melanie services which cost me nothing, since I found it so nice to make her obliged to me. Pains, tirednesses, cares, dangers were like roses to me. If a tired Melanie could not come back, I made a seat out of vines and, fixing it to my back, I carried my sister all the way to the house; this pretty girl passed her arms around my neck, and letting her golden hair mingle with the curls of the jet black of my hair, and my heart beat with joy when I felt the soft hand of Melanie wiping the sweat off my brow.

"I initiated Melanie into my great secrets, I took her down my favorite roads, to the runaway blacks.

We climbed rocks, and seeing the splendor of the sunset and the magnificence of the dawn, I tried to make her understand the little that I knew about the Eternal One; we read together what God wrote on the vault of the skies, what he traced on the sands of the sea, on the leaves of the trees, on the variegated wings of the birds. As for the other precepts, Melanie's naive and pure heart contained them all, and it was especially her, who in *learning* the sublime obligations of man towards man, only appeared to be *remembering them.* Quite young, a good action, a noble thought, flowed from her mouth and from her heart with a facility which made one believe that good and virtue were her element.

"One day, we went to the old Fimo's cave. We arrived at his retreat after having crossed the most lovely paths and having surrendered ourselves to the most sincere happiness. The setting sun gilded all the summits and said goodbye to nature, enriching it with its lovely tints of bronze, gold and purple; the air was still. A funerary silence reigned on the area around Fimo's hearth. We approached...the unhappy man had just greeted the sun for the last time!

Stretched out on a large rock covered with moss which served him as a chair, the poor, immobile black man was not breathing any longer and his open eyes, staring straight ahead, showed that the man of nature dies without being surrounded by friends, because the man of nature is afraid of death. Melanie closed his eyes, took off her veil, placed it on the poor black man's face, and, kneeling, said to me: 'Let us pray!...'

"No, from beyond the tomb, I would still hear that pure and touching voice, that tone which knocks down all the fibers of my heart!...What a glance! What feeling! Our prayers consisted of contemplating in turn the corpse and the sky! I do not know what Melanie was thinking, but I know that then my soul rose towards all that melancholy and religion have of the most grand, most sublime and most exalted. Together we rose and our eyes were in tears.

"Whatever merit the long prayers for the dead contain, I have never heard a lovelier orison than the 'Let us pray!' that Melanie spoke. Religion is a human need.

"We perceived two black men looking for their

wretched subsistence. We called them with great cries. They came recognizing our voices, we guided them to the inanimate corpse of the good Fimo. They dug a grave where Melanie chose under a coconut tree. Both of us mute and filled with a holy sort of attention, we followed them, holding hands, the two black men who carried Fimo on their shoulders. In the end we saw them set him in his last resting place: at this moment, by a trick of nature and the surrounding area, a ray of sunlight, creating daylight, shone just on the grave. 'God take him!...' I cried when the earth was cast upon him, Melanie said: 'We will no longer see him!...' We made a sort of mound, and when we were sad the black man's tomb was the altar that we came to cry at.

"On our way back, we kept silent; but in coming out of the forest, moved by all that Melanie had said, I stopped and looking at my sister, I told her with a soulful voice: 'Ah you are an angel!...'

"She only responded with a fine smile and a gracious movement of her head which are engraved on my memory along with all that she said and all that she did. That evening we did not eat, for in coming back in she murmured: 'Joseph, one is not hungry when one is sad!'

"'Divine soul!…'"

"My good Jesus!" cried out Marguerite, "you see, Monsieur," she said to M. Gausse showing him the manuscript, "you see? He cried at this part. The writing is almost erased."

M. Gausse did not respond, but his face indicated that all the strings of his benevolant and sensitive heart had contracted.

CHAPTER 9

"That was how we spent the time of our childhood. Our games and our wanderings were embellished by all that human feelings have that is naive and touching. Our bodies, not being deformed by the ridiculous clothing which style engenders, developed rapidly with the lovely proportions that nature, left to herself, effortlessly creates, and gave us the frail advantages of beauty. Our gentle liberty made our faces glow with a divine happiness.

Melanie reached her twelfth year. Her lovely build had almost taken shape; she already looked at herself in the clear water of fountains to arrange the thousands of curls which made her lovely blonde hair even more gracious. Her blue eyes were always smiling, and she had the habit of looking in a certain way which suddenly showed a tender soul given to melancholy. She covered her little feet with a sandal that was artfully woven by our blacks; and, according to the custom of the islands, she left them bare: nothing was as seductive as this young lady graced with all the lovable qualities of a woman!…Now in evoking these painful and charming memories, I recall the admirable pair which we must have formed when entangled on the side of a fountain, under a rock, in the middle of the vast antique galleries of the forest and protected by the thorny hedges, we gave ourselves over to our childish games; it seemed to me that the famous statues of Greece could not have been more beautiful, for whatever the divine fire may be which spread genius over its creations, we surpassed them by the naïveté of our attitudes, the freshness of our faces; and, like the charming shadows of the two lovers that Klopstock mentions, we had no need of human words to share our feelings and thoughts…a gesture, a smile, a glance, a kiss replacing language, our souls understood one another. Habit had made our hearts slip one into the other so that there only existed one.

"I do not know many people who would be pleased by the simple description of events which marked our years of happiness. They seem to belong to another time, rather than our modern century; but the depiction will only bore people whose imaginations have never traced the mendacious paintings of the *golden age*. Alas, I can say with pride that I know them now in my misfortune.

"One day, I led Melanie towards a place which Europeans can have no notion of. If one imagines two enormous peaks, separated one from the other at their summit by a wide space, this opening in the air would resemble an immense angle, for the two mountains are connected at the bottom and precisely form an sharp angle placed at the juncture itself, their summits form a valley with rocks above on both sides. So the lower valley was extremely narrow; each mountain, embellished by vegetation, had a miraculous appearance. On one side of the valley you saw the sea at a great distance; and on the other, a woods arranged in a circle in the middle of which a spring let its gentle murmur be heard. When Melanie was at the entrance to this vast and admirable landscape that was called the Terrible Valley, she looked at me, gripped my hand and, showing me a piece of rock in which one discovered all the beauties, a unique collection of all the resources of nature: She said, 'On this rock, under these trees which we could complete by building an elegant hut, surrounded by flowers, and farther on in there is an island located in the middle of this little lake, I would like to feel that I could be able to wait here when I saw the black man's tomb set under a taramack.'

"I led Melanie back to our house; and when she was in bed, I escaped, and running with all my strength I returned to the Terrible Valley. I went into all the haunts of the runaway blacks whom we brought food to every day. I assembled them, and bringing them to that rock where Melanie had expressed that lovable frivolousness of her sex. I said to them: 'My friends, Melanie said that she wanted a house here, so we must construct one right away.'

"Immediately seven or eight black men set to work on the bases of thirty trees which did not fail to fall, while others dug the earth, and still others collected moss. We worked all night, and the day surprised us with the work well advanced. I do not know how I went about constructing a hut according to the rules of architecture, but I have seen in parks of the wealthy artificial rustic constructions which were nothing but hovels when compared to my wild palace.

"On each side of the door there rose up thirty perfectly straight trees, which represented columns, since the gnarled trunks were fat and round, and the gaps were carefully filled with moss. On the columns we set an enormous coconut tree across, then, with the skill that blacks often show, my compatriots succeeded in setting two thick trunks at angles, which formed a pediment. At the base of the columns, they arranged the earth so that natural steps gave a base to the tree trunks, and this hut resembled the Parthenon. It was very long, and its sides were made according to the style of a facade; the blacks made the roof with mangrove leaves, and we left spaces so that the interior was lighted.

"Meanwhile the day advanced; while working for Melanie I had forgotten it!...In the end, towards evening, when I saw that the blacks could finish with my instructions on their own; I ran to the house...I entered and I saw Melanie who, with red eyes, was sitting by the door. As soon as she saw me, she began waving her handkerchief, for she was choked with joy, and she could not speak. Seeing this action I understood how sharp her pain must have been, and, in a second I was at her side...

"'Bad boy,' said Mme. Hamel to me, without asking where I was coming from 'why did you worry us?'

"'Don't scold him, mother,' said Melanie, 'see how upset he is!...Joseph,' she added with a charming naïveté, 'I will not say that you did me wrong, because you would be too saddened by it!' She began to wipe the sweat off my brow and to caress my hair with an attention that was filled with grace.

"'When I didn't see you, I cried!' she said to me; 'I did not live this day, we must strike it from the number of days that God will grant me! Cruel boy, how could you stay away from me? If it was for some good action, I will never forgive you for having left me in the house.'

"Not wanting to divulge my secret, I remained silent, which astonished Melanie. She looked at me with a pouting expression which made her charming, by the difficulty which she found in making an expression of displeasure appear on her face. Going to bed she said to me, expanding her voice: 'I do not wish you a good night!...'

"'And as for me, Melanie,' I responded gently to her smiling, 'I beg the All Mighty to spread the charm of the most beautiful dreams upon your innocent sleep.'

"At this response, she was a little confused, and went to bed muttering: 'Why did he not tell me what he did?' It seems that jealousy is a feeling whose seed is naturally inside us, and that civilization does not create it.

"The next day, my sister came to me; and, kissing me with a repentant air, she said to me with tenderness: 'I ask your pardon, my brother.'

"'You have no need of it,' and I kissed her with abandon.

"Mme. Hamel pressed each of us to her breast crying out: 'Happy children!...Be sure to keep the purity of your souls!...'

"We looked at each other without being able to understand the meaning of these words. Now I understand them!...After the meal I led Melanie off, and I brought her to the Terrible Valley by means of a path which would have her come out suddenly across from the spectacle that she had desired. Almost all of the runaway slaves had been from the coast of Guinea, and they sang one of their country's songs in chorus. This savage melody went well with the picturesque site, and it struck our ears. 'Why these are our blacks!' said Melanie arriving in the valley. She took one more step, uttered an astonished cry, she looked at me, and threw herself on my chest, and on her blossoming cheek flowed tears of celestial joy. The blacks had taken care to rake the earth and form an avenue on which golden sand was spread, making walking more agreeable. "How I love their landscaping," said Melanie.

"She went into the hut which we named the Temple. What are the words that could describe the charm of such a moment?...

"A little later, an occurance enlightened me as to the nature of the feeling that I had for my sister whom I loved too much. Among the runaway blacks there was one from the Gold Coast of an extremely ferocious nature, and the harsh treatment that he had been subjected to had only made his character worse. He fled his unhappy companions; he wandered in the steepest and most wild areas; nothing could tame him: Melanie tried. One day seeing him sitting on a rocky area she said to me: 'Joseph. It is impossible that there are any creatures who are entirely bad. You can be wrong, but no one says in the depths of his heart: "I want to be cruel;" this black man looks at the sky, but this action alone indicates to me that we shall succeed.'

"Right away she began walking and we came to this black man who did not run away as he usually did, he even looked at Melanie in a way that displeased me.

"'Good black man,' said my sister with a gentle voice which nothing could resist; 'why are you always alone? Why do you hide in savage dens, rather than live in the charming caves.'

"'Because nature has never smiled on me, and I am unhappy.'

"'Do you want us to bring you food, then you will not have to find it.'

"'No, that might be a bait to put chains on me and

bring me back to my master.'

"'But, why do you break trees? And you disturb the water of the fountains? You tear apart birds! That is evil...'

"'I have to give back all the wrong that has been done to me. Go away. I cannot see you!'

"While speaking like this, he cast ferocious glances at Melanie, for he seemed not to see me; his eyes expressed a savage desire, and then vague ideas came to trouble my brain.

"'Let's go,' I said to Melanie and my sister, pitying the unhappy black man, let a glance of compassion and naive tenderness fall upon him which caused him to tremble.

"'The wretch!' she cried, and turning around she still looked at him. I saw the black man stay in the same place contemplating Melanie; from afar he looked like a bronze statue. When we were too far for him to be able to see us, he got up and kept following us until we arrived at the habitation.

"The next day, when we were out walking carrying food to our poor runaway blacks, I saw this same black man carefully spying on us, and hiding so as to admire Melanie. We were sitting on a lawn, beside our temple, we were talking; I heard a light sound in the leaves, and bringing my eyes to the place where this trembling came, I saw the two black eyes of this black man, devouring Melanie. A mortal fear slipped its icy cold into all of my limbs, and I was seemingly spellbound by the infernal gaze of this black man. Then, I had a confused knowledge of the risk that Melanie was running, and, calling by name a black who lived just a few steps away, I succeeded in regaining my courage when I saw him come running. Right away I brought Melanie back into our habitation, with a promptness whose cause she could not guess at. For several days I went into the forest without Melanie, and I had the strength to resist her entreaties.

"Meanwhile, one morning, she begged so much that I brought her. Never, I believe, had I ever seen her look so pretty and so seductive. When we arrived in the middle of the forest, not far from the Terrible Valley, I heard a man's step walking behind us…I turned around, and I saw the black man!…A cold sweat came over me. 'Let's walk faster,' I said to my sister. Wasted effort! The black man leaped upon Melanie and took her into his arms, he ran off towards the mountains with the speed of lightning. I followed him running with all my strength, and making the forest resound with my cries of distress. Pursuing the black man, I forced him to retreat; and as long as he ran, I was at ease about Melanie's fate whose tears and sobs tore at my heart. She fought with her captor, and slowed his flight, but the latter reached an out of the way place, and there, setting Melanie on the ground, he covered her with kisses. No, never will a man know the rage that illuminated my soul! I flew with the speed of an eagle, the pointed rocks made my feet bleed, and I did not feel any pain, since the fires of anger were burning so fiercely inside me. At last, on top of a rock, two blacks appeared, like two hunters who appear suddenly to keep a tiger from devouring a young doe. At the same time I was at the black man's side who was pitilessly attacked by the two runaway slaves. Melanie did not witness this murder, for I had taken her in my arms; and as quickly as an arrow, I brought her over the rocks which I descended with a blind fury while staining them with my blood. My sister cried hot tears, obeying a vague feeling of modesty, and flirtatiousness which I could not define; and as for me, during this time, I inundated her with enflamed kisses, seeking to purify her like this and to efface the dirt of the shameless black man's kisses.

"'Kiss me well?' she cried sobbing.

"This moment enlightened me; I saw the sort of love that I had for my sister!..."

"Monsieur," said Marguerite, interrupting her reading, "our poor vicar must have cried a lot at this point too...don't you think?..." and she showed the manuscript to M. Gausse.

"The wretch!" cried the good curate.

"Well," the servant continued reading, "I did not see anything wrong with this feeling; ignorant as a creole, having no idea of legal prohibitions! And the justice of human laws, I was ravished!...I surrendered myself to the gentle charm of finding a mistress, a lover, a spouse in my sister, and I was careful not to inform her of the discovery that I had made in my own heart. A celestial joy came to cast a refreshing balm on the fleeting wound which the black man had just opened, and somehow I blessed this adventure. I came back with a sad Melanie, for the ferocious kisses of her black ravisher had stayed on her lips, and many times she brought her hand to her lips and wiped with disdain. Then I covered her with caresses, and these caresses had from that point on another character! Then I often questioned Mme. Hamel, the blacks, everyone; I was more attentive to the mysteries of nature; often sitting on the branches of a tree, I contemplated the birds with curiosity; at last a new sort of thought and melancholy came to augment my habitual reflections.

"I recall with a charm mingled with shame this delicious time, where my feeling took on a indecisive tint of divine sensuality, where I gave my sister kisses which astonished her. Confused and blushing she leaned her head on my chest, and seemed to provoke my loving caresses. Then I was not a criminal, I had a pure heart!...And then this passion left indelible traces! *It is criminal now!*...And still, despite all of my efforts, it cannot be extinguished until the cold marble of the tomb has covered me.

"A little while after this event, my sister, who waxed in grace and beauty, and whose spirit was at least at the height of her bodily perfections, became dreamy, and her charming face sometimes was covered with a sudden redness.

"One day, taking me by the hand, she said to me with a sort of solemnity: 'Come my brother? Let us go to the temple?…There I will have something to say to you…'

"We walked in silence, casting furtive glances at one another, just like Adam and Eve when they had eaten the fatal apple; it seemed that we understood one another perfectly. We arrived at our bench of moss at the foot of the temple. For other people to understand the ravishment which came to take hold of us by degrees, one would have to sit those who will read this account down at this very moment under the papaya tree which shaded us, and let them see the magnificent colors with which the mountains were adorned: the deep indigo blue which stained the middle of the rocks, their summits by imperceptible tints achieved the most brilliant gold, and their pyramidal forms jutted up in a lively fashion into a sky of astonishing purity; the sea rolled in little silver waves; the variegated vegetation of America spread out a thousand sorts of the green of the leaves that it produced; and, the setting sun gave a touching melancholy to the painting, impressing the soul with an undefineable sense of movement. It was facing all of these riches that Melanie, after having shown me with a movement of her gracious hand, said to me in an altered voice:

"'My brother, I no longer know how I love you! Your glances bring trouble to my soul and I desire you like the prisoner must desire liberty, the blind man light! I love you with love, and, I pronounce these words without knowing if there are several loves. Alas, I will never know, because I only find one in my soul. Still, after thinking about it, I saw that the love that I was enveloped in was different than the love I had for Mme. Hamel. I would like to learn from you, if when I look at you, you experience this overwhelming sensation which your eyes, fixed on mine, produces in me. I only dare look at you in se-cret, that is to say, when you are not looking at me, and then I experience an unheard of gentleness which I did not know before, and which, each day becomes stronger and more alive.'

"'O my sister!' I cried taking her hand, 'a terrible fire is burning me, and for some time I have had a new life!…We belong to one another forever! Look, do you see? I will be to you like Nehani is to his wife: you will be my spouse and I will be your husband, you are Eve and I am Adam. This is the only way!…But, we must have a ceremony, a testimony.'

"'Then we shall,' she said, 'vow very quickly, and let us take this entire valley, this sea, and these mountains as witness…Joseph, you, you must get on your knees?…'

"So I knelt, she took my hand in hers, her face took on an astonishing seriousness, and, then raising my other hand towards the sky, I said to her: 'Melanie, I vow to you always to love only you! Other women are nothing to me! You are forever my sister and my wife!…'

"I sat at her side, and she said to me with a smile and an intoxicating naïveté: 'As for me, shan't I go on my knees?…I vow…' she began again casting all the fires of love on me with a glance marked with a most enchantingly gracious tone; 'I vow to never love anyone but you!…'

"Then casting herself onto my chest she covered me with kisses. The torch of this tryst was the sun, the witnesses, the sky and the trembling sea; and nature must have smiled at the simple caresses which ended the childish scene.

"From then on, I do not know what tranquility slipped into our souls, we were happy and nothing was lacking in our contentment. Charming laughs, innocent games, candid caresses of a brother and a sister intoxicated us, and our life flowed like pure water from a stream that runs over golden sands.

"At that time Melanie was thirteen years old and I was seventeen. One morning I was digging, and my sister embroidering, when M. de Saint-André appeared on our street, and in two leaps we were in his arms. He admired my sister's astonishing beauty, as well as my extended height, and he seemed happy.

"'My children,' he said to us, 'the political horizon in France is no longer stormy: such words are a mystery to you; but, at last, your father is no longer condemned, he is leaving America. The leader of our country has given me the command of a vessel, with the grade of rear-admiral, and I have come to get you so as to bring you back to France. You will see your homeland again, and know the joys of social life: you Melanie' (and his voice adopted a tender tone which he could not conceal), 'your beauty will make you the object of the hommage of all men: you Joseph' (his voice became more severe) 'you will make up for lost time, and become educated, in order to make something of yourself, a name, so that you will arrive at an eminent position.'

"These words were the subject of a long commentary intended for me. I had trouble understanding them, and to be frank, I did not understand them.

"The next day, my father left us and was at C... selling Mme. Hamel's house. Three days later we were on a frigate, and we set out for the land of France."

CHAPTER 10

"I have already said that M. de Saint-André had, in his character, a harshness, and a severity that were terrible. I had proof of it during the first days of our navigation. He allowed no fault to slip past him, and the laws of maritime discipline, that discipline which confers a great authority on captains, were observed with a punctuality which would show how much they feared my father.

"After fifteen days, during which my father observed me attentively, and apparently appeared satisfied with me, it happened that a chief of the sailors (I do not know what rank he was) committed a mistake which was all the more severely punished since M. de Saint-André appeared to have a secret hatred for the guilty party.

"This sailor, named Argow, was one of those men whom nature seems not to have finished: short, stocky, wide in the shoulders and chest, having a big head, and a horrible expression of ferocity, there reigned, in all of that, an air of savage majesty which revealed a rare energy and intrepidness: his glance showed that in danger he executed promptly what a natural sagacity told him was the better part. For the rest, drunk, dirty, brutal, and ambitious. When, in history, Gregorio Leti and others would show me Cromwell, immediately I recalled Argow, and I thought that I saw the famous guardian of England when he appeared in parliment for the first time.

"This sailor, knowing M. de Saint-André's temperment, accepted his punishment without a word, and with a resignation that surprised everyone; but he swore, inside himself, to get back at the rear admiral and the enormity of such an undertaking did not frighten him in the least. Those who saw his dreamy expression, his dark face and the glances that he cast at my father, would judge that Argow was contemplating some bold project.

"As this sailor had a sort of ascendency over his comrades, they naturally shared their thoughts, and, before Argow had even said anything, their spirits were prepared for some sort of opening move. When their chief was free, he began to take, on the side, those whom he knew to be his friends, and he questioned them to see if they would go along with his plan.

"One night, when everything was calm in the ship, when Mme. Hamel's husband, whom they mistrusted the most, was on watch; when the officers, secondary commanders, and my father were shut up in their chambers, and unable to see what was happening: I was the unknown witness of a strange scene; for, curious as was to be expected at my age, and having noticed some movements among the crew, I hid in a cannon hole, and protected by the shadows, this is what I heard:

"'He is up there,' said the sailor to Argow, 'but what do you want to do?'

"'What I want to do,' responded Argow in a low voice and intermixing horrible curses with all of his suggestions, 'I want him to take part in our plans or go into the belly of a fish! He is devoted to the commander, and if M. de Saint-André, seeing himself weakened, wants to bring us to reason, then he would be able, on an order, to set fire to the *Sainte Barbara*.'

"At these words I realized that they were talking

about the cannon master.

"'We will never get him over here, if he is by the netting we just have to give him a shove with the elbow.'

"'A thousand cannon balls,' responded Argow in a lively manner, 'we would not have any powder, he has the key to the storeroom.'

"They stood a while thinking, but Argow broke the silence saying: 'I'll take care of it! Have all our men go down into the hold.'

"I do not know what became of the poor cannon master, all that I know is that at the time of the event, I saw the man to whom Argow had just spoken dressed up again in the particular clothes of the cannon master whom he had replaced. On hearing the order to send the crew into the hold, I slipped down there too, and I crouched in a dark corner.

"This was the first spectacle that the social world gave me: this scene had the roughest men for actors, and as they did not temper the expressions of their passions, I saw their intentions openly. Each sailor went down carefully, and some carried lanterns. All these savage and animated faces on which fear was artlessly engraved, for they still dreaded their consciences, formed a painting that was worthy to be exhibited.

"A murmur was raised when Argow appeared with his lieutenant. He went and set himself before a bundle, everyone grouped around him, some on provisions, the others on barrels, all on them in singular postures with their eyes fixed on the chief of the sedition. When the latter saw them attentive, he led his inquisitorial eyes over them, and pronounced the following discourse:

"'If I did not know you, and the captain had not punished me overly severely for such a small fault, never would we have seized the chance to make our fortunes which has been presented to us. The power and riches would have passed under our noses, without one of you having had the thought of becoming happy all in one blow, without any human powers being able to get at us, but I dared to count on your courage and your strength of character, I see now that I was not mistaken. Now we are all in this together! for M. de Saint-André would hang us all from the yard-arm, and would do the work with his officers, rather than spare even one of us.

"Flatmers, John, and Tribels have told you separately about what I am now going to explain to you in a clearer manner. In three ways, my friends, I grow angry when I consider our way of life: drag this (here was a curse) *hellstone* across the bridges; always work, treated badly, without consolations, without future, without bread, and (a curse) what have we done to warrant such a fate? We came into the world in the same way as those who are rich and who sleep in good beds, without always being separated from death by four rotten boards. Which in your opinion is better, to risk one's life once or twice in order to be happy, or to lead an existence whose greatest happiness is to sleep in-between decks and to suck air out of a porthole? But, here is my plan: the ship from Havanna is going to pass by tomorrow, there is just one boat that has seventy-six cannons, our frigate only has twenty!...Even if she had none! I promise you that we will have the last Spanish coin.

"But for that and to have the right to roam the seas enriching ourselves, and to keep everything quiet so that they will not know our whereabouts, we have to begin by getting rid of the people up there who annoy us. They are all together in the same place; when I say "to arms" we just have to aim all the cannons at the bedrooms, and then...let me act...I only ask to be in charge for this first danger. When we are masters of the ship then we will organize things better: let's go!...'

"During this discourse the faces of all these men showed a host of diverse feelings. When it was over, a sudden gesture by Argow kept them from crying out. 'Let each of us,' he said, 'come in turn before me to swear allegiance for twenty-four hours that he will take part in the plot...'

"Among the men of the crew there was only one cabin boy who obstinately refused to cooperate in this conspiracy. Argow had him kept out of sight.

"I was filled with horror. Nevertheless the danger that Melanie and my father were in gave me strength I succeeded in getting away and I arrived pale and wan at M. de Saint-André's room.

"'We are dead!' I said to him. He began to laugh. 'The entire crew has just sworn to get rid of you! Argow is the chief of the plot.' Then he began to think.

"'Where are they?...' was his first question.

"'In the hold,' I responded.

"M. de Saint-André dressed quickly, took his megaphone and ordered me to wake all of the officers.

"'To arms!...' resounded throughout the room. 'Hamel, quit your watch and close the hatchway to the hold!'

"My father was calm as if he were part of a fence. The officers grouped around him, and Hamel came to join this group that was hardly numerous. They covered the hatchway to the hold with everything that they could find, and then they heard a terrible thumping in the bottom of the hold.

"'In three minutes we will be back to work!...' cried M. de Saint-André, 'If not, you will be hanged, we can see the *Hirondelle,* I will send distress signals to them and you will not escape.'

"The deepest silence was the only response of the sailors. M. de Saint-André coldly took out his watch. 'Let those who submit say their names?...' cried out Hamel. They did not respond; the officers looked at one another uneasily, for such a silence announced some sort of trick, and they knew that Argow was capable of the most audacious things.

"Once the three minutes were up M. de Saint-André ordered all of the officers to aim the ends of their guns at the opening; and, commanding Hamel to take off the boards, he got ready to go down himself without arms…when cries of 'Victory!…Victory!…' were heard on the second level and throughout the section. Argow had demolished the back end of the storeroom, as he had taken the key to the door. At the risk of blowing up that area, he had just led the men out through the storeroom and arrived on the second bridge above where M. de Saint-André was found. He took control of the ship. Then it was his turn to close the bridge; he embarrassed the officers when the latter believed they would capture the irascible sailor.

"M. de Saint-André, looking towards his officers said to them: 'Messieurs, a little boldness and we shall surprise them!…' The officers, looking at the between decks, seemed to say to the rear admiral:

'How do you expect to get out?'

"My father began to smile when he understood their tacit question and he cried out in a low voice: 'They are drunk on their success and are not paying attention to everything. Should we risk something? Let us try being bold, and let us not lose our heads: the sea is at our level and in opening this hatch, the water will come in, but at the same time we will have to go out one by one. The ladder up to the deck is just outside the hatch. One of us will stay back to close it and get rid of the water, for Hamel will be able to manoeuvre so as to make the ship tilt.

"M. de Saint-André threw himself out first and once he had seized the ladder, we heard him climbing up rapidly. As chance would have it, the section tilted in the opposite direction, and all of the officers escaped without a drop of water coming in.

"When the last one was leaving, Argow half opened the door, and seeing me alone, was stupefied; he let me come up and ran with the speed of lightning on the top deck, for he suddenly understood M. de Saint-André's manoeuvre.

"In the blink of an eye the scene took on a formidable aspect. The staff, arrayed on the side of the top deck, fought with an audacity and an astonishing amount of courage; and the sailors, who did not expect such a sudden and vigorous attack, were obliged to give way and go rally themselves farther away. There were seven or eight of them lying out on the deck bathed in their own blood.

"It was at this moment that the terrible Argow returned furious and cursing. One of the sailors, frightened and giving up hope of success, had decided to try to become an intermediary: in the first moment of terror, the men, without listening to Argow, turned towards the group of officers; and what made this disposition of souls more stable was that the angry sailor shot the sailor who wanted to surrender, saying that they had all sworn obedience. M. de Saint-André lost everything by his inflexibility, for at the request of the sailors, he said that he would be as angry with all of them as he saw fit. His severity was so well known that when Argow cried out: 'And the convoy!…Let's go. Steadily!…' The entire crew fell on the group of officers; and, after a light combat, they had dispersed their superiors. A cannonier tied

M. de Saint-André to the main mast; all of the sub-
dued and disarmed officers were arranged around
him.

"Argow, master of the ship, ordered all his men as
was needed to manoeuvre; and taking up the whistle,
he commanded their actions and urged the vessel on
from the quarter deck where he was seated. When all
of his men were busy, he put the sailor to whom I had
heard him talk into his place and went towards the
mast where my bound father was struggling with his
ropes.

"Without being either arrogant or respectful, Argow, addressing himself to M. de Saint-André, said to
him: 'Captain, the man whom you punished so sever-
ly is now the master, he has replaced you and now
you are in the postion that Argow was in.'

"'What do you mean by this?…Use your power!'
replied my father.

"'Of course, yes, if I want to!…' replied Argow
with a ferocious glance; 'but listen, you see what kind
of a man I am, the heavens did not create me to stay a
sailor; will you swear on your honor to forget all that
has happened? Once we return to France will you

give me the rank of a lieutenant…You can! Because I come from the United States and in saying that I have this rank, you will have it given to me…Then, in two seconds I will salute you as a rear admiral, and we will sail for France. A moment ago you gave me three minutes!…As for me I give you six!…'

"On that note Argow sat down on a rope, took out his pipe, lit it, and began to smoke.

"'I will do with all of you whatever I will!…' was M. de Saint-André's sole response.

"Argow, having finished his pipe, put it calmly back in his pocket and went to the quarter deck.

"I do not need to add that during this entire scene I was at my father's side, still, I was free. As for my poor Melanie and Madame Hamel, they were locked in their cabin and I only saw them when the conclusion to this fatal adventure occured. The greatest uneasiness devoured me, but whom could I talk to? I was not allowed to leave the top deck.

"Argow profited from the presence of M. de Saint-André who always kept the rebels in danger to assume the command that was going to serve them in their pirating. He was named captain, and he himself gave them promotions which satisfied the entire crew. When things had the appearance of a hierarchy he assembled a council to consider things. He came over to tell the result of the assembly's discussions to the officers and M. de Saint-André. He offered the officers who would become pirates the retention of their rank: they all refused. Then Argow announced that he was going to deport them all onto the first deserted island that they came to.

"This command was executed. At the moment when they set my father down on the island, he seemed to recall something very important that he wanted to tell me. Argow, who refused to abandon me along with M. de Saint-André, sent him off without allowing him to speak to me. He cried out to me from the shore a sentence which I could not grasp. It finished with the words that I could make out: '...my son!...'

The intention of these pirates was to take care of us. When they were within sight of the Havanna fleet by the route along which it would travel, they put at Argow's command the sloop into the water, and set me in it along with Madame Hamel and the trembling Melanie. By a strange act of kindness Argow gave us my father's coffer and money; then he gave the order to attack, and the sailor who tossed us these things let M. de Saint-André's papers fall into the sea. The loss of these papers still causes me even to this day the worst regret; for with them I would have been enlightened about all of the mysteries that surrounded my birth, when I was able to reflect and I knew what importance such papers could be to a man's station in life and business.

"When we found ourselves, all three of us, in the sloop, in the middle of the sea, having provisions for about three days, having just lost my father, and not even able to hope to see him again, desperation took hold of our souls. Nevertheless, such is the character of those who love with intoxication that even in the most disheartening situations, even at the edge of the tomb, they find flowers on the edge of a precipice, and to lovers alone it is given to never be totally unhappy!...

"'I am not trembling anymore, since I am alone with you!...' Melanie said to me...'and I will die happy because we will die together, covering each other with kisses. Look, Joseph, we will embrace each other and when they find our united bodies they will say: "these are two lovers," and they will place us in the same tomb.'

"Madame Hamel was resigned to everything. She arranged the coffer, the money, the provisions, and she was exactly the same as if she were in her cane chair at our old house.

"I tried my best to steer the sloop by guiding it steadily towards a point where I had seen the vessels of the Havana convoy. We heard the battle cannons. A thousand frightening ideas assailed me. 'What do you have to be sad about?' Melanie said to me with a charming smile, 'we just have to let ourselves go, and death will take us when it wants to. Look, Joseph, take my head, I do not want them to find me with a blackened face!...'

"Two, three days passed and we began to ration our provisions. In the end they were used up. 'Think my children,' Madame Hamel said to us who had barely eaten anything, 'think that in the utmost necessity you will kill me!...'

"She pronounced these words with a simplicity, a

tranquility of soul which astonished us more than her proposal. We had gone two days without eating, we did not say anything else. I watched with fright as Melanie's cheeks paled, when we sudddenly saw on the horizon the white sails of a ship: 'Look!' I said to my sister and we gave ourselves over to joy. It was a Danish ship bound for Copenhagen. They took us on. And nothing else happened to us except that we went to Denmark, to cut things short, and then we could go on to Paris. In Copenhagen we found a French family who took care of us; and a short while after our arrival we left for France. In the end, one fine morning we came to Paris after having sown along the roadside all the money that one would expect from travelers like us. All of these adventures and these crossings, the gifts and our carriage, the mail coaches and the eternal tips, at last our memories of the inns, did not diminish our treasure very much. Upon arriving in Paris we had two hundred thousand francs to deposit in the bank; and, two or three thousand gold francs on our persons."

CHAPTER 11

"I come to the most painful part of my life! Alas my page will often be soaked in tears and many sentences will remain unfinished.[2]

"I was more than sixteen years old at the time: Melanie was thirteen, but, shaped by the American climate, it seemed from her expressions and her manners that she was a young lady of seventeen. All of the chastely violent fires of love embellished her eyes that were so gentle, her pomegranite lips, her flowering cheeks. Her long lashes gave her glances an expression of melancholy which she often denied, when her eyes strayed over me...

"Every second, the most seductive memories come to kill me by offering all of this gentleness which was blossoming like the flowers of a fruit. I

---

2 One thinks that a bachelor of letters would not have given the readers sentences without having rounded and completed them...and God is my witness that I have reformed, to my best, the ideas that the vicar must have had. (Editor's note)

still seem to be in the middle of the grand and majestic Tuileries when we went there for the first time, 'How lovely she is!' I heard repeated on all sides, and such gentle expressions flattered my entire soul. Melanie said that the women were admiring me; I told her that she was the object of the men's admiration, since they all adored her with their eyes. What a triumph!...What joy!...How happy we were!...

"On arriving in Paris, our first concern was, as you may suspect, to find some out-of-the-way place, whose rustic and picturesque solitude and shade could give us a faint image of our lovely America. With care and some dealing I found an abandoned mansion on the rue de la Santé, whose gardens and surroundings where the most gracious that I had seen in Paris. Once we had set up our two pennants in this place, the problem of a happy life was resolved for us for a second time. It was too short a time!...My first thoughts showed me that, as head of the family, I had none of the notions necessary to govern a fortune which I thought to be immense, when I considered it in proportion to our tastes, style, and our needs. In truth, for two beings who love one another, and

237

whose greatest pleasure is the gentle sight of each other, who are used to eating the simplest foods, one has to agree that our fortune was colossal. But after only a month I noticed that it was urgent that I learn how to do something. The customs, the mores of the city came between the naïveté of our souls and the decency of the age. I felt that I should be ready to defend our goods and our bodies, in the end that education was the basis of the spirit of man and society.

"God!...What astonishing scenes! What a laugh! How many naive observations, when Melanie and I guessed something of social mysteries. Alas! Away cruel memories!...Leave me!

"Well, for four consecutive years, I knew no other path than the one between the Pantheon library and the rue de la Santé. During this time I learned all that a man needs to know, and I learned it all alone, without a teacher, by the sole force of my imagination assisted by the powerful energy of an ardent character. I had the gentle task of instructing Melanie: here I come to our mutual vow; what we found the most difficult, was the first step!...Reading seemed like a serpent to us. Madame Hamel could not imagine the folly that had seized us, so her complaints and her reasoning made us smile. She allowed us to learn, because she thought that she saw that we were happier.

"The fatal moment approaches...Ah! I stop until tomorrow!..."

"There is an interruption," said Marguerite.

"Ah the poor children!..." cried out the good Curate Gausse, "I can guess their troubles!..."

"Monsieur," began the servant again, "can you hear you the rain that is falling in a torrent? They will detain M. Joseph de Saint-André," she said emphazing this name, "and he will probably sleep there: so we can finish the poor man's story."

As the candle had not been tapered since Marguerite had begun to read, she took care of this task; for the good curate, open-mouthed, eyes on the manuscript, would never have thought of it. The servant tapered it, put her glasses back on, and continued, "Before beginning this story of pain and eternal trouble, I cannot keep from showing the one whom I regarded as my dear spouse.

"Do you see her there, seated by a window?.. Beside Madame Hamel: her eyes are lowered to the cloth that she is embroidering, but, every minute, she looks up at me; and her glance begins to desire more than the chaste kisses which the temple in the Terrible Valley bore witness to. She often casts her eyes on the painting, which I did, in which this charming scene is represented surrounded by all of the luxury of the products of America. Each of her movements reveals a grace which one thinks that one has not known before; her virginal pose does not exclude the naive avowal of desires of a young lady of seventeen; her head is gently leaning, and her blonde hair is disposed with a seductive elegance; the tip of her little foot is visible beneath a long robe; the sweet smell of iris is exhuded by her entire body...She smiles!...And the virgin, whose throat is decorated by a black cross, surpasses Venus' smile...Ah, it is you my sister!...You speak!...What roses will be born from between the pearls in your divine mouth...

"'Joseph,' she said to me at that moment, 'we are too happy! Something bad will happen to us like Polycrate to whom a fish brought the ring that the tyrant of Samos had thrown away to conjure the whims of fortune.'

"'We are Christians, my dear sister,' I responded.

"'Joseph, the ceremonies by which one marries in this country are very different from the simple statements that we made.'

"'And how do you know that?'

"'From Finette, my chambermaid, she is going to marry I imagine. Joseph, how little we know about all of that' (what a smile!) 'just as we did not know about the sciences. Oh, Joseph! surely you are hiding something from me.'

"*Celestial soul! Pure soul! Goodbye, my grave is dug.*

"These words pronounced with the naïveté of childhood made me think: she took the expression on my face for an expression of chagrin.

"'Go ahead, Joseph, I know that you love me and that you have never hidden anything from me!' She came and sat at my knees, cast her ivory arms around my throat and covered me with kisses, imprinted with all the voluptuousness which one can put into a kiss without sinning. I still feel them! They burn my lips, and pursue me with their charm!

"'Have I hurt you?'

"'Good God Melanie, what are you saying?'

"I still think that I can see Madame Hamel get up and smile: 'Poor angels, do you know how happy you are?' she asked.

"'Oh yes,' responded Melanie, 'my brother's face is all of America to me.'

"Here, before writing the following sentence, I will remind you that I am a child of nature; and that, even though initiated in the vain delights of the world, I have never been able to conceive that there is shame in admitting, in manifesting the movements of the soul that nature has placed inside us; my sister was the same, and I do not hesitate to pronounce anathema on those who blush at Melanie's naïveté.

"For a long time I had felt afflicted by this feeling that nature had set in our souls for the conservation of its works: what my sister just said showed me that, for her too, everything was becoming clear. The vague ideas that rolled around in my head ended up becoming more clear, and I thought of everything that Melanie had said about marriage ceremonies.

"Then I began my study of law. I think that it was eight days ago that the course was opened. I opened the law!...The fatal prohibition, the two fatal lines struck me a death blow, and the penal code showed me the crime. I sought information: nature, religion, social order, everything agreed, and it showed that our love was incestuous!...I looked into my heart, and I saw the picture of my sister engraved there like a spouse!...Earth, goodness, pleasure, all the celestial joys vanished, and the black hand of crime, the cruel fate sullied all!...Before me an immense abyss opened up! And...Death was at the bottom.

"Then a fit of anger seized me, and I went out of the house, running as if I feared the fires of Sodom would fall a second time from the sky to devour us: a lion could have ripped me apart and I would not have felt anything! I was furious to the point of no longer recognizing time, place, or customs. I ran like a madman, and only stopped before a big house where a giant crowd was gathered. A man offered me a piece of paper, and asked me for money, I gave him some and I followed the flow of people. I sat down, squeezed into my seat, and I tore at my chest until it was bloody. They were playing Phedre before me! At the scene of the declaration I felt bad; and, when Phedre accuses herself and wants to descend into hell, my neighbors took me out. I went home mad, angry, intoxicated, destroyed! I was no longer human.

"The next day I was calm, pale, sad, beaten. During the night, the Christian philosophy appeared to me, the man of nature having played his role, that of the man of the world, of that man used to dissimulation, to trouble, to pains, was going to begin...Happy if, when I walked over the Pont-Neuf, my fever had suggested to me to leap into the water!...At table Melanie smiled at me, I turned my eyes away; she spoke to me, I tried not to hear the gentleness of her honey words; o torments!...o torments!...

If I wrote this for myself, at least I put here at this place, there, a warning to those souls who might resemble me, and I do not know if I should praise them or weep for them!...You should know, great and feeling hearts, you should know, you who the sight of evil makes tender and that a woman's tear makes you shiver, you should know that in a passion, even a legitimate one, there are as many evils as there were in mine. The social order is Pandora's box without hope! We are finished, there can be no infinite happiness for us! And souls that seek the immense should perish consumed by themselves.

"When I came back to myself, I began reasoning; and, in that, everyone will recognize the progress of all human passions. 'How,' I asked myself, 'is my passion a crime?...Not at all. No secret voice stopped us? And if we loved each other so, it was because the Lord willed it! Nothing happens in the universe except by his command, and he could not have desired our destruction. History teaches us that the Egyptians married their sisters!...'

"And from there, with the contributions of all of the tales of travelers, I would enumerate the countries where this custom took place. In the end, and this was the most solid argument, 'in the end, if there was only a first man and a first woman!...Either the son married the mother, or the father married his daughters, or the brothers married their sisters: what God once permitted cannot be criminal now!'

"These reasonings and a host of others consoled me for a while. Melanie forgot the passing sorrow that I felt; she did not ask me to account for it, and we gave ourselves over to all the ardor of our love.

But, it was said that I would drink down to the last drop in the chalice. In effect, one day when, sad and melancholy, I reflected on this strange prohibition, reason came and shone in my soul like lightning, but like lightning that kills. 'Admitting that my crime with Melanie was not criminal and that we abandoned ourselves to gentle embraces,' I said, 'society will always refuse to unite us, and under threat of dishonor, I cannot love her with love!…'

"From that moment, a dark melancholy took hold of my soul, and it took hold for good. I resolved to combat my passion courageously and to contain it in my chest, in taming the flames of hell: for by a strange twist of fate, it was at the moment that I learned that I could no longer love Melanie that the most terrible desires came to torment me. But, using the burning energy which consumes me, I will turn it towards the battles ahead.

"Turning my eyes sadly away when my sister showed her tenderness with a glance, I tried to flee her; but this flight had the symptoms of love which Melanie noticed. All that I said to her was not any the less attractive, my words took on the tones of melancholy, and my langorousness was revealed in everything I did or said. Leaving the house, I went to sit on a hill in the country: and there, prey to an attack of this soul sickness, I tried to put my heart to sleep with funerary meditations. O how autumn seemed lovely to me! How its winds were the object of my prayers! I wanted them to carry me away just as they toyed with the yellow leaves.

"These passionate tones of a saddened heart resembled the murmurings which trouble the silence of a forest; one hears them, but one cannot depict them. An incredible thing! I found gentleness in my troubles, and something voluptuous slipped into my soul. As for me, the most tender of friends, in the end I was the brother of my sister, yet I feared talking to her and seeing her. My hand trembled when I offered her something, and this trembling looked like hate. Paleness covered my face, and my eyes only looked at the ground. The tears that I hid from my sister were cried in secret. Tantalus' trials were real and a thousand times more cruel: each day, my sister increased her caresses, she overwhelmed me with them, because she noticed that she had the chance to do so less often. In sum, she ended up suspecting that my heart held a deep sorrow, but the true cause could never be divined by her naive soul; then, her solicitude, her tender love made her look for something else.

"At first she did not speak to me about my melancholy, because at the same time that I recognized my crime, I raised up a subject of meditation in her heart which altered the pink of her cheeks. Melanie, because she consulted Finette, because she was dreamy, or because nature desired it, Melanie, I must say, guessed the purpose of marriage, and this discovery introduced a great change into her manner of seeing and feeling. Her passion, having been like a thesaurus of all the riches of the feelings of the soul, arrived at the last moral degree of love, and entered into the terrible vein of physical passion!...Then she burned entirely, body and soul. I saw her eyes shine, her color change, a funerary and waxing pallor covered her face; I did not dare sit next to her, and the chaste young lady, keeping silent, guessed what was mutely bothering her, this inextinguishable, secret flame, was the principle of my melancholy.

"God! What testimonies of love she gave...As soon as I left a chair, she sat there and thought where I had just been thinking. She watched my steps, she awaited my returns, and, when I entered into a room, she listened for my footstep. When I combed my hair, she took up her work and was happy to watch me without saying a single word.

"One day, turning around suddenly, I saw that her eyes were filled with tears that she did not have the time to dry.

"The sight of these tears rolling along her cheeks was a dart. A knife thrust pierced my heart. 'She thinks that I do not love her, she trembles at my barbarity, without complaining!...' When she saw that her tears would make me tender she left off her work and I left off mine, she came at sat on my lap and slipped an arm around my neck!...Kissing me several times, brushing my face with her burning cheeks and with her wispy hairs, she cried in sobs: 'Joseph! Joseph!...' Her swelling chest did not permit her to say any more.

"With these heartrending words, I trembled because of our danger and I had every reason to shudder, when, raising her head a little which she had hid on her chest, she looked at me smiling with her eyes and lips, with a fine smile that was too expressive for it not to be understood. In the middle of the grace which shone on her face there was the color of the suffering of love and this gently supplicant air which makes lovers so touching.

"'Joseph,' she began again, 'I love you, and I believe that I am loved! I am beautiful, and I am your spouse!...Why,' she said hesitating, 'don't you tell me your troubles? You are suffering!...I see it. Look, my brother, between us there is a mass of new feelings which we are keeping mutually silent about. Why do you avoid me?...Why don't you look at me any longer? You have taken away my happiness...'

"'Ah! Melanie, you will know too soon all that I suffer!...'

"'No, I want to know right away, to calm your pains, I know that I can...'

"'Melanie, the cure for my problem is not in mortal hands.'

"'What is this problem?...What do you feel?...Look, tell me?' and, swaying gently, she began to lightly caress my hair; her attentive, curious face tried to read in my eyes: then noticing my embarrassment, she cried out laughing: 'Joseph, I read that lovers give each other nice presents. You still have not given me anything!...'

"'Everything on earth changes,' I responded, 'and I could not offer you something that is not perishable.'

"'You have a gold chain around your neck. I want it...' she cried with a gentle confusion, and the color of modesty colored her cheeks purple. She took my chain, and in turn put it around her neck. 'Now,' she said, 'I want to give you a present that will stay with you for as long as you live, for what is engraved on a man's soul only dies with him.' At that, placing her hands behind my head, she took it, drew to hers, opened my lips and gave me the most ardent kiss that a woman can give.

"'Melanie,' I cried in anger, 'I don't want you to kiss me like that!...Go away!'

"The poor child, shamed, flushed, went back to her chair, with the gentle feminine submission, with the passive docility which would bring pity to a tiger's heart. She not only raised her head, she cried, but she tried to hide her tears from me, and her swollen heart could not explain my savage and imperious exclamation.

"My soul wavered, I came to her side, I kissed her on the forehead, and when she raised her head, she saw my face traced with tears, then she said these touching words: 'If we have cried together, nothing is wrong!...But listen to me, Joseph, we must marry, we can't wait any longer. You see what society demands of us, so that there will be nothing to stop our caresses!'

"At this statement, I looked at Melanie with an astonished air, I broke out in tears, and keeping her hand in mine, we remained for a long time without saying anything, each of us given over to very different reflections.

"Alas! What task did I have to fulfill! So I had to teach my sister about all the barriers which separated us. At this thought I dropped her hand, I went out and began walking in the country, believing that the air would cool my soul that was aflame.

CHAPTER 12

"How could I dare say to my sister: 'We must separate, our love is a crime!' How could I resolve to break the light ship in which she was sailing? How could I go about darkening life, making happiness vanish!... And make her miserable for the rest of her existence?

"Several times I opened my mouth to speak to her without being able. One day I led her until we were under a weeping willow; and there, sitting down, I took her hand, but my tongue was frozen by the ecstatic attitude of this virgin of Correge and the love that shone in all of her features with the expectation of supreme love, so I contented myself with contemplating her in silence, in a sad trance.

"In the end, I was convinced that I could never speak to her of our eternal crime. One night, crying tears, I sat at my desk and in the silence of the night I wrote to her in basically these terms:

"'O my sister! I can only give you this name! Alas! It is the hand of the man who loves you like no one will ever love you which must separate the mortal trait. It is your brother who is going to say to you: "Die, Melanie!" Until now our lives were a dream, and here is the awakening.

"'We adore each other, our souls have met each other on all points, we love each other with all sorts of love all at once, we cannot live without one another. We must die! We are in the middle of a sea of pleasure and voluptuousness. There are others whose expectation is one of the most vivid pleasures!... Next to this laughing prairie of life, far from the ground littered with flowers, there is a wild place, a savage desert!...What sands! ...What fires!...No living water!...A scorching wind!...That is where we must go, in a word, we must flee!...Is that not death?...

"'For two months now, hell has been in my heart, for two months I have known that the love that we have for each other is a crime. Yes, Melanie, religion, the laws of the world have made it so. If in our hearts a secret voice says to us that we would not be less virtuous in breaking all of these laws, it would not be any less true that you would never belong to me legitimately. In reading the letter, see how many evils we have come to find in Paris. Ah! Why did we not stay in the vasts forests of the New World where we would have been happy!...

"'So Melanie, we must silence our desires; you must not look at me any longer; we must keep from speaking to each other; veil your blonde hair, temper the fires in your eyes, do not display the graces of your enchanting form any longer, do not pronounce those soft words any longer, with inflections of your voice that are so intoxicating, and which lead straight to the heart! For my part, I will avoid you, if I can!

"'Like two rocks without moss which are separated one from the other by an impetuous torrent that rolls them into the bottomless abyss, we will live, in the presence of one another, without being able to touch...For my sister, I keep myself from writing that it may be necessary to flee one another and no longer to see each other!...I hope that we will be able to live side by side under the protection of a stern conscience which will direct our movements, and that our precious innocence will remain like the snow in the Terrible Valley. We will carry it to our graves, and we will go and receive the recompense of our martyrdom up above.

"'All that we will have left will be the sad happiness of seeing each other, of sharing our lives, and consuming ourselves like that nymph of the fable who preserved only her voice. It is in the middle of this night, while you sleep, that I address these lover's goodbyes to you! With the day I will be reborn your brother and remain so forever. Now I will look at you like the spirit of a dear person! And each moment, each grace, each object which we depict of what we were, will be like the letters inscribed on a tomb. Everything will carry the imprint of our melancholy, everything! The notes that your hands will form as they wander across your piano, will always be notes of sadness, songs of pain…we will be happy if death comes to take us soon!

"'Goodbye, beloved beauty, the hope that I saw you cultivate, the pleasures which you dreamed, everything has vanished! We will go dormant like the trees in winter, and that season will be for our hearts the only one. Ah! Melanie, in tracing these words, it seems that my soul, and my life are going out of me, and I cannot find the strength to drive away my tears!...Alas! I would suggest that you die if religion did not forbid it!...'

"When I had written this letter, it seemed to me that one had come and lifted the iron cloak from my shoulders. I left my room, I went into Melanie's room. The celestial virgin slept an innocent sleep, her pose was gracious and when I came near to her, she murmured my name in such a tender manner that I felt the most invincible desire rise up in me. The temptation was too strong to be able to resist for long!...I set the letter on her table, and I fled without daring to look a second time.

"In what a frightening position I found myself, when the next day I had to go into the room where we dined. I was going to meet the pain which I had stirred up and see my sister knowledgeable of the crime which was contained in our glances. Ah! He who has never passed under the whip of such sorrows, does not know all that the human heart can cause in the way of misery...She came! She was laughing, and her gentle face did not announce anything wrong. 'She has not read my letter!...' I said to myself, and a feeling of compassion urged me to burn it... *Melanie had read it!...*

"This charming creature could not believe that they would have made such a prohibition and refused to believe it. Her angelic smile resembled that of a great geometrician with a little problem to solve. So the perfection of this adorable creature did not give me signs of any pain! This scene, this discussion, the astonishment, the sorrow which I feared, this first tear, and I would have to dry them all!

"We were in the living room with Madame Hamel. Melanie came over to me and said: 'My brother, you must be crazy, your letter saddened me because I thought as I read it that you had been sad, but you can be sure that you have misunderstood the laws; I am certain that they make a duty out of what you call a crime...'

"'Melanie, I wrote nothing that was not true!...'

"She began to look at me uneasily.

"'Could it be that you love someone else!...Isn't your poor Melanie pretty enough for you...' and tears came into her eyes...

"'Ah, my sister!...' I cried, 'how could such a thought have entered your mind; for the first time in your life you have caused me pain.'

"'How, Joseph, could we be criminal in loving each other?'

"At this question, good Madame Hamel set her glasses down and looked from one to the other of us.

"'Mother,' Melanie began again, 'do you believe it?...'

"'My children,' responded Madame Hamel, 'it seems to me to be inconceivable, but something worries me. I am afraid that Joseph is right.' Melanie blanched. 'As for me, I would not dare to convict you. To put an end to it, I will show you the law.'

"'Those people,' said my sister, 'they do not know nature!...Alas! Joseph, they can do what they want; I can only love you.' I gave her the penal code to read.

"'Very well! Joseph, they can punish me if they want to!...'

"At this statement, at this look, brought on by a rage that no moral barrier could stop, I seized her in my arms; and, almost stifling her, I devoured her, reaping long kisses from her purple lips and drowning my sorrows in the ocean of voluptuousness that I plunged into.

"'Yes,' I cried, 'Yes Melanie, you have just reached the height of love, that love which marches upon all laws!…Ah! You love me!…You can say it with pride!…No woman has gone so far as to sacrifice her honor for her lover. Women have sacrificed their lives, but none has yet gone so far as to use the debris of the throne of virtue, from the bed to voluptuousness…let us be criminals, guilty, but let us be happy!'

"At these words she thought a moment and said sadly: 'But no, we will not be happy if, to be so, we must abandon virtue and renounce heaven!…'

"Right away she got off my lap, tore away my arms and sat in a chair before me. Her animated face suddenly grew pale. She did not dare to look at me: Madame Hamel was thoughtful.

"'My children,' she said, 'if there are earthly laws which keep you from being happy, I only see one option, that is to take our carriage and go to Copenhagen.'

"I looked at her and said with astonishment: 'And

what would we do in Copenhagen?'

"'We would find our Danish ship to take us back to the Terrible Valley.'

"Despite my profound pain a smile blossomed on my lips, seeing that this good woman thought that since she had come by way of Copenhagen, that there was no other way on earth to go from Paris to M...

"'Mother,' I said to her, 'that would be good, if the Terrible Valley was a place where one was out of view of the Lord, but there is no such place on earth, and we cannot do what religion forbids.'

"'But if you were born in that country where sisters are allowed to marry their brothers?'

"'We are not, good mother, and we are Christian.'

"'Ah! My poor children!...' cried Madame Hamel horrified, 'what will become of you!...Wait, I will go consult Abbot Valette, my confessor.'

"'It is useless, mother, I have consulted twenty casuists. Our love is incestuous.'

"'Incestuous! My child, but that is a crime...In my day they burned you alive for that...And for other things as well! Poor children!...' and she looked at us with tender eyes.

"Melanie had not said anything; suddenly she cried out violently: 'I would rather die!…' Her expression was really fightening. She contemplated the room with a morose expression which made me tremble. Her eyes did not seem to be alive!

"'O Joseph!' she said in a painful voice, 'so what you wrote to me is true!…Here we are alone, although we are together.' (I felt like I was being martyred) 'No more kisses!…No more caresses!…' she added sobbing.

"'We will reap,' I cried, 'the funerary harvest that was sown by our ignorance!…O childhood days!…But no,' I said taking Melanie's hand, 'even if we had known the prohibition, I still think that we would have loved.'

"'Oh yes!…' she responded with a smile that pierced her tears.

"'Melanie,' I said to her, 'now that you see the danger, do you think that we can stay together?'

"'Ah!…Joseph, we will never part!…' she cried with a savage energy. This was the last spark of the fire, she fell back on her chair, I thought that she was dead. She did not move from that place until the evening, she did not say another word, nor made any gesture. For a fortnight she remained crazed like this, showing signs of impatience and changing to all appearances. She became pale, but her eyes retained an extraordinary sparkle. At night I heard her crying, and…this heavenly creature took care in the daytime to spare me the sight of her tears.

"'Joseph,' she said to me one day, 'our death will be a fine festival for us!…'

"Alas, from then on I had two sorrows, hers and mine. Our smiles, our happiness, fled never to return, the most profound melancholy marked the lugubrious shade of all our days, our moments together, our actions, our words, our thoughts, and Madame Hamel was as sad as we were. What a change! What a terrible punishment! And why?…What was our crime?…

"Our life became a perpetual battle for, despite the promise of reaping her glances, Melanie could not despoil them of their tender expression, nor could I keep myself from seeing them. Everything down to the piano keys, spoke of her passion; for I do not know how she managed to place in everything that she played an expression which gave the soul a sort of shiver. Often Melanie, wandering, would meet me in a room; she would come to me, and, taking my hand, she would look at me with intoxication, then go away quickly.

"When we went out, she leaned on my arm in such a way as to let me know that to be at my side was for her the greatest of the faint felicities that innocence allowed. I tried to encourage her by saying: 'My sister, we enjoy all that constituted happiness on earth: we love one another soulfully, we see each other, we are sure of each other's fidelity, and each of us in looking into his own heart finds the other's thoughts. We have the most beautiful of human feelings, the soul and the charming smiles, why should we be sad?...'

"'Ah my brother, the evil is done!...Talking can do nothing about it.'

"She spoke the truth. I felt it inside me. 'Joseph,' she continued, 'You are my firmest support, with a man without virtue I would have succumbed! Ah! I should pride myself on having you for a guide.'

"Seeing that our passion was ceaselessly exalted

by the deep solitude that we were in, I resolved to cast my sister into the distractions of the world. Here I will observe that with a strange piece of good luck, we found ourselves rich. Upon my arrival in Paris I had left our two hundred thousand francs in the hands of our banker, who suggested that I go into a growing business venture: it succeeded so well that in the space of four years our funds tripled and a small part of the interest was more than enough for our expenses, which were wisely directed by Madame Hamel. Then I took a team of horses, and making sure my sister had the care of a studied fashion, I led her to our banker whose salon afforded us a crowd of *acquaintances*. Balls, invitations, shows followed one after another. My sister obtained, by her beauty, a stunning triumph: all the men arrived at her feet. My self love was flattered to see that these adorations resembled the crowns which one dedicates to the statue of a goddess; the flowers die on the impassive marble. My sister always had a devouring melancholy, and in the most beautiful salons when the eyes of everyone were upon her, she only looked at one man seated in a corner; and this man, sad and dreamy, only contemplated her. The world was, for us, a vast desert free of people; our passion filled it, and we had only left our solitude, to find another which caused us to regret the former...

"I will always remember the last party that we appeared at. Melanie, crowned with roses, uniting in her person all of the perfections of her rivals without having their faults, excited a murmur of astonishment. As she had no coquettishness, and no pride, she even pleased the women. In the glow of a hundred candles, in the middle of this assembly, she came to find me in the corner where I was confined and where I was enjoying myself in silence. 'Joseph,' she said to me, 'Let us go?...People bore me, I would rather see you for fifteen minutes than to be with this crowd.' We climbed up into our carriage to return to the hotel.

"The voluptuous clothing which made my sister so seductive, the admirable light that I had just seen her in, had reignited all of my fires, enflamed all of my veins, I was calmly furious; and I was only happy when she spoke to me. In the carriage she leaned her pained head on my shoulder and said to me:

"'Joseph, I love you!…' The tone of these words resembled the last cry of a dying person; they warned me that my sister felt all that I felt. I trembled…How many things came from Melanie's supplicating sentence! Then the end of her white glove brushed my hand, and I recall that this last occurrence brought me to the peak of my ardor.

"'Melanie, I am dying!…' I responded.

"'Very well, we will die,' she said, and she kissed me with intoxication for the first time in three months.

"Let it be permitted me to stop and say that we, Melanie and I, had conquered more than all the saints together, and that we were ten times, a hundred times, a thousand times more worthy of the name of virtuous beings.

"The next day, I judged that I did not have a moment to lose, that I had to leave my sister; for her passion and mine could no longer be controlled, each day our reason was being extinguished and our love was becoming such that had we been criminals, I believe, in the sincerity of my heart, that the eternal would have absolved us.

"That was how, after many battles, when I consulted a good ecclesiastic, he told me to end the battle or we would succumb. I had to put an insurmountable barrier between Melanie and me; he advised me to become a priest. This idea waxed in my imagination and I considered it for a long time. At last seeing that each day made the combat harder, and victory less certain, I regarded the bosom of the church as a sure and sacred escape.

"'Yes,' I said one day, 'let me have the courage to flee Melanie, but at the same time let me separate myself from all humanity. Let me seek an out of the way place, where, in the most modest church post, I may achieve a life whose end I see. Let me be useful to people. I have no need of anything down here; the earth does not offer anything worthy of me since my Melanie has been taken away from me. I do not want her to blacken her splendid virginity. Let her die! I will follow her to the tomb.'

"Still, one does not plan to separate oneself from all that attaches one to life without thinking, and my melancholy became even more somber. Enclosed in my room, thinking ceaselessly on the advice that my confessor had given me, I did not see Melanie any longer: when, supplicating and crying she wanted to enter I would refuse to see her. This rudeness broke my heart; but I became cruel, I tried to harden myself by these little things. I prepared myself to strike the last blow. Our goodbyes frightened me: how could my sister let me leave? Wanting to make sure of her I resolved to hide my decision and the place of my retreat from her. The most cruel tyrants were not more cruel than I.

"Alas! Melanie, are you still alive? I dare not think about the place where you live."

"Tears again, and lines so garbled that I cannot read them," cried out Marguerite.

"Very well!" responded the curate, "they increase my pain; I am suffering Marguerite! Give me a glass of Malaga wine!...Although for the shorn sheep God measures the wind, the poor children have more than they can bear, and as there is no good horse that stumbles, the sky is my witness that I would have absolved their sin, if they had succumbed, in the knowledge that God, too, would ratify my absolution."

CHAPTER 13

When the good curate had drunk his glass of Malaga, he said to his servant: "Hurry up and finish, for this is stifling me...and I will not be able to sleep!"

Marguerite took up the manuscript again, and continued in these terms: "When I had irrevocably halted my destiny, I left the retreat; and Melanie saw in my changed features that a new sorrow was making me desolate. Using that angelic gentleness which formed the basis of her character, she suffered in silence and respected my secret; but she made me clearly see that she shared my pain, for at each instant her face, shining with the aura of divine humanity, begged me to teach her the secret that I kept closed in my heart. Her eyes seemed to go to the depths of my soul, and her gentle words were a music worthy of the eternal throne: I was unshakable.

"In reviewing the list of dioceses I noticed my name by the bishopric of A...y; the region of this town with its forest in the Ardennes, but principally the name of M. de Saint-André caused me to choose to go there rather than somewhere else. I was at my banker's where I took fifty thousand francs and deposited them with an unfamiliar notary so that if Melanie attempted a search, she would find no trace. I arranged all of our business, and I liquidated our fortune which I placed in the account book in Melanie's name; and, when the accrued interests had been dealt with, I took care of the little things, to make it so my sister would not suspect my departure and try to follow me. I bought a seat on the mail wagon, bought clothes; I sent my money ahead to A…y. Soon, too soon, everything was ready: I chose the fatal day.

"This unusual activity had singularly alarmed Melanie, and each time that I came in or went out, she spied on me with the gentle disquietude of love. She resembled a mother watching her child. At last the day that I had chosen arrived, in the morning I shivered with a violent fever.

"'My brother,' Melanie said to me, 'you are sick: what is wrong with you?…Tell me, Joseph? If not I will use my rights by ordering you to tell me.'

"'Ah! My sister…you will know soon enough! Savor this last half-day well. At five o'clock we will both be in tears.'

"'So,' Joseph, she said, casting me a frightened look, 'can we have any more trouble?...I cannot guess what it is!...'

"'Listen Melanie, love has this beautiful characteristic that the greatest sacrifices seem as nothing when they are done for the beloved person...This feeling makes the heavy light; it makes what is bitter sweet...God is my witness that I would give a hundred thousand times my life rather than cause you the least pain.'

"'Joseph, you are not the same,' she said, casting me a painfed look. 'What do these words mean? Never before have you suggested by so many sentences what you poured into the heart of...a...your sister?'

"'Ah! Melanie! How times have changed!...We were innocent and now we are guilty!...But you are right! Very well, know Melanie, that to assure your comfort, your innocence and mine, I have resolved to offer you a sacrifice...'

"'*You are going to kill yourself!*' she cried, with a sublime expression of horror and fear. She was four

272

steps away from me; her face contracted and pale as death, her dry eyes fixed on me.

"'No Melanie,' (she gasped) 'no,' and taking her in my arms I drew her towards me. This charming girl leaned her noble head with its disheveled hair on my shoulder, cried bitter tears which soothed my heart. I cried too: 'My sister,' I said to her, 'promise me that you will never try to kill yourself?...No matter how bad things get, you will live?'

"'Yes!' she responded with an angelic smile, 'but, as long as you remain on earth.'

"'Melanie! That is good! For the death of one of us will be the death of the other.' Nothing is more true. Now, set yourself at the piano! Play me your prettiest piece! Throw into your impassioned playing all the love that makes you mortal, and all of the melody, all the purity which makes you an angel. Surround this autumn morning with the most shining caresses and the greatest beauties so that these hours flow smoothly, purely, without remorse, intoxicating us!...'

"She looked at me with astonishment, and, plunged in a reverie by my enigmatic words, she sat on her stool; touched, without hesitating, a few plaintive notes, and seemed to search for the meaning of my discourse. In the end she got up, came to me, then, with that unequaled tenderness, almost of a mother, she kissed me, and said to me: 'It does not matter...you want it! I want to please you, that will have to suffice.'

"Then she made me hear a mass of sounds and harmonies, a divine melody, for me, for her it was the swan song, as soon as I heard it involuntary tears came to my eyes. Never had the idea of a separation seemed more cruel to me; I saw all of its consequences. When she had finished, I kissed the piano, the keys, her hands with an unimaginable delight: she was not surprised; this indecision which produced astonishment governed her attitude, her look, her gestures. She remained immobile, looking with her eye, in her expression, an unseen object, just like Ariane must have been on her rock, when she watched Theseus' vessel, and so that, almost a statue, she kept looking at the immense sea where she no longer saw anything.

"'Melanie,' I said to her, 'let us sing together this

admirable piece: like a last ray, like a last gust, animates the end of the day.'

. . . .

"In finishing she cried out: 'Joseph, you have very sad ideas! I would rather die than stay in the incertitude that you have cast me into.'

"'Melanie, just one word, and you would understand everything...but I do not think that you are strong enough, I would like...'

"At these words she looked at me steadily and said:

"'You want to leave me!...' Then she fell on the rug without strength and without life: her face was pale like the muslin that teased around her throat.

"Frightened, crying, I raised her up; and when she had regained her senses due to the salts that I made her breathe, she repeated ceaselessly with a tone of folly, and desperation. 'I want to die!...I want to die!...I want to die!...' I cast myself at her knees, I pulled her to me, I warmed her with the most enflammed kisses. I consoled her by the most delirious words. She only responded with one sentence: 'I want to die!...' And her wandering eyes roamed around the apartment with a frightening liveliness.

"Then looking at her with a feigned severity: 'Melanie,' I said to her, 'you do not love me!…'

"Her only response was to come and kiss me! Good God what a kiss!…Or rather what a response!…

"After an hour she was calm again, but in reality more beaten in her expression, I said to myself: 'Should I leave?…Should I not leave?…' Each time I got up she uttered a lamentable cry which made me tremble. At last she got up and came over to me and sitting on my knees cried: 'My brother, I beg you, take pity on me…do not go…you take my breath away, my life! We can stay separated by prisons, by walls of iron, if you want, but stay so that I will know that you are breathing the same air that I breathe, that you are two steps away from me, that when I give up my last breath, you only have a step to make to catch it…Happy to confess without fault that you were in my thoughts all of the time!…I will bless the severities which we will mutually endure! But O Joseph! O my only friend, my brother, stay, stay, you are everything to me!…'

"'Ah wretch!' I responded, shoving her hands away, 'do you want to lose your soul and perpetuate your evil into the other life! Weak soul! Do you not know how to make a great and proud resolution!'

"'No, I cannot!' and looking at me with eyes that reproached my abruptness: 'Joseph, if I only damned myself, then you would have been happy a long time ago!...'

"This admirable devotion which only belongs to the female species, because women add the grace and charm to it which we take away from our sacrifices, caused all of my nerves to tremble, and the least hairs of my head. I raised her up, took her in my arms and cried:

"'Let virtue perish, honor, Melanie, you have won...'

"She took three steps backward, looked at me with incredible dignity and said to me: 'Joseph, I still want to see you every day, but without crime...' The majesty which she unfolded the cold beauty of her accent drew me back to reason and I felt that it was impossible, more than ever, to stay amid such dangers.

"'I must go...' at this word she responded to me: 'very well! If there is only one crime which can make you stay...'

"In speaking like this she threw herself at me, and kissed me with an embrace filled with warmth.

"'No, no, goodbye, Melanie!...' And, looking for the last time at the room, the paintings, the piano, the furniture: 'I leave my soul in this place,' I said to her, and I went towards the door, but my sister held me tightly, not wanting to part with me, and she uttered inarticulate cries that were drowned in a deluge of tears. I separated from her forcefully, this violence on my part brought an end to her tears, and she looked at me saying: 'O Joseph!...'

"Profiting from this astonishment, I fled!...I heard her cry:

"'And our goodbye!...I did not see you! Barbarian!...Our goodbye!...'

"Uneasy, I stopped in the courtyard and noticed Madame Hamel and all of the people running. 'She is dying!...' I thought, 'well, so she dies!...It will be her greatest moment; I am going to join her.' I wanted to go back and see her, but in that instant my father's inflexibility came to my memory; and, crueler than a tiger, I opened the door and ran to the coach. I was disoriented, almost convulsive; the idea of the tender Melanie's death filled my heart with a glacial cold. I do not know how it happened that I found myself two leagues from Paris, without knowing yet how to form an idea…Then damning my barbarity, I imagined my sister's last moments!…'If she dies,' I said to myself, 'I would not be worthy of the name of a man for not having allowed her to exhale her last breath on my lips…'

"It was night, I ordered the coach driver to go back pretending that I had forgotten something. I went back into Paris and returned to the house. I leaped over the garden wall so as not to be seen, and I climbed the stair with a convulsive trembling. I slipped into my bedroom; from there I went to the living room, and without showing myself I looked in through the half open door at the scene.

"Melanie, lying on a sofa, was surrounded by women; a doctor carefully examined the least expressions on her face. I made a sign to Madame Hamel, and she came over to me.

"'Very well!' I said to her…

"'Ah dear Joseph! We fear that your sister is crazy!…'

"I shivered.

"'She cried for ten minutes whirling her arms, with horrible convulsions: 'Without a goodbye!…Without a kiss!…The monster!…' A moment ago she said: 'What will I see?…What face will please me!…' At last she began crying out forcefully about five minutes ago: 'If I only saw him for one instant!…I feel that I would be resigned!…'"

"At this moment Melanie, breaking away from those beside her, shaking off all of the women who could not hold her down, ran through the living room, with wild hair, furious: 'he is here, he is here!…' I threw myself into her arms…'So I have seen you again,' she said.

"Alas! Her smile no longer had this angelic softness. 'Melanie,' I said to her, 'I came back to say goodbye!…' 'I was sure of it,' she cried, 'I know you.' Then she kissed me with delight…'No! I cannot go through with it…'"

"But is this agony or what?…" interrupted the

good curate who was wiping his eyes.

"Monsieur," Marguerite continued, "my heart is so swollen that I cannot read any more." The servant and the master were quiet and looked at each other in silence: and, at this moment, the clock struck eleven.

"There is still some scribbling," said the curious servant.

"The poor children!..." cried M. Gausse, "They merit paradise like Satan merited Hell."

Marguerite took up the manuscript and continued in the following manner:

"At last I left, leaving Melanie between life and death. I arrived at A...y. I got out by the seminary. Far from giving my name as M. the Marquis de Saint-André, I only presented myself under the modest name of Joseph, saying that all of my family papers were lost, and that I no longer had either father or mother. When I was alone in my cell I felt the extent of my misfortune; that was when I saw that death was coming quickly. Existence became a burden to me, my soul wandered ceaselessly back to the house that Melanie inhabited. I could not do without her. At last, I painted her portrait from memory, and it has an extraordinary fidelity. This portrait is for me the sum total of my happiness. One day, fearing that Melanie would lose hope and not believe that I could finish my days far from her, here is what I wrote to her: 'My sister, I am alive!...This word alone should tell all the extent of my suffering, my resignation, my courage. I address this letter to you to ask you to support this existence, do you hear? For in writing I believe that I see you and hear you; when we have attained the age when passions die in men's hearts, when you do not have anything else angelical about you, your desires will have worn away in time; then we shall see each other again; then, we rejoice in advance for the pleasures of a very celestial existence: for, in looking backward, and seeing the reefs that we have avoided, our soul will be filled with joy. Our hearts, separated from the impurities of desire, will shiver gently. Keep this moment for yourself in which I aspire...I would like to see the time flee more quickly to arrive there. O you whom I dare from afar still call the gentle name of spouse! You are the thought of my thoughts, the soul of my soul! Goodbye! Dream that you can still make my happiness and you will live just as I live...only because of you. Take courage, hope! So goodbye, charm of all my moments. Your brother who loves you with love!...'

"I sent this letter by a rapid mail coach ordering them to mail it in Paris.

"Alas! This checked passion still gnaws at me. No human circumstance can attain my heart. At A...y, I found my uncle, he did not give me any information about my father. When I questioned him about my mother, tears came into his eyes and he looked at me with an unimaginable tenderness. It was all the more surprising that my uncle looks just like my father, and the ecclesiastical state has given him singularly austere morals. He has a reputation of sanctity which makes him the object of veneration. The fact that he was troubled when I asked about my mother seemed strange to me: for my father likewise was moved when I spoke to him about her. All of these strangenesses which would have illuminated a young man's curiosity did not touch me; Melanie's image reigned in my soul in tyrannical fashion. It still reigns. It will reign forever!...I am dying consumed by this infernal love, and I notice each day that the path to my tomb becomes shorter.

"Ah! Blessed will be the day when the good curate, whom chance placed me with..."

"Poor friend!" cried M. Gausse.

"Will close my eyes!...Well, I will give him this manuscript, and I will ask him to go to..."

"You see, Monsieur," cried the triumphant Marguerite, "you see there is no crime, no sin, and that sooner or later you would have read it."

"Then go on, Marguerite," cried M. Gausse.

"...And I will ask him to go to see, in my name, the unfortunate lady! He will bring her my last words, which will be for her the order to leave!...I would only have had a single idea throughout my entire life, and that idea, I would have it, I believe beyond the tomb. At each moment of the day I say to myself: 'Melanie is thinking of me!' She is the faithful companion of all my actions, I do not make a single movement without seeing her. O, Melanie, is it true that we will not see each other again?...The love that I have in my heart burns me with a black fire which is not sputtering at all; all that I see only has grace

when funerary thoughts are wedded to my sensations, and…I do not have a single friend whose well-
wishing voice encourages me!…No! My fatal secret
will die in my chest.

"When I spoke to my uncle my plan was to go die
in Aulnay-le-Vicomte, it…"

Marguerite was there when the little child from
the choir came running with the speed of a rabbit,
and cried out, outside by the shutters: "Here is M.
Joseph!…" Marguerite was frightened and ran to the
vicar's room putting back the manuscript in the same
place; she looked at the portrait much more attentively, arranged everything in the same way, and went
back down as she heard the doorbell ring. It was truly
the vicar who had not wanted to leave; he seemed
very disturbed to Marguerite, and his first question
was: "Marguerite, didn't I leave the key to the door of
my room?"

"Oh my God, I do not know," replied the wily servant, looking at the good young man with that
obliqueness which was the ordinary attribute of the
curate's servant's eyes; "because I have not gone up-
stairs since you left…M. Gausse," she said raising her

voice so that the curate could hear, "the poor dear man had found himself quite affected, seriously afflicted! He had dizziness as if from an attack of apoplexy that had come over him; but at this moment he is better," she added, following the young man who hurried into the living room.

"Very well, Monsieur," he said to the curate, "you are suffering?"

"Oh yes," responded the good man, *I am suffering in the heart!"* The vicar stayed a little while by M. Gausse, and during this time, Marguerite and the curate, looked silently and with respect at the altered face of the young man: there they read his thoughts for a second time and suddenly the tale of his adventures made his eyes seemed a thousand times more eloquent to them. From time to time, the curate and the servant cast meaningful glances at one another. Soon, the young Marquis de Saint-André took his light and rushed up to his room after having said goodbye to M. Gausse.

Marguerite had an even greater admiration for the nobility of his bearing which was made imposing by his long, black robe.

CHAPTER 14

You can imagine that when the vicar left, the servant had a rather long rosary to recite with M. Gausse.

"Very well, Monsieur," she said crossing her arms, "was that an adventure or what? And we are happy to know about it, since the entire village is trying to find out!…"

"Marguerite," responded the curate, "even though one wastes one's time trying to whiten black, and he who has drunk will drink, I hope that you will keep the deepest secrecy about his indiscretion, so that the name of Monsieur the Marquis de Saint-André will never leave your mouth."

"Ah, Monsieur, with God as my witness, it is buried here!" and she pointed to her heart.

"Promising and keeping a promise are two different things!…" murmured the curate.

"You will see!…" replied Marguerite quite angered that her master had placed her discretion in doubt.

This incident caused their conversation to remain there, for the servant kept her conjectures to herself without communicating them to M. Gausse who for his part went to bed still thinking of the tribulations of his young vicar. Marguerite kept her word out of spite. In vain Leseq, the tax collector, the mayor noticed that the servant knew more than they did. Had they tried to seduce her, she would have been deaf to their compliments, advances, and flatteries!…And, as Leseq was the most ardent, she got rid of him by saying that she would reveal the secret on their wedding night.

"In that case," responded Leseq, "we will keep the status quo, which means uncertainty."

Nevertheless, Marguerite, who had conceived a gentle compassion for the vicar, calmed the village so that they finally arrived after a certain lapse of time at not bothering about M. de Saint-André.

But there was in Aulnay a woman for whom the vicar was the entire universe. Madame de Rosann did not stop thinking about M. Joseph. She began to admit to herself that his being was essential to her happiness. An innocent affection drew her towards him, an infinite force which she could not tame; but, as women in general are given to explain everything by love, so that they are all love itself, the marquise hurried into the vast domain of seductive feelings. Meanwhile, though she perceived all of the dangers of such a passion, she did not even disguise the fact that at the time when she had arrived at the age which, for women, is the sure haven against storms of the heart, she succumbed and broke her virtuous existence. The image of her husband, the man to whom she had given happiness, age, virtue, nothing could dissuade or stop her. Inside herself she admired the strangeness of a fate which had ordered that she would finish her career as she had begun it.

"What?" she said, "wasn't it bad enough that at seventeen an ecclesiastic inspired a violent love in me which was beneath him!...Must I, at the end of my career as a woman, burn with a sacrilegious fire for another ecclesiastic! And fate wants the roles to be changed, so that today I fulfill the role of the one who seduced me while the one whom I love is in my place. Ah! Why was he not around when I was twenty-two!..."

Those who have experience know that our hearts give birth to untameable passions, whose workings overturn all sorts of barriers. The Marquise's passion was of just this sort.

A few days after the young priest's manuscript had been read by the curious Marguerite, the vicar went to walk in Madame de Rosann's park; he liked the place well enough because it reminded him a little of his dear America. In addition, the ruins of the old castle offered him a scene which was pleasing to his melancholy. From the hillock where he was sitting, he noticed the vast forest of the Ardennes which seemed like a crown set on the head of the friendly hills which formed the circular valley of Aulnay. At its feet, an artificial lake, rather large, separated the romantic debris of the old fortress of which only the square towers remained, solidly constructed, which they could not demolish. The moss, the ivy, covered all of these ruins; and the waters of the lake surrounded this picturesque isle. The young man, plunged in a reverie caused by childhood memories, was seated on his favorite hillock under an American tree. He was admiring the landscape that he had before his eyes, when the light sound of a woman's step resonated in the air: he turned around, Madame de Rosann was two steps away from him, contemplating him with an expression which caused a gentle emotion in him. At this moment his soul was so settled that he did not flee, as he usually did, and far from taking out his breviary, he set it down; in the end, when the Marquise was seated by his side, this woman's presence did not displease him at all. As for Josephine she trembled like an autumn leaf and did not dare look at the vicar a second time.

"Monsieur," she said in a halting voice, "I am going to be jealous of my park! For eight days you have not come to see me, and since then, this is the second time that you are wandering in my gardens…"

"Madame, the sight of this charming retreat is mute and it cannot complain if I come too often; though, if I brought you my respectful hommage too frequently, you would be able, justly, to complain! In truth there is not a man in the world who is more ill at ease than I am in a living room."

"Monsieur Joseph, you are much too modest!..." In pronouncing for the first time the vicar's name, the Marquise accented it in a way that left nothing to doubt.

"Oh! You are too good!..." replied the young man in a lively voice.

"No, my young *friend,* (for I hope that you will become my friend when you know my troubles) no, there is no goodness in that. I am even slightly egotistical, for in speaking to you like this, I am only aware of my interests and my pleasure..."

"What! Madame," cried the young vicar with compassion, "you are unhappy!"

"Oh! Very well, I will let you judge...in telling you my misfortunes, I will address myself to your heart, so that it will take my side. If you discover a secret which is known only by three people, it is because from this day forth, I confide in you the care of a conscience which I had thought was at peace for the rest of my days, and that, for the rest, I hope by my confiding in you, that I will obtain your trust and offer you the shoulder of a friend. My young *friend,* your deep melancholy has revealed your needs to me, you need a heart where you can flee your own and find consolation. Following the example of those men of yesteryear, with their same frankness, I offer you my hand, saying to you: 'let us be friends.'"

At this word, the vicar, moved by an undefinable feeling, gripped the Marquise's trembling hand: together, they shivered and dropped hands with a *sort of shame,* which is the charm of such sensations. A divine joy rose in Madame de Rosann's soul. She began in these terms, "I was born an orphan, and I did not know my mother."

At this beginning, the vicar looked at Madame de Rosann and said to her, "I feel for you, Madame, I know that misfortune…"

"You did not know your mother?…" cried the Marquise standing up. "Good God!…Yes!…You are twenty-two years-old!…You are named Joseph!… Good heavens! Would you permit me!" Then, looking at the tanned face of the vicar, tears flooded her eyes and she sat down sadly, as if a cruel memory had presented itself to her mind. She began again like this:

The Story of Madame the Marquise of Rosann

"I was born an orphan, did I say that? who is filled with the signs and appearance of gentleness, although contemplative; my liveliness only works on my insides. It is brought forth in my feelings, to grow in strength, and you should know for the little that you may have observed yourself that the more lively passions are, the more they cast us into meditation and into that lazy reverie whose delirium has so much charm, so I am tender, although upon first meeting me my spirit may seem to be cold. This modesty, which is suited to our sex, has degenerated and become indifference as a result of the education that I received.

"An extremely devoted aunt, but of that exacting devotion which makes the most futile practices of the faith the *essentials* of the religion, took charge of raising me. So I spent my childhood in a way that the memories of that time, the most beautiful of our lives, were not agreeable; I will not say any more, my young friend, my aunt is dead...but if she had lived?...I would still have to remain silent.

"Counted for nothing by my aunt, I was rarely admitted into the circle of ecclesiastics which my aunt, Mlle. de Karadeuc, surrounded herself. As I grew older, she grew more and more distant from me, so I was forbidden to appear at her house when such holy people were to be found there, and this bothered my soul for a long time. Living in such a solitude, you would think that my imagination, given over to itself, would roam vast fields; and, be it that nature wills it to be so, be it that that was the inclination of my spirit, all of my thoughts were thoughts of love, and of an imprecise love, which I cast on the least objects; it seemed that a need to love resided in me that I was not able to direct. I only considered men's characters in an advantageous manner, and still, meanwhile, I portrayed them by taking the men of antiquity for models, I imagined them to be severe, only barely able to bend under the sceptre of love. Alas! What mistakes a solitary soul casts itself into.

"The rule which kept me from going into the living room, gave to the society that assembled there the charm that results from prohibition, so that, curious like any ordinary young girl, I hid so as to watch all of the ecclesiastics come in and go out of my aunt's house. They were all of indeterminate age, that is to say of a decided age, for they all seemed to me to be between fifty and seventy years-old, and without wanting to contradict my aunt, one could see that she feared a young ecclesiastic as much as an old one. Still, from looking at them, I noticed one day a young abbot who was only about thirty. As soon as I saw him I wanted to see more of him: so, I was more attentive and I did not once fail to see him go by, and I followed him with my eyes for a long time as he crossed through the rooms.

"One day he noticed me, and I drew away quickly, but after a few minutes, I put my head forward and saw that he was still in the same place looking at the spot where I had appeared. The strength of his eyes, the astonishment of his face and his attitude, gave me an incredible pleasure, and beyond that, these little events determined my thoughts to fix themselves on this young man: he became the object of all of my thoughts, and I thought about him ceaselessly in the most innocent way in the world; following the inclination of my soul, I did not perceive any danger in endowing him with all of the perfections that I dreamed up. For a long time I contented myself with thinking of him, but there came a moment when seeing him became necessary to me; having only glimpsed him on the sly, I wanted to contemplate him at my leisure, hear him speak, and know if his soul was really as perfect as I supposed.

"I was fifteen and a half: not being unaware that I was pretty, I still did not conceive of the advantages that beauty gives; I joined naiveté with refinement of spirit that I naturally had; and, from then on I was resolved to be admitted to the living room, and I was. In truth, one day when I had just seen my young abbot enter, I hurried to make myself look good; and I went boldly into the living room. I entered, trembling I ran to sit down beside my aunt, and when I had raised my head, there was a light murmur in the crowd. Mlle. de Karadeuc looked at me with astonishment, the conversation which had been animated when I had opened the door and hesitated a moment, was interrupted; and all eyes turned towards me; my aunt did not say a word...So, casting a furtive glance at the crowd, I noticed that my young abbot was the only one who was not looking at me, and his eyes spoke to Mlle. de Karadeuc a language which was singularly displeasing to me. I did not doubt that my aunt was not charmed on the inside to see that, while her niece drew all of the looks, the youngest of the ecclesiastics kept a friendly smile for her; also I was not surprised that she did not say anything stern to me, and that she did not order me to leave. I frankly avow that the young priest's sort of disdain caused a certain movement of spite in my heart which made me want to draw his attention all the more.

"My young friend," said the Marquise smiling at the vicar, "You see with what frankness I am telling you these first happenings. Now that I have acquired experience, I have remarked what happened to me, happens to everyone. What I am telling you is, in short, the story of all loves that ever will be. I continue: I still recall the slightest words which were spoken that day, and I think that I can still see the man whom I am telling you about as he appeared. Try to imagine a young man with a noble face, but stern. long hair falling in curls on his shoulders; he is tall, his pale skin made the fire of his black eyes even more lively: his distinguished manners, his attitude, the harmony of his features, everything seduced me.

"'Monsieur,' my aunt said to him to break the silence, 'how do you overcome these objections?... That does not appear very easy to me...'

"'Mademoiselle,' he responded with a charming modesty, 'I already have made a great mistake in, at my age, contradicting people whose opinions I should respect; so I will not maintain my own opinions much longer. Only, if I am allowed to say so, the rules of the church have placed us in a dangerous position, that is to say between its laws and the laws of nature. As for me, I will consider it a crime to break my vows, I will do everything to keep them; but if, to my own misfortune, a passion, the only one for me, should be born in my heart, I would confide myself to the goodness of him who pardoned the Samaritain and the adulterous woman.'

"'So,' cried an old ecclesiastic, 'you would dishonor the object of your adorations!...'

"'Monsieur,' replied the young man in a lively manner, 'you are raising another question, which none among us can resolve. It belongs to women, and we cannot treat it at the moment. It is too dangerous, for it pertains to nothing less than to knowing if a young lady is a criminal in obeying her desires. I know that it is a crime according to our civil laws; but admitting that they are broken, I do not see what one could have to say to…'

"'Enough,' interrupted Mlle. de Karadeuc…

"In hearing the object of my dreams talk like this I found his voice flattering, his words seemed filled with frankness. I looked at him furtively, without being able to succeed in being seen by him. My aunt took up all of his attention. Ignorant as I was, I did not know that this adroit manoeuvre was designed so that Mlle. de Karadeuc would not suspect anything, so that he could come back as often as he liked. That is what happened to my aunt, flattered to the greatest degree to see that at her age she had captivated a young man whose principles seemed to be very severe and who seemed to have exemplary conduct, and whom religious ideas governed, judged that she had carried off one of the most beautiful feminine triumphs, and that she must have very powerful charms to silence the call of religion. I did not guess, at first, the secret of the conduct of Adolphe (it was of all names the one that I most liked to pronounce), and I was for a long time prey to cruel torments. My aunt allowed me to come into the living room, since my magical entrance; and I believe that it was on the advice of her friends the abbots that she no longer opposed my appearance. The coldness that the young abbot showed towards me, the lack of attention that he gave me, troubled me: I became sad and dreamy; when I saw him, my gaze attatched itself tenderly to him, and right away I fell into melancholy.

"One day I led Adolphe away since my aunt was with people. I looked at him in a touching manner, and I said to him: 'Adieu Monsieur.' There must have been, in the way that I pronounced these words, something extraordinary for he came closer to me, took my hand. I let him take it, and, squeezing it gently, he responded with an 'Adieu Mademoiselle!...' which made me tremble. I stayed on the top of the steps, leaning on the handrail. He went down slowly still looking at me, and I, when I no longer saw him, I listened to the sound of his steps!...For the entire day I thought that I heard his *Adieu Mademoiselle* and the delicious expression that he had used in saying these words. I took pleasure in thinking about our embarrassed attitude and the sort of shame which reigned in the manner in which we were regarded. In the end the memory of these fleeting sensations and that charming moment, introduced a softness into my soul that I had never known before."

As Madame de Rosann finished these words, she looked at M. Joseph. She noticed a vivid emotion covering his face, for his long black lashes could hardly hold back tears. In truth, such a tale, told with the naïveté that the Marquise put into it, recalled his own passion, but Madame de Rosann, making a mistake about the reason for his tenderness, began again with joy:

"These events are little, but they were all done in love, for nothing is indifferent: a gesture, a look form an entire epoch. It was from Adolphe's goodbye, that my hope was born. What was I hoping for?...God is my witness that I did not know; nothing is as difficult as wanting to explain the first motions of our heart. Those who have loved will understand them, for they have experienced them. It is like that in nature. There are things that can only be felt: for example, the sensation which rises in us at the sight of a starry night, or in going into a dark forest, or in listening to the sounds of the waves of the sea. They cannot be expressed, once touched the soul gives an indistinct sound for which there are no words. So it is when our senses and our hearts awaken."

"It is true!..." cried the Vicar.

"The first time, when we come back to our senses, our eyes looked with a look of intelligence which we felt one for the other when we were mutually occupied with our thoughts while we were apart. Then I was happy!...I even avow, that today this time of happiness and illusion has fled. The prism has broken. I avow that in human life there is not a purer pleasure, more graceful, more delirious, and I did not think that one could feel it two times!..."

The Marquise's eyes became moist and they stopped a moment to contemplate M. Joseph who, his head between his hands, seemed to want to reveal his tears to Madame de Rosann's sight. The unfortunate man thought of Melanie, and Madame de Rosann's tale caused his soul to have a gentle festival of melancholy. The Marquise soon began again like this: "We walked, as you see, very slowly on our way, afraid of one another, both of us religious and candid, satisfied by a look. We stayed for a long time in that state filled with charms. We had the good fortune of fooling my aunt with our secret communications. It was about this time that the persecution that they executed towards nobles and priests became cruel. One day I was sitting beside my aunt, I was reading to her from a holy book, when suddenly, the door to the room opened and I saw Adolphe. Mlle. de Karadeuc was asleep. He came over to me and said: 'Mademoiselle, I am pursued, and I only escaped the dangers which surround me by the greatest of risk. I came to seek protection in your house, and I dared to believe that you would not refuse me…'

"'Monsieur, I do not believe,' I said to him, 'that my aunt would reject you. She will be delighted, I am sure, to help you, and you…' I could not say anything more out of the joy that I felt in seeing him, so I stopped. My eyes told him all that I was thinking.

"Then Mlle. de Karadeuc woke up and was greatly astonished to find him beside me but, as he was looking at my aunt, he composed himself quite quickly and told her of the problematic circumstances in which he found himself. Mlle. de Karadeuc thought about it for a long time before responding. To me she seemed to be calculating the dangers which she herself would be running in receiving a priest and what she might get in the way of benefits in this life and the next. During this silence I trembled. At last she said with an evident repugnance, that she would consent to hide Adolphe, but only for a while.

"A divine joy took hold of my soul at this holy lady's declaration, and I took an inexpressible pleasure in all the details which were involved in keeping Adolphe out of view. So he lived in our house: it was then that, ceaselessly in each other's presence, our passion was all the more glowingly enflamed, more ardent, and the enthusiasm that all first loves excite took hold of my heart. As for Adolphe, he seemed to be suffering and battling greatly, he fought with an incredible courage, and the secret fire that burned inside him, changed him and made him pale. This young priest had been raised by a mother who was extremely pious, who had inculcated in him from the cradle the fear of God and the rigorous precepts of our religion, so that the idea of compromising the sanctity of his soul and darkening the splendor of a saintly life, to lose his reputation, had, and has always had over him the greatest reign. So, he suffered cruelly, and waged rough battles with his delirious soul."

"Come," said Madame de Rosann to the vicar, "come, let us cross the bridge in front of us and go see the ruined chapel, I will show you the only testimonial of that love that I have kept…" M. Joseph followed the Marquise in silence: they entered an old chapel, and when they arrived at the black marble altar the Marquise, raising a flute on the column, took out some papers. Then, seated on the stone bench, she took up her story again: "On the night following the fifteenth day Adolphe, not being able to resist his passion yet not daring to tell me of it, placed a letter on my night table."

Then the Marquise unfolded a worn paper and read with a visible emotion.

"'Mademoiselle, whatever dangers may await me outside, I must flee the shelter that your aunt has offered me. Even though my death is almost certain, I prefer it to the peril that I risk in the house that you inhabit!...If I write you this, it is so that you will not be surprised at seeing me leave suddenly, without apparent reason; for then, you might think that some feeling of disdain, (what do I know?) could have caused my flight, and I would not want, even for the sanctity of my soul, to cause your heart the least pain; for in the end, Mademoiselle, I feel that you have little friendship for me! Alas! Since I must retire from here, since I must flee forever, would it be permitted for me to write that I love you? The fatal secret emerges from my burning heart!...O Josephine, I know that the fire which devours me cannot reach you, and that is what emboldens me to tell you what I feel. Without a doubt you are beautiful, but how the beauty of your soul is greater than your charms. What a candid soul is revealed by a pure and chaste regard! These are the perfections which have seduced me; and it was not since yesterday, it has been for a long time. The passion that I have been combating for three months, will still make my heart beat when I die! I will conceal it my whole life under a cold appearance; and I will only live my life by gathering inside myself, searching for the traits which my heart will keep like an eternal imprint. I do not ask to know if you love me, I do not beg you to give me any favors!…Where would they lead us?…No, I content myself with adoring you from afar like an altar that I dare not approach. Only, I hope that you will have some compassion for me, that you will say of me: "There is in the universe!…I do not know where!…an unlucky man who loves me…without hope!" The idea that you will sometimes think of me will give me pleasure; and, when I am dead, I will have some of your tears…These are the only ones that I wish you to shed for me.

"Alas, Mademoiselle, if you want to assure me that you will dispose of your touching compassion, that you will arm your glances with severity!…I can respond that I…Well, I will remain, at least, in my life, I will still have a few moments of happiness to count; for, when I see you, I feel all that is pleasurable on earth! And…if heaven by chance…what do I know, makes it so that you have something more than friendship for me!…Ah! Mademoiselle, we will enjoy the most divine favors!…God!…If our souls were to understand one another! What charming concerts! What a full and pleasant life! I will only ask for that delight which in paradise one acquires by a saintly life. You fill my entire heart; you are everything to me…but I feel, I have been letting my imagination run free. I must leave, for there is nothing to all of that! So it is, goodbye, pure and cherished beauty, goodbye. I say farewell as though to the shore of a homeland that I am leaving forever! I will drag my love and sad existence elsewhere and be happy if I meet with the revolutionary axe along the way.'

"Monsieur," the Marquise began again, "you could not know how to believe in what state reading this touching and melancholic letter plunged me. For a long time I stayed with my eyes filled with tears, without being able to think: the next morning, when I met the young priest, I took his hand, and drawing him to me, I said to him in an altered voice: 'Do not leave.'

"That told him everything! He too shivered with happiness and cast me a look that made me tender. My aunt never left us alone, so we could not speak of all that was filling our hearts. So, confiding me in our mutual innocence, one night I followed Adolphe into his secret room; and there, sitting beside him, I took his hand and crying with shame I said to him: 'Ah! I love you!…'

"'Josephine,' he cried, 'Ah Josephine! You are making me die of happiness!'

"'But what will become of us?' I said to him.

"'Josephine, don't you feel an intoxicating pleasure in your heart?…That must suffice: the happy union of our souls will provide us with calm and pure voluptuousness. Let us examine a course in life in which few mortals have shined; let us separate, let us keep distinct what is material in us and let us only live the life of angels…With a strong will we will extinguish our desires, and having no more battles to fight, we will taste all the happiness that is here on earth. Happy, enjoying a felicity that will not make virtue lose its brilliant color, we will die together after having worn out all of the pleasures of the soul.'

"'So,' I continued, 'from today our souls understand one another, and when I look at you then you will understand all that I say.'

"Then we spent a delicious hour, prey to that first

happiness of love; and to that charm of first words where one dares to say everything, with reticence, movements of shame, and joy which are undefinable. This gentle moment filled by prayers, sighs, looks which one fears to understand and which one likes to feel, this enchanting moment has remained engraven in my memory, so much so, that it never appears in my imagination without causing me a secret voluptuousness which the distance of time cloaks with a tender grace.

"Our sublime resolution, taken with courage, was followed with stability and without a murmur for a while; but, young friend! How such promises are imprudent, how imperious emotions rise up in the soul, when two beings cherish each other together!..."

"Ah Madame!..." cried the vicar, then the young man distanced himself by a few steps from Madame de Rosann, he stopped and appeared to the Marquise gripped by the most lively emotion. When he came back, tears lined his pale cheeks, and all the fire of his passion for Melanie shone in his eyes.

"Madame," he said, "I cannot express to you to

what point this tale is cruel for me!…"The Marquise smiled and squeezed the young priest's hand, she cast him a look which seem to tell him that she understood his energetic sentence and that he had reason to hope. This compassionate glance caused the vicar to tremble, who became silent again beside the Marquise. She went on like this: "One night Adolphe drew me against him and said to me: 'Josephine, I must leave for nothing is less certain than the blessing of my soul and yours.'

"'What are you saying?…'

"'That I love you too much and that I can resist no longer: we have presumed that we were stronger than we are: I want more…I am not happy…'

"'Very well, speak,' I told him, 'what do you want?' His only response was to take my hand and press it against his heart. He looked at me!…Ah! I avow these simple movements told me everything! I looked at him for a long time, and my head seemed drawn to his by an invisible force. We stayed for a long time in this formidible silence: but at last Adolphe leaned towards my face, and placed a kiss on lips that I received with intoxication…then, suddenly, he drew three steps back, and said to me: 'Let us separate!...Josephine, I will love you all of my life! You will be the only woman whose name, and memory will make my heart beat!...But I love you enough to prefer your honor to my pleasure, and your future happiness to the happiness of a moment.'

"He threw himself into a corner and I heard him praying and sighing. I listened to him for a long time...I admired him, with a gentle compassion, and a vanquishing tenderness slipped into my soul. I went back to my room, and I began to reflect if one can call by the name of reflection the vague thoughts which came to inundate the soul of a passionate lover."

CHAPTER 15

The Marquise continued in these terms: "There is nothing more touching or more capable of making a woman's soul waver, than the sight of a man making efforts to respect her. This is the great proof of love which lost me: it slipped pity into my soul, a perfidious compassion. 'Very well!' I said to myself, 'shouldn't I sacrifice myself for the happiness of the man that I love!... Would it be showing a greatness of soul if I profited from another's battles? Isn't it better to choose my own misfortune, and to take everything upon my head?... Was I not barbarous to contemplate this paleness of love covering his face, without recompensing it with as much ardor and virtue... I will cry in secret for the faults that I will commit to save my lover, and before him I will be happy and laughing!'

"In the end, I found I do not know what grandeur, what sublimity in attaching myself for all my life to the same individual, even though shame would be my gain, for I believed that I must conceal everything by the most violent love and by the beauty of devotion; so that no one could blame me if they said: 'What a lover!...'

"It was by these reasonings that I succeeded in chasing reason from my heart. A circumstance came to finish the defeat of my wavering virtue: the greatest of hazards caused me to enter into my aunt's secret room; there I found the *New Heloise* I read it. In that book, I saw the faithful story of my feelings; the eloquent author of that masterpiece persuaded me that I would remain shining, pure, candid, despite my satisfied love. We were in a similar situation, and I imitated Julie...in everything!"

Here the Marquise covered her face with her pretty hands, and she remained silent for a while. At last she raised her head and looked at the vicar. He was immobile, his face had no severity on it. Then the Marquise began again: "All that I know is that men should not criticize me...My Adolphe admired my devotion. He tied his scruples in an ocean of voluptuousness, and I will have the courage to say that I did not feel any remorse!...Meanwhile, I was not depraved, I could not be so. Nothing had corrupted the lovable purity of my morals. This lack of regrets, this tranquility of soul in the middle of what the world would call by the name of a crime, should be the cause of more reflection. The severity of Adolphe's principles tormented him at each moment, and he suffered for me.

"It was in the middle of this gentle existence, it was as I grew drunk with pleasure, that Mlle. de Karadeuc became more seeing. One night when we were together she looked at me with a severe air and said: 'My niece, do you dream of the emminent post that you are going to occupy? Have you forgotten that the nobility of our family gives you the right to enter into a monastery and that the powerful ties that I have with the German Emperor and the Holy Father have promised for you a dignified place in the monastery of L..., and that if you exhibit a regular conduct... (In saying this word she looked at me with a piercing irony) you could become an abbess?...'

"'But, Mademoiselle, I have, I assure you, no taste

for monastic life.'

"'You do not love the church?' she began again with a sardonic smile.

"'I do,' I responded, 'I am religious and I believe in God, but he has given each of us the right to choose the most suitable way to attain our grace.'

"'The one which you are taking, you little hypocrite, will lead you straight to hell. Believe me,' she said angrily, 'my glasses have not kept me from seeing the looks that you are giving our young refugee. As of tomorrow he will be gone.'

"'What, Aunt, you would cast him out? You would send him to his death!…' And in pronouncing these words you can guess how I was trembling. This old woman cast an examining eye on me and cried: 'Ah wretch!…You love him!…'

"'No, my aunt!…' I responded in a broken voice. 'Ah! I beg you, don't let an involuntary glance, without intention, lose the soul of a man of the Lord!…You will be accountable for his death at the last judgement, and that is a crime that nothing will absolve you of…'

"'You see, little Satan, how you fear his departure…He will go, Mademoiselle, and do not worry, I myself will take him to a holy woman who will take him in.'

"'Mademoiselle, do you know that he will be cared for there as well as he is here? Think, that if, out of imprudence, the one whom you confide him to should uncover him, then you would cause the loss of a young man who belongs to one of the most noble families in France, a young ecclesiastic, who, if things change, could become cardinal.'

"'Everything that you say, the warmth that you put into it, only confirms my suspicions, and maybe you are more guilty than I thought!…'

"These words gave me a mortal shiver for she spoke the truth.

"'Mademoiselle,' I told her with a dignity which impressed her, 'you forget the name that I carry, and that in the end, you are the most vigilant and best of aunts…'

"You see, my young friend, if we know how to lie when we need to?…'

"Mlle. de Karadeuc looked at me, she remained

undecided for a moment, but after a short instant of reflection, she left me, opened the door to the young priest's room and led him out by the hand. This old maid could have run a convent! She set Adolphe before me, and, enjoying my blush, she told him with an air of goodness: 'I know that you love each other...'

"Adolphe paled. Before he could respond, I composed my face, and I responded to my aunt: 'What made you think that?...' My friend understood me, he looked at Mademoiselle de Karadeuc and responded to her with the same inexpressible trouble: 'Mademoiselle, I did not believe that our morals were sufficiently dissolved to give rise to such suspicions...O God!' he cried with a melancholic tone, 'What I am forced to say is already a punishment for my sins! Will this terrestrial humiliation be counted?...And what I am suffering,' he added in looking at me, 'could it erase something in the eternal book where they write our faults?'

"My aunt examined each of us in turn with a malicious curiosity: 'Monsieur,' she said with a mute anger which she retained, but which pierced through the tone of her words, 'Monsieur, I believe your words, I voluntarily gave you asylum, but it is still not safe enough for you, and my continued devotion requires that sooner or later I should have visits. To-morrow I myself will drive you to the house of one of my lady friends, and you will have nothing to fear.'

"'Mademoiselle,' I cried, 'my dear aunt, I see that nothing will efface your suspicions, very well, I am going to give you a proof whose evidence will per-haps make you…What would I not do to save a priest from the certain death that awaits him if he leaves this place.. I will leave! I will leave him alone with you,' I said with an ironic tone, 'and I will go to Aulnay-le-Vicomte, and hide in Marie's hut since she was my dear nurse!…Will that satisfy you?'

"At this proposition my aunt seemed to grow calm, and as she reflected, Adolphe, tears in his eyes, looked at me, and his moved glance told me how much he admired my devotion. Mlle. de Karadeuc consented to this arrangement, it was agreed that the next day I would leave for Aulnay. We could, Adolphe and myself, kiss and say goodbye!…What a touching scene of melancholy!...'

"'No,' cried Adolphe, 'I will not abandon you, above all in the state that you are in!...'

"'Adolphe, you will stay here? If I must fear for your life!...I would perish!...' What tears! What kisses! What cruel charm! I left!...

"I spent some time enveloped in the deepest pain, and I confided everything to my poor nurse: I could pour out tears on her friendly breast, that was when I appreciated the goodness which one experiences when one tells one's secrets to someone! — My young friend, ah! Do not fail to take that gentle liberty!...

"One night I was sitting by Marie's fire, and we were speaking about Adolphe, her husband came in and looked at me with a sad expression...We questioned him and he told us that the young priest whom Mlle. de Karadeuc was hiding had been discovered and placed in prison!...

"This piece of news that was said without thinking caused me to faint; a burning fever took hold of me, and in my delirium, I spoke only of the child whom I carried in my womb. Marie feared for me. At the moment when I was so weakened by a thousand sufferings which overwhelmed me, my nurse, seated on my bedside, thought that I was going to die…The sound of a galloping horse resounded at the door of the hut, a soldier entered!…I recognized Adolphe! …He flew to my bed of woe…Joy had the same effect on me as pain. When I came back to myself, Adolphe held my hand in his; and when I was up to listening, he told me the violence of his passion had not permitted him to withstand my absence, and love had inspired the strategy in him which had caused my pain.

"In truth, if he escaped Mlle. de Karadeuc would only be confirmed in her conjectures, and would imagine that he had fled towards me. 'So,' he said to me, 'I quieted your aunt's mind by surrounding her with attentions and hommages which she was infinitely grateful for. I abolished all trace of a suspicion in her mind; and when I had her back to her first friendship for me, I wrote to my faithful friends, my brother among others, to fall upon me disguised as policemen one night by chance at Mlle. de Karadeuc's house, and to take me away from her!…He executed this tricky manoeuvre so well that my aunt thought that she would die of sorrow when at midnight they came to make a thorough search of her house and when my brother, to whom I had indicated the secret of my well-concealed hiding place, with a sabre knocked the wall in where the secret door was. I played the resigned one, I consoled your aunt who accused herself of imprudence; and I left her, happy to be able to come and find you. My brother gave me a uniform, I ran from woods to woods, at night, and…here I am!…'

"O intoxicating joy!…o pleasure!…I have savored this period of my life, all the pains and voluptuities of a longer love, for I was approaching term, and sadness would soon place its iron hand on my heart.

"My young friend," said the Marquise showing the young priest the park of the castle, "you see this charming refuge. It is filled with memories for me!…These fields, these beautiful fields, have seen me happy for three months!.. As happy as a mortal can be!…For these three months, free, without care!…Loved, adored by Adolphe, I did not ask for anything from heaven except to remain like that for the rest of my life.

"The first punishment for my crime was inflicted by Adolphe himself, when he saw that there would always be a heavenly witness to our love!...He became dreamy; through the questions that I asked him, I saw that he was thinking of the future, and he even was jealous of the tenderness that I would feel for my child. That was when he told me to leave Aulnay, to bring the fruit of our love to light in another place!...

"No one noticed my state, for I had the cruel courage to dissimulate it up until the last moment, and I remained pure and virginal in the eyes of men!...What wrong I committed towards society!...Alas! I only hurt the being that I loved the most!...My poor child!

"To confuse Mlle. de Karadeuc, we told Marie what she was to tell my aunt, that I had been obliged to seek refuge with one of her relatives because they had made searches in the village of Aulnay to come and arrest all of the nobles whom they could still find; and, once the first wave of the search had passed, I would return to her. So Adolphe brought me away, he was the one who helped me with everything. His love was shown in the care that he took for me. But alas!...The barbarian took my child away, and...I did not see him again!..."

Here the Marquise cried for a long time!...

"All that I know," she began again, "was that Adolphe, whom I begged to give the child my name, called him Joseph!..."

"Joseph!" cried the vicar with signs of surprise, and his face aflame! Madame de Rosann looked at him with pleasure.

"You are named Joseph too..." she said.

"Where did you give birth?" he began again, seizing her arm and looking at her.

"Ah! Far from here!" she responded, at Vans-la-Pavée!.." And all the time she was prey to a lively anxiety as she examined the young priest's face.

"Wretch that I am!..." he cried, "don't I know who I am!...Still a priest!..." Then he fell into a reverie that Josephine respected.

After a long silence during which the young

priest looked furtively at Madame de Rosann, she began again: "Besides, Adolphe came to tell me that my son was dead: he took great care to announce this fatal news to me, but, dare I say it! I never believed in the reality of what he said!...A secret feeling cries out to me that my son lives!...So, you can expect, when I notice a child or a young man, I have a heart that is heavy with a tenderness which searches an outlet from the heart that is swollen!...

"Ever since I have had only misfortune...Adolphe emigrated, I returned to my aunt, and I lived in tears because, according to the nature of my character, a passion was to make great ravages in my soul... What a melancholy seized me!...I was inconsolable at the loss of my child and of my friend. I received his news. He assured me that he loved me, and still a secret bitterness reigned in his letters. It seemed that he was weeping for his mistake, and he did not dare to reproach me for he would have had the utmost infamy!.. Ah! when someone's character is too religious, they have a shade of degrading fanaticism and are capable of many cruelties. You will judge!...All I had left was the great God!...To be scorned by the one whom I loved so much, for whom I sacrificed everything!...For I loved, my young friend, as much as one can love here on earth!...

"After my aunt's death, I came back to live in my dear Aulnay-le-Vicomte. M. de Rosann saw me and loved me. I found contentment in the bond that we contracted, but I kept silent about my transgression. He still does not know about it!...

"Soon an amazing regime came to replace the excesses of the revolution. Then the sovereign reestablished religion on its altars, Adolphe was recalled and obtained a significant post six years ago, while I ran with intoxication to see him again!...Never will this scene leave my memory. He was at his house, I went in, and he did not recognize me, but the servant told him my name. This gratuitous insult pierced my heart with a deathly chill.

"'Ah what!' I cried, running to him, 'Adolphe does not recognize his Josephine!...'

"Then he said to me coldly: 'Here you are Madame...'

"He sent everyone away, and we remained alone!...I thought that this great severity, this reticence would cease. No. Alas!. No...

"'Josephine,' he said to me, 'You have married?...'

"This question made me tremble. Ah! I gathered in this moment all of the untruth that I had sown in my youth!

"'Cruel!' I cried, 'it would have been nice to remain faithful to you and be received like this!...'

"'Josephine,' he continued in a serious tone, 'I still love you.'

"Despite the deep tone which accompanied these words, his coldness, his pale and stern face, destroyed the conviction that I burned to have.

"'Josephine,' he continued, 'you have a husband!...'

"'And do you believe,' I told him with emotion, 'that I have come here to put one over on him? If that is what your words mean, you do not need to say anything else!...O Adolphe!...Adolphe...' despite my pride I broke out in tears.

"'Religion...' he began again.

"'Enough of your religion, and look at me like you once did!...'

"With this sentence, he cast me a glance of horror and disdain.

"'Goodbye!...' I said to him, and I raced out of his house, swearing that I would never see him again. The dryness of his speech, his dark attitude, his repentance had overwhelmed me."

"So my young friend, do you believe that there is a man stern enough to condemn my fault, when it has been followed by two such punishments: the loss of the one who could have made my crime glorious, and the cold disdain of the one whom I loved so much!...Ah! There are crimes (if it is one) that heaven certainly punishes down here!...You see that I have in my soul vast subjects to think about, and they are so vast because I have not had any children by M. de Rosann: Heaven has cursed my bed!.. Alas! The tears that I cry in secret, will they rectify my wrongs? Our religion, which makes repentence a virtue, gives me hope!...But, good God!.. What would I become if I did not tame the new sparks that my heart is enflammed with!..." she looked at the vicar.

The latter remained plunged in a deep reverie:

the simple and naive manner in which the Marquise had recounted her story: the place, the memories which were awoken in the depths of his heart by this woman's tale, her tender tone and the look which she cast him as she said certain sentences that she developed that were evidently for him, everything helped make him dreamy: he did not even hear the last sentences of the amorous Josephine, who did not dare at first to interrupt this melancholy. Nevertheless, after a few moments she said to him: "Let us go back to our bench on the lawn, these ruins, these vaults, set one to thinking!…"

She leaned on the young priest's arm, and they returned in silence to sit under the cedar.

"Very well, Monsieur Joseph, you are not talking to me?…"

"Madame," he responded, "I cannot say anything to you, I am incompetent in such cases, for I always absolve those who suffer and who suffer such torments."

"You are worthy of the holy ministry which you perform!…Ah! Come over sometime to give me gentle consolations, I feel that they refresh my heart!…Alas!…It is still aflame!…I fear that a cruel destiny is pursuing me…Ah! If you knew…"

She turned her head aside and cried.

"Come," she said, "come, my young friend…you will represent for me the one that…I lost!…"

At this moment the castle bell rang lunch. The Marquise, looking at M. Joseph said to him: "If you do not fear having a poor lunch, give me the pleasure of accepting half of mine!…"

The thoughtful vicar followed Madame de Rosann without responding. One would have said that a secret charm was acting upon him and forcing him onwards in spite of himself.

CHAPTER 16

We left our vicar plunged in a profound melancholy following the Marquise all the way back into the castle dining room. He was at table beside the Marquise, but he did not know where he was. When Josephine offered him something, he raised his eyes and saw on the face of one of the servants who was serving him a smile whose sardonic expression caused him to shiver.

This servant was standing, a napkin on his arm, just across from the young priest; he was only balanced on one foot, his slightly cocked head followed the general thrust of his body, and this posture added to the irony that was expressed on his face. His eyes, with their piercing look, also embarrassed both the Marquise and her protegé. This glance halted M. Joseph's ecstasy, and threw his soul into a vague disquietude which tormented him.

This servant, named Jonio, was one of those creatures who is devoured by a desire to move up in life and out of the station in which fate has placed him, one who has *philosophized* enough to shake the yoke of conscience; and one who will make use of all possible means to arrive at his aim. At last, by a special favor of nature, he had the sort of style and manners whose candor excluded all suspicion of his principles. He seemed to be attached to M. the Marquis of Rosann, in whose service he had been for some time; but he served him with such zeal since the trust that M. de Rosann had of those in power since the restoration of the Bourbons gave him hope; and he looked on his master as the first instrument that he would employ for the establishment of his fortune.

The vicar was soon rid of the importunate presence of this servant, for Madame de Rosann, reading a sort of disquietude in the vicar's eyes, and seeing that he was looking at Junio on the sly, set him away immediately.

M. Joseph naturally had compassion for those who were victims of passion, so the Marquise found the rigid vicar much more affectionate than she had hoped; she enjoyed this change as if it were the first step that the young man had taken towards her.

"My young friend," she said with an affectionate tone of voice, "I hope that someday you will confide your troubles in me."

"Alas, Madame, I would tell them to you, if friendship could offer me consolations, but there is no solace for my sorrows, and it would be to needlessly afflict a friend if I told you my adventures."

"Never," responded the Marquise, "to participate in your sorrow, even in vain or as you say: needlessly. Two wretches find themselves stronger to support their misfortune, when they are together, and their hearts understand one another."

"Ah! Madame, your misfortune is at its greatest!...You will find your son!...But I!...The fatal *never* is engraved on all of my wishes, even hope is forbidden me!..."

"Poor child!..." cried the Marquise, and with such a friendly air that it was impossible for the vicar to be astonished by this exclamation which seemed to win, for the one who pronounced it, all the rights of friendship.

The Marquise led the vicar into the living room: there, after a few insignificant sentences, Madame de

Rosann set herself at the piano. She began carelessly and from memory a piece by Haydn. At the first notes the vicar shivered, he approached, and Josephine, noticing the young man's attention, continued to release all of her feelings into her playing...She turned around, the vicar, with moist eyes, immobile, had the attitude of a prophet; and he religiously gathered the sounds that the Marquise drew from the harmonious instrument.

"Madame," he cried, "without knowing it you have caused me the greatest pleasure and the greatest pain!..."

The unfortunate man, hearing his sister's favorite sonata, thought that he saw Melanie herself!...He let himself lean back on his chair, hiding his face in his hands, and the Marquise ran to his side out of respect for M. Joseph's pain.

For Madame de Rosann this morning was one of the most delicious moments of her life; she savoured that pure happiness, without her conscience even reproaching her for it. When the vicar left she took it as a pretext to go see her former nurse to be able to accompany the young priest all the way to the castle gate. Her heart bubbled with joy and loved walking beside the being who seemed to carry her entire soul with her.

When the vicar found himself alone, he began reflecting on the affection that Madame de Rosann had for him, and his entire heart murmured. The memory of Melanie did not disturb at all the new gentleness which slipped into his soul. Meanwhile, he kept up his guard against this waxing feeling and resolved to go to the castle less often; but Josephine was too wise with those womanly ways which overcome the greatest obstacles to leave the young priest in the presbytery. At each moment, she created pretexts. Marie helped her singularly on these occasions. As soon as Madame de Rosann got mad at one of her servants and sent him away, Marie consoled the afflicted one immediately, counseling him to go find M. Joseph, and to get him interested in his plight. The vicar came back asking for a grace which was given as soon as he spoke. At times Marie went to tell the vicar of a poor family's needs; and in the hut, M. Joseph found an angel of goodness who had preceeded him. Madame de Rosann came on foot so as not to give her good works the luster of prideful philanthropy. She had need of the company and the arm of M. Joseph. Along the way, gentle conversations, delicate and charming words, tender, appropriate, became so many blows struck by the Marquise on the heart of the young priest.

All of these cares were disguised by too much good naturedness and spirit for M. Joseph to notice: meanwhile, he began to reflect on the pressing cares that surrounded him. When he spoke to the good curate about his embarrassment, M. Gausse did not know what to say: informed about the ardent love of the young man for Melanie, he was not unaware that M. Joseph's heart could not contain any other similar sentiment; but, on the other hand, he would have been enchanted to see his vicar cast into a passion which would cause him to forget the being whom an insurmountable barrier kept him from approaching. Then the good curate was content to smile with a certain style; and he unleashed two or three proverbs which enveloped his secret thoughts, and which M. Joseph's candor prevented him from understanding.

The result of these reflections by the vicar was

that he should have renounced going to the castle, not because he conceived suspicions about the nature of the feeling that Madame de Rosann had for him, but because he believed that he was committing a sacrilege towards Melanie in finding pleasure by being with another woman, and that, for the rest, he was failing, in some manner, the vow that he had made to separate himself from all humanity.

This incommutable decision was executed with rigor, and Madame de Rosann's most subtle intrigues failed before this decree by the young priest who was back to contemplating his dear portrait. Madame de Rosann was desperate.

Her love, reached its peak, could not support such a privation. One morning she risked writing the following letter to the vicar.

Letter from Madame Josephine de Rosann
to M. Joseph

"It seems to me, my friend, that you are often neglecting your Josephine! Is she still Madame the Marquise de Rosann to you? I believe, to tell the truth, to have done enough to win the title of *friend*. Reciprocate!...Think that you owe me many consolations. Only you can banish the sadness which overwhelms me...For a month now you have not come to see me. I am waiting for you, alas! I feel that you are becoming more and more necessary to me. In truth, think of the happiness of an adult when he finds his true friend, and you will see that I do not have cause to be happy...In the end, my young friend, I wish it for you; and this word must suffice..."

It was unfortunate that the Marquise ordered Jonio to go bring this letter to M. Joseph. When the domestic entered Madame de Rosann's room, he noticed a passionate expression on her face which the least observant man would have guessed the cause.

"Jonio," she said, "take care to bring this letter to Monsieur Joseph himself; if he is not there, then bring it back!..."

The tone, the look of the Marquise said everything, and her eyes followed the paper into Jonio's hands as if this letter were her lifeline.

Once Jonio possessed the letter he thought of retaining it. But he thought to himself, if the note does not say anything, then it is useless to intercept it. As he thought this he was in the avenue of the castle, he walked slowly, when a man came up to him, and after having read the address of the letter the man said: *"Tu quoqou Brute,* and you also Jonio!...*Indulges amori,* you are adding to the basket! *Quo te Moeri perdes?* You run off to the vicar; go! *Tineo Danaos et dona ferentes,* be afraid of being hit by the rod when you are carrying chickens."

"It is you Monsieur Leseq..." said the preoccupied valet.

"Luckily for you! Can you not know what the entire village thinks of Monsieur Joseph? Madame de Rosann loves him, *et traxit per ossa furorem,* she has the devil in her body. There is something for us: *oportet servire marito,* we must enlighten the husband, and we will win, *funus,* a job in *circumvallationibus in customs vel aerario,* or in contributions."

"You think that this letter is a love note... Ah!...How can you tell?..."

"That vexes you," said the curious schoolmaster who ran no risk in the affair. *"Ego sum alpha et omega,* I

340

am unique in such sort of expeditions! Go!... Our fortune has been made, and we will go *vertere materiam,* light the firecracker. Come to my house, I still have a bottle of wine, that is all that I have left of what the curate gave me."

Jonio went along with the schoolmaster who boiled water, and hanging the letter above the vapor, he removed the sealing wafer, he opened the letter without damaging the seal, and read the letter out loud, as Jonio trembled with joy and hope. The letter was put back together again so skillfully that it was impossile to think that it had been opened.

"What news!..." cried Leseq, "I will know more than Marguerite!...Ah that," he said looking at the valet, "I hope that if Monsieur the Marquis de Rosann rewards you, then you will not forget me...Keep the letter and when you learn something new come and tell me..."

Jonio came back to the castle, he affirmed to his mistress that M. Joseph had just read the letter in his presence; and, asking him to give his respectful greeting to the Marquise, he added that he would bring his response himself.

The vicar, expected with an unequaled impatience, did not come. Madame de Rosann, seated by one of the windows on the side that looked out on the avenue had her eyes more often on the field than on the work that she had in her hands to keep busy. In the evening, the sound of a team of horses was heard in the avenue, the Marquise looked with a trembling glance; and she saw the carriage of her husband M. de Rosann. An inexplicable feeling slipped into Josephine's soul, to give an idea, one must mix everything all at once, spite, anger, the sort of mood that one has against the person who has just interrupted one's projects: again, the Marquise united all of that with a certain sort of aversion without that being the exact feeling.

At last her husband, for the first time, was a burden to her and annoyed her merely by his presence. An importune remorse rose up in her soul, as the light carriage came towards the steps. The Marquis, having noticed his wife at the window on the ground floor, had given the horses a violent lash of his whip to make them go faster.

The man of a fifty and a few years, but still of a

young build and face, leaped lightly out of his elegant carriage and rapidly went up the steps, buttoning his blue frock coat that was decorated with the ribbons of several orders. He was surprised that he did not find his wife in the vestibule, he opened the door to the antechamber and, not seeing Madame de Rosann, thought that she was indisposed. He ran into the living room and then he saw the Marquise who had slowly gotten up, and advanced halfway through the room.

"I see," he said with a slight smile, "that you were expecting me?...My lovely wife..."

"Certainly not," responded Josephine coldly as she was still thinking about the vicar.

At this utterance, the Marquis looked at his wife with surprise, and began to examine the careful clothes that embellished her, thinking that it was a careful game he replied: "Josephine, a presentiment warned you without doubt of my arrival for you are dressed with an elegance and an attractiveness which proves that you are playing your astonishment well!...Marvelously..."

"Ah!" cried the Marquise coming back to herself,

"I see that this is enough play!…" And she kissed M. de Rosann, believing to put into this kiss all of the grace and charm of before, but it was a married kiss, in all the sense of that expression: and the Marquis, while giving his wife a cold caress, could not keep from thinking that something had happened to the woman that he loved.

A moment of silence followed during which Madame de Rosann could not say anything, for her troubled soul did not dictate anything to her, and she began to weigh the value of what she had to say.

"Very well! Dear friend," cried Monsieur de Rosann, "since our marriage until now this is the first time, I believe, that you have gone without troubling me with questions!…"

"But M. Marquis, I do not know which of us should be reproached, I am only quiet because of your silence."

"You have a dreamy air about you, and you are not looking into my eyes…"

"I could say the same to you!…"

"Ah! Josephine! Turn your eyes to mine, and you will read how ravished I am to see you again! So you did not hear the crack of whip that I gave my horse, it would have told you everything…I rushed all of my business in Paris, I left the Chamber before the end of the session just to surprise you! But you, have you ever thought about me…Have you longed for me?…How have you spent your time here? What is new in Aulnay?…Tell me?…" In finishing these words, the Marquis went over to his wife took her arm and kissed her hand with ardor.

"Monsieur, I am *enchanted* to see you again, but, I would have wished that a word from your *dear* hand had warned your Josephine, even if it were only to keep her from the reproach that you have made, so, (for I see that I have failed to fly out onto the steps), well, you would have met me in a carriage along the route, waiting for you with *an unequaled anxiety,* and, when you would have given your horse a stoke of the whip, my driver would have given *two*…even ten to my horses, to hasten the *enchanting* moment of our reunion… In the end I do not know how to convince you of my tenderness for it seems to be the style to doubt it, I would not have gone all the way to A…y."

"You would have only done one ordinary thing!"

replied the Marquis, piqued by the irony that Josephine placed in the way that she pronounced the words that she had just said.

"Another time," she began again, "I will go all the way to Septinan. Then will you find that twenty-five leagues is enough?…If that did not suffice!…I would go all the way to Meaux."

"One cannot overly cherish the one who loves us!" murmured the Marquis.

"Reproching one's love is a little bit too much!…" said the Marquise striking the floor with light and repeated little taps of her foot.

"I am wrong, Madame, I am wrong!" said the Marquis with a concentrated spite while twisting his gloves violently.

"Non, Monsieur, no, I am…I should always remember that I was Mademoiselle de Vauxelles, and that you were Monsieur the Marquis de Rosann…so that my duty is always to be lowly…and to only see you as a benefactor…even as a master!…"

"Ah Josephine!…Josephine!…" cried M. de Rosann with a deep pain.

At this tone Madame de Rosann resumed her natural goodness, had a feeling of shame, and abhorring her cruelty, she threw herself into the arms of her husband: then with the dissimulation that is natural to women, she kissed him with an expression which resembled love, and said laughing: "You will agree, my friend, that these little storms are necessary to feel the happiness of a good marriage?..."

Who would not have been fooled by such a strategy? M. de Rosann begged forgiveness and received his pardon: meanwhile slight suspicions remained in his soul, but they were so vague that he was astonished to be hung up on such thoughts.

Madame de Rosann told him of Laurette's death! And to be sure she did not forget the vicar. In speaking of Joseph, the Marquise seemed to be walking on hot coals; M. de Rosann, noticing that his wife feared to speak as much as to remain silent, pressed her; and a black notion invaded his soul as increasingly the Marquise's expressions became more animated as she recited the young man's perfections.

"Surely he has come to the castle?" he asked.

"Rather often," as the Marquise responded M. de Rosann had his eyes fixed on Jonio; he saw the compassionate, ironic smile wander on the lips of the servant, which had disturbed the vicar so much; it had a terrible effect on the Marquis. He did not say anything else, and was content to look at his wife with a scrutinizing eye and seemed to be trying to read her soul. Jonio contemplated his master with an interested curiosity, he tried to guess if M. de Rosann would be jealous enough that he would not disdain the one who enlightened him.

"My dear," said M. de Rosann, "you should know that if you speak of this again, I will not ascribe any meaning to it, but you should agree that you had a reason not to come out to me, for you must not have seen my carriage."

"To use your careful language," responded Madame de Rosann laughing, "I begin by denying you the right to pose me that question; but I truly want to lift the uneasiness from your spirit, although as a wise woman I should leave it to you: ah! Well, vassal, your sovereign avows to you that when you entered, she was entirely occupied with the means of obtaining a grace for an unfortunate woodsman, whom they just condemned to six months of prison, and whose absence will leave an entire family in misery. I thought that I should write to you on the subject in Paris, and I was also thinking of sending our young vicar to help these unfortunate people."

"You are quite occupied with this young vicar…"

"Quite, dear vassal, and I will occupy myself even more with him if I notice that he makes you jealous, for it would bring us back to the delicious times of our first love."

The tone, the expression, the irony, the fine coquettishness which Madame de Rosann employed in this response blew away the strength of the cloudy suspicions of the Marquis. Still, a disagreeable opinion of the vicar slipped into his soul, it would not have taken much for this opinion to have become hate.

By an extraordinary coincidence, M. Joseph came to the castle that very night; and, only seeing Madame de Rosann in the presence of her husband, she could not tell if his visit was in response to her note from earlier in the day. The young vicar, meeting

M. de Rosann, behaved towards him as was his habit. He was severe, reserved, cold and gave free reign to the disdain and mistrust that he had for all humanity. In this way he talked down to M. de Rosann who had not thought that he would meet a being whose manners and words belonged to the highest class of society. The Marquis, wounded in the superiority that he tacitly felt towards M. Joseph, conceived a hatred for this character, and he would have had the singular suspicion that the vicar's soutane hid a lover of high degree: he surprised several of his wife's glances which confirmed him in this opinion, as well as M. Joseph's affected politeness towards Madame de Rosann.

The young man kept coming back to the castle for several days, and these visits were not of the sort that they would change M. de Rosann's opinions. He was dreamy, abrupt, and began studying his wife with care and the attentions of jealousy. One could easily conceive this feeling in M. de Rosann who was, in truth, a constantly happy man. For a number of years he had believed himself to be loved by his wife; and having found everything in her, felt strongly attacked when he had arrived at an age when one desires a faithful companion, and saw his happiness disappear like a dream.

Meanwhile the Marquise seemed even more emboldened, since the presence of M. de Rosann made her position more dangerous, and her passion, irritated by this risk, became exasperated and grew furious.

One day the Marquise went towards Marie's house, she went in and came into the room where the vicar once gathered the first hommage of her regard.

"Marie," she said, "I defy everyone, run to the curate and warn Monsieur Joseph that the family of Jacques Cachel, the imprisoned woodsman, is dying of hunger!.. Tell him to be there tomorrow, but, nurse, do not tell him that I will be there..."

The nurse faithfully accomplished this mission: the vicar promised that the next day after dinner he would go into the forest, to Jacques Cachel's house, and Marie informed Madame de Rosann of the time when the vicar would be with the unfortunate family.

CHAPTER 17

Jacques Cachel's hut was situated on the slope of one of the hills which surround Aulnay-le-Vicomte. At that time a poor but rather pretty woman lived in it and had for company three little children as well as misery and hunger. You should have seen this desolate mother, covered with rags, watching a pot of potatoes boil, and keeping her children from grabbing them before they are cooked! She cried for her children's misfortune, for her husband's pain, before thinking of her own misery. She was overwhelmed with work and groans because this work, excessive as it was, did not procure her a wage that was sufficient for the needs of her little family. She turned her gaze towards the hole which served as a window and she was happy to see the rays of the sun display the magic painting of an autumn sunset, for she thought that during the night her children would not complain of hunger, and that sleep would take away the memory of their sufferings. Her sad gaze was not that of someone who was unfortunate who only worried about himself, rather it was the gaze of a mother who cried for others *besides herself!*...and who are more than she was. She cried, even though she knew that her tears are useless. She cried!...Could anyone bear the spectacle of a woman's tears?...The poor Madelaine contemplated the riches of the valley, and asked the heavens why there are so many inequalities in the distribution of wealth. "Ah!" she said, "if I were rich, I would do good!..."

With this exclamation said in a low voice, she heard a light sound, gentle and pleasing. She noticed the panting of a tired person...The children went out and came in again with fear and surprise carved on their innocent faces that were worn with care. Madelaine looked and the Marquise appeared!...

"Very well, my poor child you are unhappy and you have not told me?..." Madelaine was surprised, she cast herself at the feet of the Marquise and kissed her glove.

"Come on, my girl, get up. What does that mean? I do not do what I should..." The peasant tried to speak, to express her recognition, but words failed her, and the poor woman did not know that she did not owe Madame de Rosann anything. If the vicar did not exist, the Marquise would still have helped her, but she never would have wounded her delicate, white feet on the stones of the forest!...Let us have the consolation of believing that human passions can sometimes produce good through their evil!...

"Look Madelaine," said Madame de Rosann, sitting down, "here are some coupons for the village butcher, he will give you what you need, and here are some for the baker. As for money, ask Marie at the castle; she will give you some hemp to weave, and you will be well paid for it if you do the work..."

Happy, a thousand times happy! The one who, without a witness has reaped in a hut such a tear flowing on the cheek of an unfortunate person who has been helped! This lovely discourse that pronounced recognizance with just a look and a tear!...The Marquise caressed the little children with an affability which doubled the gift. She looked at the ruined hut, and could not conceive that human beings could live in such a log cabin.

"Is it true?" responded Madelaine. And at this

humble response, the Marquise promised herself that she would be the one to furnish the surprise for the poor woman by repairing her hut while she was absent.

At this moment the Marquise shivered, for she heard the rapid step of a man; and, long before Madelaine made it out, Josephine recognized the sound of the vicar's footsteps...He stooped to enter into the hut and Madame de Rosann greeted him with a fiery regard. Her soul was entirely agitated for the disorder of her feelings was at its peak. Her passion had categorized its forces to deploy them at this moment. During this minute, the Marquise chose what she would say to the young man: "I love you!" for she attained this degree of desire, in which everything else is indifferent, she arrived at this summit that was so high, that one does not perceive either laws, or time, or earth, in the end where one is alone with one's beloved, where everything else has disappeared, except her and him.

"I beat you here!..." she said smiling at the astonished young priest.

"So you have left me with nothing to do!…" he responded blushing under the inflamed regard of the poor Marquise.

"Let's see," she began again, "I gave her bread and work…What have you brought?"

"Hope," he responded, "yes my poor Madelaine, you will soon see your husband again! I just wrote to the Monseigneur, and I believe that they will lessen the Cachel affair. Another time he should be more prudent, for he would have no protection if he tried it again. Send your children to school; I will take charge of the expense. Poor woman! How you have suffered…What a bed!…"

"Go get some linen at the castle!…" cried Madame de Rosann.

After a few moments during which the vicar gave soft consolations to Madelaine, he left with the loving Josephine. The poor peasant followed them for a long time with her moist eyes; and coming back in she kissed her children out of pure pleasure, without fear, giving flight to all of her tenderness.

The Marquise walked beside the priest. She glanced at him at times by casting her eyes aside in a charming manner, and she rejoiced in the admiration of the young man who contemplated the picturesque beauty of a horizon decorated by the strange fires of the sunset. The blue, the pale green, the poppy red, were mixed with inimitable tints of fire, silver, and gold, and the sky resembled one of those treasures of precious stones that are told about in Oriental tales. These celestial stones cast their fires on all the objects in the valley, and each tree, each roof mingled its reflections with the sky, its own color: so that the grains of grass seemed to contain diamonds, the trunks of the trees seemed bronze, the thatch roofs colored with a reddish brown, and the most original and astonishing plays of light agreed to plunge the soul in a reverie which the fall of the leaves made profound. The silence which reigned between the Marquise and the young man was only interrupted by the sounds of the village bell. This harmony brought the gentle melancholy which had seized their souls to its peak, so something voluptuous slipped in and prepared them for hearing tender words. Then, a sudden sound, a rapid movemnt would have broken the spell of the spectacle. To be sure, the Marquise could not have chosen a lovelier exhortation.

"What a scene!..." she cried, "how it uplifts the soul, it inspires the love of heaven and detaches one from the earth! It shares this power with the most noble of our passions..."

"Ah yes!..." cried the vicar next to her, seizing the Madame de Rosann's hand, as he would have siezed that of the black man Fimo: "your words," he said after a moment of silence, "your words are in harmony with all that is happening in my heart!...Alas!..." A divine joy rose up in the Marquise's soul when she heard these words which applied to Joseph's past life; she interpreted them in her own favor.

"My friend," she continued, "despite the severe countenance and the wild manners which you affect, a secret instinct has always told me that you possessed one of those souls susceptible to exhaltation, burning, which only conceive what is great and sublime, that in the end you understand love, that feeling of a hero..."

"Too much!..." said the vicar with a somber energy which charmed Josephine.

"You must know how to pardon with nobleness the errors of the soul into which an untamed passion casts us, you employ this forgiveness which is so rare for victims, you weep for them, and your gentle and tender compassion eases their wounds with the fresh balm of consolation. It has never occured, I am willing to wager, to your noble spirit to send away with coldness or repulsion someone who is unlucky at love."

"What savage of the African deserts would be able to!…" cried the young man with the intensity of a criminal who pleads his case.

"Then," began the Marquise who was confused by her happiness, "you would never push away from your chest the being who would seek refuge there?…"

At these words, pronounced with an inexpressible tone, the vicar contemplated the Marquise's face, and, despite himself, was forced to admire the sublime expression which love made shine from it. Josephine, profiting from the silence, began again: "Do you recall that once the Athenians condemned to death a child who killed a dove that had sought refuge on his heart?..." The vicar tilted his head, still looking at the Marquise. What a gentle movement. It intoxicated Josephine...She believed that she was understood.

"Very well, my friend, if a woman presented herself before you and said: O Joseph, I cannot forget the pride in your eyes!...I love you! The little piece of road that we have walked together on that path which they call life has made me want to walk the rest of it by leaning on your dear arm...My hands are filled with flowers, let me crown you and let me adorn what I love above all my riches? Without being able to boast that I possess youth or beauty, I can respond with a fidelity that brings me no honor for it costs me nothing...Do you see me? Since I am crazy about your rare smile: don't you have something to tell me? Ah!...Just a sigh would set me on the throne of happiness... very well, Joseph?"

The innocent candor and the aegis formed by his love for Melanie kept the vicar from understanding this discourse. He was immobile, and took an unspeakable pleasure in seeing the Marquise. A confused murmur raised up in his soul; it seemed to him that a feeling was born in him…

"What do you say?…" said Madame de Rosann with a pained tone.

"But Madame, what good is such a fiction? Such a thing would never happen."

"Ah, Joseph!" cried Josephine. "I am that woman!…"

At this word, the vicar took three steps backwards and stood plunged in a deep astonishment. His face even had an expression of horror on it.

"Yes!…" continued the Marquise, "know that I have counted on your heart…Ah! My young friend! Blush for the two of us, for the violence of my fatal passion keeps me, as you see, from all restraint: I am unworthy of the daylight! But at least learn about all that I suffer: yes, from the moment I first saw you, I felt that fate had given me to you, I belong to you forever, despite myself, from that moment a fever took hold of me and has been devouring me, I only see and desire you; I am as unhappy as a creature can be, and just now I envied the lot of the peasant whom we just helped! Now, I will not have the misfortune to envy anybody, my misery will be the greatest of all! I conceived the crime and nothing is holding me back. Oh Joseph!..." a deluge of tears followed this torrent of words.

The frightened vicar ran towards the village, but Madame de Rosann rushed in front of him and stopped him, crying out in the midst of her tears: "Joseph, you are fleeing me! You despise me, let me see you again, it will be for the last time!..."

"Madame, do you think...about what you are doing!...A crime!..."

"God!...What a punishment!...The disdain of he whom I adore!...Cruel man, have you never loved?..."

The vicar stopped, for the memory of all her troubles touched him.

"In the name of the heaven that you cherish, let me say goodbye to you!" cried Madame de Rosann with a terrible energy..."Grace!...Grace for those who love! A look and I am happy!..."

"Madame, think of your name, it will tell you all!..." In pronouncing these words the vicar cast the poor Marquise one of those lightning glances which pierce the soul, by a cold disdain and a cruel irony.

"Good God!...It is my death!..." and Madame de Rosann fell on a hummock of grass. The vicar was already far away. Nevertheless, not hearing anything any more, he turned around and saw in the evening glow the Marquise lying pale as death. He ran back to her, the cold sweat of fear seized him at the sight of her. He picked up this woman calling her gentle names, he accused himself, he pressed her against his breast. "Madame!..." he cried, "I will love you!..."

At this moment she opened a dying eye, and cried: "What a scene!...I will die of it!..." She fell without strength.

All of a sudden there was the sound of a horse team, and then M. de Rosann's carriage appeared and M. de Rosann himself ran to his wife's side. Before she could regain her senses Josephine was taken into the carriage, and the Marquis, as he got into the carriage beside his wife, violently seized the vicar's hand and said to him: "Monsieur, we will find out about this affair, do not try to escape me!..."

The vicar remained alone in the place where the Marquise had avowed her passion to him; out of habit he looked at the landscape, the sky, and the fleeing carriage. After a moment of reverie, he walked slowly back to the presbytery, thinking about the strangeness of what had happened. His virginal candor and his good heart were such that he hoped the Marquise would feel all of the trouble that he felt. "Ah!" he cried when he saw Melanie's portrait, "she is doubly unhappy, for her love will never be shared!..."

This scene was, as one should guess, the subject of conversation for the entire village. Marguerite defended the vicar and was the only one to imagine that the young man had rebuffed Madame de Rosann. In acting like this Marguerite was not motivated by M. Joseph's interest; no, she had felt the vicar's rigor, and she would have been in despair if someone other than Melanie had moved the impassive ecclesiastic. As for the good curate, when his servant told him of this singular adventure:

"Each is the child of his works," he responded causing the pages of his prayerbook to crack.

When the Marquise arrived at the castle they had to send her to bed right away, and she did awaken from her long swoon only to fall into a terrible delirium.

"Ah, what!" she said to her husband, "you disdain me?...Ah, when will you love me for an eternity, when will you overwhelm me with the most gracious smiles, when will I at last be at the peak of happiness!...I cannot forget your glance...You know? That glance...not a word...no, it is a rock!..."

Then, raising herself on her seat, and rolling her wandering eyes, she seized Marie's arm crying...

"My son!...Let me see my son again...and I will die happy...I have loved my husband greatly," she began again with a fine smile. "Oh yes, I still love him...with friendship—with love you say?...No... no...a being has taken everything away!...In my room!...Joseph!...Joseph!...Goodbye!"

M. de Rosann, sitting on a chair at the foot of his wife's bed, remained plunged in a solemn sadness, he had sent an express letter to A...y and another to Paris...He could hardly bear to look at the delirious face of the one that he loved so much. A horrible fever took hold of Madame de Rosann, and, when the bouts ceased, she became prey to such a weight on her chest, that one doubted that she would live, when her eyes were closed and her face was pale, she leaned her beautiful, discolored head as if she would have wished for a coffin. The Marquis spent all of the days and nights by his wife's bed, incapable of making a single movement, having no thoughts which were not concerned with the dear invalid.

At last the doctor from Paris arrived. He observed Madame de Rosann for several days and declared that when the fever and the momentary sickness had ceased, the Marquise would still languish: that her morals had been too thoroughly shaken, and that the slightest misfortune that might result would be a melancholy which nothing could cure her of; that, in the end, if this violent shaking, if this melancholy were caused by a love, a passion, it would only disappear when it was fully satisfied. As it was impossible for the Marquis to doubt the friendship that the doctor had for him, this decree cast him in the greatest consternation. All that remained was for him to seek the cause of the Marquise's state, and by what event she had been found almost dead beside the vicar, in the middle of the valley of Aulnay-le-Vicomte.

He had to go from misfortune to misfortune! One morning, Josephine was resting and he was hoping for her imminent cure when he saw her face seeming so gentle, which, during this innocent sleep, seemed to have returned to health. Maybe a dream in which she saw the vicar was causing her soul to rejoice!...Suddenly Jonio came in, and, approaching his master, asked to speak to him. M. de Rosann got up, followed his servant, and stood with him by the living room windows.

"Monsieur, I believe that I have given you more than one proof of my attachment to you since I have been your servant."

"What does that mean?...Have you had a quarrel with one of your comrades?"

"No, Monsieur, but I have heard people speak about what the doctor said about Madame the Marquise's condition."

"Very well!"

"Monsieur, I beg you to understand that one must be very devoted to you to voluntarily submit to your anger, by showing you what we should hide in our hearts, for I know that our job is to see everything, understand everything, and to forget…"

"Jonio, you are making me impatient!…" cried the Marquis.

"Monsieur, give me your word of honor that if, by what follows from the testimonial that I am going to make to you that I become hateful to you, although you recognize my usefulness, you will take charge of my existence, by placing me in some administrative position!…"

"Ah! Jonio, are you joking? I order you to speak."

"Monsieur, I will not speak until you have solemnly vowed to care for me, for I know that even though I am going to tell you the truth, there will come a time where you will be stirred up against me, and that then you will prefer my misfortune to that of someone dear to you."

"I promise what you want," responded the Marquis.

The clever Jonio disguised his emotion of joy, for M. de Rosann observed him carefully; then be responded like this: "Monsieur, the day after his arrival here, Madame the Marquise (the Marquis shivered) saw Monsieur Joseph…Since that time, Monsieur, she has thought only of him, since that time they have not ceased being together, and the entire village knows what you alone do not know!…"

"Wretch!…" cried the Marquise. "Do you dare to spread such calumnies!…" But M. de Rosann stopped because in the depths of his heart, a voice called out that Jonio was right.

"I expected that, Monsieur, so I have not come before you without proof!…"

"Proof!" cried the Marquis, "so it is true that this suspicion is real; Josephine loves that young man!…And she is dying for him!…"

"Nothing is more true, Monsieur, the ambitious vicar is inciting Madame's love to elevate himself at the expense of you, Monsieur."

"And your proof?…" cried M. de Rosann suddenly.

"Monsieur, what proves how certain I am about what I am telling you is that I now present you with a letter whose contents I do not know: I would not be permitted for a million francs to unseal a master's letter, but I wager my head, M. the Marquis, that this note is a love note and that it indicates a rendez-vous."

The Marquis, after examining the seal, opened the fatal paper with rage, and read it greedily. A sudden pallor came over his face, and he cried: "It was the day of my arrival!...So that was why Josephine was cold to me.. Go!..." he said to Jonio with a somber anger.

The Marquis closed the letter and went back into his wife's bedroom. The most horrible despair tortured his soul, and a cruel rage took hold of him when he saw Josephine's gentle face...What to do?...A thousand plans were destroyed just as soon as they formed in his soaring mind. Madame de Rosann awoke.

"I am better!..." she cried softly. "My friend, why aren't you at my bedside?...I want to get up! Ah how I want to go to the park to the hillock which is found across the castle's ruins."

"Why?..." said the Marquis drawing near.

"To die there!...for I feel my strength abandoning me."

"You said that you were better?"

"M. Marquis, isn't it better to die when one cannot live any longer except surrounded by shame?" she said in a pleading voice while taking his hand, "do not ever imagine that I do not love you…but remember, that before dying I want to see the Vicar of Aulnay again!…"

"I am going to send him to you, Madame!" cried the Marquis with a terrible look; "but in seeing him, remember that it will be for the last time!"

"What do you mean to say?…Monsieur the Marquis!…You are going to kill him!…Frederick!…"

The Marquis left quickly leaving his wife with the pain of a horrible convulsion.

Marie came running and lavished care on her mistress. In the middle of her delirium and ready to give up her last breath, the Marquise cast a last piercing cry: "Marie, I am dying!…Stop them!.. Ah! If I saw him!…" This latest event had so inflamed the blood of the unfortunate Marquise that she was at her wits end. Leaning on her pillow, she could not even speak, and, to express her thoughts, she weakly moved her white and delicate hands. The nurse, crying a torrent of tears: cried: "She is dying like Laurette!…My dear cherished girls!…Both of them!…I can't bear it!…"

"Again Marie," said the Marquise with a dark anger, "if I saw my son, my death would be almost pleasant!…O my son I would not have shivered at the sight of you!…Not to have rejoiced in one of your smiles!…Ah! Marie, what afflictions!…The subject of secret tears all of my life, my son!…The thought of all my moments, and I will die without seeing him!…Happy are those who give up their last breath surrounded by children!…O God! Take all of that into account…if I could just see our young priest again!…"

Madame de Rosann, tired from all of this heartrending discourse, fell back as if dead.

"I think that I can see Laurette!…" said the frightened nurse.

At this name, the Marquise made a last effort, she raised her eyelids, and tried to make a sign that she found Laurette to be happy…At this moment she cast a feeble cry. The vicar was at the door. He had arrived silently, and he looked with pain on the feeble face of the dying woman.

"Madame," he said approaching the funerary bed, "Monsieur the Marquis himself has sent me."

Madame de Rosann, for her only response, seized the vicar's hand with her burning fingers, and, with a delirious gesture, she brought it to her lips and set a kiss of love on it.

"Alas!" she said, "I am surrounded by angels!…I alone am unworthy…You make me love my husband, even more than I loved him…" she added feebly.

"He is gone!" responded the vicar, "and he came to beg me to come see you…"

"A great and generous soul!…" cried Madame de Rosann, "all of that my friend," she said, "commands me to die!" In finishing these words, a divine joy shone on her face, she looked at M. Joseph with as much voluptuousness that she thought was permitted by her nearness to the tomb.

The vicar aided Madame de Rosann with the most tender and affectionate consolations. In hearing this dear voice, Josephine felt her horrible moral pains calming down, and the more sensible that she felt by the presence of M. Joseph she got him to stay at the castle to try to re-establish her health.

CHAPTER 18

The Marquis de Rosann, prey to the deepest sadness, went towards the road to A...y. After having long thought about the affliction which overwhelmed him, he took a reasonable position: namely to let the vicar procure by his presence some amelioration in the moral sickness of his wife, while at the same time he ordered Jonio to watch over their meetings and to assure him as to just how far the intimacy of these two beings had gone: he, during this time, went to A...y to ask the bishop for a sudden and firm order by which the vicar would be forced to leave Aulnay-le-Vicomte right away. Then, for his part, he would bring the Marquise to Paris in the hope that the pleasure of being there would complete the cure that the vicar had begun.

"To be sure," he said to himself, "as things go, in the depths of my heart I cannot be angry with the poor Josephine...passions are born involuntarily inside us! And Madame de Rosann's malady, the speeches that she makes in her excess of delirium prove that she is fighting her passion…I cannot complain about her, nor moan about her and my fate!…Her death would be the greatest of evils for me, so I must sacrifice everything to allow her to recover her health."

As soon as he had arrived at A…y, he headed for the bishop's residence. His carriage entered the court and the straw on which its wheels rolled indicated to M. de Rosann that M. de Saint-André must be quite ill. In truth they refused to allow the Marquis to enter into the bishop's bedroom. Then M. de Rosann addressed himself to the monseigneur's secretary.

"Monsieur," said the Marquis to the young abbot, "you must know Monsieur Joseph, the vicar of my holding at Aulnay-le-Vicomte."

"Yes, Monsieur, do you have some complaint against him?"

"On the contrary!…" cried the Marquis, "I am so interested in him that I have come to beg the Monseigneur to find him some place more suitable to his merit."

"He would not take it…" responded the secretary flicking a piece of feather that was found on his sleeve.

"You astonish me,?…" said M. de Rosann stupefied, "so he has come to A…y…"

"On his own," interrupted the secretary, "he asked the monseigneur to send him there."

"What sort of person is he?…" asked the surprised Marquis.

"Only the Monseigneur knows!…" replied the young abbot with an air of mystery that made M. de Rosann tremble.

"When I would have him named cardinal," he cried with spite, "then he would leave Aulnay!"

"I do not believe so," said the secretary with refinement, "and if your lordship wants to make someone cardinal address yourself to someone else who will not refuse you!…"

"Monsieur," replied the Marquis, "as I am not one of M. de Saint-André's heirs, I will not unravel any of his last depositions; could you send me in to him?"

"Very well," said the young priest curving his

spinal bones before the nobleman who was an intimate friend of the president of the council of ministers: he guided the Marquis de Rosann by a secret stairway, and suggested that he not make much noise. M. de Rosann heard the prelate's voice and these words came to his ears.

"I institute Monsieur Joseph, Vicar of Aulnay, my sole he…"

At this word M. de Saint-André stopped to listen to the sound of the men coming up his stairway. The Marquis knocked three times on the door and entered without waiting for the bishop to respond. M. de Rosann found the prelate lying on his chaise longue by the only window whose blinds were drawn, so that the day shone on him and at first made the white shade of his severe face disappear. The room bore witness by its noble simplicity to the character of the man who inhabited it.

"Monseigneur," said the Marquis, "I beg you to give me a moment's audience and will offer you the same in Paris at your request."

The prelate began to smile softly, and after having

made a sign to the notary to retire, he indicated to the Marquis a chair that was situated by his chaise longue.

"My son," said M. de Saint-André, "if some sin has brought you to us, I advise you to go turn the key to the lock of the first door by the stairs, for, since my secretary has misunderstood my orders once, he might do so again."

While M. de Rosann hastened to close the door, the bishop rang and ordered one of his men to have everybody withdraw from the neighboring rooms: then he cast a blanket of purple silk over his legs, and shaking the little piece of tobacco that was resting on his purple soutane, he turned towards M. de Rosann uttering a sigh that was caused by suffering. Then he looked at the great crucifix that was placed on the wall across from him, and confiding his hoary head to his right hand, he said to the Marquis, "Speak."

As the Marquis opened his mouth to respond, the prelate freed his hand with a liveliness that contrasted with the sort of solemnity of his movements, set his right hand on the Marquis' arm while asking him with a visible emotion: "And how is Madame de Rosann?"

"Alas," responded the Marquis sighing, "she is at death's door!"

"Death's door!…" cried the bishop suddenly sitting up, "and…I did not know about it!…It is true that for six months I have been secluded!…"

"It is on the subject of Madame de Rosann that I have come to see you," said the Marquis.

At these words the bishop changed color and looked at M. de Rosann with an anxiety that one cannot describe, he even moved his semi-paralyzed leg, without even noticing.

"What are you saying?…" he cried, "explain yourself…"

"Monsieur," began the Marquis again, "a month ago I was the happiest man in France: rich, well favored by the Lord, having as much power as a wise man could have, still healthy, in the end, resting on the breast of a woman whose only thought was for me, spending my life with a virtuous angel!"

"Ah yes!.." the prelate interrupted, "she was the

model of virtuous women, and a year of living with her as a *wife* would erase a thousand faults!..." In saying this the bishop raised his eyes to the sky and his face seemed to grow young again.

"Very well!" M. de Rosann began again in an altered tone, "all of my happiness has been broken by a man and that man!...is our vicar."

"Joseph!..." cried the prelate with fright.

"Yes, monseigneur, Madame de Rosann is dying of love for him!..."

The bishop stood up, he wandered his room prey to a cruel agitation.

"O my God!" he cried. "God of peace!..." Then, crossing his arms he stared straight at the crucifix and said to it: "all powerful God give me the strength, give it to me!..." At last, after a long silence he turned to towards the stupefied Marquis and said to him:

"What have you come to ask me? Who has asked you to ruin me?...Why choose me as confident for your troubles?...What do you want?..."

"Monseigneur," responded the Marquis, "I came

to beg you to place the young priest somewhere else so that Madame de Rosann can forget him!...And recover her health."

"There are things written in the sky!..." cried the prelate slowly; "and it is folly to want to stop the course of the will of God!..."

"What are you saying?..." M. de Rosann began again, "you know the priest?..."

"Yes I know him!..." repeated the old priest energetically.

"Who is he?..." asked the Marquis placing himself before M. de Saint-André.

"God himself would have to be kept ignorant!" responded the priest seriously rasing a finger towards the sky.

"By God! I want to know!..." said M. de Rosann with a despotic tone.

"My son?..." responded the prelate softly.

"Tell me about the life of this man, and I will give you a cardinal's hat!"

"Monsieur," said the bishop coldly, "I am almost in my grave! Honors no longer mean a thing to me. Power," he added ironically, "cannot touch me, and all that concerns me now is the state of my soul. I must obtain pardon for an eternal fault. Earth no longer concerns me."

"So you are refusing me everything!..." said M. de Rosann in with an annoyed expression.

"Return to Madame de Rosann," responded the prelate gently, "announce my coming visit to her. I will drag myself, even dying, to your castle... and...my presence will re-establish peace..."

"So you will remove the vicar?..."

"On the contrary," cried the prelate in a strong voice. "Listen to me, my son. Old men's words are wiser than you would think. Have you often thought that you have no heir, that your name will die with you?..."

M. de Rosann uttered a deep sigh and raised his eyes towards the sky.

"You too should consider that the favor which you enjoy could vanish at any moment and that for a long time you should have profited so as not to allow your holdings to die with you..." The tone that prelate added to these words, his deep gaze, denoted an ambition, a desire, announced vague projects; the attitude of the old man struck M. de Rosann in such a manner that he remembered it for a long time.

"What do you mean?..." he asked in an uneasy tone.

"That is enough," responded the bishop, "I am tired, and...I will see you soon..." With that he gave him a benediction, he opened the door himself for the Marquis who left mechanically and prey to a reverie caused by the prelate's last words.

M. de Rosann climbed back into his carriage and regained his castle. He ran to his wife's room with a haste which showed how much he loved her...He had a vivid sense of joy in seeing Josephine was up, she was sitting on a couch, with dark eyes, her attitude melancholy, which showed that she was still aflame. M. de Rosann could not keep himself from shivering in thinking that this sad improvement was due to his arrival. The Marquise stood up painfully, walked slowly towards her husband, cast her feeble arms around his neck and kissed him with joy.

"My friend," she said, "without Monsieur Joseph you would never have seen me again."

The Marquis dissimulated the pain that this naive phrase caused him. He looked at Josephine with a touching compassion, and then they were seated beside one another.

"My dear beautiful woman," he said, "the Bishop of A...y, Monseigneur de Saint-André, is coming to see you soon!..."

"He is someone I must see again before I die!..."

That night, Jonio, who understood human hearts rather well, took M. de Rosann aside and said to him: "Monsieur, I swear to you on my head that madame's sickness only stems from the fact that the vicar is a fanatic whom through the love of his position has become carried away with himself so that he does not want to respond to her love...I heard their conversations, and I am sure!..."

"Jonio!...Jonio!..." cried the Marquis, "once I am in Paris I will get you the job that you want!..." The Marquis, overcome with joy, ran to his wife's room; and, without asking about the cause of her happiness, overwhelmed her with tender caresses and cares that touched the heart.

The very next day, the Bishop of A...y arrived at the castle of Aulnay-le-Vicomte. When the Marquis noticed the prelate's carriage, he descended and offered him an arm, and he led him to Madame de Rosann's room.

The unfortunate Marquise was in her dressing room by the chimney where the portrait of the ecclesiastic whom we have spoken about was still hanging. Josephine, seated on a chair and her eyes fixed on the color of the rug, thought that she saw the noble and touching face of her idol. Tears rolled from her eyes, and her attitude sufficed to reveal the meditative contemplation of an unhappy lover. All of a sudden she heard a step, she shivered, the door opened and her husband appeared, leading M. de Saint-André. Madame de Rosann lowered her eyes and the priest did not dare to look at Josephine.

"Madame," he said with an emotion that he could not conceal despite long practice and the experience which age had given him to hide his passions from the eyes of men; "Madame, as soon as I learned of your suffering, I came running, as you see? To take part in them."

"Monsieur," she said, "You must have worried for a long time!…"

"For a long time," said the prelate with an air of reproach, "no, Madame, no!…I have not been able to for long."

"It is as if you were speaking Hebrew," the Marquis interrupted, looking carefully at the deep emotions of his wife and the prelate.

"My friend," said Josephine looking at M. de Rosann with gentleness, "I beg you to leave me alone with Monseigneur, and to take care that no one comes near here!…"

The Marquis got up and left!…What a moment!…After ten years, the Marquise saw the object of her first love!…Despite the coldness that religion had given to his soul, the bishop could not repress the movement of gentle voluptuousness which made his heart shiver when his lover cast him her first glance, marked by all the grace of memories. Although the most austere virtue would have for a long time detached the old priest from all that the earth could offer in the way of pleasure, he was forced to approach; and an untameable power caused him to seize Madame de Rosann's hand saying: "Josephine!…"

Her only response was to point out the portrait on the chimney. The austere prelate cast a rapid glance at it, felt his heart beat, felt his vanity flattered when he recognized the portrait that he had given to her when she was Mlle. de Vauxcelles, his first and only passion. He brought his gaze back to the pale Josephine, and he noticed that what he had come to say required greater care, for she would never be strong enough to stand the news.

"Good God!" he cried, "how could I aggravate my fault at the moment when I am almost in the tomb…Good God, will you pardon me?"

"It is not a crime to see me," responded the Marquise.

"You do not know how I still love you!"

"Don't I. After the greeting that you gave me when I saw you ten years ago at A…y."

"Josephine," cried the prelate, "excuse me! I fear losing by some imprudence the consideration which I am surrounded by: this air of sanctity, this reputation without blemish would have vanished, and...if I must admit it, I feared myself! I felt that I still loved you and the severity that I armed myself with was all too necessary to me!...As for you, Madame," the prelate began again, "as for you, whom my face has not remembered for long..."

"Ingrate!..." cried the Marquise, "when I should have forgotten that lover, the father of my child would never have been indifferent to me!... Adolphe? I still love you!..."

The tone of this last sentence was spoken with an unequaled energy, it indicated the type of feeling that Madame de Rosann kept for the prelate.

"Ah, I would have loved you even more," she responded with a sigh, "if you had left me my son!..."

"How, Josephine, can you dare to use such language towards me, when your features show that you are the victim of a criminal passion..."

"Monseigneur, are you the one to reproach me?..." she said casting him a lightning glance.

"Yes, Madame," responded the priest, "because when one has a son..."

"I have a son!...I have a son!..." she cried with delirium, "So where is he?...Ah Monseigneur!... Adolphe?..." and she cast herself at the bishop's knees; "have mercy and tell me everything...Give me back my son..." she cried with that burning energy, with that heartrending voice of a mother hoping to see her only son for the last time in her life.

"Madame," cried the priest in a low voice as he stood up, "Madame, think that people can hear us!...Just a word and we are lost!...You, your child!...Everything!..." Monseigneur de Saint-André's fright told just how much he cherished his saintly reputation.

"So he is not dead!..." asked Madame de Rosann almost out of breath, and whose eyes devoured the icy heart of the stern bishop.

"No!..." he responded with an expressive smile.

"Powers of heaven, my soul is breaking!..." and the Marquise fell almost senseless onto the sofa. "Adolphe, what a torture you are putting me...in the name of God!...If you want to efface your faults in the eyes of the Eternal, don't let me languish...tell me, you have seen him?..."

"Yes..."

"You named him your son!...You..."

"No!..." responded the prelate energetically, "no one can know about our sin, even him!..."

"Ah I recognize you!" cried the Marquise in tears, "I recognize the man whom religion pushed to the extreme, and made inaccessible to the most beautiful feelings that are in a man's heart. Adolphe," said Josephine seizing the arm of the priest, "tell me where is my son? What is he, or I will tell the whole world about my shame and yours."

"So the secret will die there!..." responded the bishop coldly showing his heart, "unless you promise me to observe exactly all that I require of you."

"Oh, I guess your game!...What! You have not wiped out all human laws, virtue, glory, and future life to greet your son with a paternal kiss!...Ah God!...I would sacrifice this mortal life and...the other just to see him for ten minutes!..." Having said this the Marquise fell on her chair and remained immobile. The bishop seizing this moment of weakness drew closer so as to speak to her:

"Leave me?" she said, "Go, despite your penitence you will not go before a God whose greatest title is that of Father!...Letting a mother languish and torturing her!..."

"Josephine, you must know who your son is! The heavens want it, after all that I have done to destroy this living proof of our crime!..."

"Destroy!..." cried the Marquise with a sublime cry of fright.

"If he was able to escape..."

"Ah!..." and Madame de Rosann was able to breath.

"If he was able to escape," the bishop began again, "it was because God wanted you to enjoy his countenance."

"And I am forced to listen to such talk!..." said Josephine with a tone of profound pain.

"Josephine, listen to me..." the bishop continued, "Look at my white hair...Soon the tomb will receive the man whose only passion was you! Let this whitened head cover itself with the fatal shroud without stain; you will not have to keep your promise long. I am going to rip away the veil which hides you from your son, but vow to me, that as long as I live, you will not tell him about the mystery of his birth? Will you imitate me, Josephine? Will you content yourself with the delicious shivering of your breast at the gentle sight... Keep in yourself this divine joy...When I am dead, you can say: 'I am your mother...' Until then keep the secret in your breast, for our son's interest demands it, you can still adopt him some day!...Then keep yourself from pronouncing a single word which could jeopardize his fortune...It will be brilliant...At that price you will know your son."

"Adolphe, Monseigneur, I vow everything!..." she cried with liveliness.

"You have understood me..." the priest continued expressing the contrary with his look.

"Yes!..." she responded briefly.

"Swear on the Gospels?..." said the prelate.

"Above all I will swear on my child...but," she added with an ironic smile, "the Bishop of A...y should know that Madame de Rosann keeps her word."

"That is true!…" replied the prelate recalling that no indiscretion had betrayed the secret of his sin, just as Josephine had once sworn, "Madame," he began again, "your son…"

"Is…" she said growing pale, trembling, blushing, and hardly breathing.

"At least, Josephine, lie down, gather your strength, you should wait…"

"My son!…My son!…My son!.." she repeated with a growing energy.

"He is…" said the priest looking at her.

"Hurry up. I'm dying…"

"It is Joseph!…The vicar…" cried M. de Saint-André.

At this name, Madame de Rosann fainted, it seemed that a bolt of lightning had struck her heart. In seeing Josephine lying on the floor, the bishop lost his head and tried to run, but then he felt his heart weaken when M. de Rosann came running and saw the spectacle of these two creatures devoid of life…He ran out again to find smelling salts…Then the Marquise came back to herself and began crying with a crazed rage…"My son!…My son!…" The bishop held her in his weak arms saying:

"Madame!...Your vow..." Madame de Rosann looked at the frightened priest and was silent; but her gaze reproached the priest for his barbarity.

"My friend," she said to M. de Rosann who came back in at that moment, "My friend,...now I am living!...I am cured!..." She was no longer on earth, her joy was that of angels.

"My son," replied the bishop addressing himself to the Marquis, "I promised to bring peace into your house, and I have fulfilled my promise!...I hope that this effort will not cost me my life, goodbye." M. de Saint-André got up, but one of Josephine's glances made him stay, she came to him and drew him into the adjoining room: "Barbarian, you will not go see your son?..."

"You mean with you?..." he said with a smile and a look in which all the fire of his younger years and his first love appeared.

"That is the way to regain all that you have lost."

"Monsieur the Marquis," said the prelate, going back to M. de Rosann, "Madame has just made a vow, I will take her to see that she accomplishes it, you will see us soon."

"What, my beautiful wife," cried the Marquis, "you who can scarcely walk, even supported by two women, you speak of leaving?"

"My friend," she said, "I am not the me of a moment ago, I am another woman, and you are the winner!…Goodbye my vassal!…"

She walked off with an incredible lightness, smiling at all nature: never had the sky seemed more lovely to her, never an hour, never a moment was not more delicious. She set herself beside the bishop who ordered his coachman to drive them to the presbytery.

The good curate was at table with his vicar, the young man was sad as usual, dreaming of Melanie.

"How is the Marquise?" asked M. Gausse.

"She is going quickly to her grave, just like…Melanie," he added within himself. "Poor woman! I feel sorry for her, on the other hand the abyss is a bed of roses to the unfortunate."

"I prefer my feather bed," said the curate jocularly "That hurts me," he began again with a sad air,

"Madame de Rosann is so good, so loveable!...bah! God is wise, my young friend, the Marquis will remarry, he will have children who will inherit his patrimony: still, old husband, young wife, put love into the earth; and although love and lordship do not want companions, if he remarries, he could have children...but, there is no horse so good that he does not stumble, one nail chases another. Marguerite?..."

"Ah! Bah!..." Marguerite looked out the window, she came running crying out:

"Here is the Monseigneur!..." then she ran off to get the door arranging her bonnet along the way. M. Gausse and M. Joseph hurried into the living room, and it was from this room that they went to meet the bishop and the Marquise. I would like for a painter to faithfully represent the first look that Madame de Rosann cast on her son...She admired him herself!...Her moist eyes had lost the fire of her criminal passion, savored greatest voluptuousness that a woman was able...Ah! What energy, it took her not to fly into the arms of this handsome young man, and cover him with maternal kisses. Good God what a trial!...

The bishop took the young man's hand, which excited his mother's envy, and testified all of his love by a gentle squeezing of the hand. They sat down, M. Gausse, despite his hatred for Latin, recited as a compliment the *nuc dimittis* to M. de Saint-André, who thanked the good pastor by a movement of his head. The good man, in his joy, at first thought that the visit was for himself, but after a moment's reflection and the look of the Marquise who could not take her eyes off of the vicar, made him lose his enthusiasm.

Madame de Rosann no longer knew where she was: for her, the humble living room became a palace embellished by the gifts of the first fruits of her maternal feelings. If I emphasize this fatal moment, it is because there are not colors to depict the charm of it, and it passed as quickly as the line which you have just read. The Marquise had returned to the castle, she found herself in her chair and the bishop had long since left on the road to A...y, when she imagined that she had dreamed it and had not lived anything but a single minute: the minute when she saw her son. That evening she went to bed thinking of M. Joseph, and she must have woken with that same thought. Happy, a thousand times happy!...

One should, with a little imagination, guess all that happened in the village, the bishop's visit to the presbytery started a rumor. Marguerite had a long conference with her master, whom she tried to persuade that M. Joseph was the bishop's son; but M. Gausse responded that each is the child of his works.

CHAPTER 19

Such an event had a visible influence on the Marquise's condition, and if she found strength for the first moment when she woke up the next morning, a great weakness overwhelmed her faculties. In truth, at the moment when the bishop had shown her son to her in the man that she had loved with ardor, by a secret impulse of nature, a terrible revolution took place in her spirit. This situation, one of the most extraordinary, the most unheard of which could happen in a woman's life, could have caused her death, if, in the middle of this total revolution in her feelings, the ineffable joy of maternity had not arisen.

In the end, when she could reflect on it, she found herself miserable.

"So what!" she said, "I must see my son without speaking to him...He will flee me, for he will take all of my looks and all of my words for proofs of love, of that love which I abhor! Ah! How I am much happier to be his mother! Oh! How I wish I had never spoken to him, and that I could erase the memory of that scene in the valley…What a son!…Skilled, handsome, virtuous!…Ah! When can I say to him: 'Joseph, you are my son!…' But alas!…It would be to tell him: 'My son, you do not have a name, your father denies you, although he loves you!…' Alas yes, as Adolphe mentioned, his fortune depends upon my silence!…If Monsieur de Rosann could love him!… What if, one day, in front of everyone and not in secret, I could name him my son?…He would have a name!…Unfortunate mother, be quiet!…What a trial!"

That was where she was in her reflections, when M. de Rosann entered looking at his wife uneasily.

"Very well, my lovely wife, how are you this morning!"

"Very well, very well, I am cured…Sit down there, by my bed…Good!"

"Are you cured of everything…body and soul?…" asked the Marquis.

"Yes," said Josephine, squeezing her husband's hand; "but listen, my dear child, if you want to see me always radiating happiness and health, let me be with M. Joseph often and do not be suspicious…"

At these words the Marquis shivered and looked at his wife with a vivid worry: "My dear friend," he said, "you know how much I love you; for you but think for yourself about the dangers that you would expose yourself to!…If you are better, let's leave for Paris instead!…"

"Never!…" cried the Marquise, "I want to stay in Aulnay for my whole life!…"

"What are you saying?…" began the Marquis again stupefied. Then: "What sort of peace did the bishop bring you?" he asked himself.

"Monsieur," Josephine replied drawing her husband near her with a graceful gesture, "You who deal daily with the secrets of the states of Europe, and who must know a lot about how to guess other people's thoughts…will you listen?…I would really like to know why a young man of the age, the bearing, and the spirit of Monsieur Joseph confines himself to Aulnay!…He is sad…for what happened to make him become a priest?…" These last words were said with a tone of regret.

"Madame," responded the Marquis, "one only tries to discover secrets that are useful…"

"My dear vassal" (this was the Marquise's favorite term), she said changing her thoughts suddenly "tell me what are your feelings about the young priest?…"

"I hate him…"

"Because I love him!…"

"Maybe…"

"I want to make you love him!…And you know, my beautiful knight, that when I get an idea…"

"I am lost!" said the Marquis laughing.

So it was that each day the Marquise annoyed M. de Rosann, trying to make him change his opinion of M. Joseph. She put such grace into it, she surrounded her husband with such care, concern, and love, that the latter did not know what to think: all of his ideas were confused and were lost in an inextricable labyrinth, and he admitted to himself that women were incomprehensible creatures. But, what happened between the young priest and Madame de Rosann came to trouble him more than before, and his jealousy, growing from day to day, soon knew no limits.

In truth, once the Marquise learned that it was no longer a crime to see M. Joseph, she saw him often. At first, as she was too weak to get up, she asked for the young priest; and kept him for a long time at her bedside; then, when she became convalescent, she walked in her park leaning on the arm of the vicar whose help she chose with a visible pleasure, and these marked preferences were heartrending for M. de Rosann, who, for the first eight days, did not leave them alone for a minute, and a terrible rage agitated his soul when he surprised the moist looks that his wife cast at the young priest.

One morning (it was the third time that Madame de Rosann walked in the park), she went with M. Joseph and her husband to the ruins of the old castle, when some business obliged the Marquis to withdraw and leave them alone.

"My friend," said Madame de Rosann to the young priest, "if you should recall the woodsman's hut…Try, I beg you, to forget that horrible scene? For now my feelings for you have taken another turn, and I do not love you any more than a mother would…You never knew your mother; I never saw my son. He would have been your age…Let me give you that gentle name, and if you have some friendship for me, the illusion will almost be a reality."

"Ah, Madame!" replied the vicar, "I can assure you that it will not be difficult for me to have feelings of that sort for you, but, if you want me to speak with an open heart, I fear…"

"Ah do not think," cried the Marquise with liveliness, "let yourself go entirely!…"

"I even would regard," continued M. Joseph, "this walk as the last. You are perfectly well recovered, on your face you have the blossom of health…You are no longer sad, and your melancholy has fled…I should no longer be with you…There, where unhappiness reigns, that is where I live…Look at my forehead, each day it grows paler."

"Joseph! So you will not tell your troubles to your mother?"

"Oh! no…" cried the young priest.

"My friend," said the Marquise, "you could not know how much I would taken pleasure in consoling you. Ah! Believe me, women who are true friends, know the art of curing the wounds of the soul…And if you could guess to what extent I love you...Without my virtue receiving any flaw, ah! Joseph! if you had any idea, you would not refuse me...Can you imagine," she said with a touching tone of voice, "can you imagine a chaste love, a feeling which has not been frightened by even the appearance of a loving caress: in the end, a holy tenderness, whose testimonies are pure like a drop of dew which adorns the calyx of a morning flower; take exactly the notion of this beauty of feeling, and you will understand what I feel for you...Can you, my young friend, my son, make this sentence replace in your memory the fleeting words that I told you in the middle of the valley, and replace them so that no trace remains..."

"Ah!" cried Joseph, "you have depicted all that I think of you! For you have vanquished my misanthropy, and beside you alone, I forget my vows and my troubles, and everything...in the end."

"So come and confide in me," said this mother whose eyes enjoyed contemplating the tanned face of the vicar. "I imagine," she added, "that your troubles are not without remedy, and that your pain rests on causes which are not real."

"Alas," cried the young priest to himself and turning away his eyes filled with tears, thinking: who could make it so that I was not Melanie's brother!...

"What are you thinking of? You have not answered? Come on, Joseph, you are my son...by adoption, have confidence in your mother."

"Ah! If only that were true," cried Joseph, pouring out a torrent of tears. He sat on the lawn, and hiding his face in his hands. "O Melanie! Melanie, what joy!" he said through his sobs.

"What is it?" asked the Marquise who cried when she saw her son crying.

"Very well!" replied the vicar, "since you are a true friend..."

"Ah, I have proven it to you, right here, where I told you my secrets...Joseph," she said looking at him with a deep emotion, "if you had for a mother (imagine that this is a supposition) if you had had for a mother a woman who, like myself, would have known you in an illegitimate manner, what would you do when you found her again?"

"What I would do!" cried the vicar inflamed with the distrust that he always had for ceremonies and social barriers; "what I would do! I would cast myself into her arms, and I would, before all the world, proclaim that she was my mother and that she was virtuous!…I would go to the ends of the earth to live with her, and surround her with love, so that the shame and the unjust approbation of men could not attain her."

"Joseph! Joseph! Who told you?"

"Nature!" he cried with an incredible strength, showing the sky with a delirious gesture. "Ah!" he said, "if only I had stayed in my deserted isle with the runaway slaves!…Then I would not die young, sad, and consumed by an eternal passion!"

Madame de Rosann threw herself on the priest's neck and kissed him with a delight that no one could describe.

"I can't take any more!" she responded, "I am suffocating!…Joseph, until tomorrow, come to the castle, by way of the park. You will come up the stairs secretly, I will be in my room, and I will arrange things so that we are alone."

"That is it!…" cried M. de Rosann when the vicar and his wife had left. He had come upon them surreptitiously and hidden behind a clump of trees, he had heard these last words.

"Ah!" he began again, "I see what the Bishop of A…y came to do to me!…O the men of the church are an infernal race!…They take the world for their seraglio, and help each other out. Yes…Monseigneur de Saint-André came according to some Jesuitical arguments, very cleverly, raising doubts in Madame de Rosann and even giving her absolution…But what interest could he have?…O rage!…I want to cast light on this mystery!…Or rather, I know what I want!…"

M. de Rosann was suffering all day long, he looked carefully at his wife with an Inquisitorial care, and his eyes seemed to seek out the most secret thoughts in the depths of her soul. A horrible torment tortured his heart when Josephine turned on him her eyes filled with gentleness and innocence, and he saw her face filled with contentment and happiness, when he felt her caresses overwhelm him in such an affectionate way that he was surprised… Then the thought that she loved the vicar poisoned everything, and he would have voluntarily torn his chest at the thought that everything was feigned and that she was trying to fool him…He swore to take his wife away forcefully and to bring her to Rosann or to Paris. In the end, his rage at its peak, he thought of avenging himself on the priest and Josephine.

The next morning he set Jonio up in ambush, so that he would warn him when the priest appeared. But Madame de Rosann did not allow him the leisure of being able to come and disturb her meeting. She went in to her husband's room, which was something that was out of the ordinary; and sitting on his knees she said to him with a gracious gesture and a charming tone of joking happiness: "My love, vassals should faithfully obey the slightest orders of their masters, you know that…"

"So that is where we are!…" cried M. de Rosann, "I see…"

"Ah!…You are definitely forbidden to mutter…" interrupted Josephine kissing her husband. "Will you listen? Since it is the sovereign's will that sets the vassal to marching, he would rather break himself into a thousand pieces rather than dissatisfy his master."

"And all that," began the Marquis, "is to tell me..."

"To wait patiently on my will..."

"Ah! That is too much!" cried M. de Rosann.

"How is it too much!...Not enough? Nothing is ever too much. Ah! Truly one would give oneself to trouble of loving you with all that one had in one's soul, one would cover you with the prettiest caresses, one would try to please you, and one would have no influence over you!...Why are pretty women born?..."

"Josephine, remember what you have just said, and try to practice its precepts...just for today."

"What is this!...Your tone announces a rebellion, I believe, let us go. I demand that you get in a carriage and that you go to A...y where you are to bring me back all of the new novels that have appeared since my arrival in Aulnay."

"What is this new whim?"

"Ah! Ah!" cried Madame de Rosann laughing, "have you ever seen a woman who gave reasons for her whims...but, everything changes...what would you do if we did not have them?…Ah! Nonetheless, when I go, I will take care to govern you, to leave my die in one of your hats, to imitate Charles XII who wanted to send one of his boots to the senate in Stockholm."

"I am hurrying, Madame, I am hurrying!" M. de Rosann's sardonic expression made Josephine tremble once again. Nevertheless, the Marquis called for his horses and took off at a great gallop. Soon Madame de Rosann lost sight of the carriage, and she went into her room. "At last," she said to herself, "I will know my son's troubles!…"

"Madame," cried Marie, all out of breath, "the vicar is here!"

"Good, my dear nurse, act as my sentinel so that no one interrupts us."

The nurse ran into the vestibule leaving all of the doors open. As Marie arrived in the antichamber she found herself face to face with M. de Rosann who had let the horses go on without him and whom Jonio had just warned that the priest was going up to Madame de Rosann's by way of the secret stairway. Jonio had even take the precaution of locking the outside door, so that M. Joseph could not get out of the room.

"Monsieur," cried the nurse bravely, "Madame wants to be alone…"

"Shut up, you old nut!…" and the Marquis went past. But the nurse, forgetting her age, ran even more quickly and arrived in the room shouting; "Madame, your husband is here!…"

Right away, the Marquise closed the door and locked it, begging the priest not to say a word. At this moment a terrible thought frightened her, at the risk of making M. de Rosann unhappy she would have to explain to him why she was interested in the young man.

"Madame," cried the Marquis shaking the door, "open up right away, I want you to!…"

"I prefer not to," she responded.

"Jonio," said the Marquis, "go get the masons and have them wall in the other door! Madame," he began again, "you are not alone?…"

"No."

"Open up right away, or I will break down the door!…"

"You are free to, Monsieur Marquis, but if you break down my door, you will open the door to a convent for me, and you will not see me again in your life."

"What do you want me to do!..." he cried kicking the door and striking the clock on the chimney by which he was standing with his cane; "I am aware," he said in a fading voice, "that you are with the vicar, but he will pay for it with his life."

"So kill me!..." said the vicar coldly, as he opened the door.

This sang froid along with M. Joseph's noble and imposing attitude froze the Marquis.

"Joseph!..." cried Madame de Rosann, "go away!...And you, Monsieur Marquis, under the pain of seeing me die, do not touch a single hair on his beautiful head!..." The ecclesiastic went away slowly, showing a noble majesty and the calm of innocence.

The Marquis was stupefied as he watched him leave, and, after having allowed a convulsive movement to escape him, turned suddenly to the bedroom and entered. Madame de Rosann said coldly to him: "Close the door, for what you are going to say surely merits the honor of a lock!…"Then she added when he came back: "What do you want from me?…"

"Madame," cried the Marquis, pale and trembling with rage, "Madame… do you dare to ask me?…At last my eyes have been opened and I do not feel for you any more than the only feelings that you merit!… The horror!… Ah, what! A *creature* whom I drew out of misery, that my hand raised to the level of the highest families, who owes me everything!…Lowers herself, degrades herself…A country vicar!…Still, Madame, if he were a distinguished man, if a passion founded on what one recognizes as a duty drew you in, excused you; but no…You descended even lower…"

"Monsieur Marquis," cried Josephine with a sublime tone, "you are dishonoring yourself!…"

"Ah! I dishonor myself," he began again, "ah! In this affair I am the one who will imprint the mark of dishonor on my forehead!…" He walked around the room with agitation.

Josephine, mute, pale, stunned, did not dare open her mouth, she felt that everything was against her; and that, to justify this imprudence, she must, at the end of her career, admit the fault of her youth, before a man who, seeing that he had been fooled from the first day of his marriage, perhaps would no longer believe her!...She let her maternal love be overwhelmed, out of pride, by a host of considerations which imperiously told her how to act.

"Very well, Madame," continued the Marquis crossing his arms, stopping before her and casting her a horrified glance; "very well, don't you have anything to say to all that?...Nothing, nothing, *wretch!*...Ah! From today on I will become a master, and you will know just how far my anger can go!...Will you say something?..." He cried moved by that feeling of rage which desires responses in order to nourish its fires with the torrent of curses that they would suggest. The Marquis could not add anything, his furor stifled him. The Marquise stood up, stood before her mirror and re-established the order of her hair, she said calmly without looking at her husband:

"What do you expect me to say to a man who goes so far as to spy on his wife? You left for A...y, at least you said so, and monsieur hides himself!...A great man!…A peer of France hiding!…Is that diplomatic, who taught you such noble tricks?…" she added with a slight smile which concealed her embarrassment.

"O peak of infamy! How, Madame," said the Marquis, forcefully seizing his wife's arm, "how could you…"

"Monsieur," she interrupted, "at least put some passion into your caresses, you see?…" and she showed him—the arm on whose soft skin M. de Rosann's finger marks remained imprinted. He made a motion of regret, but continued: "How do you dare to reproach me for my trick, what about yours!…Child of hell!…"

"Mine," she began again, "I never hide anything…If you had asked me what I was doing this morning, I would have told you." And Josephine's face remained calm.

"You would have admitted that you were waiting for that devil of a vicar!…"

"Yes, yes!…" she repeated in a lively tone, as she was getting delirious.

"Let us test your forthrightness…Did you write

to him?..." asked the Marquis striking her with a piercing glance.

"Yes."

"You were the one who asked him to come?"

"Yes...a hundred times, yes, Monsieur!...And I cannot do without that young man. In the end," she said with spite, "I will have him ceaselessly, always, incessantly, at all times, at each minute at my side!...Take back your gifts, your dowers, your presents, your luxury?...I will go with him far, very far away, alone, and I will be happier than I have ever been...There, you wanted it, and I have told it to you, and I will not regret it, my heart will be pure...Ah! So what, good God! Men pretend that a piece of parchment, a wedding present, gloves and gifts, doweries, manors, a word of Latin that we do not understand, should take the place of all of our feelings!...And that we should become for them a field, a holding, that our marriage contract is a bill of sale, that the products of and the bare property of this conjugale earth belongs to them...In any case, what about fallow ground?...Ah! what tears one must shed bringing a daughter into the world!...Yes,

unfortunate as we are, the love of a huband is sometimes crueler than his disdain. Alas! So our happiness
depends on a look, a gesture. My faith, I do not want
to live any longer, it is too hard under these conditions!...And what pleasures do we get?...This is one
at this very moment!...But in truth it is awful..."

The Marquis, pushed to the edge by this deluge of
words, cried: "Madame...Madame! You are hurting
me!...I am stifling!..." And he advanced towards
Josephine with a dark anger; he presented his hands
to her in such a manner that she believed, in seeing
his eyes sparkle, that he had come to kill her. An icy
fear took hold of her.

"Monsieur!..." she cried, "help!...Help! Ah..."

"What is wrong, Madame, I came to say goodbye..." in saying this he was pale and trembling.

"No, Monsieur the Marquis, I am the one who is
leaving. Mademoiselle de Vauxcelles will find a haven
with her cousin the Duke of Ivrajo. *That unfortunate
creature* has friends who do not suspect her and who
are still powerful, I believe!..."

She stood up with an incredible dignity, and, taking a couple of steps, she turned, looked at M. de

Rosann with that air of pain and contentment that Rubens captured in the face of Marie de Medicis, and she said to him: "You love me, M. de Rosann, I can see it…I will not say if I love you, if, despite all appearances, there is nothing to all that you believe… No…I am silent!…Goodbye…I await you."

"Josephine!…" and the Marquis cast himself violently at her feet, "I beg of you, a word, just one!…My heart needs one, one single word!…I need to know that you are virtuous!…"

"That," she said, laughing while gently caressing her husband's forehead, "that is a little less conjugal!…At least the shape is right!…So believe me, Monsieur! Get up! I am only worthy of horror…*a wretch, drawn from misery!* Still, Monsieur, I was once named Mademoiselle de Vauxcelles!…You have forgotten something!…" Her tone and look were then filled with a gracious tenderness.

"Ah! I forgot it," said the Marquis with a remainder of spite, "but, you too!…" he began again, "take this?…" And he presented his wife with the intercepted letter. She took it and blushed!…

"Ah you are blushing again!…" he said with a sardonic smile…

"I will always blush for you," she responded, "and for myself! For I cry tears over my momentary error about the young priest!…When I wrote that letter, Monsieur Marquis, I loved the vicar with love and…Quite violently!"

"And now?…"

"I still love him," she said, looking at M. de Rosann with the greatest tenderness…"In truth, my dear vassal, we must admit that we are surrounded by villainous people!…Who gave you this letter?…"

"Josephine!…I promised…I must…"

"Go on, I want to know," she said in a masterly tone; "do you love me?…Will you say it?"

"Jonio!…Who…intercepted it…"

The Marquise turned towards the bell's ribbon and pulled on it lightly with no sign of anger. Marie arrived.

"Marie," said Josephine, "tell Jonio to get out of the castle within half an hour! He is no longer in Monsieur Marquis' service; and if he presents himself before us, tell him that he will go to prison for more than a day.

"My dear vassal, without your asking, I grant you pardon for your outrages: nonetheless I am the one who must become a supplicant."

Immediately Josephine got on her knees with an air of obediance which makes any woman touching; she looked painfully at the stupefied M. de Rosann, who sat down. A few tears rolled from her eyes, she sighed, then she said in a plaintive voice: "I must finish it, M. de Rosann, I must tell you the truth; I will not ask you to keep it secret since I am sure that you will…"

"Get up, Josephine, it is your vassal's right…" said the surprised Marquis.

"Ah!" she said, "there is no vassal! This attitude is the only one which I should adopt and I will lose all of my luster…"

"But what do you mean to say?"

"Monsieur," she replied, "you recall the melancholy state that I was in when you became sweet on me?" (The Marquis inclined his head slightly.) "Well, didn't I refuse you for a long time?…"

"Yes…"

"The pain which I never told you about, didn't it

last a long time…Did it worry you?"

"A lot."

"Thank you," she replied with a smile.

"Josephine!…"

"Monsieur," she said with an invincible repugnance while crying a torrent of tears, "I committed *a sin* which I never told you about."

At the sight of Josephine's pained expression the Marquis felt tears welling up in his eyes: he looked steadily at her.

"Monsieur…the pain was caused by the supposed death of my son…"

"A son!…A son!…" cried the Marquis with an unimaginable joy, he ran around the room like a crazy man, "you had a son!…Before our marriage!"

"Good God!" cried the Marquise falling down; "good heavens! He is not angry!"

"Me angry?…" said Marquise de Rosann taking Josephine in his arms and pressing her against his heart. "My Josephine!…" and he covered her with kisses.

"This son…is Monsieur Joseph!…" (The Marquis sat down, and stupefied, drew the wife onto his knees who monitored the least movements of her husband's face.) "They did everything possible to lose him, they sent him to the West Indies!...Fate, chance, have brought him back to the place where he was nursed and to his mother's sight...fooled by nature, I loved him...Oh! Quite with love!...Now...*he is my son!...*" Nothing could show the tone of these words.

"And his father is Monseigneur de Saint-André, the bishop," added the Marquis.

"Silence! Monsieur, silence!...Let your mouth never open upon such a mystery...Dear vassal! Discretion..." and she kissed her husband.

"I swear it Josephine!" For a long time silence reigned; in the end the Marquis, looking at his wife with intoxication, said to her: "So you still love me?..."

"Oh yes!" she responded.

"My lovely woman," said the Marquis gently, "we do not have any children..."

A celestial joy inundated the heart of this delighted mother. "So?" she asked greedily.

"So," continued the Marquis, "we will adopt Joseph. He can have my name. I will get the king to let him succeed me in my estate; and he will be rich, for the bishop made him his sole heir. The young man is good," began the Marquis again in a flattering voice. "He is proud; he is educated; big, handsome, he will amount to something."

"Frederick...you are making me die of happiness!..." And the fainting Marquise let her head fall onto the tender M. de Rosann's chest.

"I can tell that I will love your son!..." This gentle word and the Marquis' caresses brought Josephine back to life.

"And I," she said, "I will bless this event; now my life will be complete. The poor child came to tell me his troubles! My dear vassal," she said with seriousness, "remember that the vicar does not know that he is my son, that I swore never to tell him; promise me that you will keep this secret until the monseigneur dies, and even until we have adopted him."

"So we will only be happy in secret?..."

"We must," she said with a sigh, "we must in his

own interest and for his future."

"Ah! How happy I am!" cried M. de Rosann. The two happy and calm spouses came down to dinner overwhelming each other with the signs of a tender love.

The conclusion of this scene which had affected everyone surprised those living in the castle...

CHAPTER 20

While this scene took place in the Marquise's room, another one was taking place in the presbytery. The young priest returned to the curate's house with slow steps, having serious reflections.

"So what!" he said to himself, "Madame de Rosann's love has not been extinguished. Each day it reawakens. It is as strong as Melanie's. My presence will maintain it, and I will cause the unhappiness of two people...It seems that I bring misfortune to everyone around me. It follows me!...Let's go, I must leave this place...this beautiful place which I love so much and where I counted on dying..."

When he was at the gate, he cast a glance at the park, on the ruins of the old castle, he sighed and said: "I will not see them again...Goodbye!...I must go away forever. By some sort of fate, I must abandon all that I love." Then, thinking of his dear Melanie, he went slowly to the good curate's house.

Marguerite, as she opened the door for him, was struck by the changed face of the young priest.

"What is wrong, Monsieur?" she cried.

"Nothing, nothing, my good Marguerite."

M. Joseph de Saint-André went into the living room. He entered quietly and sat beside M. Gausse who was reading his breviary, that is to say, who made all the pages of it squeak as he reviewed them all with one single stroke under his fingers.

"Very well, my friend, what is bothering you? You are even sadder than usual; let me kill your sorrow before it kills you!…"

"Alas, my old friend, you have told me of your affection; I have need of advice."

"You speak gold, a sound advice is worth…"

"I hear a sound," said the vicar, interrupting one of the curate's favorite proverbs.

"My dear vicar," began M. Gausse again in a low voice as he leaned towards the young man's ear; "Marguerite has always thought that, if the Lord permits extreme heat to make wood come apart that it was to please the servants…It would be easier to draw a bill of exchange between Gascogny and Limousin than to keep her from knowing all that is said…Also, when I discuss something important, I customarily call her and tell her to keep the secret thinking that honoring her in this way will stop her tongue."

"So let us speak in low voices!" said the vicar.

"The poor woman will damn herself!" replied the curate with a tone of goodness, "and for ten days she will almost kill me to find out what it was about."

"Let her come in," cried M. Joseph.

Marguerite came in!...

"Monsieur," replied the vicar, "it is certain that Madame the Marquise de Rosann loves me..." At this sentence, Marguerite drew close to the vicar; and the curate looked at him with an astonished expression.

"You only just noticed?" cried M. Gausse.

"I have known it for a while," responded M. Joseph seriously, "but I believed that her passion would cure itself; I believe that every day it grows worse, and that Madame de Rosann presents different faces to fool herself perhaps, but today Monsieur the Marquis could not fail to know that I am the cause of his misfortune... I must make it cease!"

"Certainly," cried the curate, "it is not man's fate to be the misfortune of our fellow men. There is someone up above who will reward us for it."

"So, Monsieur Gausse, I am going to leave you."

"Leave me!" cried M. Gausse, "Oh! my child, one knows where one is; one does not know where one is going; what have I done to make you want to leave? Can I follow you, I? Where the goat is tethered it must graze! Stay, my friend, stay."

"Oh no! I must go, and even right away! At least it will not be out of fear!…" he cried with an inflamed face. "If you see Monsieur de Rosann tell him that the 'marquis' hidden under the humble soutane of the vicar does not fear anyone, and that he knows how to sacrifice himself for his happiness!…" In saying these words the young vicar got up, and ran into his room. He took the portrait of Melanie, his manuscript, his papers, and came back down.

"My dear child," cried the curate his eyes filled with tears, "what will happen to me! What will happen to the unfortunate ones!"

"I leave them a father."

"My dear friend, you are abandoning a poor old man who was pleased by the thought that you would close his eyes…I loved you Joseph!…So did this valley, these fields, this modest habitation…this gentle existence!"

"I must say goodbye to everything! Monsieur," he began again after a movement of tenderness, "I leave you my books, and that is a feeble sign of my esteem."

"Ah!" cried the curate, "I will never go up to your room; I do not like tombs."

"Loveable, simple man," said the vicar with emotion, "you too, you are from the Americas!…"

"Poor child! Be happy!…And so that I may be of some service to you, let it be engraved in your memory that one is never criminal in obeying the laws of nature."

The vicar looked at the curate with astonishment. M. Gausse painfully lifted his leg from the stool on which it was set, and using M. Joseph's arm, succeeded in getting up. "Let us go my child. I want to lead you as far as I can…Go! Your devotion, the goodness of your heart, have touched my soul. Whatever you do, you will go to heaven!"

"Monsieur," said the young man, in an imposing tone, "and you Marguerite, promise me never to open your mouths about me! Do not tell anyone that

I have left…for two days…by that time I will be *far away,*" he added with a dark and sardonic smile. "If they come and ask for me, find some pretext, that I am out shopping, indisposed, whatever…"

"We promise you," said the curate and his servant.

"Goodbye Marguerite," said the vicar with a tone that made the servant shiver.

"Goodbye, Monsieur…Ah! If you would listen to me," she added with a fine air waving her white cambric smock, "you would not go!…There is something beneath Madame de Rosann's feelings, and…"

"Marguerite," said the vicar, "goodbye! A secret premonition is drawing me away. I must flee this valley."

Marguerite, teary-eyed, followed the vicar for a long time admiring his handsome form, his noble manners, which contrasted with the heavy bearing and the friendly air of M. Gausse. The two priests went towards the road to A…y; and when the curate had gone a hundred steps beyound the village, he kissed the young priest goodbye with cordiality saying to him:

"Goodbye! Be happy! It is a law of nature!…"

Then, sitting on a stone, he watched M. Joseph leave with great strides. M. Gausse must have been very moved not to have said a single proverb.

When he arrived back at the presbytery, tears flowed down his cheeks; and, in seeing Marguerite, he said with a pained tone: "We are alone!" Then recovering that old man's spirit which sees in a glance the least details of all that afflicts them, he cried: "Who will preach for me?"

"Monsieur," replied the servant, "I was biting my tongue so as not to tell him that I think that he is the son of Madame de Rosann and the bishop, and that means that he is not the brother of Mademoiselle Melanie."

"Ah the wretch!" cried the curate, who fell into a deep reverie.

Meanwhile our hero went rapidly and soon arrived at Vannay. In crossing the village he went quicker.

"Let the devil take the priest!" cried a man who, his arms crossed, from his threshold surveyed the two directions of the road alternatively. His look denoted that of an innkeeper.

The young priest raised his head believing that the exclamation was addressed to him.

"And what have I done to you?" he asked the host.

"Nothing," the latter responded bruskly. This response convinced the vicar that the exclamation did not concern him. Then he noticed that the building before him was an inn. He entered saying: "Come on, my friend, I am going to show you that we need not send all priests to the devil." The innkeeper cheered up when he saw that at least he would get a traveler.

"Let ten of them come!" he cried, bothered by his idea. "All that would not keep Abbot Frelu from hearing my wife's confession every fortnight! But also, the first time, I will give him a terrible absolution!"

Joseph's intention was to buy any sort of carriage in Vannay which could function like a post coach, and he looked in the courtyard to see if there were not something which resembled one. In fact there was an old post coach (if the ruined hulk still merited that name) lodged in the shed. As it did not occur to the innkeeper that a young priest could have need of a coach, he said to him: "I will have to burn it some day, since that is all that it is good for; and it reminds me too much of the biggest loss that I ever had; anyway, I will bring the shaft into the living room so that I will always remember the hundred crowns that I lost, and to make sure that my travelers are solvent. That and my wife; they are two sore subjects."

"That did not cost you a hundred crowns?" said Joseph.

"Yes," responded the innkeeper, "but it is there like a relic and the hundred crowns are dormant."

"Will you sell it to me?" replied Joseph going towards the shed.

The innkeeper let out a heavy sigh, and he would gladly have taken back his words.

"So I only say stupidities," he muttered to himself. Joseph examined the coach.

"Look, Monsieur, here are wheels that could still go all the way to Russia, and which could still climb the Euxin bridge, although the Emperor made it out of iron; the blacksmith here offered me two hundred francs for it. But it would be too bad to destroy it...The body is good, and they do not make coaches like that...It's from the old days when workers took pride; what cloth! When it is brushed, the leather is old, I agree, but you could oil it…and polish it: give me eight hundred francs, and I will sell it to you."

"But my dear man, it only cost you a hundred?"

"Yes, Monsieur, you are right, but my hundred crowns have been dormant for ten years."

"I'll take it," said Joseph, "get it ready."

"Let my wife do what she wants today!…" he cried in his joy. "I don't give…won't complain." He began cleaning up the coach; and, so as not to be putting one over on the vicar, checked with the blacksmith who decided that the coach *could still go.*

Joseph was obliged to spend two days in Vannay, for the carriage was fixed up slowly, and the lovely hostess put on airs beside it.

"Still, if he were a priest like that," her husband said," but Abbot Frelu…I still hope that he never comes again."

"And my conscience?" said his wife.

"I'll take care of it," he responded.

At last the coach was restored, and Joseph continued on to A…y at great speed for the innkeeper had warned the driver that the passenger did not worry about money.

While the vicar was fleeing, the Marquis and his wife, burning up with desire to see their son again, had sent Marie to the presbytery. The nurse arrived and at the door she found Marguerite who, with her arms crossed, was sadly shaking her key chain.

"Hello, Mademoiselle Marguerite."

"Hello, Madame Vernillet, what are you doing over here?"

"I came on behalf of Monsieur the Marquis and Madame, to invite Monsieur Joseph to spend the evening at the castle, this evening, right away!"

"Ah, Monsieur Joseph!" began the clever servant who was in her own element when it came to dissimulating; "it seems that he is veritably anchored at your place! He is going to become cardinal that young man! His parents will be happy...And how is Madame de Rosann? And your Michael and you? What is new over there? Jonio has been sent away, Leseq told me that...The schoolmaster makes for a good bug...he told me that it was about a letter...in-

tercepted; Ah! That is a betrayal of one's masters...
How could something like that enter into the head of
an honest man..." Marie made use of one of the servant's sighs to slip in: "Will you tell M. Joseph that
monsieur and madame are waiting for him?"

"I will!" Marguerite went up and came back
down. "Monsieur Joseph is not here!...I thought that
he was still in his room...but no! I did not see him go
out...Ah my dear friend, we have so many problems
in *our situation*...I am alone here...just the kitchen
and the bedrooms. Two men!...That is something!..."

"Goodbye Mademoiselle Marguerite..."

"But I will go back with you..."

And Marguerite kept talking until Marie had arrived at the castle gate.

The Marquis and madame were not satisfied with
the nurse's response, and the evening passed without
their being able to see the young priest. The next day
Marie was sent back with a letter.

"I will give it to him," said Marguerite. The Marquis waited for a response. There was none. Marie's
third trip came, and this time the servant said confi-

dentially in a low voice that M. Joseph was ill. Madame de Rosann, alarmed, came herself with Marie; and she ran down the avenue when a man dressed in black and twisting a hat, who appeared to be of wood he was so hard, presented himself before Madame de Rosann.

"If Madame the Marquise will permit *infandum renovare dolorem* to let the cat out of the bag."

"I don't have any money, my dear..." and she walked even quicker.

"You are not, Madame, *jactu sagittae,* but a rifleshot from the castle, you will not go any farther *si fas mihi loquendi,* if you give heed to what I say."

"Go to the castle and say that I sent you!" and the Marquise ran.

"Madame," said Marie, "it is the schoolmaster."

"Ego sum, that is to say, received by the university. Madame," said Leseq, *"doli sunt.* You are being fooled...*decampaverunt gentes,* the vicar has left..."

At these words the astonished Marquise stopped short and she looked at Leseq with fright. "What are you saying to me?"

"Yes, Madame, *vulnus alit venis,* that must cause

you pain; but *ab ovo,* from the depths of my school, I saw Marie go to the presbytery four times in two days; *gallus Margaritam reperit,* Marguerite finds a way *illudere vobis,* to make Marie walk, for *vidi,* I saw Monsieur Joseph say his goodbyes to M. Gausse, and he is still away...*habemus reum confitentem,* which means that he no longer felt comfortable..."

"Silence you impertinent," cried the Marquise, "and be careful what you say about Monsieur Joseph...if he is in Aulnay, I will..."

"That is the *quos ego* of Neptune..." cried Leseq. "What a lovely translation!"

"If he is not here, I will give you fifty louis to show me where he is."

"Madame, in two days you will know..." and Leseq ran off hastily. *"Dux femina,* fortune is driving me forward!" he cried.

Madame de Rosann continued going towards the presbytery, where she was convinced of the truth of Marcus Tullius Leseq's words by the testimonials of the curate and his servant.

We are going to leave Aulnay-le-Vicomte, in saying goodbye to the good curate, his servant, and the mayor-grocer, for we must follow the tracks of the young traveler. His coach, drawn by two horses that were spurred on by good lashes of the whip, and by words which the Abbess of the Andouillettes would have had so much trouble pronouncing, carried him towards A…y without his noticing, for he was plunged into a deep reverie. The last words which the curate had said made him think that he knew his story, and that sufficed to cast him adrift among his memories. This reverie meant (good God, if one wanted to find out the initial causes!…) that the driver noticed his passenger's indifference, and drove to an inn where he usually had every one get out.

In the main street of A…y, everyone admires in passing the golden letters which form the big sign, Hotel-d'Espagne; it was into this renowned house that the driver had M. Joseph enter. The young vicar let himself be led to his apartment, where they officiously brought everything that belonged to him.

"Will Monsieur eat at the host's table? It is well served; and a big banker from Paris, who arrived a little while ago, is there so you could not do better!"

"As you wish," responded the young man softly as

he remained thoughtfully in his chair. Ten minutes later the driver came up.

"Monsieur," he said swaying, "you are an honest man, aren't you...or...you are...not!...what I mean, sss...you see that these...sss, I am bringing you...I...sss, bringing you your gold coins...which I want...you saw two like me!..."

M. Joseph took back the sack which he had forgotten in the carriage and which the driver had noticed. "My gen...eral, my father...you will think that...to eat...for out of conscience I drank."

M. Joseph was so preoccupied that he gave him a five franc piece..."long live all the sovereigns of Europe!" cried the driver. "I am an old sol...dier and clever...like that one is not s...s...s...seditiously... caught!..." And he threw his hat into the air.

How could the vicar hear and see all of that? He was thinking of finding Melanie again, that is to say, to go live in the house next to hers, and, without telling her, enjoy observing all of her movements and contemplating her life. He began by ordering some common clothes, and, as his hair had grown back on the top of his head so that his tonsure was almost effaced, he flattered himself by thinking that he would no longer be taken for an ecclesiastic.

He was in the middle of these reflections when they came to tell him that dinner was waiting; he came down mechanically, and mechanically sat across from the big banker who had come from Paris a few days previously. He was an extremely opulent man, dressed in a beautiful black suit, with extremely fine cloth, with a hard face, but he tried to make it agreeable by meticulous grooming: his beard was well kept, his straight hair carefully arranged, his demeanor, the jewels that he wore, in sum the grace with which fortune gilds its favorites took away the fear that he initially inspired and changed it to the respect and consideration which one gives to riches. He came with a man who seemed to be his associate, but whose deferential air, simpler dress, gave the impression that he was not on the same line as the big banker, and that the material genius of the one followed from afar the conceptions of the other. Despite the care that the banker took to give him gestures and his discourse an air of affability, at each moment he betrayed his lack of education and an innate rudeness, which denoted the calling of a warrior. Also the mistress of the hotel, having once been in high society and having fallen on subsequent misfortune, noticed that the banker and his companion tried to disguise the fact that they were *beasts with a little spirit* and nouveau riches, was amused by them and laughed into her sleeve.

"Your bishop, is he a *good child?*" asked the banker, "will he pay me all that is coming to me when he sells me his lands?...If he knows that it is next to mine, then he will skin me like a merchant vessel taken by a corsair, what do you say grandmother?"

At the sound of this voice, Joseph quickly raised his head and tried to confirm his suspicions. He had just heard the voice of Argow, the pirate, but at the sight of everything that was disguising the sailor, the young vicar hesistated.

"Has Monsieur been to sea?..." he asked the banker. The latter looked at the young priest, and, looking at him with an unease that he hid under a light smile, he responded curtly, "no, Monsieur."

At this negation the surprised vicar looked at Argow (for it was he) with more attention, and he could not keep from thinking that he had before his eyes the author of the conspiracy which had broken out on his father's ship. Meanwhile Argow had such assurance in looking at Joseph, that the latter dared not persist in his suspicions, dreaming of the whims of nature, and examining all the circumstances by which the ferocious sailor of the frigate, *Daphnis,* had transformed himself into the rich capitalist of the Chaussée-d'Antin.

"I came in time, because they tell me that the good man is getting ready to go. I already spoke *this morning* to his business manager, and tonight I will sign the bill of sale."

"Monseigneur de Saint-André is not dead yet," replied the hostess.

"No," replied Argow, "that old boy did not seem to be *rotten* to me!"

"That is a name which you must recognize!..." said Joseph with irony looking at Argow with a questioning air.

"On my honor young man," replied Argow getting angry, "you have sworn to get into my business, but do not stick your nose in...I am not a *friendly prince!*...It seems to me that in polite society one is not so curious?..."

"If it is him!..." murmured Joseph, "then I will avenge my father!..."

"Speak up!...My friend, I like for people to explain things to me, and if M. Maxendi, your humble servant, owes you anything, bring your claim...He will pay it."

"M. Maxendi has nothing of mine that I know of!..." replied the vicar, "and I took you for a sailor named Argow!..."

"A sailor!..." cried the banker, "why I couldn't tell a mizzenmast from a fine field; and let them give me a dry hold if I know what a crow's nest, a top deck, a poop, a between-decks, or a hatchway are...I have always lived on the rue Victoire, and I have only navigated on the waters of the Seine; although the sailors there do not know much, and their nutshells are not worth a good sloop. A fine sail they manoeuvre under a free flowing tent, and ram everybody under the water line, is that not true Vernyct? Still we have used their little boats to go to Saint-Cloud. By the way, good mother, you have forgotten the punch with arrack last night!…That is our milk, for us! It rinses our throats better than your teas."

"You can see that these gentlemen come from Paris, and know only the finest things, for it is the fashion of the best people to *rinse their throats* after a ball."

"You laugh, grandmother, but be careful that you do not need to be fixed!…Like a pretty frigate that has been broken by an oversized reef!…"

At this statement Argow and his companion let out big laughs which made the hostess blush.

"Are you gentlemen going to see Monseigneur the Bishop tonight?…" asked Joseph.

"Yes, my dear sir," replied Argow, "is that all right with you?"

At this moment, Joseph thought that he should at least go and warn his uncle, Monseigneur de Saint-André, and ask him permission to leave his diocese. The friendship that the prelate had shown him, the desire to present him with his thanks, and to warn him that he could avenge his father, if his buyer was named Argow, incited him to go to the bishop's house. In sum he was burning to learn from the mon-

447

seigneur's steward if it really was Argow whom he had just seen, and then to tell his uncle to arrest the sailor right away. He arrived at the bishopric where the concierge told him that a half hour ago the bishop had recieved a letter that despite his pains had forced him to leave, for he got in his carriage and left on the road to N..., ordering, unusually, for the driver to go at a great gallop.

Nevertheless, as Joseph was known to all the members of the house, not as the Monseigneur's nephew (for the bishop and Joseph had never told anyone) but as a man who was cherished by the Monseigneur, they let him into the room. The vicar sat on a chair beside his uncle's bed, and he waited patiently for the return of the prelate to whom he was going to say goodbye!

Daylight faded, it became dark, and Joseph, lost in his habitual reverie, was not aware of what was around him. The bishop and M. de Saint-André arrived at the bishop's residence without a sound.

"Yes my brother, because your son escaped," said the first, "since he exists, I must tell him that he is not my son!...Joseph, is, you say, in this department. I will run to see him and ask him where my daughter is!..."

The vicar, stupefied, felt his entire body freeze, burn, and such was the power of his emotions that he remained impassive as a statue!...What a discovery! He remained silent and listened carefully. The man who had pretended to be his father had just spoken.

"My brother," replied the prelate, "I beg you to wait, to make this avowal until I die, which will not be long..."

"How could that bother you?...Joseph only carries that name in his birth certificate. Neither Madame de Rosann, nor you, no one is compromised: Joseph is an orphan born in Vans-la-Pavée, and that is all...you leave him everything, Monsieur de Rosann adopts him; everything is in order. As for me, I cannot bear this trickery; I have survived enough troubles without needing to make more for myself, and all that will lead to them, if it has not already produced them. My first care on landing was not to run to Paris. No, I came to see you, and I am going to find my daughter over land and sea."

"But tell me how, by what miracle, am I seeing

you again? For the last fifteen minutes that I have been with you joy has kept us from speaking. Who could have gotten you off of that island! Ah the Lord willed it!…Tomorrow I myself will say a mass of the actions of grace for this miracle."

"It is truly a miracle my brother, I am the only one who escaped hunger, thirst, and it was one of those English ships that had been at Saint-Helena, which, by the greatest of chances, came to stop at L… In addition my troubles have ended. What I want now is to find my daughter, to be employed in sailing, and to take revenge on my renegade sailors who stole three years of my life, and who are known by all the governments as the most infamous of rogues!…Ah that, you are well in the Court? You can help me…for they must have forgotten me, everything has changed!…So much the better for us!…"

"M. de Rosann will introduce you at Court. He is almost the favorite."

The young vicar had fainted. The terrible effect of these words upon him had overwhelmed him. In waking from his faint he found himself alone. At one and the same time he had just learned that Melanie was not his sister, that Madame de Rosann was his mother, the bishop his father; the story that the Marquise had told him earlier had been his own. These new notions, the barrier that he had raised between Melanie and himself, everything was overturned in his mind; he got up, and rushed around the room. He saw the Marquis de Saint-André's wallet; he opened it and saw Melanie's birth certificate, and her mother's death certificate. A vague idea that these things would be useful to him flew through his mind, he imagined Melanie in the distant future as his possession; he took them with the aim in mind of proving to his sister that it was no longer a crime for them to be in love; then he left by the secret stairway. He ran; he flew; he arrived at the hotel; he asked for coach horses since he intended to leave in six hours for Paris. He wanted to see his Melanie: in his soul there was only one idea, that was Melanie; it was that pure lover, gentle, tender, faithful, who was his dear sister. To see the delirious movements of the young priest one would think that he was attacked by madness.

The hostess and everyone who saw him looked at him with astonishment, and they spoke among themselves of the sudden change that had occurred in the face and manners of a man who, at first, had seemed so cold, so severe, so tranquil. His delirum was such that he could not even say a word.

Also, it is impossible to render the millions of thoughts that invaded the vicar's imagination, since he had just learned that there were no barriers separating him from his dear Melanie. He took his lover's portrait out of his breast pocket, and he covered it with enflammed kisses for a long time. One more sentence added to his state of exhaltation, another degree in the multitude of his thoughts, and he would have become crazy. Succumbing under the effects of such rapidity, of such imaginative activity, overwhelmed by this news which gave an entirely new face to his existence, he fell on his bed and slept.

Chapter 21

While M. Joseph slept, a scene took place in the bishop's residence which unfortunately he did not witness, for it would have told him about the danger that Melanie was in.

Argow-Maxendi and Vernyct, his accomplice, after having sunk more than a hundred merchant ships of all nations, escaped the death which human justice had prepared for them in the United States in a most miraculous manner. Here is how: Argow and Vernyct were captured by an American vessel. Taken to C...T....they were condemned to be hanged along with two hundred of their accomplices; these pirates, wealthy with several millions, could not save themselves because in the United States nothing can stop the course of justice. Then, the English besieged C...T....The pirates, ashamed of dying by the gallows, asked to form a French brigade which would fight all day long against the attackers. They gave their word of honor, and promised to set aside their fortunes out of caution; and added that once the siege was raised, they would return (that is to say the survivors would) and be prisoners again; they thought that they would all die with their weapons in their hands. [3]

This strange proposition was accepted. Argow assembled his men, whipped them up until they were intoxicated: right away they went and attacked the English. As soon as a battery was established they rushed to strike it. The enraged pirates fought forcefully against the batteries, profiting from the loading of the cannons that were firing at them to climb into the openings, and capture the pieces. Their fear of dying by hanging caused them to perform miracles.

Then, the fury with which they attacked the English forced the latter to raise the siege, and the authorities, convinced that the city would have been taken except for the help of these hardy criminals, granted grace to thirty of them, who loyally came back to their irons when the siege was raised. Among these thirty were their chief Argow and Vernyct, his

---

3 The fact is historical. (Editor's Note)

lieutenant, who were still alive. This lesson was enough to teach the ferocious corsair to consider spending a peaceful life. He disguised himself to try to escape the justice of each government whose commerce he had greatly wronged, and he succeeded in coming to Paris with his fortune: he changed his name. That is to say, took his true name of Maxendi, and he tasted the balms of repose. We will soon know what happened next.

At this time, he was in A...y, to buy a property that the bishop wanted to sell. This property was situated next to his, made him the sole possessor of a vast forest beside which he had erected his castle of Vans-la-Pavée. He had already had several conferences with the bishop's business manager; and, while our vicar slept, he went to the bishop's residence to sign the contract.

When the bishop and his brother left the room where Joseph had fainted, they went into a little room where the monseigneur had ordered a tasty supper to celebrate the arrival and happy return of his brother whom he had thought dead: M. de Saint-André the elder sat at table beside the bishop, and his first words were: "Have you by chance seen your son again?"

"I have never questioned him for fear that my tenderness towards him would betray me, but it seems that he has had great troubles: he came to the seminary about a year and a half ago, and I obtained a dispensation so that he could become a priest."

"He is a priest?" cried the rear admiral with a motion of fright.

"Ah well, what's wrong with that?" asked the bishop.

"Alas!" responded the sailor, "see what troubles our arrangement has caused! Your son loved Melanie. He must think that she is his sister, and in desperation became a priest!...I should have united them. Now I ask you the grace of leaving Joseph in his ignorance. Try to get from him the name of the town where Melanie is living and right away, for tomorrow I want to go see my dear daughter! He will never marry her; he cannot now. Ah! How beautiful Melanie must be! What a charming smile she had for me, as well as for her brother; with what joy I saw that Joseph could be worthy of her, and become a *statesman!* I've said it all, my brother. But how events could have changed my Melanie! Did Joseph follow his sister? Ah, what cruel incertitude!"

These words enlightened Joseph's father, who, guessing the secret misfortune of his son whom he had heard using the name Melanie, felt a deep sorrow. There was a moment of silence, during which the bishop, his eyes on the room's green wallpaper, wondered if he possessed enough influence to have Joseph's vows broken by the Pope, which was almost impossible! When all of a sudden one of the bishop's servants, coming in to serve them, asked his master if Monseigneur had seen M. Joseph the Vicar of Aulnay-le-Vicomte.

"Is he here?" cried M. de Saint-André.

"He should be," responded the servant.

"My brother," continued the rear admiral, "see him. Ask for him. But don't let him see me; for then he will still think that I am his father!...Since he is a priest...we will not tell him the secret of his birth until I have married off Melanie!"

"Patience, my brother," responded the bishop, "all is not lost."

They searched everywhere for the young vicar. At last the concierge said that he had left, after having waited for the Monseigneur.

"Since he is here at A…y," said the bishop to his brother, "you will know where your daughter is tomorrow. I will ask Joseph, he will tell me."

As the Monseigneur finished these words, a servant came to tell him that the buyer of his property had just arrived; he asked for him to wait in the next room.

"What, my friend," said M. de Saint-André, "a man who is bringing us seven or eight thousand, a million francs certainly merits sitting at our table with us."

"Have him come in," the bishop said to his servant," and set two places, for there are two of them I believe."

Argow and Vernyct entered: M. de Saint-André raised his eyes, shivered and cried out: "by faith the heavens are just! And they have suddenly taken all of my troubles away!"

At this sound and M. de Saint-André's look, the audacious Argow dissimulated the fear that overcame him; but Vernyct, seeing their certain fate, paled and stumbled.

"May I know what causes Monsieur's astonishment?..." asked the pirate, bringing his hand to his pocket to assure himself of the presence of the little, extremely flat English pistols that he always carried with him.

"What, rogue..." cried the booming voice of the rear admiral, "you don't recognize Monsieur de Saint-André?...And you think that I do not know about your horrible pirating that is known in all the courts!...Fortunately you cannot escape again."

"Monsieur, if Monsieur Maxendi, banker, owes you anything..."

"No, he does not owe me anything; but, I, I owe him a judgement by a naval court, a court of justice...and Monsieur Maxendi who is nothing less than the pirate Argow, will end his days in a bath of sticks or six feet of earth."

"Monsieur the Rear Admiral, think that they do not hang men who have five million francs!"

"Are they yours, you infamous crook?..." and M. de Saint-André began ringing the bell as if he would break it. "Don't they belong to all the unfortunate people that you sent to the bottom...Look, my brother, you have before you a man who has killed three thousand people."

"You are wrong!..." interrupted Argow shaking his head.

"Do you dare to deny it?" continued the rear admiral angrily despite his sang froid.

"Oh! That is not it! I don't deny a thing," said the pirate with a ferocious smile, "but you must correct your calculation; now it is three thousand and one," he added looking at M. de Saint-André in a way that made him understand that he was contemplating his death; but M. de Saint-André did not see it.

"Good God!" cried the bishop, "what perversity!..." and he raised his eyes to the sky.

"But, Monseigneur," said Argow, "perhaps they died of yellow fever!..."

"My brother," continued the bishop, "take this wretch out of my presence!..."

"Wretch!" cried the pirate fiddling with the diamond trinkets which garnished the gold chain of his watch, "don't I have a retinue, gold, aren't I well dressed? A wretch!...No one can see my conscience...I have drowned it...bah!" he said with an indefinable gesture, "I did like everyone else!"

"Get out, unfortunate man..." cried the bishop.

"Ah! Your benediction, Monseigneur! The just only have to act that way and things could not be better." What a smile came to wander over the lips of this horrible rascal!...

"My brother," said the priest in a feeble voice, "seeing this man makes me sick; have him go, I beg you."

"I would be very annoyed!..." said the rear admiral who after having rung was eating peacably as if Argow were not there.

"What do you intend to do?" asked the bishop, astonished at his sang froid.

"Arrest him..." replied the sailor. Then M. de Saint-André stood up. He went into the neighboring room. He ordered the servants to be ready for anything, and he sent one off to the police station to ask for help; for Argow's calm attitude made him uneasy.

"Monsieur," the pirate said to him when he came back in, "look." (The pirate showed him his pair of pistols.) "You see, this will keep me from being a bird of the gallows for my American business when they took me without these biscuits," he said, moving his arms, "taught me never to go out without taking precautions. Listen well, Monsieur de Saint-André!..." The rear admiral was still eating...Argow turned towards Vernyct and, seeing him uneasy, cast him a look of pity. "Vernyct," he cried, "are you one of my friends?" At this word he pulled a pair of pistols from his side pockets.

"You understand, Monsieur the Rear Admiral, that we have four shots, and that it will not be easy to arrest us; but there are ten reasons why they will not arrest us at all..." At these words M. de Saint-André looked at the pirate.

"First," continued Argow, "no one has heard you!...If they had you would already be dead. Ah! You can cast me those lightning glances all that you want, that is...no one heard us, which means that we can kill you, you and your brother without a sound; and we will leave without being arrested because we will be taken for *bankers of consequence* and in two hours I will be far away!…Secondly, Argow is not my name, and before you can gather witnesses to condemn me, I will have conned the guard, and I will have the key to the town. Third, 4, 5, 6, 7, 8, 9, I will not tell you because you do not want to hear them!…"

"What insolence!…" cried the bishop.

"It is not insolence, Monseigneur. It is to reason correctly, and as I am of high society, I will not get angry at what you have just said!…If we were at sea, then you could go bless the fish; but I am in company…all that, Monseigneur, will not stop our business."

At these words, a servant signaled M. de Saint-André that the police had arrived.

"Tenth, as it is time that I finish I see, tenth, my admiral, you have a daughter?…" And in asking M. de Saint-André this, he cast him a terrible look which made the intrepid rear admiral shudder since he was attacked at his weakness.

"What are you saying?..." he cried.

"Do you love her?..." asked Argow with an ironic smile and moving the jabot of his shirt. M. de Saint-André, interdicted, looked at the pirate without responding.

"You see Monsieur the Rear Admiral, that although arrested, my trial would be far away, and I would not be buried so hastily; but if you say a word, if you send me to prison for even two hours..."

"Then what?" asked M. de Saint-André angrily.

"Then...you will never see your daughter again! ...Isn't she named Melanie? Isn't she blonde?..."

"What, you infamous brigand!..."

"Take away my titles, but I will not call you a rear admiral."

"How is it, scoundrel, that you are destined to torment me...curse of my life!...O destiny!..."

"Aren't you the curse of my life?...I have your daughter; you have a feeble hold on my life and my reputation, we can do business..."

"Wily scoundrel!..." cried M. de Saint-André smiling, "you think that you can get out of here by a trick? It will not save you!"

"Imbecile, despite your spirit," replied Argow, "don't you think that I would have asphyxiated you when I saw you with your brother, if I did not have a way to contain you."

"That's all a trick!" replied the rear admiral.

"I must conclude...look, Admiral, see. And if you are a good father, leave me alone, and we will agree in good faith to argue no longer. I have a word of honor that I can be proud of; I have proven it...promise me not to chase me, and I promise to refuse the advantage which fate always gives me over you by some inconceivable luck." In finishing these words the pirate presented an opened letter to the rear admiral. It was by Melanie addressed to her banker.

"Monsieur, I can no longer consent to the union which you propose, as advantageous as it may be; still, as you have presented me without my consent to Monsieur Maxendi, I think that he would be fine, that it would be proper to make him understand that my refusal is because of no disagreeable thoughts towards him; and for proof of this good will, I consent to go to your party tomorrow. If you would be so

465

good as to send me your coach, I will be obliged…etc. Melanie de Saint-André."

The banker's letter read: "Mademoiselle, if you permit, Monsieur Maxendi will take pleasure in offering you his coach to bring you to the ball tomorrow. It is a very feeble mark of good will that you would give him…. William Badger."

"So what!" cried M. de Saint-André looking at Argow.

"So what! My coach was a private coach, which quickly brought your daughter where I wanted. One of my men, an old sailor and an expert in these things, was sitting by the drivers; and he paid them, telling them that his masters were sending their daughter to the waters at V…"

"Scoundrel!" replied M. de Saint-André in a feeble voice, "who suggested such an idea to you? What were you thinking? What interest do you have in her?"

"Oh, I hide nothing from my friends," as he sat beside M. de Saint-André. "I will tell all…But first, send your policemen away and the men that I hear nearby?…"

M. de Saint-André, covering his eyes with his hand, began to think. He quickly realized that he could promise all that Argow wanted, so that he would give him back his daughter, and that after that, his brother or someone else would draw the vengeance of the laws on the head of this bold pirate. Taking his hand from his head, he signaled Argow that he consented; and the sailor, going towards the policemen, told him that M. de Saint-André knew a suspect man in the village, and that he would go with him tomorrow to the police captain. He told them also to tell their chief to wait for the rear admiral: then, passing by Vernyct, he ordered him to go right away and show their passports and to ask for a horses for midnight, an hour, and to come back right away. Then Argow went back to the chair beside M. de Saint-André, and told him with a sang froid equal to that of the rear admiral who had recovered from the great emotions which had just afflicted him.

"Monsieur, when I came back to Paris ten months ago, I made the acquaintance of Monsieur William Badger, an honest boy whom I saved from bankruptcy. To repay me for the service that I rendered him, he advised me to marry, saying that with a fortune like mine, (I have five million, Monseigneur), I should have a wife to help me enjoy life; he added that he knew of a young lady who would render a true service in marrying me; that she had come five years ago from America, that she was beautiful, touching, rich,(for it was he through a lucky manoeuvre had increased her fortune), that she did not know society, lived alone with sorrow, and that a bon vivant like myself would cheer her up. I am not handsome, but I am, you see, strong and quite healthy. I have strong shoulders, and I am not given to melancholy. I consented. When he named Mademoiselle Melanie de Saint-André, a secret joy rose up in my heart, and I disguised it. In truth, Monsieur, you are my fiercest enemy; you alone in France can betray me, for almost all of your officers must be dead and my accomplices as well!...Wouldn't it be a master stroke to become related to you...Your daughter did not want it! Besides, not being able to furnish your death certificate, I would have needed her brother's consent...He would have recognized me...In Paris the marriage officials are not easily fooled. So I made a public declaration that two of my sailors had seen you fall into the Atlantic from a gunshot. With this notice I will go to the place where I hid Melanie; and there, with a few *bells and whistles,* I will make the mayor believe whatever I want, and I will become...your relative...I adore your daughter...She is sweet, we must agree!"

"Give her back to me, Argow," said M. de Saint-André, "I swear to you that I will never betray the secret of your past life..." Tears covered the cheeks of the rear admiral..."Argow," he added, "give me back my daughter, before God, I promise to do everything that you ask."

"You will never open your mouth about all that you know about me."

"I swear it!..." said M. de Saint-André with a tone of good will which was hard not to notice.

"Very well," replied the ferocious sailor with an infernal smile, "I swear on my word as a pirate, *only to give your daughter back to you...*"

"When?..." asked the rear admiral.

"Tomorrow night!...At this time!...I have to go get her!..."

"Argow, I trust you!...And I forget all of my hatred. I abjure all of my desire for vengeance!..."

"And I," replied Argow, "I trust you...goodbye, Monseigneur, goodbye, Monsieur the Rear Admiral!..."

The sailor went slowly to see if there was anything to fear. He came back and said: "You should not be surprised if I leave tonight!...Your daughter is far away!..."

He left the two brothers together. In the antechamber he met up with his lieutenant Vernyct, who had executed his orders.

"Let's go, Vernyct!...And let's take a close look at the rooms that we go through!..." The two pirates looked at the height of the windows, the stair, the courtyard, the door. When they had left, Vernyct asked Maxendi why he wanted to know the layout of the bishop's residence.

"What I want to do," cried the sailor in a low voice! "I cannot trust the secret to anyone. For this scheme I will only trust a woman."

"A woman!..." repeated Vernyct laughing and looking at his captain.

"Lady death!" added Argow with a frightening smile. "Let us go around the bishop's residence," he said, "for all of this information is necessary, along with resolution!...For we must assure our existence!..." When they were across from the garden, the sailor looked joyously at the walls which were not very high and at the roofs of the bishop's residence which were covered with chimneys. At this sight, Argow stopped his plan and went back to the inn.

As he was walking through the streets Argow came upon a young wretch of about seventeen. The young man was from the Auvergne and his clothes showed that he offered his back to anyone who was buying.

Argow stopped and began to consider his pitiful and hardly clever face.

"How much do you make, my boy?" he said to him carefully.

"As much as you," replied the messenger.

"How is that?" asked the sailor astonished by this reply.

"Yes, I have my earnings and you have yours!" replied the man from Savoy drily.

"You are singularly pleasing," said Argow with surprise.

"I have pleased many others."

"Enough said," said Vernyct quickly, "do not anger this great man."

"My friend, do you want to make your fortune?" asked Argow.

"Of course!" responded the young man.

"Very well," continued Argow, "how much would make you happy? Think, try…but happy, so that you could not desire any more."

"Ah for that I would need Mother Veronica's field, a house roofed with tiles, a garden and…oh I could have all that for twelve thousand francs, and I would marry Jeannette!…Oh! I would marry Jeannette even though she is richer than I am! She told me to go earn enough to have a wife…Oh! She would be astonished!…"

"My friend, you can earn those twelve thousand francs right away!…"

"Earn them!" cried the man from Auvergne opening his eyes wide, "you mean earn them legally?"

"Legally!" responded Argow, "your conscience will have nothing to reproach you for, but you must have tact…without which you will only earn twelve cents…"

"What is your plan?" asked Vernyct in a low voice.

"My friend," continued Argow without responding to his lieutenant, "follow us. I will give you a big package; you go into the bishop's residence; you ask the servant to let you into Monsieur de Saint-André's room, the rear admiral, who came today. Go into his room; give him the package and take care to see where his room is located, if it looks out on the garden or on the court, if it is in the right wing or the left wing, and you report these details to me exactly, I will take you with me to my castle, and I will count out, this very night, your twelve thousand francs. Then at least I will have made one person happy in my life!…Do you understand?"

"Yes…but, what do you intend to do?…What is the purpose of this information?…"

"That does not concern you. Do you want to marry Jeannette and earn twelve thousand francs?"

"Yes."

"Let's go!…" The man from the Auvergne began to run.

"Now do you understand?" Argow asked Vernyct.

"No."

"So what, keep going…"

The three of them arrived at the Hotel d'Espagne, and Argow made up an enormous package of papers, laundry, and everything that he could find, he set it on the little Auvergnat's hooks and the man ran off to the bishop's residence.

"Will you tell me your plan?" Vernyct asked Argow when the messenger had left.

"It should not be spoken between four walls," said Argow into his lieutenant's ear. "Can't you see that there is just a door a thumb's width thick that separates us from the neighboring room and that one can even see through the cracks," he added fixing his eyes on the door.

After half an hour the Auvergnat returned and gave Argow the information that he had asked for and also swore by his Jeannette that it was accurate.

"I believe it," Argow said to him, "but I will have proof of it. Did you see Monsieur de Saint-André?"

"No. He had just left by carriage with the monseigneur to go look for a young man who came earlier in the evening."

"Wait for us at the door to the hotel."

The Auvergnat left.

Argow went and changed and invited Vernyct to do as well. They put on the old clothes which they always wore to smoke and drink in the morning; and in these outfits, they escaped from the hotel without being seen except by the Auvergnat. Argow, looking at his watch saw that it was not yet nine o'clock, and he made use of the time to buy ropes and iron braces. They walked through the village; and when eleven thirty sounded from the cathedral, they went towards the bishop's residence.

CHAPTER 22

Fate would have it that a dark night protected the undertaking of Argow and his accomplice. They arrived behind the wall of the residence's garden. Vernyct cast an iron brace up into a tree attached to an end of rope that was strong enough to support the weight of a man and in which they had made knots of rope at regular intervals. As soon as the brace had been secured in the branches which formed a fork where they joined, the two pirates slowly went up the makeshift rope, and when they were in the tree they drew the rope and the entire package to them.

They were in the garden and soon found themselves against the side of the facade which reached to the ground. Argow measured the facade with his eye.

"He told us that the room looked out on the courtyard…the two windows are the only ones on the left wing, so that wing will receive our visit…Good, there is a chimney; it is that one!"

"But how will we get up on the roof?"

"That is the question, the problem to resolve,"

said Argow, "and for that we only have an hour…We can't keep the horses waiting since that would look bad. They will have to come wake us in our beds." In pronouncing these scattered phrases, the sailor contemplated the facade.

"Are you light, Vernyct? For I am fat now, so I would not dare to try it."

"What?" asked the lieutenant.

"Look! You have to attach the rope to the balcony on the second floor by climbing over the leaves of the slatted shutters on the first floor: once you are on the balcony, you bring up the rope above the shutter on the second, and from the second to the roof. The jutting part formed by the cartouche on which someone's coat of arms is sculpted will make it easy to fix the brace to the roof."

Vernyct hesitated for a long time, but in the end was resolved. Argow pulling a ring off his finger, a poisoned needle in the liqueur with which savages get rid of their enemies,[4] gave it to Vernyct so that he

---

4 When a savage wants to kill one of his enemies, he goes to a party with him, after a long hunt: he places himself immediately above the person

could annihilate without sound those who would oppose his operation. Then he began to watch, and to examine everything while the lieutenant accomplished his tasks.

Vernyct succeeded in fact in placing himself on the cartouche, and he placed the iron brace between two uneven boards. Argow hung from the cord below to test its solidity, and raised himself up to the top. From there they walked on the roof to the chimney above M. de Saint-André's room, and after removing the cap on it, Argow went down it making as little noise as possible. When he was at the level of the apartment he listened to see if the rear admiral was asleep.

---

whom he wants to poison; and, when at the end of the meal, the great cup from which everyone drinks is passed hand to hand, the savage drinks, his enemy imitates him and falls down dead, without the avenger being harmed in any way. Furthermore, this is how the Americans cause the liqueur to dry, and when it only leaves a compact residue, they make it into a powder and fill their needle with this deadly powder. (They call it Peygu.) When the cup comes they drink, but they lick after having drunk the powder hidden between their nail and the skin of their finger. No one can escape their vengeance: this is the most heavily used. (Taken from the *Voyage of Sambuco*.)(Editor's note.)

After this check, Argow let himself fall down into the hearth. There he listened again and dared to look around the room. M. de Saint-André was fast asleep. The sailor got up, ran and stuck a needle into an artery. The unfortunate man opened his eyes, saw Argow, he wanted to cry out…he died.

"His rope is at an end!…" said the pirate. Immediately he went back to the chimney and up to the roof. He redescended by the rope into the garden and from there got out into the street. It was one o'clock in the morning, and the two corsairs hastened towards the Hotel d'Espagne. Argow was as calm as if he had kicked an empty bottle. His accomplice followed him; and if someone had followed them like this, walking through this deep night, they would have thought them to be the very pictures of crime followed by remorse……….

The vicar slept, and he was prey to the pains of a troubling dream. He saw his Melanie again, amid the purest and most vivid delights, looking at the *head* of her dear Joseph. Then a mortal pallor came over his forehead, she became immobile and cold, on her mouth wandered the smile of innocence, and by the way in which her eyes closed, the vicar noticed that her last look, before closing her eyes had been at him. Then, after this painful gesture, he saw Melanie surrounded by an extremely bright fire; her face was like that of a saint, her clothes were seemingly threaded with silver; her hair was disheveled; her pose ethereal, in this state she rose up towards the sky and made a motion with her finger for him to follow her. He found himself on earth in a terrible state. Trying to obey his friend's gentle command and not being able to, he grew angry and raised his arms; but something corporal kept him attached to the earth…In the distance, he noticed the marble of a tomb that rose up slowly, and M. de Saint-André showed his head, only he was dead!…And farther on, in an indistinct manner, Madame de Rosann was sketched, and he saw her tears, without being able to recognize her… He awoke with a start, he listened, and his own name, pronounced emphatically, struck his ear. Then, he got up and saw the light shining through the slats of the door which separated him from the other room.

M. Joseph approached, and he tried to distinguish who the men were who were speaking at this hour...He recognized Argow and his accomplice.

"It is his supposed son!...I tell you..." repeated Argow, "and while they are searching for our horses, we should..."

"We should," interrupted Vernyct, "we should resolve something...The old maid is going to betray our plans!...She escaped...You just heard what Gorbuln said. That was an imprudence."

"Bah!...If the girl is well locked up, I doubt that the old woman will know how to get back. She does not know anything!...And besides, she will stay near the castle, we will go there and watch....You always give up..."

In saying this, Argow held a roll of paper with which he rapped on the table.

"What do you have there?..." asked Vernyct.

"It is nothing. It is the little one's diary. What she wrote every day!...Pitiful!..." and he cast the roll on another table.

"Very well, what do you plan to do? The horses are coming! Have you paid the hostess?"

"I think that because the young man is asleep!...It will not cost us anything to make him sleep far away!..." These words made Joseph shiver, for Argow, in pronouncing them, indicated with his finger the door through which the vicar was looking; and for Joseph to die without having seen Melanie, although their love was now innocent, would have been the bitterest and most horrible death. He shivered and looked around his bedroom to see where he could flee and have the pirate arrested.

"He recognized me," continued Argow, "and he is a man who will come after me!...There is nothing to fear, like all young people, when they are exhalted. Their self-interest, danger, nothing can stop them!... And...look, let's go!"

No," said Vernyct, *"he will die like the other one!... And the doctors can just as well...two!...The same symptoms!..."*

"That is the first good reason that you have given me...still, think that no trace remains...that nothing could discover...It strikes the blood!...The blood chills!...It is a sure thing!..."

"I know full well that the devil will not find us

here! Because we plan to make a tour of Columbia…take distinguished letters, set ourselves up in their service, and tell off the Spanish. We have to forget this particular affair…"

"Coward!…We will only go there at the last moment. England, Sweden, Denmark, Russia, aren't we blessed like at Ch…T…You go…the safest place for us is Paris…"

"So you will leave the little one…"

"No…I want to marry her…I love her!…" At this word Argow's hideous face took on a singular look of power.

"So you are going to give Gorbuln orders?"

"Yes!…" This prolonged "yes" spoken, Argow was still thinking of his plan. As courageous and intrepid as the vicar was, he shivered; and seeing the terrible eyes of the pirate fixed on the door, he could not keep himself from thinking that he had been seen.

"Look, Vernyct, I must fulfill my desire!…"

"Argow, my friend, it is a useless crime, believe me!…If he follows us!…Then it will be time!…And I will admit that it is necessary!…"

In saying this Vernyct listened as if to hear if the

horses were coming, and the vicar read on his face the desire that the lieutenant had to leave…

"Let's go," said Argow, "the horses are not here yet. I have time!…" Argow went out and was followed by his accomplice who was still talking.

Never had the vicar loved life as he did at this moment. He knew all of its value, he would have defended himself like a lion; but he had seen Argow without arms, and a vague notion of betrayal slipped into his soul. A secret presentiment told him that he would have to be tricky. Then, he had the presence of mind to remove the peg of the hinge of the connecting door to Argow's room, and at the moment when Argow entered into his room from the hallway, he slipped into the two pirates' room. The sailor, having forced the lock, went forward without light into the vicar's room.

M. Joseph saw him plunge his hand into the bed several times!…At this moment the carriage horses that Joseph had asked for appeared out in front of the inn along with Argow's. Vernyct cried: "Argow!… Argow, there's our Auvergnat with the inn girl!…"

"It's done!" said the pirate in a low voice, and he

raced to the stairs along with Vernyct.

Joseph, stupefied by the danger that he had just avoided, remained immobile; and he held without noticing it the roll of paper that the sailor had cast aside with disdain. The vicar, hearing himself called, reappeared in his room. He fixed the door and the servant told him that his carriage was ready.

"Did you know," he asked the young woman, "where those execrable rogues ordered their driver to go?"

"To his castle in Vans," said the big man.

"Was he astonished or surprised?"

"No, he was laughing!..." replied the servant.

"He laughed, my child!..." cried the vicar... "Look, my girl," he added, "I am going to give you a mission which I hope you will carry out!...Go to Monsieur de Saint-André...my f...my protector, my uncle... tell him that Monsieur Joseph came to pay him his respects at about eight o'clock; and that he was forced to leave right away without being able to see *his father!...*"

"What!" cried the servant, "you are the Monseigneur's nephew?"

"Yes," said Joseph giving a five franc piece to the servant, "and keep, my child, keep this coin; if you are in love someday!...Remember Monsieur Joseph...and...if you marry the one that you love, then think again of me!..."

The servant, moved by the tone that the young priest added to these words, accompanied him all the way to his carriage. He gave the order to go to Paris and promised the driver a tip which was the reason why all of the inhabitants of A...y were awoken by the slap of the driver's whip...

Just as the vicar was carried off with lightning speed and the servant went to close the door after having followed the carriage with her eyes, a voice was heard saying: "*Qui potest capere capiat* which means to say, my lovely child, that in moving up, one cannot go too far!..." And he kissed her two or three times in succession...She began to cry.

"Hush! Hush!" Leseq began again, "you are a servant in the best hotel in A...y, so, it was here that our vicar, Monsieur Joseph, must have come."

"A handsome young man, tanned, who rushes to

Paris without waiting for the clothes that he ordered!..."

"No, my young priest has enough...He is not like me!...*Vestes usatas semper.*"

"The monseigneur's nephew!" cried the servant. "He seemed sad,...in love!..."

"That's just it!..." responded Leseq. "Where is he? Where is he going?"

"He stayed here all day, he just left for Paris, and..."

Leseq, without waiting for the end of the harangue, had climbed back on his horse and galloped towards Aulnay-le-Vicomte to tell Madame de Rosann about her son's flight, to receive the twelve hundred francs that had been promised, to make Josephine desperate at not knowing more; and without doing more or less, attend all of the gatherings that they would have in the village since Joseph had left.

Meanwhile, the vicar, confined in a corner of a bad carriage, reflected on the events which had assailed him during the short evening. His thoughts found new material in the risk that he had just run, the rascality of Argow and his impunity: the scope of his ideas obsessed him; but at last, he came back to Melanie whom he was going to see again. He transported himself by the strength of his imagination into the room which she occupied, and this gentle reverie subjugated him entirely. It chased away all other ideas, even the memory of his mother, Madame de Rosann, whose ingenious tenderness had at first softened him. When he had climbed into the carriage he had cast the roll of paper in a corner like something that annoyed him, and leaning on one side of the carriage, he remained for a long time in that semi-sleep which comes from long thoughts.

That was how he arrived at Vans-la-Pavée.

It was in this village that the first stop since A...y was located. Vans-la-Pavée touched on one end of the forest which Aulnay-le-Vicomte and its charming valley terminated on the other end in such a picturesque manner. At the start of this immense forest, the imposing castle was to be seen which once belonged to the family of B...and which Argow had bought a year ago.

The cessation of the rapid motion of the carriage, drew Joseph out of his melancholy; he asked the driver where he was.

"Vans-la-Pavée!..." he responded. Joseph leaped out of the carriage and mentioned his intention to stop there for a few minutes. He asked to speak to the master, and soon was introduced into the room of the postmaster, who, by chance, was also the mayor of Vans.

"Monsieur," Joseph said to him, "twenty-one years ago a young woman..."

"That was before the Revolution," said the mayor-postmaster-innkeeper.

"Yes, Monsieur, a young lady of quality, disguised probably, came here to give birth..."

"That's all they do!..." the mayor-postmaster interrupted, "before, like after the Revolution, children are always what they're up to...those women..."

"But my friend, that is what we are in the world for!..." said a young lady sitting on a chair.

"Now I am lost!..." cried the mayor-postmaster aiming his rather aged face at the vicar.

"Monsieur," began Joseph again, "I want to know if the woman whom the young lady stayed with still exists."

"Certainly," responded the woman, "that is the sister of the concierge at the castle of Aulnay-le-Vicomte. I recall that story perfectly…a church man, a young woman, pretty like all loves…"

"That is it, Madame," said Joseph. "Monsieur, I beg you to have the goodness to tell the mayor to send the child's birth certificate…"

"I am the mayor!…" cried the mayor-postmaster. "I hold this post through royal favor…"

"Monsieur, I will leave you the price for the certificate, and beg you to send it to Paris to the address that I am writing below…"

"What a handsome man!…" muttered the young woman.

Joseph could not hear anything else but the mayor's voice scolding his wife. As he left the building, the vicar thought that he should at least go see the hut in which Madame de Rosann had brought him into the world. He was told of Marie's sister's dwelling place, and a driver took him to the end of the village, on the side of the forest and the castle. The vicar knocked at the door of the almost ruined hut, covered with a thatch roof. A wrinkled, decrepit old woman opened the door and she poked the embers in the fireplace to light up the hut. In this vacillating light, Joseph cast a rapid glance on this temple of misery, and a gentle but painful feeling took hold of his soul

"Ah!" he cried: "This is where I began to breath for the first time. This is where I cast my first glances, my first cries! O mother, how I love you! O tender and gentle woman, whom I reproach myself for not having seen enough! Here is where you suffered!...Hello dear hut...I will fix your ruined roof, I want the person living here to be happy!...As happy as a mortal can be!..."

"What! You are the one whom that poor little lady brought into the world!..." cried the old woman, "I am the one who received you in my arms: the ecclesiastic was there..." and she showed a worn chair. "You mother suffered..."

"She suffered!..." said the vicar with a touching tone of pity.

"On this bed which was better!..."

"It will become what it should be!...Poor woman, what misery!..."

Joseph, seeing an inkwell, wrote to Madame de Rosann.

"O mother! I am writing to you from the hut which resounded with your cries. It is with a heart which is penetrated by that gracious recognition which is called *filial love* that I address myself to your heart...I know, now, the motif of your kindnesses, and your attentions!...And I rebuffed you!...Oh!...I will come back to Aulnay!...I burn to cover your sacred face with my kisses!...My soul is prey to a deluge of gentle and charming sensations. Permit me to greet you with the gentle name of mother, from afar, it is true, but fate requires it...One day, leaning on your chest, I will tell you the secret of my troubles, which now have a cruel remedy...I admire the strangeness of the events which have kept me from you. I want you to believe that since a desire still holds, in spite of myself, the first place in my heart, yet the most sincere of my wishes is to kiss you!...If fate were not taking me on, I would have flown into your arms just as soon as I learned the secret of my birth, and your admirable devotion. At this time still, everything in me is quiet at the memory of your pains, and the sight of this cherished house, where, secretly, I saw the light of day!...This event from your youth makes you dearer to my heart, because I feel all that my love owes you more than another mother!...Hear in reading this letter, hear the voice of your son thanking you, seeing you, placing all of his soul on paper. Imagine that in this place, I have attached the idea of the most respectful and most tender kiss that a son has ever given; your image is beside me, I see you on the bed. I cry, thinking that I hear you moan, and this cottage seems to be a palace to me!...Goodbye!...

The wretched woman who lives here is poor, I want us to enrich her together. Together we should repair her roof, this first of our actions should be shared, and only this woman is capable of bringing you this letter. Joseph."

"Take this, grandmother," said the vicar filled with emotion, "in the morning go and present yourself at the castle of Aulnay-le-Vicomte, ask for Madame de Rosann."

"Never, I would not dare…" said the ashamed woman.

"Go! Go!…You will be well received when your give her this letter…" And the vicar, letting his eyes wander about the broken down hut, went out accompanied by the astonished peasant woman…

Leaning against the door, the driver, immobile, was looking far away. The vicar asked him what he saw.

"Look, Monsieur, do you see, over there, on the castle terrace?"

The first tints of dawn hardly permitted him to distinguish objects; nevertheless, Joseph noticed on a little terrace above a river, a young lady sitting in the middle of great greenery, and that she was singing sadly: the distance only permitted them to hear the indistinct sounds of an extreme melancholy. The young lady remained immobile: her attitude and her pose made one think that she was considering the precipice like Sappho must have looked on Leucade's leap before drowning. This woman, wearing white and seated in a picturesque manner on the fortifications surrounded by water sighed with songs of love, whose tender modulations seemed to come from the air. The undefined wave of colors of the first rays of light, made the spectacle extraordinary: also these circumstances plunged the vicar into a sort of ecstacy. He tried to see and hear her, without being able to catch a word or distinguish a trait…

The imagination, that friend of the Romantics, would have thought to have glimpsed one of those ethereal girls that Girodet and Gerard have placed in their paintings of Ossian. This woman, like a light, ample vapor, appeared like the spirit of ancient feudalism, crying out at the sight of herself cut off from the world and deploring the ruin of her castle.

"That is," said the driver, "the unhappy young woman that M. Maxendi brought here. They say that she is crazy, and those that have heard her talk think that she is crazy with love!"

"They say," began the old woman again, "that she

is no crazier than I am and that M. Maxendi kidnapped her."

"What!...That is Argow's castle!..." cried the vicar, drawn from his reverie, by the name Maxendi. Nevertheless he did not follow up on these words, because an irresistible charm constrained him to return to contemplating this spectacle which inspired a painful presentiment in him: a vague fear flew through his spirit, for lovers fear everything.

At this moment, a more distinct modulation came to Joseph's ear. He seemed to have heard Melanie; but, attributing this idea to the fixation of the image of his love in his imagination, he let himself be led by the driver, without noticing. For in climbing back into the carriage, he kept looking at the castle, whose imposing appearance and vast constructions were gilded by the first fires of daylight. With the last glance that he cast he thought that he saw the young woman waving her handkerchief. This gesture made him shiver.

"She is asking for help," he said, "I would like to see her!..."

"The horses are waiting, Monsieur."

"She is unfortunate!…I am happy!…Nothing can take Melanie away from me!…Why don't I stay to find out about this adventure!…What is an hour to me?…"

"Monsieur, Monsieur," said the driver slapping his whip.

The vicar left…

Chapter 23

I know of nothing more terrible than the solitude that occurs when great and strong souls have received a violent blow which casts them into that deep meditation in which their spirit finally gets lost. The spectacle which the Vicar had just witnessed had been like a dream to him, and this dream continued for a long time, because of the rapidity with which he was being driven and by the disposition of his soul. Without sleeping he had all the heavy sensations of a dream, and this dream was stifling in the vague fear that the last modulation of the young lady's voice had imprinted on the vicar's soul.

Joseph arrived at the gates of Paris, and he was still tapping his knee with the roll of paper that Argow had cast off with disdain. He ended up being astonished by the constancy with which he held on to the papers; and glancing at them, the thought that he had to read them came back to mind: he unrolled the neglected paper, cast his eyes over them, recognized

Melanie's writing, and all of his blood seemed to go out of his heart!...He paled and leaned on the green Moroccan pillow which garnished the corner of the coach.

"So that's it," he thought, "it was Melanie that Argow was talking about! She was the one that I saw!..." A frightening series of evils unrolled before his eyes. His mind wandered, he became unable to think; his brain seemed to dissolve. At last he brought his eyes to the fatal paper and read what follows:

Melanie's Journal[5]

"I am better, but I am alone!...O my brother, I

---

5   Mademoiselle Melanie de Saint-André's journal would easily have filled three hundred printed pages. Using the taste and discernment that a bachelor of letters can have, I reduced these amorous meanderings to their proper size. The writings of lovers are all cowardly, diffuse, filled with repetitions, and it is not a little task to condense them. Also I ask forgiveness for the incoherencies, the delirious expressions of these fragments, and remind you that they are not my own. It is by these same reasons, that I am permitted to cut off many things in the manuscript of the vicar. I hope that readers will praise me for this delicate application of conscience.

can only think of you!——When the dawn appeared I found my house to be big, sad, empty, and the rooms are odious to me. It seems that they only present me with a uniform gray color; everything wears your mourning!...My soul is wrapped in crepe, which muffles the least sounds that it makes.

I want to write a word to you each day and speak to you as if I had you at my side. Ah Joseph! A day is long since I do not see you any more! I cannot live my rational life. It is impossible to consider this; I try to form reasons, but my eyes wander across the ceiling, the furniture. I am looking for something that is no longer here. I live in a tomb in which nothing smiles at me.

. . .

Joseph, my friend, my nights are worse than my days! The most frightening dreams assail me. This morning I began to make a notch on a piece of wood to mark each day and see how many I will go without living!...What are you doing?

. . .

You left a feather pen on your bureau. I took it greedily and that is what I will write with from now on!.. When I first picked it up I thought that I possessed you...A moment later I cried!...I saw that I had nothing but an overly strong memory!...

...

It is midnight; I am alone; a night light is illuminating my room: not a gust moves the air; everything is quiet, beside me, under me, above my head. I am in the heart of the deepest repose...A worry is bothering me; my head is heavy!...In the middle of the calm reigns a terrible trouble for I have seen you!... Yes I have seen you,...you whom I dare not name! You noble face appears to me brought by a dream cloud, and this vision has inundated me with a gentle joy and balm like the fugitive smell of a flower from the fields. Your soul soars in this room which is too small for my emotions!...O my dear spouse! I feel you at my sides, you burn my ribs, love! Draw back this magic painting! For I only caress a light smoke. God!...What power! In this unperceivable world my soul has traced, has fixed a portrait designed by the most voluptuous crayon! Only roses!...How they smile at me!...What a crown!...Although nothing exists, and I see it!...Reverie of love!...Night of flames!…Joseph, I am dying!…

　　　…

Today I have remained pale, immobile, without thinking of anything, and without feeling any tiredness in my soul; your image pursues me; Mme Hamel is before me; I do not see her. The servants go by; I do not hear the sound of their footsteps. I do not think at all about your delightful form, and I see it; I do not hear your voice, and it rings in my ears. I do not see what I see, and I see what I do not see. What charm!…Maybe someone can tell me why I feel thoughts without really thinking?…*I think that I am a cloud!…*

　　　…

I am going to die young; for me voluptuousness will not do away with the liqueur of its divine chalice; I am devoured, undermined: my poor mother Hamel shivered this morning. She said to me: 'Melanie! you are quite pale!…your eyes are shining. The curls of your hair are disordered, you did not get ready!…you are not careful any more.' *'Is he here?'*… I responded. 'O my daughter,' she said, 'do not descend into the tomb, for our hands are eternally joined, and you will drag me with you.' 'No, no,' I said, 'I will not die, as long as he is alive…dead, I will go to rejoin him since the tomb will be our wedding bed. Death will hold the torch of our consummation…and the night of our funeral wedding will be eternal.' Madame Hamel shivered, poor woman.

· · ·

Joseph! I received your letter!…I kissed the cherished characters a thousand times…They will always be on my heart! They would burn there if they were not already calcified. Yes, my dear, yes I will follow your orders, and I will live for you! I will wait impatiently for the time when everything will be dead except our hearts…which will never die. I am too joyful to express something. Goodbye for today!…I am going to sit down, and all day stare at the air as I look for your gentle image!…

· · ·

Joseph, our banker came, he was surprised to see me so changed. He was pained when he learned of your departure. He seems to want to take a lot of interest in me!…I believe that he is a very honest man and a fine soul.

· · ·

The banker, M. William Badger, came back and he said that I should marry…He proved it to me. I tried not listening to his blasphemies. Me marry!…Oh Joseph I would rather die a hundred times.

· · ·

Today M. Badger brought me a man named Maxendi. He displeases me, his looks are disagreeable. His face has a sort of energy that does not inspire those who see it except to think that this moral strength does not produce good effects…

· · ·

Good God!…M. William Badger wants me to marry M. Maxendi. I just came from a ball at which I suffered death and passion. They shouted in my ears that M. Maxendi has five million francs, that I would be a sovereign queen.

'What, my dear little one,' Madame Badger said to me, 'that does not astonish you!…But see how all of the mothers and young ladies greet Monsieur Maxendi. See how they name him with their eyes. He is the only one here…'

'Madame,' I responded, 'Monsieur Maxendi does not please me and will never please me.'

Madame Badger left me, and I sat beside poor mother Hamel, who, dressed sumptuously amidst this striking feast, nonetheless tried to sleep as decently as possible. Madame Badger came back to present me with M. Maxendi, and I was forced to dance with him. I do not like the man at all, and everyone wants me to cherish him...

Joseph I must tell you the truth, the least feelings of my heart belong to you! So I will tell you that amidst the enthusiasm created by the spectacle of the most beautiful women in Paris, the riches, with the freshest ornaments, amidst the conquests of luxury I felt a feeling of pride to see me proclaimed by everyone's regards the queen of the assembly...I was dressed simply, with this muslin dress which you gave me, a whimsical crown garnished my head as it suffered from love: this simplicity made me notice all the more those whose hair was embellished by all the fires of diamonds. Ah! I only shone because some spark of the fire which consumes my heart came to make my face resplendent...so it is to you that I owe this triumph! My eyes often wandered to the corners where my Joseph used to be seated, and there my soul addressed all its conversation, all its prayers to you.

...

They are proclaiming me M. Maxendi's wife...I do not know how it is so, but truly these worldly people have a way of making you talk, to interpret the slightest look, the slightest smile...Ah Joseph! Why aren't you there to cast off the seductions of these salon people...

...

If I did not trust a decided '*no*,' I believe, in truth, that they would marry me in spite of myself to M. Maxendi...I cannot believe the fierceness of these people! What is it to them if I marry?...Can't they leave a poor girl in peace when all she asks is to weep alone when her heart has been given forever.

...

My friend! Joseph, will you pardon me, I acted unwisely, I am lively, light, after all I am a woman. They brought this M. Maxendi to me again; I received him; he came back the next day, I refused him at the door…I wanted to go out, my carriage was broken…You can guess how!…M. Badger wrote to me that after what had happened I had commited a great dishonesty; he thinks that I should go to the ball that M. Maxendi just invited me to…I responded that I will go but that I intend to say in the middle of the assembly that I cannot marry anyone, because I am married. M. Badger should send me his carriage…

. . .

This morning, Joseph, I am sad, it was M. Maxendi's carriage that came to get me, I did not have time to say 'no…' Besides it is the last time that I am going out…Joseph, today is the day that you left me! This day should be unlucky for me!…A horrible presentiment afflicts me. At every minute my heart swells, and I am uneasy…I was just at the window: there are men in the road; they are talking together; their faces displease me. They seem to be pointing to my house with their fingers…O unlucky day!…Everything that I imagine appears to me in a disagreeable light, I am more beaten than if I were walking towards my death...I scolded Finette for nothing;...The poor child began to cry, and the sight of her tears caused mine to flow...

Joseph, I am dressing for the ball...I am dressed. Madame Hamel looks at me with astonishment: she says to me that I have changed frightfully...The carriage arrives...goodbye dear!..."

That is how the tender Melanie's journal ended...In finishing it the vicar was no longer a man; he tore at his chest, and, blood flowed on his clothes. He took out his handkerchief to dry it *without noticing that it was blood*...At this moment they brought him into the rue de la Santé: he went in to Melanie's house...Finette was at the door.

"Finette," he said crying, "Melanie, Melanie!..."

"Do you know where she is?" asked the chambermaid..."Ten days ago she left for Monsieur Maxendi's ball, and she has not come back. I tried to go to M. Badger's, but they said that he was not in and that everybody was in the country."

"In the country in winter!..." cried Joseph. "How

stupid you are!...Finette," he began again, "I beg your pardon...O poor Melanie!..."

With that the vicar went precipitously up into the house and wandered with a savage delight through all the rooms that were filled with Melanie's aura. He rushed to the bed that she had slept in. He kissed her feather pen, her piano...He kneeled before the dressing table that she had left to go to Argow's supposed ball. He cried at the charming disorder of the bedroom. He gave all the signs of a true mania...and Finette, stupefied, looked at him with astonishment which she could not get over.

"Where is Mademoiselle?..." she asked.

"Where she is, Finette!...She is at the bottom of a prison...in the power of the most infamous brigand that the sun has ever shone on!...Only I saw her like a light smoke without knowing that it was she...O Melanie! I swear to rescue you, to avenge you, and the sword of the law will fall on that fierce pirate's head."

"Ah! How poorly Mademoiselle must be," said Finettte, "She likes her little things so much!...She is without a chambermaid. Who will take care of her? Who will dress her?…Ah!…Ah!…" And Finette began to cry.

"Do I have money!…" cried the vicar suddenly, "do I have enough!…" And he took out his purse and his wallet.

"Gold! Here have some!" said Finete opening the drawer to the desk. "Look the drawers are full of it."

The vicar took all that he found.

"To wage a war," he said, "that is all that you need; let's go Finette!…"

Joseph went down the stairs and got back in the carriage.

"Monsieur," said Finette, "you are bleeding!…"

"No…no…driver, a louis for a tip and split the air for me on the way that we came. I have to be in the Ardennes by tomorrow."

"In the Ardennes!…" cried Finette, "O my poor mistress!…"

At each stop the vicar cast away money crying: "Horses! Horses! A runner up ahead, a louis to the driver, I will pay for the horses which you can kill!..." and the vicar drawn by four horses went like lightning...

Let us leave him to drive as quickly as an ambassador going to a meeting! And let us go back to Vans-la-Pavée.

Chapter 24

The postmaster of Vans-la-Pavée also owned a renowned inn. As he was in addition the mayor of the place, the rowdier members of the village pretended that more than one marriage sketched in the innkeeper's garden finished legally in the mayor's office. As soon as a dispute arose among drinkers, the mayor appeared at the same time as the barman; and despite the law that requires bars to close at nine o'clock, and though after ten o'clock they were still dancing, the mayor was gentle as an angel on this point, and as postmaster he reconciled everything.

M. Gargarou (that was this character's name) was worthy of being a minister of state, although the name of Gargarou does not lend itself to noblement or to being named a peer of France: whatever the case may be, those of our princes who passed by Vans-la-Pavée did not judge it worthy of anything but a mayoralty: also the good man was proud of his position! And although a bon vivant, hardly annoying, obliging, there was one subject that he never joked about; that was the devotion that all good Frenchmen should have for the *government*. One could have gotten him to do anything for the *government*: for him the word *government* was a talisman; and when I passed by Vans-la-Pavée, I was convinced myself that he did not know the form or basis of our government.

We left him sleeping next to a young and pretty wife. We will not take him up again at that moment, for his honor. In the morning he went out to visit his stables and show his face to the help, for he was very careful. After this general visit, he went into the big black smokey room that served as his living room.

"My wife is not up?…" he asked.

"No, Monsieur," responded a rather pretty servant who was holding a cup of broth.

"Who is this breakfast for?"

"For the old woman that has been here for the last eight days, and whom we only see in the morning and the evening…she is sad, you know?"

"I fear that she is *following some whim*," began the innkeeper again, "that she is plotting something against the government...A woman who does not say anything, who seems sad...If she were young then we could interpret her sadness...but...in the end, it is not clear, and I will speak to her! When one is the mayor one owes the government the actions of a police officer."

Buttoning his sport coat that was spotted in a thousand places, he went towards the corner where the old woman was patiently waiting for her dinner. She offered the most singular contrasts in her clothing. Her lace bonnet had a great knot of ribbons that were very distinguished and that attached under her chin by white satin ribbons: her face had all the character of gentleness and a touching goodness; but the veil of a profound suffering was cast over her face: she did not notice the kashmir which covered her shoulders; and, an elbow on the dirty inn table, she raised her eyes towards the blackened ceiling as if to ask for help from heaven. Her dress did not match the luxury of dress of her *bosom:* one would have said with reason that she had just gotten out of sumptuous clothes only to keep in terms of the art of dressing one named I believe an *underskirt;*[6] and this rather thick cloth skirt was garnished with a simple thread, contrasted all the more with the rest, which was dirty, and her silk stockings and black satin shoes were foreign and also had their share of mud. This description should give an idea of the whimsicality of this old woman, and her tears indicate rather well that it is Madame Hamel.

"Madame," said M. Gargarou, "you seem quite afflicted…Perhaps the business which brought you to our area has not gone as you had wished? Do you need anything?…If you do not say anything, we cannot help you."

---

6 I only risk this term with the greatest circumspection, not knowing if it is proper or improper to place it in this work; for I humbly declare to never have left the rue de la Femme-Sans-Tête, on the ile Saint Louis, to go to the Latin quarter, where the gracious Muses stay, who are naked, if one will believe the fable…And, having never been able to introduce myself to a lady of the world, this expression is the fruit of my conjectures… Perhaps when I have the signal honor to be licensed in the arts, this title will make me important enough to be able to obtain a favorable glance; and then, in my next work, I will say more about over and underskirts, if there is any need.(Editor's note.)

"Ah!" responded Madame Hamel, "unfortunately I am old, I do not know anyone around here, and I can only cry about the unfortunate event which has happened to me; for where could you find people to serve me, when I need people devoted to me!"

"How is that, with enough money one finds devotion…in everything…but, do you have bucks?"

"Alas! All that I have for money is what I brought with me to go to the ball…"

"Ah! You went to a ball?…" said the mayor-innkeeper with an air of curiosity.

"Yes…and they took me away…" cried Madame Hamel crying.

"Ah you do not have any money?…" began the mayor-innkeeper with fright, looking at Madame Hamel's bonnet and shawl, already adapting them to the head and shoulders of Madame Gargarou.

"No…I do not have a girl any more!…No…" the poor old woman dried her eyes with a lovely batiste handkerchief: "the barbarians! They refuse to imprison me with her!…"

"She is crazy!…" said Gargarou to himself. "Ah! ah!" He began again seeing the paper that the vicar had left on the table; "This is what the young man asked me last night...*Charge everything to M. Joseph chez Mademoiselle de Saint-André rue de la Santé*...and then he left five francs."

"Joseph!...Joseph!..." cried Madame Hamel, "he was here..."

"Ah well! Now what is it? She is crazy...Hey Jacqueline!"

"Would it be possible..." continued Madame Hamel, "show me that...yes...it is his writing...the poor child!...Ah! If I had seen him...then my daughter would no longer be in prison..." At that, without waiting for her breakfast, she went out and off towards the forest.

"Oh!" said the mayor-postmaster-innkeeper following her with her eyes, "I believe that the poor woman is not trying to harm the government! She seems to have enough to pay...so, leave her alone."

When Argow's men had lead Melanie to the castle at Vans, they had pitifully chased Madame Hamel away, for they feared her age and experience. The foreman's wife cried and begged to be left with her daughter in vain, but nothing could bend the determination of the pirate's men: so she went out of the castle in a ball dress and stayed at the inn by paying with her white satin coat. Then, every morning she stayed at the castle; and, sitting on a rock, she contemplated the castle window where Melanie was; and when the young lady walked on the terrace, she spoke with her. Then in the evening, she went back to sleep at the inn. So one can guess where the good woman was running to when she learned that Joseph had passed by Vans-la-Pavée that very night...

She hurried her step, and risked running despite her age to arrive at the stone which Melanie always looked to when she got up. Melanie had not left the terrace that was almost ruined and surrounded by water; she was still at the place where the vicar had seen her... She looked at the village and from afar she recognized her second mother.

"There she is," cried Melanie. "Nothing stops her, cold, rain! And she risks everything to see me, as if she were a lover!...O worthy mother, receive my homage! Before you arrive, let my thoughts surround you with thanks!..."

"My daughter!...My daughter!..." cried Madame

Hamel, from as far away as she could see Melanie, "*he* came, *he* came…rejoice…*he* is not dead!…"

"Who mother?"

"Joseph!"

"So that was *he!*…" said the pale and shivering young lady sadly, "my heart told me so…O my mother, can you imagine that last night finding my room too small for my pain I came out here guarded by two spies who will not leave me…I sang painfully that song that marked our last looks and our goodbyes: 'Like a last ray, like a last gust, animates the end of a lovely day.'

"All of a sudden I saw a light appear in that hut…that sudden light which struck my soul as if it were a ray of hope; I cannot explain what I felt. Without thinking that it was Joseph, an involuntary presentiment cried out to me: *'If that were he!…'* You see that I am, mother, still prey to such thoughts… And you tell me that it was *he!*…"

"Yes, daughter!…But why should we rejoice?… He fled like a shadow! He went off to Paris, for he asked for something in the village and wrote that one should send it to him at the Rue de la Santé."

"He is coming to see me!...He is going to see me!...and...I will not be there!...O my mother! What a trial...Take me from this odious prison, where I am dying..."

"My daughter, do not say that word...You cause me too great a pain...Let us wait for Joseph!..."

"But how will he know that I am here..."

Madame Hamel thought for a long time, and after having gathered up the sum total of her intelligence she cried: "I will write to him!..." Melanie leaped with joy, clapping her hands.

"O mother! Write, write quickly!...If I see Joseph again, then we will be saved!...Write!..."

As she finished these words a footman, with a forbidding face, came precipitously towards Madame Hamel: "Let's go, old woman, you cannot stay there..."

"What! I can't stay here...Do you own the earth?"

"Yes! Go away!..."

"What do you mean to say?..." cried Melanie. "Didn't you tell me that it was the will of the master of this castle that I should rule like a sovereign..."

"Yes, Madame," responded the footman respectfully, taking off his hat, "but only so long as your orders are not contrary to the surveillance that we are
to keep up around the castle…and Monsieur
Navardin has judged that this woman can no longer
come near here."

"Then why don't you lock her up with me?…I
want you to!…" responded Melanie.

"Monsieur Navardin, does not want it…Madame,
without that…"

"Let's go!" said Melanie, with a somber resignation, "goodbye my mother!…"

Madame Hamel did not have the strength to respond, she cast on her daughter a painful glance and
went away until the footman was happy with the distance that she was away. There she waved her handkerchief slowly, and Melanie responded to her by
making the same gesture.

"Madame," said another man to Melanie, giving
her a respectful look, "it is impossible for you to stay
here, if you continue to make such signals…"

"But my dear Monsieur Navardin, am I really a
prisoner?…"

"I did not say that, Madame, but, I am responsible for you with my head, and the man whom I am dealing with, if you were to escape, he is a man who would…"

"Very well! Monsieur Navardin, your head is in a great deal of danger," said Melanie with spite.

"Then Madame you will no longer leave your rooms!…Go back in…"

"And if I don't want to!…" replied Melanie proudly.

"I will force you!…" cried the sailor casting her a ferocious glance.

Melanie cried, lowered her head and followed with slow steps the ferocious Navardin. The latter lead her into a sumptuous apartment, in which she remained for ten days. She sat on a chair; and setting her lovely head in her hand she set herself to thinking of her brother, whose cherished image had appeared to her that morning. The weather was singularly foggy. The vast room only had two big windows garnished with curtains of red lampas in such a way that darkness reigned: Melanie became more thoughtful, and a strain of sorrow was mixed with her other thoughts.

What is going to happen!...They still have not spoken the name of the man who kidnapped me, but everything leads me to believe that it was M. Maxendi...He seemed to dread it...If he is rich, powerful, and helped by men who regard his orders as absolute, how will Joseph rescue me?...He will risk his life...but no, M. Maxendi cannot marry me against my will. There are laws!...O Joseph!...Come ... come...

At these words, she took a worn letter from her bosom, each fold of which formed a sheet, a green silk thread connected all the pieces. The young lady unfolded it with a careful precaution, and her eye *revisited* the cherished characters...Cursed love that I cannot tear from my heart!...she cried after having read, you will still shine at my last breath!...

As she pronounced these words, a loud noise was heard in the courtyard of the castle. It was Argow, Vernyct and the Auvergnat who had come from A...y by twisted roads.

"Very well, Navardin, what is new?" asked Argow.

"Captain, your young chicken is still here, crying, dying, talking of killing herself; for the rest, she has not been difficult to watch…She is nice like a twenty-four cannon frigate.

"And what did you do with the old woman?" asked Vernyct.

"We put her out the door right away."

"Unwise!.." cried Argow. "Unwise! She will tell everyone all around that we have kidnapped her daughter…Catch her again!…and put her right away under a good lock and key until we have achieved the perfect end to our business. Vernyct," he added, "you will take charge of the fortress! And you, Navardin, put yourself in a carriage and take this man to the Auvergne. Give him twelve thousand francs. I will send them to you at Clermont, by way of Badger."

At these words Navardin cast an oblique eye on the pirate to ask if it were necessary for the Auvergnat to die along the way from a heart attack, but Argow responded to him: "Go on, do what I say and nothing extra." The sailor looked at the astonished Auvergnat and shoved him towards the carriage crying: "Let's go!..." They left.

Argow, after having asked in what room they had placed Melanie, went towards the bedroom where the vicar's tender lover listened attentively to the rude sound which interrupted the silence of the antique castle. She stood up when she heard his steps: she ran.

"Ah!" she cried, "it is you, Maxendi!...So I am saved!..." The naïveté of this exclamation made Argow smile despite himself.

"Mademoiselle," he asked her, "how have you found your stay?"

"If they had let me wander about, I could have given them my opinion."

"What!" cried Argow vividly, "I ordered them to leave you free."

"So! Monsieur," Melanie interrupted, "so it was by your orders that I was kidnapped?...With what pain I am forced to change my opinion about you...I esteemed you Monsieur!..." she said with a tone of reproach; "And to what end? Why? What is your purpose in acting like this towards me? Do you know what risk you are exposing yourself to?"

"Mademoiselle," responded the criminal, trying to soften the roughness of his voice and face, "do you believe that I did not see on your face a strong indecision when there was a question of our marriage...You do not know, Mademoiselle, what an excess of love can cause a character like me to do...Have you never examined the effect that you produce on the souls of those who see you...Ah! Mademoiselle, you have illuminated a terrible passion in my heart!...I vow to you this love with the frankness that distinguishes energetic souls. I desire your legitimate possession. It alone can keep me from dying..."

"Well, you will die, my dear Monsieur Maxendi," she said graciously inclining her pretty head, "for never will a man have anything from Melanie...She has given her all!..."

"By the thirty cannons of my last frigate! You have lied!..." cried the angry criminal, "and when I abducted you, it was to force you to marry me...How could you reappear in society after having spent a fortnight with me?"

"I will no longer go out in society."

"Fine! But you will not leave here except dead…or my wife…"

"As for dead," said Melanie, "death seems to be the only thing that I wish, so it would help me!…As for your wife, that will never happen!…Never!…"

"But, my little villain, your smiles and you tilting head will not keep you from being in my power, and I can do with you what I will."

"No…no…"

"How is that?…"

"Because unfortunate people always have one refuge which cannot be taken away."

"Which one?"

"The tomb."

"Oh! I will certainly keep you from dying."

"Monsieur Maxendi, thought and death are the only things that are beyond the power of tyrants and villains. Nothing stops them…"

"What, Mademoiselle, you would refuse this luxurious life filled with joys and pleasures that I offer you? Do you think that you control everything, to begin with me, with the despotism that lets a captain command a sloop? Your self-love will be satisfied on all points! You will be a queen. I defy you to form a desire that I could not satisfy, even if it included killing someone (Melanie shivered) you will have the choice of *killing who you will*…and…"

"All that is the same thing," Melanie interrupted gently, "one of my dreams and a minute of thought give me more joy than all the pleasures that you uselessly spread before me."

"But, little flute, you do not know what a husband is, how useful one is, how tender one is, all the voluptuousness that he brings, you know nothing."

"That is true, but I know," she said with a fine smile, "that I love even better than a lover."

"Ah! If that is all," cried the sailor.

"All!…" said Melanie, "it is my turn to respond to you, Monsieur, that after what I have seen of you, it is impossible for you to *love,* for a true lover does not afflict the person that he loves."

"Ta…ta…ta…ta…" began Argow again angrily. "As for that, little nut, watch out for your head!…It is too pretty for your lovely eyes to be closed permanently. You refuse me?…"

"Yes!" said Melanie with a movement of horror.

"But one has motives," said the pirate, bending the rigor of his character at this moment in an astonishing way before Melanie's naive simplicity.

"I have mine too, Monsieur Maxendi!...For it is not out of aversion, nor a feeling of hate that I refuse you. Any man, even a prince, could not wipe away this refusal...Do you hear me? I love!...I love forever!..."

"Ah as for your blessing, little woman, do not pronounce those words before me with that look and that tone!...Believe me, do not play with fire."

"I love," she began again, "a being who will ceaselessly have my love...I will die a virgin!..."

"This being," said Argow contemplating her with a hellish smile on his lips, "did this being accompany you on the vessel that brought you back to France?"

"Joseph!..." she cried, "my brother...yes...yes... he is the one! Oh my beloved," she said deliriously, "yes it is you!...Cherished image...were I at a stake I would still see you..."

"And you believe, " began the pirate again, "and you believe that I do not have the means to keep you from dying and to marry you!...Let's go my lovely child, you will be Madame Maxendi! When you have five million like I do and twelve devoted men, one has all that one could want. No human power," he cried staring at Melanie in a way that made her blanch and shiver, "no human power can get you out of here: and before I give you up, I will kill you!..."

"Monsieur!...Monsieur!...Help!...Help!..." cried Melanie aghast at the horrible expression of his face.

"Help!" he repeated with an ironic tone, "you forget that no one here has ears or eyes for you!...Everything belongs to me. Do you think in good faith that I would let your lover come here?"

At this thought, Melanie remained like a marble statue and looked at the pirate with an expression of stupor that is impossible to render. Never had her chaste and pure spirit, her divine spirit been able to conceive the idea of such villainy; and, at this moment, Argow seemed by his attitude and the ferocity of his face to be veritable *crime* itself.

"I know where Joseph is," he began again with a sardonic smile, "I saw him last night, and I can tell you," he added tightening his lips, "that you will never see him again!"

"What! You know that he is in Paris…"

"Paris!" said the surprised pirate; "isn't he dead?" he said to himself.

"He came by, I saw him," began Melanie, "and…"

"You saw him?" asked Maxendi again.

"Yes, the fleeting sight refreshed my withered soul: the unlucky man was going to Paris…"

At this moment her face had a divine expression, one would have said that she was one of those saints whose head is surrounded by a celestial halo.

"Ah! He is in Paris," said the criminal, "that is good, I did not know it."

Melanie cried with desperation, when she saw that the candor had given him a weapon against her.

"My beautiful child, I am going to send my men into the field, for that Joseph will have to come back through here…Then, in a little while, you will have to choose between my hand and the death of your lover…So I have sworn it, and it is a great miracle…"

"Good God!" cried Melanie, "Where am I? What am I?..." And she let herself fall onto a chair while crying a torrent of tears.

"You see," said Argow coldly, "the extent of my love, it makes me capable of the greatest excesses...My queen, I leave you to reflect on these propositions...But I want to give you a thread to draw you out of the labyrinth which they will draw you into: remember well that in what I say, in what I do, there is only one step; and this step, it only takes a minute, a second to take it. Goodbye...Do not cry, tears are useless...Make a resolution! And...there is only one good one."

"Good God!" repeated Melanie twisting her arms in desperation, "won't you help me! I am suffering almost as much as when Joseph said goodbye to me."

Argow contemplated her, for she was more than beautiful; then he went away casting her a masterly glance, and leaving her in a horrible state of suffering.

She cried the entire day, all night, she would not take anything; and her overwhelmed soul, almost delirious, could not form a single reasonable thought.

CHAPTER 25

Argow came back into the living room of his castle where, at that moment, Vernyct and two former pirates who were helping him were trying to out drink each other with punch.

"Oh, oh!" cried the master criminal, "hold your glasses! Do not lift your elbows! We will have to use the thumbscrews nowadays."

At these words the three sailors looked at Argow with astonishment as he came and sat down next to Vernyct…

"So tell us, the man?" cried Argow at him shaking him suddenly, "how is it that the young man from the inn is not in our Lord's fields?"

"If you do not know yourself, who know everything, how do you expect me to know cap…tain," responded the drunken Vernyct.

"Ah! The brutes!" cried Argow, "it would never have worked, you cannot take…"

"Ah! What if, my su…per…ior, if we still took…"

"…(this replaces the horrible curse that Argow made) listen to me?…" And in saying this Argow seized the big crystal punch bowl and cast it out the window; "the first person who gets drunk before my marriage, I will lock him in the cellar in a giant champagne vat."

They all looked at the pirate with fright.

"Vernyct," he cried slapping him on the shoulder, "are you sensible now?"

"Present, my captain," responded the lieutenant shaking off his punchy fog.

"And you Scalyvt, Ornal and Carilleyn, are you ready to work?"

"To arms!" they cried.

"That's good," said Argow with a softened air. "First you are to go neaten up the castle: dress decently, even sumptuously: you, Scalyvt, try not to always bury your hands in your pockets; Ornal, do not scratch yourself; and you, Carilleyn, do not put a single leaf of tobacco in your mouth; let no one swear…if you do, the cellar! It will replace the ship's hold. In the end, my children, although this may be difficult for you, adopt for me the manners and the tone of high society, do not speak all at once, do not interrupt people, no gestures, no criticisms…Imagine, Ornal, that you are a duke, Scalyvt a marquis, and Carilleyn a baron. Vernyct, tell the cook to distinguish himself, to make for us for tomorrow three servings, all our men will be invited, we will put a Swiss guard at the door to the castle, and the gardeners will rake the paths, and will clean up the little woods at the entrance for me, along with everything that is falling in ruin! Do you understand me?"

"The captain is in fine spirits," said Scalyvt to Ornal in a low voice. "He is capable of anything…"

"Do you hear me?…." Argow repeated.

"Yes," cried the four criminals.

"Then battle stations!" responded Argow.

"Forward!" said Carilleyn, "may Saint-Elmo's fire consume me if I understand what he wants to do, but forward!"

"Very well!" said Vernyct when he was alone with Argow, "what are you up to?…"

"What am I up to? Marrying Melanie: and for that, given all of the difficulties, we must *broadside* the mayor of the town, so that he is not overly scrupu-

lous about our titles, and at all costs to make him believe that hares are rabbits...So you will go on behalf
of Monsieur the Count Maxendi, invite him to a
sumptuous meal tomorrow; and as we must take all
precautions, you will make him understand that a
seditious person, hidden under the name of Joseph,
should arrive in these parts; and that he should seize
him and guard him when he does, and you will place
a nice spy, Gornault for example, in ambush in the
village. Go get dressed, take a carriage, and observe
the village mayor's character a moment to find out
how I can get a *hold* over him."

"But Argow, my friend, your head, your excellent
head, is it well? How can you marry that girl...Are
you crazy? Wouldn't it be better?...Do you understand me?..." he added looking at Maxendi, "and
once you have satisfied your desire, give her the slip."

"I love her, Vernyct, and to keep your head, respect her. If she makes me angry, and she refuses to
marry me, then I will always be able to do
that...Let's go, march."

Vernyct went murmuring, and thinking that this
marriage was the height of folly; for he said to him-

self: once Argow is married, his wife will send us all away. He will become thoughtful. He will become attached to life. He will leave us there like dead dogs…And I'll be deviled, if one can joust with him, he is wise; what he wants, we have to want. If this marriage should fail…without its being our fault, for he would knock our heads off."

Thinking like this, Vernyct got dressed. The carriage was gotten ready and in an instant he arrived at the mayor's. The latter, seeing a carriage arrive at his door, rubbed his hands, and made room for Argow's lieutenant.

"Monsieur, aren't you the mayor of Vans…Can I have the honor of having an immediate meeting?"

"Monsieur!…Monsieur!…" said the mayor, troubled by this deference which flattered his pride…"Monsieur, sit down!…Enter, do me the honor…"

Vernyct entered into the room where Madame Hamel was sitting beside the mayor's wife to, whom she was telling her troubles.

"Honey, quick, a chair…Surely Monsieur is part of the government?"

"I am," replied Vernyct crossing his legs and leaning on his chair. "I am the intimate friend of Monsieur the Count, who for the last year has owned the land around Vans…"

At these words, Madame Hamel, squeezing the hostess' hand, paid the greatest attention to what Vernyct was going to say to M. Gargarou.

"Maxendi," began the pirate again, "greatly regrets that his business and the cares of public affairs have detained him in Paris until now, for he greatly loves your region, and he intends, nevertheless, to live here in the summer. He has sent me, Monsieur the Mayor, to invite you to dine with him tomorrow. He especially wants to meet you; and he has, I believe, some business to discuss with you. There will be almost no one there. We will be a small committee with the Marquis Scalyvt, the famous Ornal, and a German baron…"

"Monsieur," interruped the mayor who felt more than joy, "are these men also part of the government?…"

"Of course!…" cried Vernyct making a disdainful gesture, "these are all friends of the present minister, they are very influential…"

"Ah!…" said M. Gargarou, "I would like to double my position, if these men would take an interest in me. Monsieur, from here to A…y there are two mountains, and three between here and Septinan, you can see what injustice…"

"You should," interrupted Vernyct, "be very attached to the noble family which governs both us and the state, Monsieur the Mayor…"

"What, yes, I am attached…" cried Gargarou.

"Very well! Then you will understand that it is very important to foil all of the perverse plots which would harm the happiness of the friends of legitimacy."

"Legitimacy!…Ah! My wife is right there!…" cried the mayor slapping his forehead, "*legitimacy*. I must write that word down, I can never recall…the government of the legitimacy."

"Monsieur," Vernyct began again seriously, "I would warn you about a man named Joseph… (Madame Hamel shivered) as an enemy of the government, a seditious person, and it is very important to the minister to arrest him, for he holds the secret of a conspiracy...You understand me...he should come to this village. If you arrest him, you will become at least a sub-prefect!...Bring him secretly, immediately, to the castle and send us the..."

"Sub-prefect!..." cried the mayor. "Dear! Dear!..."

"Shut up you big beast!..." said his wife in a low voice!..."All that glitters is not gold."

"In addition," continued Vernyct, "I will leave a young man here who will be a great help to you; he is alert, strong, well afoot and sharp-eyed...so," he began again, "you will do us the honor of coming to dine with us tomorrow..."

"What? Certainly," said M. Gargarou leading the lieutenant out, his hat in his hand doffing it with every step.

"Very well! Dear, you see!..." cried the mayor who could not retain his joy, "my position will be doubled, I will be a sub-prefect...but," he said, "this Monsieur Joseph...that was the young man from the day before yesterday...Oh yes! he certainly looked like a traitor, a dark air...hey! He lives," he cried, drawing from his pocket the note that the vicar left, "he lives…" (he put on his glasses) "Rue de la San-té…" The mayor-postmaster-innkeeper withdrew to reflect on this important matter.

"O my God! my God, how everything is con-fused," said Madame Hamel to Madame Gargarou, my poor head cannot take it! Who told Monsieur Maxendi that Joseph was coming back, when I only just mailed my letter?…What can I do?…"

"My poor lady," responded the hostess, "I am sin-gularly interested in that handsome young man whom I saw yesterday, and it is impossible that he is a bad man…"

"Him a conspirator!…But those are lies…He is the son of a rear-admiral."

"Of a rear-admiral," cried the young woman… "Listen I do not think that Gargarou should be mixed up in this business! That character who was just here did not seem to be who he claimed to be. We always see great men when they travel and this one did not seem up to the mark. Listen, you must go to the next postal stop towards Paris. There you can wait for the young man who loves the young lady… and you warn him to disguise himself as a peasant. He can come here on foot and I will say that he is one of my cousins."

As she finished these words, an old woman came into the inn and came up to Madame Gargarou…"ah Madame, I have come to pay you what *we owe*…that young man who visited my hut really put butter on my bread."

"What young man?…" asked Madame Hamel.

"A big, brown, handsome man, the son of that young woman who…you know the story…" said the woman.

"Yes…" said the hostess, "so what?"

"So! He gave me a letter to bring to the Marquise de Rosann, on the other side of the forest…They took me into the prettiest castle! Into the rooms!… Lady!…He is a peer of France!…Once she had read the letter, she ran to her desk and got me a sack of twelve hundred francs…And she uttered many cries of joy!…She said that she would come here…"

"The Marquise de Rosann," cried the hostess… "Let's go, let's go, I will tell Gargarou that he should walk prudently in this affair…this young man…Go on mother," she said to Madame Hamel, "hurry to the next postal stop and watch for him…"

Poor Madame Hamel set out and despite the bad weather, arrived at Septinan distancing herself with regret from the place where Melanie was.

"Is your husband my brother's shepherd?" the hostess asked the old woman.

"Yes, madame, at your service!…"

"Very well, I need for him to show one of my cousins how to do it…and for him to keep everything that I say secret…" The old woman went, happily, to tell the entire village of the fortunate event which had rescued her from her misery. The hostess had a big quarrel with her husband on how he should behave towards M. Maxendi; but the mayor, swollen with ambition, forbad his wife from mingling in *government business*. The wife got angry with her husband and there resulted a big discussion which was marked by what is called in parliamentary language *an opposition*. Madame Gargarou decided to help Joseph's cause; and on the contrary the mayor chose M. Maxendi's cause.

The next day, the mayor dressed in his best and went towards the castle where the tender Melanie was pining away. A big footman, well-dressed, announced him in the living room by the title of M. the Mayor of Vans-la-Pavée.

Argow came before him and, in succession, they introduced the pirate's four friends. The mayor was astonished to find himself in the company of such noble characters, and they did not wait to seat themselves at the table. M. Gargarou did not get over his astonishment when he saw the luxuriousness of the table settings, silver, crystal, and fine wines which they changed frequently.

"Monsieur the Mayor," said Argow, "you had no doubts about the reason for which I begged you to pass by my castle…"

"No, Monsieur," responded the Mayor respectfully.

"It is for a marriage," the pirate continued casually. "Being in a way the lord of the village, I did not want to get married in Paris…By the way Monsieur Gargarou, they tell me that you want to see your position doubled?…"

"Ah! Monsieur," cried the mayor-postmaster-innkeeper, "that is a dignity which they have not given me for a long time, you who have traveled over this road, you know how hard it is for me, on both sides…"

"They will double it! Don't they need an ordinance, a law?"

"A law, I believe, Monsieur."

"Ah! A law, a little law," said Argow looking at his companions.

"We have the majority, we will pass this law…" said Vernyct, "it is a trifle."

"Monsieur the Marquis," added Argow speaking to Vernyct, "that is your affair since you are the friend of the minister of the interior."

"Monsieur the Mayor," he began again slapping the postmaster on the arm, "I would like for this marriage to take place promptly, and one of my friends should send me an missive from the minister of justice which will make it unnecessary for me to make a second publication of the fact. So, you can begin to prepare. First I will give you all the information, and, next week, we will dance here…"

"But your future wife?…" asked the mayor-postmaster-innkeeper.

"She is here," replied Argow, "but as she would have been the only woman with six men, you can imagine that a young lady, my cousin, of whom I am the protector..."

"Is it going to be the young woman whom you brought the other day?" asked the mayor-postmaster-innkeeper. "They say that she is crazy..."

"Crazy!" said Argow, "she is a little: that is to say, she likes a *barefoot* boy, a rascal, and she is marrying me with a little repugnance; but after she has been married a fortnight that fantasy will pass. I tell you that because we are good friends, and you will see that she is a little chagrined, perhaps..."

"But," replied M. Gargarou, "does she have her father and her mother...because..."

"They are both dead," said Vernyct. "Go on, Monsieur Gargarou, Monsieur the Count's nuptial present to you will be the doubling of your position..."

"Monsieur the Mayor," Argow took up, "as I am going to have a lawyer come for our marriage contract which you will sign, I hope!...He will edit your official act; for it is quite tricky, and then you will just have to sign..."

"I will just have to sign!" repeated the mayor slightly tipsy from the wine, "and I will have my position doubled, because you are in the government."

"The government of the state..." continued Ornal.

"And the legitimacy," said Vernyct.

"Yes," began the mayor again, "the legitimacy of the government, of the state, of the realm...I am attached to it and no one can say that I am not a good Frenchman and an honest man. Then my position should be doubled, you understand, Monsieur?"

Argow, seeing what kind of man he was dealing with, judged that he would have no opposition in the plans that he was hatching from that quarter. He poured him glassfuls so often, and his companions gave him such a good example, that M. Gargarou and the four sailors became completely drunk. Argow promised everything that the mayor asked for, in the name of the government and the surety of the throne; then he invited the mayor to come to dinner in three days, because then, the supposed lawyer would have arrived and edited the act of marriage, for which Argow would have to ask for the necessary pieces, and fabricate the most essential ones.

Poor Melanie spent these three days in a deathly sadness. Her windows looked out on the beginnings of the forest, and, the trees bare of leaves, the fields deserted, nature resumed its mourning clothes, forming a spectacle in harmony with the sombre thoughts which assailed her. The young lady grew paler each day and was desolate at not seeing Madame Hamel. Now she did only one thing which was to go to the window and contemplate the winter sadness, and to come back and sit in her chair thinking still of Joseph, no longer desiring his arrival in the place where M. Maxendi was all powerful for this ferocious abductor had sworn his death. She felt that if Joseph did not fall into Argow's power, the latter could not present her with the cruel choice of the death of her brother or her marriage.

While these things took place in Vans-la-Pavée, Madame Hamel had gone on foot to Septinan; and this poor woman, taken out of her normal character by these sad events, had an activity of body and spirit that was truly astonishing. She stayed on the road from Paris all day, and at night she lay awake listening for the slightest sound of a stopping carriage to see if Joseph were there. Impatience, uneasiness, kept her in quite an extraordinary state for her; her weak head was almost deranged, for she found herself in a sphere that was quite distant from her sphere of indolence and tranquility; but the unusual attachment that she had for Melanie and her brother sustained her.

Finally, at the end of the second day, a courier arrived hastily at the postal stop, and asked for four horses which would be paid double. They were in a hurry. Madame Hamel stayed at the door of the stable, her feet in the mud, her satin shoes almost worn out. After eight minutes she saw Joseph.

"My son!" she cried, "do not go any farther..."

"What! It's you mother, Melanie, Melanie!... Where is she? So that was she!"

"Get down and stay here...Finette hurry!..."

The vicar, pale, beaten, devoured by chagrin, squeezed Madame Hamel in his arms, and kissed her crying, "Melanie, where is she?"

"My son," said the old woman in a low voice, "let us leave here. Leave your coach and come secret-

ly…You are dealing with a tricky man, capable, powerful, and one cannot take enough precautions… come Finette…"

"Ah!" cried the vicar, "I am going to recruit an army, and either the men that I hire will abduct Melanie, by force if necessary, or I will die!"

"He is going to lose everything…" cried Madame Hamel, "my friend, listen to me. The first step that you take in this region, they will arrest you. If you are in prison, then how will you save Melanie? They can take her away if they know that you are here!"

"I will follow her," cried the vicar.

"No, my friend, you will have to disguise yourself as a peasant and Finette as a peasant woman. Finette has to pass for your wife…Then, in this disguise, and when you are safe from evil plots, you can find a way to rescue Melanie from her prison which is Maxen-di's castle."

"Argow, mother, it is the same person who raised the mutiny on our ship." Madame Hamel remained mute with fright. "My son, save her, Argow is capable of killing her."

The vicar, admiring the good sense of Madame

Hamel's advice, went to the Septinan post office and paid for the horses, asking them to keep his coach and to keep it ready to leave with good horses. Then he came back to the inn with Madame Hamel where he took off his fancy clothes, and combed his hair down over his forehead like peasants do, and put on the costume which the careful mother had already bought in advance. Finette borrowed the old clothes of one of the inn girls, and Madame Hamel also put on a country costume. All three of them walked together towards Vans-la-Pavée. Along the way Madame Hamel told the vicar about what had happened.

Fortunately for them the postmaster at Vans, M. Gargarou, was not in the main room of the inn when Joseph presented himself, for in seeing this young cousin of his wife alongside Madame Hamel, he would not have failed to have grave suspicions, since she had avowed to him that she knew M. Joseph.

"You cannot stay here, cousin," said the pretty hostess carefully, examining the young vicar with her eyes. "You would be in too much danger; for M. Maxendi has made my husband such a fanatic that all he thinks of is arresting you. If you want to succeed in your undertaking, go to the hut that you visited four days ago; and you will find two nice people who are devoted to you…You will take a shepherd's cloak, and you will wander about the castle…You are in love aren't you?…Well you must address the rest of your questions to the god of love…"

The vicar left Finette and ran with an astonishing rapidity towards the dear hut. The husband and wife were warming themselves by the fire when their door flew open with a bang. They turned around, and Marie's sister recognized her visitor.

"My friends," he said, "you must hide me…The woman at the inn warned you…If she did not, think about keeping silent about me; and I will pay you for your discretion!…I am for all the world a poor peasant, and we are going to lead flocks together…Let's go my friend, let's take our cloaks and go…"

"Just a moment my dear sir, the sheep do not go out now, they are at the farm."

"Then let's go find them…for I am dying with impatience…" and the vicar, wearing a humble shepherd's cloak, went out hastily and stood in the doorway looking at the castle which contained his dearly beloved…

A short while later, Melanie was at the window. She was contemplating the fields with a tear-filled eye…without being able to tell, through the cloud of her thoughts, whether she did or did not want Joseph to come. She saw a herd of sheep, directed by two men, advance towards the moat around the castle.

"Are they happy?" she asked herself, "they are free, but as for me, I am imprisoned!…"

The herd approched closer and closer for the dogs, spurred on by their master's voice, were nipping at the sheep to make them go faster. This strange behavior struck Melanie. She opened her window, and setting her arms on the cold stone, rested on her elbows trying to guess the motive behind the shepherd's conduct. She took an interest in the sheep. "Alas!" she said, "the man is a despot. Always absolute when he commands, he does not put any kindness in his actions!…And those poor beasts cannot come fast enough!…"

One of the shepherds sat on a stone and the other

imitated him. Melanie experienced a sense of joy in seeing the sheep at peace, and the dogs resting at their masters' feet. Suddenly she noticed one of the shepherds come forward and advance in the field. She shivered involuntarily thinking that she recognized Joseph's shape. She rubbed her eyes fearing an illusion. Her heart beat with an extraordinary violence. She was barely breathing…At this moment Joseph sang in his pure and light voice: "Like a last ray, like a last gust, animates the end of a lovely day."

He revealed who he was…Melanie did not see anything else, happiness cast a veil over her eyes, she felt ill…She succumbed under a feeling of pleasure…She awoke from this spell to hear Joseph's gentle tones. The air brought his words with an admirable purity. Ah! Nothing can depict the charm of such a moment…Let those who have loved imagine it!…After almost two years to see each other again!…And to see each other separated by a cruel distance, to see each other in the middle of winter, to recognize each other by this gentle song, whose first modulations made their hearts agree. What poetry at

this tender moment!…How they now exist together!…Melanie, the imprudent Melanie waved her
handkerchief, to tell her brother that she had heard
his voice. The vicar put all of himself into this gentle
contemplation, happily forgetting the place and the
circumstances, and waved his…

"Let us go, Monsieur," said the shepherd, "here
comes a man on the run!…Come this way if you will
trust me!…"

This man was the sailor charged with surveilling
the part of the fields that Melanie's windows looked
out on. He came to walk around the two shepherds,
and seeing Joseph's hands he said, "It seems my
friend," he said, "that you have very white hands for a
man of the fields?"

"What is that to you?" asked the shepherd.

"I was not speaking to you."

"But I, I am speaking to you," said the shepherd.

"Your friend," continued the sailor after having
sized up the two shepherds: "you who have on a cambric shirt to guard a flock, could you tell me what
sheep are doing in a place where there is not a blade
of grass?…"

"Once again, what is that to you?" cried the shepherd.

"What is that to me? You are going to see!..." And the brigand blew three whistles.

"You are on my land, and you do not have the right to bring your sheep here," he cried.

"Ah! So I don't know my business!..." responded the shepherd.

As he finished these words three big footmen came on the run and the sailor called to them to grab Joseph. A fight started, and at first the dogs gave the shepherd the advantage; then the vicar seized the moment in which he had succeeded in throwing off the two men who had attacked him, and he took to flight running towards the forest with the speed of an arrow. The footmen, abandoning the shepherd, began pursuing Joseph; but the shepherd sent his dogs after the brigands who were stopped in their tracks and forced to defend themselves from bites. Meanwhile, Joseph, having been raised in forests and mountains, was much too agile for any of the men chasing him to be able to approach him. Melanie, whom the fight had left trembling more than the few leaves that were still on the trees, watched with joy as her brother disappeared into the forest...

Right away Argow was told about the presence of his rival, he doubled the guards around the castle, and sent men out into the field overjoyed that Joseph had come to present himself to his clutches.

CHAPTER 26

Night came quickly, and the vicar was still running with the same speed through the immense forest that he had entered. After two hours he began to feel tired and in want. Then he walked slower, tenaciously directing himself in a straight line to arrive at the other side of the forest.

Entering into a road that was more frequented than the ones that he had just crossed, and whose deep grooves indicated the passage of carriages, he heard the movement of a cart in the distance, the slap of a whip, and the whistle of a driver. He ran towards the place where this sound came from to find out what part of the forest fate had led him to.

"My good man," he said to a peasant who was of an enormous size, "can you tell me where I am?"

"A half league from Aulnay," responded the big cart driver.

"But," began the vicar again, "your voice is familiar…Aren't you Jacques Cachel, the wood and coal man who lives on the heights?"

"Ah! It's Monsieur Joseph!" cried Cachel. "Ah! Monsieur the Vicar, I cannot tell you how grateful I am for the help that you gave me. You can have all of me, body and soul... You are the cause of my little fortune, for I furnish the wood and coal to the castle at Vans, and I would have lost the business if I had been sent to prison. The monseigneur obtained a grace for me; and your goodness, along with those of Madame the Marquise have put me one a peak... Body, soul, and goods, I am yours, Monsieur Joseph... But what are you doing at this hour in this forest? While for eight days all of Aulnay is beside itself! Everyone is weeping for you!... Monsieur the Marquis has left for Paris to go find you... They say that you are a great lord. Monsieur Leseq, Monsieur Gausse, Mademoiselle Marguerite, keep talking about you and your story. My wife told me everything... my poor wife, ah! How your return is going to surprise her!... The monseigneur came to look for you too, and there are some who say that the bishop's brother died the night of his return, through the machinations of hell!"

"Monsieur de Saint-André is dead!" cried Joseph,

who had not said a word until then, for a good reason. In truth, as soon as the woodsman had spoken about the access that he had to Argow's castle, the vicar was lost in thoughts which he was only drawn out of by the news of M. de Saint-André's death.

"Jacques," he continued, "can I count on your devotion and your discretion, which the volubility of your tongue does not give me a good impression of?"

"Monsieur," responded Jacques Cachel, "you can count on me, like you do on yourself...I will prove my discretion to you and my devotion at the same time and place..."

"Let's go quickly to your hut, because I am hungry, and I am tired..."

Cachel lashed his horses with his whip, and in a quarter of an hour they noticed the light which shone out of the skylight of the almost deserted hut.

"Come on, wifey, open up? It's me!...Go in, Monsieur, I am going to put my horses in the stable which, thanks to Madame the Marquise we have been able to build..."

"Shh!" cried the vicar stopping the astonished exclamation that Cachel's wife was going to utter, "shh, good mother! And wait for your husband. I have something to say to the both of you."

The woodsman came back in, the vicar sat between the husband and his wife: they drew near the fire that Cachel stirred up again; and when M. Joseph was assured that the children were asleep he spoke in these terms: "My dear friends, above all keep in mind that you must solemly promise me not to open your mouths about my presence in these parts, that is the main point. Now, Cachel, I promise you two thousand francs if we can succeed in rescuing from the castle the young lady that Monsieur Maxendi is holding there. For that we will need courage, skill, discretion, haste and limitless devotion. The first thing to do will be for you Cachel to go to the castle everyday to find out what is going on there and to keep me informed."

"No problem, Monsieur," Cachel interrupted, "tomorrow I am bringing coal there, and the day after tomorrow six cartloads of wood...I know the concierge and the head cook."

"Good, good, Cachel!" cried the vicar transported with delight, "we are going to dream up a way of getting me in, for I have to see Melanie...Tomorrow, at sunrise, you will go buy a horse that is known to be a good runner and keep him ready for any developments."

"There is Monsieur de Rosann's horse, if we could borrow it from Marie."

"Do you know," asked the vicar, "the internal layout of the castle?"

"Monsieur," responded the woodsman, "there are two wings and a facade: the great stairway is at the junction of the left wing where the principal living quarters of the castle are located. The stairway leads to a vast gallery and the rooms of the west wing where the young lady is. As for the great rooms, they are on the ground floor by the great facade..."

"So," said the vicar, "to get to Melanie's I must go through the courtyard, into the vestibule where the great stairway begins, and...her room looks out on the country...very well! Cachel, tell me now, where is the kitchen that you surely bring your coal to."

"The kitchen, Monsieur, is right on the ground floor of the west wing, and the door is not far from the steps."

"Cachel," cried the vicar, "tomorrow I will place myself in one of your coal sacks, and I will risk myself in that labyrinth…Do not go until nightfall…O happiness! I will see Melanie!"

The vicar ate a frugal meal which his hunger made succulent, and he lay down under his coat, advising once again the husband and his wife to be discrete. Despite his tiredness, the vicar could not sleep; and all night Melanie was the subject of his thoughts. M. de Saint-André's death gave him the hope of having Melanie for he already was discussing inside himself just how criminal it would be for him to marry the woman whom he had thought to be *his sister*…or rather, carried away by the danger that Melanie was in, carried away by the violence of his passion, he put off to another time the examination of the serious questions which his desire to marry Melanie gave rise to. He only foresaw one thing, his sister's happiness, her joy, and his well shared love…

The next morning, Cachel's wife started sewing a sack that would be big enough to hold and hide the vicar, and when everything was prepared, Joseph set out along with the woodsman, taking care not to arrive at Vans castle until five or six o'clock at night. When they were about to leave the forest Joseph climbed back on the cart and slipped into the black sack that was destined for him; and the woodsman, whistling and slapping his whip, drove straight towards the castle. When he was at the door of the last gate, the sailor in charge of guarding this area came forward and said: "Who is it?" because it was rather dark.

"It's me," cried Cachel, "I could not come earlier because the rain had ruined the road."

"Very good! You are going to be well received by the cook, Master Jacques Cachel. There is a big dinner and he has been cursing you for an hour. He just sent an extra chef to see if you were here."

"Then don't stop me..."

"Ah, that is true! You are part of the house! Go on! But you see, the plans are confused: yesterday there was an engagement with the enemy, and they are chasing him. They have doubled the watch. It is not a little thing to guard a lady when she has a lover who wanders about... Go on."

Jacques followed the avenue, past the courtyard, crying stop and swearing about the roads. He led his carriage all the way up until he was opposite the kitchen door.

"Will you come now!..." cried the angry chef, "by my cotton hat! You will lose the business Monsieur Cachel!" And the chef made a sign to one of his boys, the cooks assistants who set to work climbing on the cart and tossing down sacks.

"Hey! Hey! Cook's helper!" cried the frightened woodsman, casting the young man down and seizing him by the collar; "I do not touch your food, do not break my coal." Cachel promptly took up a sack and carried it into the middle of the kitchen.

"By heavens Monsieur Lesnagil, you have no idea what the roads were like...My horses almost died in the mud..."

Cachel returned to his carriage and arranged several sacks along the wall placing Joseph next to the stairs: "come out," he said to him. "I am going to amuse the cook for a good half hour."

Joseph climbed out of his sack and threw himself

into the antechamber. He heard the noisy voices of the guests, for it was precisely the day when the mayor came for a second time to dine with M. Maxendi. The vicar shivered involuntarily. He climbed up the stairs quickly and arrived in that dark gallery where he assumed Melanie's room was located. He wandered down the hall and he saw, from afar, a thread of light escaping onto the tiles through the gap that there always is between the door and the floor...He risked opening the door...He went in...

Melanie was sitting on a chair reading her letter. She raised her head, looked into the shadow. She uttered a cry and fell down as if dead when she recognized the vicar's face...The latter covered her with the gentlest of kisses which made her come back to life. The kisses were the expression of a voluptuousness that Melanie still did not know. She raised her drooping eyelids and cried, "At last, it is you!"

"*Melanie*...I only have a moment, a quarter of an hour, and I am running the greatest of risks. Try to be sure that we do not get surprised."

"You take away all of my ideas, by your presence...I am crazy...What to do?" Her pretty face, shining with all the joy of love, took on the distinctive character of a face that is thinking: her pretty forehead wrinkled; then smiling at her brother like Venus looking at Mars, she cast him an intoxicating look saying to him: "I have found...since it has to do with your safety."

Then she went to the table where there was the remains of her dinner, and the fragile remnants of some nuts, she went quickly out and ran to spread them out in the gallery; then running with the lightness of a zephyr, she closed the door, locked it, and said, "Joseph, we are alone, now..." and she ran to sit on her brother's knees.

"Melanie!..." he said with an almost trembling convulsion, "how much do you love me?..."

"Joseph!...Like in the past, and your face has come to rekindle the fire, for the ashes which covered it, have flown everywhere..." and she leaned her lovely head on the vicar's shoulder.

"Always the same smile!..." he cried.

"Always!" she responded with melancholy and that melodious tone which ravishes the soul and inspires a feeling of pain in it, nevertheless without causing harm, "Cruel man, how you left me! I hope that you rescue me and that we are never apart again!..."

"Yes!" cried Joseph with energy.

He did not know how to tell Melanie about the mystery of his birth. This piece of news should only be announced with great care.

"How I love that promise!...It just," Melanie continued, "it just rang in my soul with an astonishing power...Yes, my brother, we will live together! Come on, we will suffer less from battle than from separation. Let me kiss you...For two years I have not savored the nectar of a kiss..."

The vicar kissed his lover in a voluptuous way.

"Joseph!" she said, "what do you mean by that?"

"I want, *Melanie,* to tell you without my lips forming the words...ah!...I fear your joy."

"What do you want to say?..." And she looked at Joseph's face, with an uneasiness that was not at all pained. "My brother!..."

"Melanie!...." responded the vicar emphasizing the word.

"My brother, why don't you give me the gentle name of sister since you came you have not pronounced it...Ah, what is that to me," she cried as if delirious. "Don't I see you?...Am I not your gentle friend?...Ah, I will not try to compromise the spirit of my joy with mysterious words. Very well, yes! I still love you with ardor! If that is what your interrogating eyes are asking...Yes I love you with an unvanquished, invincible furor...Which will control me until the tomb...But let us forget all of that? Let us keep this instant pure and brilliant, so that in the midst of our affliction we find a flower...You are not saying anything, my brother...And your eyes are devouring me...Ah! yes, they have said enough...Lower your eyelids with their long lashes, I want to cover them with kisses!..."

"*Melanie,* you see me..." said the vicar slowly adding a thoughtful and deep tone to the sentence...

"But my love, what do you mean to say?"

"*Melanie,* when I left you I swore not to come back until we could love each other *without crime.*"

"Without crime!...What a thought! Joseph!

Brother."

"Do not call me your brother…"

"Aren't you!…" she said in a languishing voice, and all the color went out of her cheeks, she grew pale. She hid her head on the vicar's chest. She lost her feeling of happiness. Joseph's tears, those tears running with love flowed down onto the pretty face that was almost dead.

"That is what I feared!" he cried, and lifting Melanie up, he tried to warm her with the most ardent and numerous kisses.

"Melanie! Come back," and he tried to raise her again.

"My friend," she said barely opening her lovely blue eyes, "I am dying…I will die! Ah many kisses…For two years I…Joseph!…You mean to say that we are not…and ring for Finette!…"

"Melanie, you are in Argow's power."

"Argow!…" she cried standing up with great haste caused by her indignation, "that pirate who took away our father?…"

"Melanie," the vicar continued seating her on his knees, "do not shout so loudly!…Listen to me? M. de

Saint-André is dead…He was not my father, and your mother was not my mother…*Your love is innocent!…*"

"Innocent!…My brother, yes, *my brother,* because I still want to give you that gentle name!…Innocent!…Oh let me kiss you like that day when you rebuffed me!…So what!" she cried, "Joseph, you are sad, what is it?…" she said passing her hand through the priest's hair, with a divine ravishment.

"Melanie," he said with chagrin, to change the subject from the cause of her sadness, "how can I smile when I see you in this castle, without having found a way of getting you out?…"

"That is true," she said. "It is sad! But love's flame is not in vain, and…I will light…" She cast him one of the most gracious smiles…

At these words, the rapid footsteps of a man caused the sound of nutshells being stepped on to resound in the gallery.

"It's Argow!…" cried Melanie, "we are lost!…Where can I hide you?…"

The vicar was overcome by a stupor.

"Let's kill him!…" he cried…

"No, no, hide yourself in my bed!..."

"Mademoiselle, open up!..." said Argow in a thundering voice...

The vicar hid himself between the two mattresses: Melanie reestablished the disorder of the bed, and got ready to go open the door.

To become acquainted with this new development one must transport oneself back to the time just before the pirate's arrival in the dining room whose door opens out onto the vestibule where the stairs begin. When the vicar went hastily up, the guests, in the middle of their meal, were trying to ply M. Gargarou with wine.

"Let's go, Monsieur the Mayor," said Argow, "yesterday you made the first publication of the bans, in four days you will marry us...Let us drink to that celebration!..."

"You will end up making me see my position *doubled*," said Gargarou, laughing with a fat, frank laugh which is the sign of countryfolk.

"You see? Here is a lawyer who will save you the trouble of writing up the contract...He will compose the marriage contract; ah, he is clever!"

"Is he part of the government?..." asked the mayor looking at him.

"Of course."

"I must admit Monsieur the Count that you are a famous bon vivant, and those around you are not given to melancholy...I am astonished that with your money you are looking for a problem like mine."

"What do you mean to say," asked Argow staring at the mayor.

"Ah yes!..." responded Gargarou, "marriage, isn't...it..."

"Ah!" interrupted the pirate, "love is a terrible thing..."

"Yes," said the mayor, "especially for women, because when mine..."

"She is pretty," said Vernyct.

"Too pretty!..." responded the mayor with melancholy, "for my reply to you...No I will not reply..."

All the guests began laughing, and praising M. Gargarou's spirit, telling him that he would eclipse many people in Paris and that he was not made out to be just a postmaster.

"Oh yes," he said, "I should furrow around in the government!..."

"Go on," responded Argow, "you understand politics..."

"Ah, that, Monsieur the Count," the mayor continued slapping Argow on the belly, "do not interrupt the flow of my ideas... We are alone, you say that love is burning you up; this young lady must be quite pretty!..."

"Divine!..." cried the pirate.

"Divine!... Would it be possible to see her?..."

"No," said Argow.

"It is not," said Vernyct, "that Monsieur the Count would not like to, it is that he cannot," added the lieutenant, who could not have asked for more than his Captain and Melanie getting in a fight and the marriage failing to come off.

"I cannot, double rascal!"

"Ah! It is going bad!..." said the mayor, "curses are prohibited!..."

"If I wanted her to!... At this very instant she would come down!... But you are drunk..."

"No," they cried together, "that is a poor excuse..."

"My friend," said the mayor, "if she does not come, we will think that she leads you by the nose!... And that is a bad sign...from the nose in front!..."

"Silence, Monsieur Gargarou!...I will cut the throat of anyone who speaks ill of my fiancée..."

"It's going bad!..." said the mayor in a low voice...."ah well, bring her, that youngster!...We will not eat you alive!..."

Argow, afraid that the mayor would get angry and seeing that he needed him, besides being urged on by the jokes that his accomplices were assailing him with at the moment, stood up and said to them:

"I am going to get her, but death of God! if someone tries a trick and is not respectful, then he will have to deal with me!"

"Ah!" said the mayor, "we are all in the legitimate government so there is nothing to fear."

So Argow left and went up to find Melanie.

"My queen," he said to her, "what is wrong with you? You are trembling!..."

"It is the wind which blows, the cold, and solitude."

"In that case come my little wife… Come…preside over the end of our party!…"

"No!…I want to be alone…" she cried with a terrible energy.

"What is this strange wish?"

"Address me as lady!…I am a woman!…"

"Yes, but I, I am a man!…"

"What does that mean? In France I do not have to obey…"

"I am from America," said Argow lowering his brow, "my beautiful friend. Can you tell me by what chance your dress is black like coal?…"

"The wind blew cinders on me…"

"Young lady, you are a flower," said the pirate casting her a lightning glance. "Be careful not to raise the storm that breaks the oaks!…" And he began looking around the room with a frenetic curiosity.

"What do you want from me?…" Melanie continued with a gentle tone of voice which covered the horrible fear that ran through her. Seeing Argow contemplating her bed with a terrible attention, she ran to him, took him by the shoulder, forced him to look at her, and cast him an enchanting look:

"So what do you want from me?…"

"For you to go down!…Into the dining room!…"

"I will go down, Monsieur Maxendi," she responded with an air of submission which disarmed the pirate. He approached her and seized her…

"Monsieur!" she cried, "I am not yet your wife!…" And a mortal fear chilled her, as she saw the bed move, which meant that Joseph could not contain his indignation, probably imagining things that did not exist.

"Let's go! Follow me?…My angel," said the ferocious pirate to her.

"Oh! Monsieur!…No!" she responded with a gesture filled with grace and expression, "I am not dressed, and I am covered with ashes, at least I have to put on a dress…in ten minutes…That way at least in obeying *your orders* I will be in control of my appearance which has never been denied any woman."

"Very well! I will wait for you," said the suspicious

criminal, sitting down.

"Can I get dressed in front of you!...Go away, I will join you."

"Little siren!..." the corsair cried opening the door, "I trust your word, and I will announce your arrival..."

"Yes," she said with a gracious smile, "be my aurora!..."

She listened to the sound of the pirate's footsteps, and when she could not hear them any longer, she took a chance and stepped out into the gallery, and went all the way to the stairs...She heard Argow's voice mixed with those of the other guests, then she ran with the lightness of a hind back into her room. The vicar was already out of hiding...

"Melanie, I was overcome with rage!..."

"And I with fright!...Go on, my friend, how can you get out of this hell?"

"Before leaving, Melanie, let us agree on part of your deliverance which I just thought of...Whenever one o'clock of the day or night, no matter which, sounds, be in your room hiding in a corner of your bed. When we give a rifle shot, if the ball goes into your room, it will tell you that a moment later something important to you will happen; be it a rock shot by a sling and which will be wrapped in a letter, be it an arrow that brings you a note. Count on it tomorrow, my beloved, keep on your guard!...And we will not wound you!...Goodbye, receive my parting kiss..."

"Joseph!...We will see each other again!..."

"What, Melanie, you doubt me!...But before three days are up I want us to be on the road to Paris!..."

"Let's go, I believe you since you say it...Goodbye." And throwing themselves into each other's arms, they shared a last kiss in which all of the fires of love resided.

"Oh," said Melanie, "Joseph, how gentle!...Let's go. We'll leave!..."

She went first into the gallery and Joseph followed her from afar, ready to run back to hide in Melanie's room at the first sound. They arrived at the stairs, they went down into the vestibule, and as the

vicar slipped into the courtyard to regain his place in
the coal sack...Argow opened the door to the dining
room...

"What, Mademoiselle, you said that you were going to get dressed..."

"Aren't I..." she responded growing pale. Argow
looked out into the courtyard.

"Who's cart is that?" he asked...

"Monsieur," said Jacques Cachel, "you were out of
coal, and I could not come any earlier...Monsieur
Lesnagil, you don't want the rest."

"Go on," said Argow, "get these sacks off of the
steps...and on a day that I have company!..."

Cachel felt the sacks to know if Joseph had returned, and seeing that he was indeed filling his sack,
he cast two or three in front of Argow: the sacks
thudded in front of Argow, then he took the sack
with the vicar, and set it down gently just as the pirate, turning towards Melanie, said to her:

"Well that dress!..."

"How could you expect me to change, I did not
have anybody to help."

"And you knew it when you sent me away you little trickster …"

At that moment, Jacques Cachel, looking at Melanie, said: "You have nothing more to fear!…"

"Who are you talking to?…"

"You have nothing more to fear, Monsieur Lesnagil," continued the woodsman without responding to Argow, "for you have enough coal to last at least a fortnight; until tomorrow!…"

Cachel drove off with a crack of his whip making his horses gallop.

"Enter, Mademoiselle," said Monsieur Maxendi, and taking Melanie's hand, he opened the door crying out: "Here is Mme. Maxendi!…"

A murmur of astonishment began at the sight of the lovely Melanie whom the presence of her lover and the danger that he had just faced had decorated with the most ravishing colors…

"Mme. Maxendi!.." she said with energy, "never Messieurs! A marriage needs consentment, and, even with a sword over my head, I would not say 'yes.'"

"Bravo!" said Vernyct, "that is energy…very good,

Monsieur the Count."

"Monsieur the Count," cried Melanie, "the one who is taking the name of Maxendi is none other than a pirate named Argow."

"You lie!...serpent!" cried the angry Argow. "Shut up, young lady if you do not want..." He looked at her with such flashing eyes that Melanie became silent in an instant.

"You have seen someone, Mademoiselle?..." he said calming down.

"I do not hide a thing, I just saw a moment ago the man that I love, and within two days I will be rescued from this place!..."

"Devil, how this is problematic," cried M. Gargarou, "you did not tell me about this, Monsieur the Count."

"Shut up you imbecile!..." the criminal replied to him.

"Bravo!" said Vernyct, "he will not get married."

"Young lady," said Argow, in a low voice, "you have roused a storm, and you will die for it."

"I vow," she said with a naive smile, "that I was dying of sorrow, at the moment when I just learned that

I can marry Joseph since he is not my brother!…"

"But where did you see him?…" asked the astonished Argow.

"A moment ago," she said.

"Where was he?"

"In front of you."

Argow let out a terrible curse, and cast terrible looks around the assembled crowd.

"You lover is here!…" he began again with a somber air that spoke of death, "you will marry me!…"

"Never," she cried, "and if anyone here has any power, any authority, then I implore him to take me out of here, to use his power; for I have been carried off by force, and that is a crime!…"

The energy that Melanie used was sublime, and Argow, fearing that despite his intoxication the mayor would have grave suspicions, had a footman come and bring Melanie forcefully back to her room.

CHAPTER 27

The furious Argow ordered them to make the most vigorous search, which proved to him that no one could have gotten into the castle without being seen; nevertheless it was impossible to doubt that Melanie had seen Joseph again, since she had learned the details of his pirate nature, which he had taken great care to conceal. He fell into a strange perplexity, but he was not a man to remain down for long. The obscurity which surrounded this sudden adventure, the energy displayed by Melanie, the suspicions that the words of the young lady might excite in M. Gargarou's spirit, everything led the pirate to decide to strike with a big blow. He thought about it all night long, and even the next morning, he resolved to put his plan into action, to outdo the undertakings and presence of the dangerous enemy that he had in the person of Melanie's lover.

This plan was to leave right away for the village of Durantal, situated amid the mountains of Dauphiné, a charming secluded spot, where he owned a castle and a considerable estate which he had not yet visited. He ordered everything to be made ready for his departure; he asked M. Gargarou for horses, and invited him to lunch so as to know what effect the previous night's scene had had upon him. In case he was suspicious, the pirate had to decide how he would allay the mayor's suspicions.

These preparations took place as secretly as possible so that no one would suspect M. Argow's plan. Still, as they did not distrust Jacques Cachel and since Cachel had spent the whole night on the edge of the forest, he knew right that morning that the pirate was going to be taking a big trip, for the kitchen master paid him for the coal and refused his wood saying that they were going to the Dauphiné.

Hearing this news, Jacques unhitched one of his horses and rode recklessly to the hut; and mounting the vicar on another horse, he told him as they came back towards the castle about the sailor's new plans. Joseph hugged Cachel for his devotion, and he began to think about what he should do at such a juncture. But we know that love did not always hold its lit torch for him, for it is blind. It holds it to enlighten lovers, so the vicar had quickly formed his defensive plan.

"Cachel," he said to him, "do you know many woodsmen in the forest; and could you gather a group of them in a short time?"

"In an hour, I will have ten or twelve; what must we do?..."

"We must, my friend, post them at the edge of the forest and arm them to the teeth. In addition we must block the road with your cart, and I will come and rejoin you shortly to give you your last instructions!...Melanie is ours..."

Cachel hastened through the forest, and Joseph went to the village at Vans. In approaching M. Gargarou's inn he hid his face, and began looking about carefully to see who was in the main room. As he watched, the postmaster and Vernyct came out; frightened, the vicar hastily escaped at a rapid clip towards Septinan. When he was at a distance, he turned around and saw Gargarou and the lieutenant go off towards the castle. He came slowly back to the inn of the Big Green Integer. He entered boldly after having hitched his horse to one of the iron rings which were on the wall; the hostess was alone. As soon as she saw Joseph, she made him a sign to proceed with caution. She lead him to an upper room, where Madame Hamel and Finette were staying.

"Madame," said the vicar, "Melanie will be mine, if only you will help me..."

"What do we need to do?..."

"Didn't Maxendi order horses?..."

"Do you have a driver whose devotion we can count on?"

"Yes, a handsome man, who does everything that I ask!"

"Very well, Madame, if the thought of saving the unfortunate lady from the hands of a ruthless pirate touches you, and the reunion of two beings who adore each other moves you, then it is in your hands: send this driver to Maxendi, and have him bring poor horses; here have a hundred francs!"...(And the vicar cast a roll of Napoleons on the table) "Here are two thousand francs for him, if he will consent to follow my orders."

"What are they?" asked Finette, Madame Hamel, and the mayor's wife all at once.

"They have to do with," continued the vicar, "having his horses chomping at the bit when he leaves the castle driving Monsieur Maxendi through the forest; and there, not being afraid of anything that happens when he finds himself stopped by two carriages."

"If that is all it is, then my young driver will serve you marvelously, and just out of affection for me!..."

"That is not all," began the vicar again. "I need you Madame Hamel, and you Finette, to go and wait for me in Septinan, for you to have a carriage and horses ready and have them hitched up all the time!... You will wait for us...go, run!..."

"For that I will need a little letter for our compatriot," said the lovely hostess, "and I will write to him, right away. Catherine, ink!..."

"This is not a whim, Madame, but tell me, I beg you, would you know in the village a good archer; for you surely have a corps of them here as they do at Aulnay-le-Vicomte."

"Certainly, and the most skillful, the cock around here, is your shepherd..." responded Madame Gargarou.

"Now," began Joseph again, "I only need a rifle

loaded with shot, and some paper and ink."

In a moment the vicar had all that he asked for. He wrote to Melanie telling her to follow Argow, putting on great despair, and to be very frightened when the horses take the bits into their mouths so that nothing seems contrived, and not to awaken the clever pirate's suspicions; but at the entrance to the forest twelve waiting men will capture the criminal and rescue her.

Having explained everything, he went out of the inn leaving Madame Hamel astonished, for she did not understand any of it, leaving Finette and the innkeeper's wife who understood everything, he ran to the shepherd in the house in which he had been born and whose cloak he still wore, so that he could take care of the rest, and warn Melanie.

While the vicar took all of these steps with an activity which made the moments seem too short, Argow, having left his belongings to Vernyct, having ordered, and arranged everything, finished lunch with M. Gargarou to whom he proposed going on a trip which he had intended to take with his fiancée.

"Has she become less mutinous than yesterday?

For she accused you of things that are contrary to the spirit of the legitimate government…"

"The folly is over!…" responded the sailor, staring at the mayor with a look that tried to guess what he was thinking. "The night brought wisdom, you will see…"

Right away Argow, leaving the mayor under Vernyct's guard to whom he gave a meaningful look, went towards Melanie's room, who, despite the cold, had her windows constantly open, since Joseph had warned her of the danger signal which he could send. Also, she took care to stay in a corner everytime the hour on the great castle clock struck. These little cares, the wait, and the hope, had made her less somber and less thoughtful; she sang and dressed carefully. In sum, her room, which had seemed sad to her, had become a palace since Joseph had brought her hope.

She spent the night amid the most delicious reveries. "Since he is not my brother," she said to herself, "we can marry…We will enjoy an untroubled, cloudless happiness." And with that she devoured the future, constructing a thousand projects, dreaming of a thousand luxuries, naming Joseph without blushing, and stopping her thoughts at the wedding night's pleasures, with a rare complacency.

For her, this night was almost happiness itself; for to the dawn of pleasure, hope is like the dawn of day, beautiful, splendid, fresh, elegant, gracious; and I do not know if the pleasure in reality is more voluptuous than the pleasure hoped for by thought!...I leave this problem to be decided by those wiser than myself!

When the soul is so disposed, a young lady who is candid and naive like Melanie smiles at all that approaches her: also, when the ferocious pirate entered, she left the window and ran towards him with the innocence of one who offers food to a serpent. All her traits excluded happiness...

"Mademoiselle," said Argow, "you must follow me right now; and consider that if you utter one word that is disfavorable to me, if you do not appear as you should be with the one whom you are going to marry...I will break you like a glass."

"Certainly, M. Maxendi, you will not kill me; for life, since yesterday has become too precious to me...but with all the desire that I have to please you today, I cannot go with you until eleven o'clock has struck…"

"What is this new whim, my queen," said the criminal looked at her carefully, "does it hide some trap like your desire to dress last night?…"

"How could it conceal a trap!…I believe," she responded tilting her head in a seductive manner, "are we not all *traps,* us women?…:"

"Yes, but we are all power, us men, and I want you to follow me right away."

"You are wrong, my dear Monsieur Maxendi, you do not want it!…You believe that you want it…." began Melanie again, trying to gain time. "I am convinced that in two seconds you will not want it any more…"

"How is that? Satan's little daughter!…"

"If I promised you to kiss you, here when eleven o'clock has struck!…And to follow you afterwards, wherever you wish…"

"Kiss me!…Follow me!…" cried the pirate stupefied by this expression of malicious coquetterie which was contained in her pose, her face, and in Melanie's eyes. "In truth, I want nothing more!…Women are all strange!…"

"Let's go," she said smiling lightly. "The bargain pleases you…"

"What time is it?" cried Argow drawing out his watch. It was just ten seconds before the needle arrived at the sixteenth minute. "We are going away!…" he said looking at Melanie with an ironic air.

"I will not contradict myself!…" responded this charming lady.

"I accept," cried the sailor and he threw himself at Melanie to seize her in his arms and kiss her.

"It is not eleven o'clock!…" she cried energetically defending herself. Argow had taken her, and held her in his arms; she turned her mouth away with repugnance, and this combat took place before the window…Eleven o'clock sounded! Hearing the sound of the brass, Melanie wanted to withdraw from the fatal window. A rifle shot was fired, the bullet took off one of the curls of hair which played against the young lady's temples, scraped the pirate's ear, and lodged itself in the door…

"A thousand cannons! Death and fury! Satan incarnate, I will pay you for that!...I see your brother, and in a little while I am going to have him under good locks. What a shot!...Let's go, *to battle stations! To your posts!...*"

In shouting like this the sailor ran into the gallery and flew to capture Joseph himself. Melanie, alone, did not have time to throw herself back, to fall on her knees and thank God that the pirate had changed his mind, thinking that they wanted his life; and as she got up an arrow whistled, and joined the bullet in the door of the room. The young lady leaped upon it with the avidity of love. She seized the note, tossed the arrow into the moat, and after having read the note she swallowed it and looked to see what was happening in the field. Trembling like a pursued warbler, she saw her brother and the shepherd flee on their horses with the speed of a cloud chased by the north wind. The pirate remained confused with his men, for they were all on foot. Argow, furious, swore at them, and seemed to give them orders to capture Joseph, if he came back; but, soon he would leave them, and come back to the castle. With fright she heard him advancing down the gallery, and he appeared before her in an unparalleled rage.

"Let's go, African snake, will you follow me?..." he said staring at her with an absolute gaze.

Melanie, frightened, followed the criminal who lead her into the dining room where the honest Gargarou was having great trouble reasoning with Vernyct about all the toasts that the latter drunk to him.

"Ah! Ah!" he cried seeing Melanie, "there is the future wife of Monsieur Maxendi. So she is more reasonable this morning! Let's go, my administrator, what day will you marry them?...I am all set..."

"Yes, but now I am not," replied Argow angrily, "and we are going to steer to the side...You know what I told you, Vernyct," he added looking at his lieutenant. "Watch for him, and if he reappears, do not miss him!...Monsieur the Mayor," he began again, holding out a hand to the postmaster at a sign from his lieutenant, "if you would like to lead us a little of the way, I will give you the necessary instructions..."

"To double my position…"

"Yes," replied Argow ironically, "to double your position."

The horses were harnessed to the pirate's carriage, and the young driver seemed to be having a great deal of trouble controlling them; and if the mayor-postmaster-innkeeper had not had his vision slightly altered by that sparkling product of the Champagne region, he would have seen that his driver was behaving in such a manner that although he was seeming to restrain the horses, he was pricking them with his spurs.

"We gave you new horses!…" he said supporting the trembling Melanie, to whom the driver made a clever signal. When the young lady had gotten in, the horses started to draw her away, but he restrained them, playing the game perfectly; for as soon as M. Gargarou and the pirate had sat down, the horses left as if there were a legion of devils chasing them.

Melanie uttered high cries…"We are going to tip!…Where are you taking me!…Help!…"

"Do not fear a thing, my beautiful little lady," said

M. Gargarou. "Monsieur the Count," he said to Argow, "is this a good carriage?"

"Yes," responded Argow.

"Then we will go all the faster. The young man is a good driver, he is one of my wife's cousins."

"Very well, where are you taking us?..." asked the pirate.

"Help!...They are kidnapping me," Melanie was still crying.

"Where am *I* taking you?" said the driver, "it's the horses because I am no longer the master of them!" ...(and the clever rascal spurred them.) "This is the first time that they have had a carriage."

"You see," said the postmaster, "they have taken the bits between their teeth."

"Go by the forest!" cried Argow, "I do not ask for anything better."

"I will go there if I can!" responded the driver who followed the road into the woods seemingly carried away by the horses. Melanie was still crying out; Gargarou consoled her repeating that there was no danger; and Argow, uneasy about his prey, spoke to the driver who did not listen to anything.

At last the carriage rolled with a frightening rapidity down the forest road. From afar the driver noticed the two carriages. He asked for passage by shouting and striking his whip, but the carriages remained immobile. This palpable danger greatly moved the postmaster, who feared for the lives of his four horses, who might break themselves against the carriages; the driver and the postmaster cried at the top of their lungs; Melanie trembled with fear, for she knew that this was the place where the rescue would take place. Argow looked ahead to brace himself for a crash and save Melanie; and the noise was such, that no one heard the sounds of the horses that were following the carriage.

After a minute, the carriage arrived among the other carts, and the two front horses hit them and fell. Melanie uttered a cry, the driver hopped out, Gargarou trembled and Argow felt himeslf seized and gripped by ropes which were wrapped around the middle of his body in such a way that he could not make a move; he swore like the *Thirteen Cantons,* and ended up breaking the carriage by the efforts that he made to escape from the power with which Cachel pitilessly gripped him. The vicar seized Melanie joyously. Two men contained Gargarou; and the other three, with their rifles aimed at the Argow's servant's chest, kept them from opposing the rescue.

The pirate, foaming with rage, was strung up so that he was forced to remain immobile like an inert mass. They tied up the Mayor without listening to his opposition and they placed all three of them on a cart. Argow, like all those with great character and who think of *power,* did not say anything and contemplated the vicar with a concentrated rage. Gargarou, like all imbeciles who believe that cries and complaints can change destiny, quieted down so that he could say to the woodsmen: "I am the Mayor of Vans!...Untie me!..." They did not listen. He sought his driver with his eyes, but the clever young man had hid himself.

The vicar order Cachel to fix the carriage. They brought two horses to replace the two that had died. He put Melanie back in the carriage. When all was arranged, and Cachel's accomplices had left the vicar said to the woodsman:

"You will lock up these three men in your cellar; and you will hold them until an express mail gives you a letter from me, telling you what to do with them. Feed them! Keep them from escaping! And, in your interest, try to make sure that their cries are not heard. If this rescue gives rise to any law suits, let me know right away and I will make them cease...understand?..." And the vicar gave a purse of gold to the honest Cachel. The woodsman covered the three captives with sacks and had the horses trot towards Aulnay.

When the vicar was alone with Melanie and Cachel was far away, the young driver reappeared and brought Argow's carriage at a great gallop back to the inn. Melanie, when she learned the part that the hostess had played in her deliverance, left her a gold chain as a souvenir. Joseph paid her well for the two horses that had been killed and paid the driver once again who drove them right away "belly to the ground," to Septinan.

There Melanie and Joseph took up their own coach, and the driver was instructed to take the carriage back to the castle at Vans.

The young lady, overwhelmed with joy, kissed Madame Hamel and Finette; and the coach flew towards Paris with all of the speed of a Gascon lawyer who has just found out that his cousin in the ninth degree has been named a minister.

CHAPTER 28

What scenes of love! What a gracious voyage! Melanie overwhelmed her brother with roses. A deluge of enchanting caresses inundated him, and despite the regret which began to gnaw at him, he could not refuse savoring this charm which was no longer so criminal.

"Joseph," said Melanie carried away by the speeding carriage, "Joseph, we are going to marry. We are no longer brother and sister; that is to say, we will be so forever, but we will add to the gentle feelings of our childhood, those feelings which a wife owes her husband. I won't be pale any more, and you are the one who will give me the new beauty that my cheeks will be glowing with...Isn't that so Finette?... Joseph, you are not saying anything, you are looking at the countryside... It is sad, and we are happy, why, because our hearts are delirious, and in seeing me, you seem to enjoy the appearance of happiness, so why are your eyes seeking the winter emblem of sadness?"

"Melanie," responded the vicar, "don't you imagine a resounding joy?..."

"Oh! no, no, my love, my life, my happiness, no, I know the august silence of delight; but," she added smiling and taking her own hand away which the vicar had held to his forehead, "shouldn't a young lady speak little...Still, Joseph, this babble of intoxication displeases you, I am going to be silent..."

"Yes, be quiet Melanie!"

The young lady no longer said anything, and she began to look at her *brother* with a sort of uneasiness. "Since when," she murmured, "have Melanie's words not been pleasing to Joseph!"

"My sister," responded the vicar holding back his tears, "I believe that I have proven to you that I love you...Celestial girl, virgin!" he added letting a tear fall on his *sister's* astonished face. "I can only adore you, why suspect my feelings? Go...I will give you the greatest proof of love that a man can give..." He stopped. "And..." he said, "for the peak of happiness, you will not know..."

"You are crying Joseph," (and Melanie cried) "you are crying!...What is wrong with you..."

"Melanie, I am crying out of happiness!"

She looked at him with a fright that she was not aware of. She was careful not to open her mouth; and during the rest of the trip, she looked with the curious care of love at the least gesture, the least look, the least word of the vicar.

The latter, noticing his *sister's* uneasiness, tried to dissipate it by shaking off the melancholy which had taken hold of him from the moment when he began thinking of the new barrier that he himself had raised between himself and Melanie; but his gentle caresses, his words could not dissipate the cloud that had formed in the young lady's soul.

Soon they were in Paris and found themselves back at their lodgings on the Rue de la Santé. As they went in Melanie gripped her brother's hand and led him into the living room. With a graceful gesture she showed him the seat where he had been sitting before leaving, and she told him, "That was where I was thinking of you!...Ah!" she began again, "I was thinking about you everywhere."

The vicar fell into a melancholy that was as deep as the one that had taken hold of him when he had found out that Melanie was his sister, and that he could not marry her. Meanwhile this perpetual reverie had a certain charm; for in this new position, the social prohibition was not the same; it was not as strong, but Joseph's battles with himself were not any the less violent. His mother's story kept coming back into his memory and not finding anything in his heart to make him distrust either Madame de Rosann or M. de Saint-André, he made use of this adventure like a shield. One can easily judge the violence of these battles, if one thinks for a moment of the religious spirit that the vicar was imbued with. The fidelity of his oath, his conscience, his belief in religion, everything made the tearing of his soul a thousand times more cruel; for beside these bonds rose up one of the most passionate and most pure loves that has ever entered into the heart of a man. This strange suffering of the soul cannot be described; the imagination cannot conceive it for it would have to apprehend the vicar's entire soul.

"Well," he wrote, "if I marry Melanie, won't she remain pure? She does not know about my being a priest. She will still be virtuous. I alone would be the criminal, and then who will know about it?...God, I am a wretch! my conscience tells me, but won't He pardon so much love?...And besides that, isn't Melanie worth eternity? What lover would have made such a big sacrifice!...Yes, Melanie, yes, celestial beauty, I will marry you. I cannot suffer the sight of your eyes which turn towards me languishing any longer. It is a weakness to wait...besides, the good curate, didn't he tell me, as he left, that one is not criminal in obeying nature. Ah! I believe that simple soul...Ah Melanie! Gentle spouse! If you ascend to the heavens, you will beg for my pardon and your hand will draw me out of Hell!...O anguish!...But what, Joseph, that is egotism. You do not dare to sacrifice yourself!...Let's go, wretch, take courage."

. . .

"No, I cannot, for then Melanie would just be my mistress! She would not know it. She would believe that she was my spouse, but I, I would know the opposite, and that is a delicate affair, an honest man would not do it. Rigid virtue does not want me to marry her. Let us die!...Yes, but she is dying!..."

. . .

"How she smiled at me a moment ago!...O divine face!...O Melanie! I will marry you...this moment has decided everything!...The women's faces shine with a certain grace that nothing can define...O let me forever engrave that moment in my memory, for a ray from heaven has fallen on Melanie and revealed to me that she will be my spouse! Besides, priests used to be able to marry! Our brothers the Protestants, who are of the same religion, marry. I will not be guilty!..."

. . .

These phrases give an idea of the exact situation that Joseph's soul found itself in. He only had two thoughts, two *notations* in his soul: "Will I marry?...Yes." Then his melancholy became gentle and Melanie hoped. "Will I marry her?...No." In this instance of virtue, he was somber, savage and his worried lover cried in secret.

One can tell that Melanie must have been chagrined. She participated all the more in Joseph's preoccupation since she did not know about it; she could not imagine what could make him like that at the moment where happiness surrounded them; but as she loved with that gentle submission, that respect which the one who loves the most has, she did not dare to question her brother. She looked at him crying, she deplored his lack of sharing with her and devoured her own sadness.

Nevertheless, after a few days, one night when she was sitting in a corner by the chimney they found themselves alone, Melanie got off the easy chair and came to sit on Joseph's lap as he looked sadly in turn at *his sister* and the fire, and gave her caresses filled with grace and sweetness. She ended up setting on Joseph's mouth a long loving kiss, and passing her hands several times through his hair while staring curiously into his eyes, said to him:

"Joseph, it has been eight days since we came back and were reunited; and you have not smiled at me…Do you know that the dawn of marriage is hardly brilliant…My friend, for eight days I have respected the secret of your melancholy…Do you know that that is a lot for a woman…It is too much for you, to hide the cause of your sorrow!…Why are we not together now?…I will not suffer it because I really doubt that it can be delayed, for you love me, don't you?" (He made a pained sign with his head)…"Very well! what is with you, Joseph? Pour your sorrow onto my chest, it was made for that…I am sadder not knowing, than if I knew…Let's go, Monsieur!…For I will call you Monsieur…When people tell me that the horses are ready, I will say: Monsieur is he dressed? This Monsieur will be Joseph, my brother, my husband…"

These words marked with a childish grace reminded Joseph of the scene in the Terrible Valley; they drew him from his lethargy, right away he thought that in truth he was not alone, that his sister shared his sorrow, that she had been a witness of it, and that their confidence demanded that he give a reason for his melancholy.

"Melanie," he said with emotion, taking her hands and staring at her.

"Oh Joseph! Do not look at me like that, I am afraid…You pierce my soul…"

"Melanie," he began again, "I am sad for good reason, and I will tell you why: I have no name, I am a natural child, in the eyes of the world this birth brings with it a sort of stain, and I experience shame to…"

"O Joseph!…Joseph," Melanie cried interrupting him, "I know you poorly!…For I did not think that you were capable of such pettiness and…You do not know me at all, if you thought for a moment that this social misery could enter into my soul…O my friend, I blush for you!…Cruel man!…"

"Divine soul!" cried Joseph, his eyes filled with tears, "who would not sacrifice his soul for you?…"

"What, my brother, is that what you were worried about!…I am glad that we spoke of it."

Then the vicar dissimulated with a movement of false joy that made Melanie shiver.

"Ah," she said, "I will not see you sad any longer, and we are going to marry!…" Joseph covered her with kisses and withdrew. When Madame Hamel returned and Melanie naively told her the subject of Joseph's sadness, the good woman got angry for the first time in her life and cried: "I do not recognize the boy I raised!…"

Two days later, as Joseph still had the manners and

words of sadness, Melanie seized on a moment when he was shut up in his room and knocked.

"Who's there?…" asked a brusque voice.

"Oh I do not respond to such a tone! Speak otherwise, Joseph, and I will tell you that it is Melanie."

"You can come in, my sister!…" he responded gently.

"That is it!" she said with a charming naïveté. "Why, my friend," she added drawing near to him, "are you fleeing me? For two days during which I am kept from all that supports my existence…speak to me, my dear, the sound of your voice will make my suffering cease."

"Pardon me, my sister, but a disposition of the soul, whose yoke I cannot cast off, is saddening me. My senses are erring, obscured, and the notions of good and evil are indistinct for me…"

"And so," Melanie interrupted, "because you are in this state you are fleeing me? It seems to me that if ever my soul began languishing, I would seek you out to dispel it. I recall that once I found myself like that, it was during your absence, suddenly I thought of you, of your gentle words, and your charming form...and all my sorrow flew away!..."

"You win! *Demon*..." the vicar cried...and he pressed Melanie against his heart.

The young lady looked at him with an inconceivable astonishment for this word, this action, were marked by a taint of craziness..."What is wrong Joseph?..."

"What is wrong!...I will marry you...I betroth myself to you forever!...We will be happy Melanie, if Death does not hear us!..."

"What you say frightens me!..."

"No, no, do not be frightened! Now," he added with a sardonic laugh, "I am going to be happy, very happy!...I have just taken up my role!..."

"What a voice!...Joseph, my friend, you suffer...Joseph?"

"Very well what is wrong with you?...I will marry you..." After a moment of silence, he told her seizing her forcefully by the arm:

"Melanie, I beg you, promise me...listen!..."

"I am listening."

"Tell me," he began again with a melodious and

plaintive tone of tenderness, "tell me, if to belong to one another you were only able to be my mistress, what would you do?"

She titled her head towards the ground.

"Do not hesitate!" cried the vicar, "it will be our death!…Respond, yes!…No!…"

"Joseph," she responded with the flame of love in her eyes, and on her lips the gentle smile of innocence, "I do not hesitate."

"Then what would you do?"

"I would drown my infamy on your chest!" she cried with a burning energy, "I would be so virtuous, good, tender, that no one would have the courage to condemn me and my love would enforce the silence. Besides, Joseph, that does not concern us, it is up to me to consent if my lover is so bad as to agree…"

"I will marry you! I will marry you!" cried Joseph with a cry of horror.

Since that scene, which was terrible by the expressions which animated these two charming beings, the vicar drowned his regrets. He asked for M. de Saint-André's death certificate, that of his birth, and they published their bans at the Town Hall and the church. Melanie was at the summit of happiness, and the vicar, leaving the bounds of strict virtue, surrendered himself to the delights of his passion with the fervor that men of his character carry in their virtues as well as their abandonments. Melanie, constantly turning her head towards that of her beloved, was at last satisfied with the ardor of his love.

"I have found you again!..." she said to him; "you are the Joseph of the mountains, the one who once wrapped me in vines to carry me back to our house..." And these gentle words were followed by even softer kisses.

The day of their marriage came slowly for Melanie, too quickly for the vicar.

"Melanie," he said one morning, "I have not given you a wedding present. You do not see one..."

"Do I need one?" she interrupted, "the most beautiful present that one can offer a spouse, is the husband's heart...and...I have it..." she said with a fine smile.

"Look, Melanie!..." and the vicar presented to his

future wife the portrait that he had painted in his seminary room.

Melanie shivered with surprise.

"My sister," began the vicar again, "on this day I sacrifice to you…" She looked at him.

"No!" he cried, "I cannot say it…"

"Do you love someone else?…" she asked with anxiety.

"Good God! Melanie, that is the second time in my life that you have asked me such a question. It is too much for my heart!"

It was at midnight, in the church of Saint-Etienne-du-Mont, that they were supposed to make their last vows: the ones that the imaginations of most people have surrounded with the most pomp and the most trappings by having the God of the skies intervene.

The solemn hour of the wedding night arrived. Melanie, dressed like a wife, was resplendent with a celestial beauty.

Never had a crown of orange flowers been set on a nobler, more beautiful, purer head. The vicar contemplated her in this ravishing attire and this gentle spectacle made all of the murmurs of his heart silent.

"Joseph," she said, "we have picked a very somber time…to marry: I do not know what cold is chilling me beforehand, when I imagine that we are going to find ourselves…alone, in a dark church, at midnight, in the shadows, in the silence, and…It will not be a party."

"You are really a woman," responded the vicar with a disdainful smile. "What evil can befall us? We are rich, we are in love, we do not fear anyone!…Very well, dear Melanie, who stops us from being more happy, to flee the world and go against human law?"

"No, no," she replied, with a light smile, rapping her pretty fingers with a handsome fan, and presenting her foot in front of the fire, "no, I want people to admire our happiness for a moment! Let them know that you possess Melanie! I want to reappear as your companion…And when you have gathered the incense of their envy and I have satisfied the pride that society has given me, when I have seen how the looks of envy will be turned towards you, then my Joseph, we will flee to the Terrible Valley, to the Bermuda Isles, wherever you want, on a deserted rock, as long as you are there, it will be splendid…"

"Melanie, it is eleven thirty, and our horses are stamping in the courtyard."

"Clever dear, you are rushing me…I guess your game…I want us to come back here as much as you do…We are alone, aren't we? For that is only said between spouses!…But you see, Joseph, I am cold and it would be scandalous for a wife to get cold…"

They stepped into the carriage and arrived in a few minutes at Saint-Etienne-du-Mont. The church was not lit, the chapel in which they were to be married was located at the back of it, and the candles did not cast triumphal glow. Joseph, upon entering into this basilica, had a feeling of fright which obsessed him for he was not able to chase it from his soul.

"Do you see it?" he cried.

"What?" said Melanie.

"Death!…" responded the vicar.

"You are joking?" replied Melanie…

"No, no, look!…"Then the vicar showed Melanie that the first object that came into view was a dead head on a black cloth. In fact the church had not taken down the funerary trappings which had served at a burial, because there was going to be another one the next morning.

Melanie shivered and an icy cold slipped into her soul.

"Joseph...Why make me sad?..."

"O my sister! I beg your pardon!...Let's go...keep going so that it does not follow us..."

They arrived at the altar: no one was there yet. Joseph left Melanie kneeling beside Madame Hamel and their people, and he went towards the sacristy to rush the priest. In going in, he took off his coat and began dressing as if to say a mass.

"What are you doing?" asked the sacristan.

He looked about with an astonished air and responded: "I am almost crazy...I am so happy..."

At last the vicar was on his knees beside Melanie. A priest arrived to marry them: he was one of Joseph's former confessors...He drew back with fright ...He came down, took Joseph to the side and asked him: "Aren't you a priest?..."

"No!..." cried Joseph, "I am not a priest!...

No!…No, Monsieur!…"

"If that is so," began the good old man again, "I was mistaken…excuse me."

Joseph kissed the hand of the venerable priest. The latter, astonished, said to him: "why are you kissing my hand?"

"I am not a priest!…" Joseph repeated.

To be sure, such a ceremony, done in the middle of the night, was rather imposing. The darkness, altered by the trembling glow of the candles which reddened the pillars slightly, an old priest imploring heaven, and among these circumstances, a young lady, the love of nature, lovely with all possible beauties, formed one of the most poetic paintings of our religion: but what makes the scene even grander was the presence of the young husband, whose pale, haggard eyes cast about him the deep look of someone who is committing a crime. Fortunately, gentle Melanie did not look at Joseph! And her entire soul implored for union with the eternal for such was the beauty of her heart that this celestial vision effaced all of her charming desires.

At the moment where the priest turned around

to speak to the couple and he stopped because of Joseph's pallor since the latter's face contrasted with that of the pure Melanie, a great noise was heard at the church door, and hurried steps were heard in the hall. Joseph turned around and in the distance he saw a woman shouting: "My son!...My son!..."The vicar rushed forward, he had recognized Madame de Rosann, and he ran to meet her.

"My son, what are you doing!..."

"Mother, be quiet," cried the vicar, "be quiet!...Be quiet!..."

"How can you marry?..."

"Silence, listen to me!...Do you love me?..." he asked with energy forcefully seizing the Marquise's hand.

"I love you!..." responded Josephine, raising her eyes to the altar; "good God! He asked if I love him!..."

"Very well, my mother, if you do not want to see me die..."

"Die!..." she cried with fright.

"Yes, die," responded the vicar. "Turn around!

Keep silent! I will come and see you, I will bring my Melanie to you, and above all, mother," he repeated as if delirious, "never let the fatal secret of my state as priest leave your mouth…If Melanie hears of it…I will die!…"

"My son, let me see!"

"No, no, mother, tomorrow, early, as soon as you want, but now…"

Madame de Rosann remained stupefied…Joseph, who had turned around, had seen the curious Melanie looking at the Marquise with anxiety, and he hurried to rejoin his wife.

"Joseph," she said, "who is that lady?…"

"That is my mother!…" Joseph responded.

"Ah!…" cried Melanie.

The Marquise hid herself behind a pillar and silently contemplated the august ceremony, which told her of all the vicar's melancholy and the importance of the secret which she would have to keep.

"My daughter!…" said Madame de Rosann kissing Melanie.

"Since you are Joseph's mother, I will indeed

cherish you!" said the young spouse whom the Marquise clutched to her breast.

"Go, you will be happy!…" said the Marquise.

"Look, Joseph," replied Melanie, "can you see how the dead head is smiling at us…it is a lucky sign!"

"Alas!" said the vicar, "how can you say that?…"

"Very well, my children," began the tender Marquise again, "are you crazy enough to worry about that?"

"Mother," responded Melanie with a charming smile, "it is because we are truly intoxicated!…"

"Charming!…" cried the vicar.

Joseph, Melanie, Madame de Rosann and Madame Hamel came back at one o'clock at night to their lodgings on the Rue de la Santé. After the first moment of joy, Madame de Rosann, having kissed her children, felt that she should leave them alone…

Melanie, after having cast a last virgin look at Joseph, was the first to leave, followed by Finette and Madame de Rosann.

She went into that room which was decorated with the most elegant luxury. She smiled at the sight of a faint white glow that was almost fantasmagorical which escaped from a lamp contained in an alabaster vase: she looked at the sumptuous bed, the arrangement of the furniture, and did not dare look at Finette since her chest was palpitating.

"O mother!..." she said, throwing herself against Madame de Rosann's breast, "How happy I am!..."

"Yet you are crying?..."

"I am crying out of instinct........."

. . .

Finette came to close the marriage room, and Madame de Rosann, shedding a tear, withdrew. If Finette smiled, I can also smile! But I should imitate her, and put a lock on all that I am entitled to think. Then smile if you want!...Let your imagination exercise itself and fill in the lacuna that I have left! Will you fill this page with voluptuous ideas?...As for me, I will not do so, for I love Melanie too much; and the future frightens me....

. . .

. . .

So we will draw the curtain as well; and we will meet Melanie again when her gaze no longer has that gentleness, that satisfaction which shines in the eyes of a spouse; when the ardent flame will have become moistened, and love will no longer hold up anything but a pure torch in place of its sputtering flame. During this time we will see by what chance Madame de Rosann attended her son's wedding.

CHAPTER 29

While all of these events took place in Paris, strange things were happening in Aulnay-le-Vicomte; and to fully recognize the motivations behind this other adventure, we must go back to the time when Jacques Cachel brought Argow, his servant, and the poor M. Gargarou back on his cart.

The woodsman arrived without problem back at his hut, and after having opened his cellar, he moved his captives there one after the other, and when they were all there, he looked at them crosswise and said to them: "Do not think of crying out, for I am not nice when I am angry!…You will be treated well, and set free when I have received the order…"

"Monsieur," interrupted Gargarou, "are you attached to the legitimate government?"

"That is to say?…"

"If you are a good Frenchman you should not detain a mayor named by the king."

"Sing something else," said the woodsman.

"Listen," responded Argow, "if you release me inside of two hours I will give you a hundred thousand francs…"

At this proposition the woodsman left, and ordered his wife to bring food to the prisoners, but with plugged ears so that she would not let herself be beguiled.

Still, despite the prisoner's silence, and the discretion of Cachel and his wife, one could not stop the news from spreading; and as it spread through Aulnay-le-Vicomte by the means of Marguerite and Leseq we will introduce the reader into M. Gradaval the mayor-grocer's shop.

"*Because* you see," said the latter, "Jacques Cachel has added a stable to his house, and he buys many things from me which he pays for with gold. He has become rich,…because…" Here he looked at Leseq.

"Yes," finished the latter, " it is clear, one does not get rich suddenly without some trick, *sine turpitudine,* and *latet anguis in herba,* as Cicero says, 'There is some snake in the grass.'

"Listen to me," said Marguerite setting a pound of sugar on the counter…"Madame Vernillet's sister, the concierge at the chateau, came yesterday; and she said that the big lord of Vans-la-Pavée was someone who did not smell like balm, and that Monsieur Joseph's sister, who is not his sister, he had kidnapped; for it is a story that you do not know and which I will tell you some day; it is very interesting, there are pirates, yes, it was a pirate that Monsieur Joseph said was at Vans."

"Fiat lux," cried Leseq, "that is to say, give us a candle to see clearly into what you say, *age quod agis,* do not chase two hares!…"

"In the end," began Marguerite again, "it was she who said that our vicar kidnapped a girl, and that the big lord is a scoundrel. According to what Madame Gargarou said, who was brought to our side, and I maintain, I repeat, and I claim, as I maintained a moment ago that Jacques Cachel is in it for something. At the castle in Vans they would really like to catch him; but as one knows the saints must be honored, says Monsieur Gausse, and Jacques no longer goes to the castle."

"Fortunate senex, happy Leseq," cried the school-

master, "I see another twelve hundred francs to earn," and he flew off like an arrow.

"What did he say?" began the mayor again opening his eyes wide. "Where is he going?..."

"I do not know," responded Marguerite, "but what I know is that he is a clever guy, and that if he wants me to make his happiness...Monsieur Mayor," she said, "if he earns twelve hundred francs a month like that, he is a good match..."

"Bah! Business is not good!" responded the mayor.

Marguerite told everything to the good curate who easily guessed that the young lady that the vicar had kidnapped was Melanie.

"I can clearly see what will happen," he responded to Marguerite, "but each is the child of his works."

Meanwhile Leseq raced to the castle, and when he was in Madame de Rosann's presence, he took his hat off respectfully and said to her:

"*Risum teneatis,* be joyful, Madame Marquise, with care and action I have discovered where our vicar is."

"Very well," responded Madame de Rosann, "where? Tell me, let's hear, hurry!"

Leseq twisted his hat. "Madame," he said, "Jacques

Cachel saw him the other day, and he…"

The Marquise rushed outside, leaving Leseq alone. She saw to it herself that her men were getting the horses ready, and she drove off to the woodsman's house.

The first thing that she noticed on entering was on the chimney the address that Joseph had given the woodsman to write to him, in case of trouble. Then, Josephine, without saying a single word, seized the paper, went running back down the mountain as fast as she could go, to the great astonishment of Cachel and his wife, and she went to A…y, with her horses at a gallop. She took the coach and went to Paris where we saw her again.

The sudden departure of the Marquise gave the inhabitants of Aulnay-le-Vicomte a lot to talk about; Leseq among others got the idea that Cachel's hut contained some mystery, and began wandering around it, spying on what was happening there. One morning he entered, under the pretext of telling Madame Cachel to send her children to school because the vicar had paid for their education.

"Oh! Oh!…" he cried, seeing the woodsman's

wife making a soup that was too large for her house-
hold, "Oh! Oh! Mother Cachel, so your children are
eating a lot?…"

"A lot," responded the housewife.

"Ah, that's a leg of lamb, a chicken!…"

"It's a party in house!…" said Madame Cachel.

"Now you are important people!…" responded
Leseq casting furtive looks around the house.

"That is nobody's business!…" responded the
woodsman's wife curtly. "What do you want from us
this morning?…"

"I came for your children…" at this moment Argow's laugh broke out below Leseq's feet.

"What devil is down below us?…" he asked.

"My husband is drawing wine with one of his
cousins."

The more Cachel's wife grew impatient, the
more the clever Leseq pretended not to see her, staying and rummaging around with his eyes.

Then Jacques Cachel arrived from the forest
striking his whip.

"Ho there, wife!…open the door?…"

Right away Leseq understood that there was some

mystery and he swore to discover it. Saying goodbye to Madame Cachel, after having cast her a sly wink, he returned to Aulnay-le-Vicomte.

The next morning, he went with the judge to the mayor's shop saying that they needed to talk about an extremely important affair...When they were seated in the back of the shop, the schoolmaster began talking in these terms: "Messieurs, you are the two great authorities of the village, *consules Romae.* Well, you know if up until now I have failed to serve you, to be useful to you, today the *magnum practicum* presents itself—a great occasion to *ire Corintho,* to increase your rank, and to make the names of Gradaval and Marignon famous. There is in this commune, chief villains, counterfeiters, or great scoundrels, you choose!..."

At these words, the mayor and the judge looked at the triumphant Leseq with an unparalleled anxiety.

"*Florentem cytisum sequitur lasciva capella,* these words of Cicero mean that a judge should pursue criminals, *trahit sua quemque voluptas,* one does not argue about tastes! but if you believe me, there is one step to take."

"But," said the judge, "explain yourself, and if you find a way to make me a judge at A…y I will give you my post here at Aulnay."

"If you increase my business…"

"Everything will happen," replied Leseq. Then he told them about all that he had heard at Jacques Cachel's house. "You feel that *rem tetigeris acu,* you will put your finger on the wound in making a judiciary visit to the woodsman, to do this announce that he is keeping prisoner there the scoundrels from Vans-la-Pavée, whom the government is looking for; or he is the chief of these criminals, or at least, he is making counterfeit coins, *falsos nummos.* For where did he get that gold which he pays you; and he has bought thirty bottles of Bordeaux."

"And good wine at that!…" cried the mayor.

"This is becoming very important," said the judge.

"Leseq," said Gravadel, "in my life I will not try to hang a man!…"

"Monsieur the Mayor," began the judge again, "state security requires…"

"Yes, yes," Leseq interrupted, "we must *coercere la-*

trones, pursue the criminals!…" At that the schoolmaster, raising himself to lofty considerations, proved by his speech that they should encircle Cachel's house and discover the mystery. His eloquence drew in the mayor and he was resolved that at nightfall Gradavel in his sash and the policeman in his robe would meet with their attorney and Leseq to visit Cachel's hut.

In fact, at eight o'clock in the evening the squadron set out, followed by the field warden, and M. de Rosann's guard, who were policemen. Arriving at the woodsman's door, Leseq knocked brusquely: *"Attolle portas,* that means to say, open up, it's the law, the King, etc."

"You see," cried Cachel's wife, "we have gotten into trouble for keeping the brigands."

"Who are you?" asked Cachel.

"Open up, it's the law!…" said the judge.

Recognizing this voice, the woodsman opened the door and the official squad entered into Cachel's house.

"Jacques," said the judge, "you are marked as harboring people whom you should have delivered into the hands of justice…We will search your house, unless you prefer to tell us the truth."

"Go on, tell them everything," his wife added.

"Cachel," began the judge, "after your last advanture, if you are found guilty of anything it will go badly for you…Tell us truthfully…"

"By God, Monsieur, I was going to tell you: in my cellar I have three brigands who had kidnapped the girlfriend of our vicar, Monsieur Joseph. They were going to take her away to the Dauphiné, when a month ago our vicar stopped Monsieur Maxendi's carriage since he is, it appears, as you would say, the chief of the brigands of the sea; and he charged me with guarding them until he wrote to me, to tell me what to do next."

"It's a criminal affair!" said the judge; "a chief of brigands!…If it was the one that they pointed out to the royal prosecutor at A…y, what a discovery!… Cachel, you are going to follow us, and put the criminal in our hands."

"Yes, officer, but you will assure me that nothing

will be done to me for having arrested and detained him…"

"No, no, you will even be remunerated!…"

At these words, Cachel, judging that this was all that the vicar desired, to be free of Argow, thought that his prisoner would be even more secure in the hands of the law than in his own keeping; and so he led everyone into the cellar, and when the assembly had all gone down, M. Gargarou began crying out: "Messieurs, I am attached to the government…and I am…"

"Be quite, crook," Leseq responded to him.

"How am I a crook," replied Gargarou, "I am the mayor of Vans-la-Pavée."

"The mayor of Vans-la-Pavée,' cried M. Gravadel, "it's true!…This is Monsieur Gargarou."

"Ah! Monsieur Gravadel! " said the mayor-post-master-innkeeper, "you are a good Frenchman devoted to the government, I hope that you are going to free me from my bonds and give me justice."

"Monsieur," responded the judge seriously, "you find yourself implicated in an criminal affair of the first order; for it is nothing less than armed thefts and attacks committed at sea...So you are with pirates?"

"No, Monsieur," began Gargarou again, "I am a postmaster, sincerely attached to the legitimacy, and I am innocent."

"What is your name?" said Leseq to Argow.

"I am Count Maxendi."

"Maxendi!..." began M. Gravadel again, "you have been denounced to all the mayors of the region, as a man to be arrested right away! The royal prosecutor at A...y wrote to us."

"And I read the letter!..." said Leseq.

Argow looked at them all proudly and said: "That may be, Messieurs, but I am innocent, the estimable Monsieur Gargarou will affirm it to you and for the rest, to prove to you that I do not fear the light of justice, untie me and I will follow you. If you think that it is necessary to put me in prison, I will go there with pleasure, for I am certain that in twenty-four hours the *qui-proquo* will cease and that on the contrary it will be I who can claim the vengeance of the laws to punish my assassins..."

"Ta...ta...ta..." said Leseq, "Monsieur, you were

the one who kidnapped the girlfriend of Monsieur Joseph our vicar…"

"What!…" cried Argow, making his most lively joy obvious, "Joseph is a priest!"

"You are," responded the schoolmaster, *"habemus reum confitentem,* he betrays himself."

"No, no, I do not betray myself, my friend," responded Argow becoming calm again, "let's go, Messieurs, be done with it…"

Upon Gravadel's commanded they untied M. Gargarou, who, after thanking the group, fled without waiting for the rest. Argow and his servant were given over to two guards; they led them to Aulnay; and, as there was no prison, they locked them up in Leseq's school and named him the jailkeeper.

This arrest caused many tongues to waggle, and as in anything there were two opinions. Half of Aulnay regarded Maxendi as a scoundrel, and the other half as a *victim.* The opinion of this latter half was greatly disconcerting to the judge and M. Gravadel, who greatly feared being compromised, for the prisoner's assurance, his clothes, his opulence, strongly supported the reasoning of those who claimed that the mayor and the policeman had been led astray.

But an event occured which delivered M. Gravadel from his unease. Argow began by sending Leseq to buy sugar, bread, six bottles of liquor, liqueurs, smoking tobacco, tea, and other provisions in such a quantity that the mayor found that the pirate had very good manners and that he was not as devilish as people said.

When everything had arrived in the prison, Argow implored Leseq to help him make a punch, and politely invited him to drink.

"You seem to me," he said to the pirate, "an excellent boy, and I would be very annoyed if something bad happened to you!…"

"And I too, *me quoque*," responded Leseq.

"Do you sometimes ruminate?" the criminal asked him.

"Almost always," said the schoolmaster.

"Very well! Will you listen to me?" began Argow again, "for me there are only two ways of being: either I am criminal, or I am innocent."

"Aequum et justum est, nothing is more true."

"If I am criminal,' said Argow, "I am sure that you

would regret having had a man's head cut off for the rest of your life. For it is possible that even though I am innocent they could find proofs…but there are not any…If I am innocent, you are gravely compromised, and one does not impudently arrest a man like me…in any case, what devil could be mad at you if I happened to save myself through the funnel of your chimney…do you hear me? You will have no responsibility, nothing can harm you, I offer you *a hundred thousand francs,* to open the door for me tonight…"

"A hundred thousand francs!…" cried Leseq, "where are they?…"

"Take them!…" cried Maxendi opening his wallet and counting out the banknotes, "there, you see them!…"

The schoolmaster remained stupefied.

"That is not all, I want to shield your conscience from any remorse: if I ask to flee, you must naturally believe me to be guilty…That is not so, I want to leave because I want to avenge myself, and in three days I need to be in Paris. If I stay here one night longer, they will transfer me to A…y, and there I would have to wait for my business to clear up: but, can you imagine a delayed vengeance?...As long as I need it at this very moment, I enjoy the spectacle that a word can produce...let's go, my firend, let's drink, and think of that..."

"A hundred thousand francs for opening a door!..." cried Leseq, "wait, I will consult Monsieur Gravadel and the curate..."

"Imbecile," said Argow stopping him, "do they need to know about it?...Listen to me first of all: you tell me that Monsieur Joseph, a big young man, handsome, brown, is a priest."

"What, that is our vicar!"

"Very well! My friend," cried the pirate, "go on decide yourself!...For in two hours it will be too late."

"I fully believe that it will be too late," said the schoolmaster, *"equites,* that is to say that the policemen will come, we are waiting for them..."

"In that case," began Argow again, "I only give you three minutes!..." The pirate put his watch, garnished with gems, on the table and while Leseq reflected, he took off his ring and searched for his needle crying: "Everything is against me, I want vengeance!…"

"*Ego prendo,* it's a deal!…" said Leseq.

"You have done well, friend," responded Argow, putting the needle back into his ring. "Let's go!…"

"And the hundred thousand francs!…"

"I leave them there for you,…" said Argow, "take me out of the village, and you can come back and get them."

The schoolmaster led the criminal and his sailor all the way to the forest path; and after having wished them a good trip, he went back to his school and clutched the hundred bank notes. Then feigning a great sadness, he closed the prison door and went to the policeman and the mayor whom he told that the two criminals had escaped out the window. As he was finishing his litany, the royal prosecutor and his men arrived in Aulnay to seize Argow. The people of Aulnay told them of his escape, and right away the policemen set out in pursuit of the criminal.

The latter, careful not to go to his castle, went to Gargarou and took a coach to Paris.

Chapter 30

It is impossible to describe the happiness pure and sweet that reigned in the rue de la Santé! the gentle Melanie, having all that she had hoped for, ressembled a newly cannonized saint among the heavenly throng. This calm voluptuousness does not offer any features to the art of the poet or the writer: it is like the painters of paradise who cannot paint the spirits, because once someone told them: "They have all possible happiness." Everything has been said, for there is no nuance in perfection; it is good and evil mixed together which alone can make things comprehensible. In the end, the passion of these two beings purified itself even in that state where men's passions take on a tone of sensuality. The fate of these two charming beings was to give to everything that they touched the quality of gold like the fabled king. In truth, they ennobled everything by the charm of their manners, the beauty of their souls, and the perfection of their qualities.

Madame de Rosann was not out of place in the

middle of that touching and perpetual scene of a love that would survive that which kills love. She kept very silent about her son's terrible secrets, which she did not even speak to him about; and this tender mother experienced Joseph's happiness absolutely as if it were her own. She could not leave Melanie whose gentleness, beauty and charm won her over. In the end, Madame de Rosann wanted to make this happiness last and to set it apart from all possible threat, to place it outside the grasp of the devouring hands of evil, to use her honor and that of the Marquise de Rosann to end her son's promises, and to revoke his priestly vows. She found a relation in the ambassador to Rome, and the Bishop of A...y knew one of the cardinals who was an intimate friend of the Holy Father. So, without telling her son of all of these steps which would crown him with success, she looked forward to the fine day when she could make her Joseph entirely happy by bringing him the papal letter which would secularize him again, and the order from the king which would make him heir to the title and holdings of M. de Rosann.

So everything was prepared for the couple's happiness, and fortune seemed destined to smile on them forever. Alas! The demon had decreed that the monster who had afflicted their family would pursue them ceaselessly.

Although the vicar had succeeded in silencing all of the cries of his conscience; or at least to listen to them without allowing the chagrin which devoured him to appear on his face, Melanie was not without guessing that her husband was not content.

One evening Joseph was obliged to accompany M. de Rosann to a diplomatic meeting and Melanie found herself alone with Madame Hamel. The young woman uttered a sigh, looked at her second mother and said to her, "Mother, have you noticed how my Joseph is sometimes dreamy?"

"My daughter, it is quite simple, men often think about the great ventures that they are concerned with."

"But, stepmother, Joseph is not dreamy because of that...Look, stepmother, let me explain my thinking to you. I am so happy that I can compare myself to a pure sky whose gentle and calm azur has no clouds; very well, to be sure Joseph ressembles an enchanting sky, but he has about him that mist that one sometimes sees in the air when there is a wind and one is on a high mountain."

Madame Hamel remained astonished contemplating Melanie's face which shone with grace, and on whose forehead all the poetry of her ideas appeared; Melanie began to smile, recalling that never had the good woman ascended to the height of a poetic idea; and she began again like this: "Listen to me, mother."

"I am listening. I enjoy it, but I do not understand you."

"Look," said Melanie, "look in the mirror, do you see that spot which darkens its shine?"

"So what?" said Madame Hamel.

"So," Melanie began again, "that spot is Joseph's spirit, and the other part of the mirror is mine."

"Where do you go to find everything that you say, little girl?" said Madame Hamel. "You are joking with me...Joseph is happy; he does not have any sorrows."

"Yes, mother, he has...That is to say that he is happy; but his happiness is not complete. I fear that either he has a chronic malady which is gnawing at him, or that he did not find in me all that he thought that he would find…I will ask him!…" she said shedding a tear.

"What an imagination you have!" cried the good woman.

"No, mother, I am not making anything up. Unfortunately, my soul is *too much like his*. I feel by contrast what is in his heart; for he does not have a thought which is not mine, and I maintain that he is not the same as he would have been if, having never thought that we were brother and sister, we had married in M…"

"But who is making you presume all of these things?" said Madame Hamel, setting her glasses on her knees and looking at the clock which was striking eleven.

"Mother, sometimes I look at him, and he does not smile at me. Often, in sleep, awakened by dreams or unease, I feel his forehead to assure myself that he is still there; his forehead is burning. He speaks, and in his sleep he seems to be fighting with strangers who want him to be a priest…In the end, think what you want, cherished mother, I feel that he has something in his soul. Yesterday, when he heard a bell at Saint-Etienne-du-Mont, he said, 'There is another happy one!...' His tone said even more than his words."

"Melanie," the good woman interrupted, "it is late...goodnight!"

"Goodnight!...You should have stayed anyway since Finette is out..." She is deaf, the poor mother, she said to herself; in fact, Madame Hamel had not heard and she had gone.

Melanie remained alone in the big living room, counting the minutes, thinking that each coach belonged to Joseph. After a moment of reflection, she cried: "Bah! Maybe Madame Hamel is right, I am making up worries..." After fifteen minutes she said; "I'm cold...my soul is shiverring on its own, something is going to happen..."

She looked around the room, listened amid the silence, checking for sounds. From afar she heard the rolling of a coach: the rolling approached...her heart beat. "Oh!" she said, "It's Joseph!..." In truth a coach entered into the courtyard, she leaped forward, feeling a general shiver!…The door opened…Argow appeared…Melanie fell on her easy chair, chilled with fright.

"You were expecting your husband!…" said the pirate with an execrable smile. "My lovely fugitive, have no fear of me…Look, I will stay right here, and I promise to behave…I only condemn you to one pain, that of hearing me…"

"That is a horrible trial," Melanie responded, "and I want it to end…"

"No, you will not escape me! I took everything into account; you are mine!…"

Melanie was prey to a deep horror, seeing that the ropes to her bell were cut.

"One does not walk away from a man who wants vengeance," said Argow, "for I have taken every precaution: your husband will not be back for another hour. Your servants are not here. Finette is away, and they are keeping her. You are in my power…But I will not touch you!…I abhor you!…" he cried energetically. "Yes, to relish this minute of revenge I have cast like a spider an invisible web. Since I must be a demon, I will be so until my last breath!…And as a servant of Satan I will do all the evil that I can. Since you refused, cruel beauty, to hold out your hand and draw me out of a life of crime."

"Ah! Don't talk to me like that…"

"Don't talk to you?…What I am going to tell you will ring in your ears until your death!…It is coming, there is a sword over your head, it hangs by a thread, I am going to cut it!…"

"No, Monsieur," said Melanie with a light smile, "my happiness and my life are no longer in your hands…"

"Child," replied the criminal with a deadly laugh, "I told you, I am extreme, and the day that I become virtuous, I might be too virtuous!…But at this moment, I only want one thing—*to avenge myself!*…And I warned you once never to stir up the tempest that destroys forests, because you are just a flower!…"

Melanie was speechless, her eyes staring at the energetic face of Argow who remained calm and looked like a statue.

"A last drop of pity remains in me," the pirate

continued, "and I leave you a minute of happiness, before causing, forever, sorrow to devour your young heart."

Argow fell silent, then, after a moment, he said: "Do you love Joseph?..."

"Oh yes!..." and a smile came to wander on Melanie's icy lips.

"Your love is based on respect?"

She made a gentle movement of he head.

"It will end," began the pirate again.

"Do not finish. The lie dishonors the man!..." cried Melanie.

The pirate began to laugh, and said to her:

"Melanie, you think that you are beautiful, virtuous...You are nothing but an infamous woman; your marriage is *nothing,* your husband is a *priest!*...And you are...*a concubine!*...You blush?...You can stop, people like you never blush."

"I am dying!..." cried Melanie, "I am dying!... Help! *Ah! I am wounded to death, I can feel it.*"

"Joseph, that rare man," continued Argow, enjoying his victim's agony; "that Joseph whom you so cherished, is a scoundrel. He lied to you!…He abused you!…"

"No, no," she said, "my brother is virtuous!…" Her cry of love was heartrending.

"Virtuous?… Like you…You are plunged into debauchery, infamy…"

"Is that all?" replied Melanie calmly, containing her terror.

"No!…" said Argow coldly, "that is nothing!…"

"What do you mean that is nothing?…" cried the young lady shivering.

"Yes, you are going to come to my feet, I am going to see you!…" he said with a hideous expression of rage, pointing to the floor. Melanie stared at him intently like the lamb that trembles before the African *boa* constrictor.

"To your feet!…" she murmured feebly with the tone of a crazy person who laughs at his own suffering.

"Yes," replied the criminal, "I want my vengeance to be striking. Do you think that I am satisfied with the sorrow which will assail you?…No, no, I want all the world to know that you are infamous, that Joseph is going to be hanged!…"

"Be quiet, be quiet!…Monsieur Maxendi,…by grace, be quiet!…"

"Be *hanged,*" he began again emphasizing each syllable of the word; "a criminal trial will be known everywhere: 'Melanie de Saint-André is nothing but a concubine!…' And you will not find a person in France who will not say it to your face!…You will not be received in society. Your mother will not want her daughter to come near; and, from tomorrow, a letter will be brought to the office of the attorney general, to tell about your crimes. My revenge will be aided by the revenge of the law."

"Monsieur Maxendi, if to avoid such a disaster, you want me at your knees, to be sure I will drag myself…" Poor Melanie, seeing a sort of hesitation on the pirate's face, advanced slowly towards him on her kees, took his hands and looked at him with an expression of supplication which would have tamed a tiger. She said to him: "Argow, if you ever had a mother that you loved!…Then by that gentle memory I ask you to spare Joseph…I have had, for the last ten minutes, death in my chest. I have felt the fatal blow of its scythe. You should be content with a victim such as I!... You will be the one who has killed me!... If...what you have just told me is true..."

"You can tell," the pirate said coldly, "if Joseph is a priest, then he is tonsured, and whatever care he takes to hide the top of his head from you..."

"That's true," she said with fright...

"You only have to look!"

"Argow," she began again, "I beg you, keep the secret?..."

"What will I get out of it?"

"One less crime," she responded.

"Very well, so be it!...I consent...Goodbye Melanie, we will only see each other again in Hell!..."

The pirate went softly away, leaving the vicar's spouse still on her knees in the middle of the living room. She remained in this posture for a long time, as if she were lost in a deep meditation; and she held out her hands saying: "You promised me!...Look," she said, "he is not there!..."Then she got up, sat in her easy chair, leaned her head on one of her hands, set her elbow on an arm of the chair, and she was not drawn from her preoccupation until a gentle voice said to her: "Very well! Melanie, my love is sleeping, I believe?…"

"Who is speaking?"… she responded with a distracted air.

"Ah Heavens! What is wrong with you, Melanie?…"

Then she looked and recognized her spouse, and this celestial creature, disguising her sorrow, responded:

"It's you Joseph, I was sleeping…How unfortunate that I did not hear your coach, so I could not run out to the stairs and be brought back in your arms!…"

"Melanie," began the vicar uneasily, "you have been crying!…You are pale, changed, your eyes are no longer smiling, what is wrong with you?"

"Listen," she said, "Joseph, I had a horrible dream!…It bothered me, and I must have cried in my sleep."

"Then why didn't you go to bed? It's one-thirty…"

"It is a sacred time for us," she said forcing a smile, "and besides, today we have been married for a month…"

"Melanie, you are trembling!…" cried the frightened vicar.

"That is because I am cold!"

"You are cold, and yet here is a fire that is burning ten feet away…"

"It does not matter, my friend, I am all ice…all!…" she began again, "oh no, my heart will always burn…Joseph, warm me with your kisses… Look, sit down there…" And Melanie indicated her brother's ordinary place to him on the loveseat. The vicar set himself on it. Then the young woman took Joseph's head, and set it gently against her chest that was palpitating with terror.

"What is with you tonight, Melanie, your heart beats with an extraordinary violence! What is with you, my dear?…You are hiding something from me, I repeat for your eyes do not look at me with that charming expression of love which always animates it…A feeling that I am afraid to name is mingled with it…"

As the vicar spoke these words, Melanie, holding her spouse's head captive in her pretty fingers, gently caressed her brother's hair...A secret horror kept her from looking at the tonsured place, which was not so effaced that a trained eye could not recognize it. Fate urged the poor, unfortunate woman on...She cast a furtive glance...

"Melanie!" cried Joseph, "Melanie."The vicar took a vial and made her smell salts. She remained immobile. He covered her with kisses!...Ah that caress, it opened her eyes, and closed them suddenly. The vicar, frightened, having no idea what could kill Melanie, lavished the most touching cares on her.

"My friend," she said in a weak voice..."I thank you..."Then, seizing the vicar with a terribly energetic grip, she squeezed him with all the power of love, kissing with this voluptuousness that the idea of a sacrifice makes more ardent and almost *frenetic*.

"Melanie," began the priest again with a tone of reproach, "can you imagine such a scene in the middle of a happiness that is *pure?*"

"*Pure!*..." cried the young woman with fright; but suddenly getting hold of herself, she said;

"Joseph…my chill has passed…it has given way to a fever…look…" She took the vicar's hand, and brought it to her forehead, he shivered with fear, finding Melanie as burning as if torrents of flame had replaced the blood in her veins.

"My friend," she said, "do not be astonished at seeing me sick…I love you too much to live…Souls that direct their moral strength towards one feeling should be quickly consumed when their passion is too strong."

"Melanie!" cried the vicar taking ten steps backward, "now you are making me chilled…"

"Come, come, dear! Come and banish all of your fears…You know that women have moments of folly…That an overly serious consideration made in the middle of this night, when I was alone…That dead head that we saw in the church of Saint-Etienne-du-Mont the night of our marriage came back to my memory; a thought came into my head…My spirit found itself with a bad disposition…What can I say to you?…Look, come, a kiss will fix everything!… Do not go away!… Joseph!" she cried imploring him:

"I feel strong enough to love you more than ever!…"

Then, chasing away the clouds of funerary sadness that were found marring her forehead, Melanie cast her deathly chill and her horror into the depths of her soul. She kept quiet with an admirable sense of devotion, and put on the stippled robe of joy, her most brilliant and most voluptuous one, she covered herself with joy forever, and her illness only made that much more progress.

Nevertheless, this strange scene struck the vicar, who became more thoughtful and who began observing with astonishment the increase that Melanie's love took on after this fatal evening. In truth this victim of love, crowned with flowers, like those who walk towards death in their youth, doubled her testimonies of tenderness, imprinting them with such a burning charm that the vicar could not help believing that something supernatural was at work inside Melanie.

Is it not before the tomb that joys are more keenly felt and that the grip of life has more strength?

CHAPTER 31 THE FINAL ONE

After several days, Melanie, devoured by the sorrow which silently undermined her, was obliged to remain in bed. She fought for a long time before taking this cruel step, for she felt that she would only get out of her bed to go to the tomb. But one morning she tried to play one last piece for the vicar before whom she still forced herself to appear well. She set herself before her piano. Her feeble fingers could not cause the ivory keys to make sounds...Then tears escaped from her lovely eyes. She got up and leaning on the cherished instrument whose tones pleased Joseph so much, she painfully went back to the loveseat. Still crying bitter tears, she leaned her head on Joseph's chest; and as she had not slept a wink in three nights, she fell into a light sleep.

"Mother Hamel," said Joseph in a low voice, as soon as Melanie was asleep, "do you know what internal suffering has made our poor child become so pale?"

"My friend," the excellent woman responded, drawing near and showing the vicar a face marked by a fatal sadness, "do you think that I waited for you to ask?...Do you think that I do not love this angel on earth, that I have not noticed how she grows thinner every day?.. Each day her pallor becomes more and more terrible. Once she adorned herself with roses, with gracious crowns to please you, yesterday she crowned herself with black flowers!...Yes she told you laughing that it was the style...the style, Joseph, is in her heart. Her lips are becoming white. Her noble smile that is so loving when she looks at you is sad when her eyes fall on me!...Do you believe that I have not noticed all of that?...My son, for three days I have been questioning her...The poor child did not want to say anything: but go on, Joseph, she is forcing herself on you!...For she is out of strength: I often take her hand, and never have I found her to be without a horrible fever...You do not see that she wants to disguise her suffering from you so as not to afflict you, just as you would towards her...Joseph, there is no time to lose...I assure you that Melanie is quite ill...Look?...Even in this touchingly innocent sleep, her cheek is devoid of those lovely colors which made other women despair; and under her white skin, there is a funerary color…"

Sobs kept this poor woman from going on: this speech, the longest that she had ever made in her life, could only have been uttered by her on such an occasion.

The vicar, immobile with horror, looked with crazed eyes at the gentle movement of his companion's breast. Her half opened mouth seemed to devour the pure breath that escaped from Melanie's discolored lips. This grand vision of celestial eternity which shines on the face of a dead young virgin already appeared on the gentle face of this admirable woman. These terrible signs which the vicar had noticed at Aulnay, in the delirious features of Laurette, caused him to shiver and he felt inside himself a horrible convulsion move his innards.

"Celestial angels…" Melanie murmured faintly in her sleep, "you will not disdain me!…I am pure…I only loved too much…that was my only crime!…"

"What do these words mean?…" said the vicar.

"When will I sleep forever?.." Melanie was still

murmuring waking up and casting about her uncertain looks of waking. A tender expression animated her face when she contemplated Joseph and Madame Hamel.

"Melanie," said the priest, "you owe me an account of your slightest feelings…I require that you confide the secret of your pain in me."

"Joseph, I would have told you everyting when I would have told you that I was suffering, my friend," she said, "I am ill…very ill…but I tell you because you are big and your soul is strong, you should not be astonished by anything."

"But Melanie, who could…"

"My love," she responded with a smile, "yes Joseph, my blood is boiling, nothing can cool it any longer, for at each moment the sight of you heats it again…and…I would rather die than not see you…"

"Die!" cried the vicar who for the first time, saw the full extent of the danger that Melanie…"Die!…"

"Joseph!…" she responded with a frightened air, "do not be so little a master of yourself, for your pain will kill me. Imitate me, my friend…and let's live all of our lives without sorrow! Surround me with joy, flowers, smiles, love, and all that human life, luxury, feelings, and hearts have of what is splendid. If I must die of this illness that is devouring me, you cannot keep…so your soul is strong enough to conceive what is necessary, since I am weak, I believe it; I am taking my last steps on the golden sand like that which you spread on the paths that lead to the Terrible Valley!…Yes I live!…The sorrow would still be too much, to die like this, and the happiness of my manners…"

Meanwhile the vicar's stupor was too great, and Melanie cried out painfully: "Joseph, you are ahead of me!…" She fell on him, and it was with great pain that they carried the dying lady to her bed.

Right away a servant climbed on horseback and went to get a doctor. He came, drew near Melanie; and after having examined her, he put on a jocular air and cried: "All that this pretty woman needs is some dissipation and the countryside."

"Yes, Monsieur," she said: "the countryside…the heavens," she added in a low voice. "Joseph," she began again, "and you mother, go away…"

They left with tears in their eyes.

"Monsieur," said Melanie, "I only have three days left to live! You must have guessed the cause of my affliction?...The terrible event that changed my role as wife was a cruel scene...Nothing can save me, for I have the conviction that I must die... You knew it didn't you?"

The doctor remained silent.

"Look, Monsieur, I am responsible for myself up until my last breath, I am going to be happy and laughing. Promise me, just swear to me, to fool my husband, and to persuade him that it is nothing, and that I was frightened by a trifle. Tell him to fool him all the better, because," she said laughing, "it is admirable for us women to trick you even on the subject of death. Tell him to take care, as well as Madame Hamel, to take away the ideas that have been slipped into my head. For what I imagine can delay my cure. It is too strong. It harms me, and if one does not change my mind, I will begin to languish...Then my husband will not offer me the cruel spectacle of his pain...and I will take with me into my tomb the hope that he will survive me...I will no longer be an unfortunate woman..."

The doctor, struck by this speech, looked at her with surprise caused by admiration. "Ah! Madame," he said, "if this is your death, then how have you lived?"

She began to smile, and said to him: "Do you promise me?"

"Yes, Madame…"

"So," she replied, "you will come from time to time, and, each time you will tell them that I am much better…They are at the door" she began again, "come on, my friends, enter!.." she cried softly. The vicar came in and looked in turn at Melanie and the doctor.

The latter got up after having written a meaningless prescription. Madame Hamel and the vicar hastened to follow him…He was faithful to what he had just promised Melanie so the priest and the old woman came back with smiles and satisfaction.

"Melanie," said the vicar, "in a month you will dance at a ball. If then Madame de Rosann has obtained the decree making me a peer of France, we will have here a superb assembly to celebrate your convalescence: it is nothing, my well-beloved." He spoke for a long time on the subject of that divine angel who slowly came to agree with the vicar's feelings.

Never had Melanie been more touching, more gracious, more caressing than in this last part of her life. Not a complaint left her mouth; and to dissimulate, she disguised the cruel marks of her illness under careful make-up, so that she preserved a sort of freshness. The fever animated her coloring with a shade that made her brilliant with beauty. She perfectly resembled a candle at night that, ready to expire, casts a last glow that shines with a thousand sparkles. Even her spirit had a gentleness, a sweetness that felt like heaven.

When the fever ceased and her face took on a livid tint that was the messanger of death, she became pale, disordered, her deep iron eyes darkened and her discomfort was too evident. She pretended to want something rare, and she required that it was her husband who needed to go get it. The vicar was fooled. He went and ran around Paris. When he came back with the flower, the jewel, the book, the desired finery, he found Melanie radiant.

In these last moments, she overwhelmed her husband with proofs of the violent love that had held her since her younger years, and Joseph was astonished by this frenzy of love!...A man who knew Melanie's secret would have burst into tears if he could have guessed the admirable thoughts that were making Melanie act like this.

Madame de Rosann was fooled by her son about the gravity of her daughter-in-law's illness, and even though she came to see her often, she did not conceive that Melanie was ever in danger: she laughed and cried with her; and the vicar's gentle lover was prey to a celestial joy when she noticed that everyone except Madame Hamel had fallen into the trap that she had laid. As for poor Madame Hamel, sitting on Melanie's bedside, she foresaw death and contained her sorrow with a heroic courage. This old woman was admirable for her sang-froid. She showed her sensitive soul and united the firmness of Cato with the warmth of her gender's feelings. She seemed in the bedroom of her cherished girl to be tranquil, calm. She helped her in a thousand little ways with the love of a mother and the punctuality of a soldier.

Meanwhile her eyes stared at Melanie and guessed the secret thought behind each gesture. Madame Hamel knew that her girl was going to die, and she said to herself with an unimaginable sang-froid: *"I will follow my girl…"* She got ready for her death as if for a pleasure trip, as if she were going to visit a newly acquired property.

One morning, it was in the month of March, Madame de Rosann came running into the apartment; and her son, seeing his mother's horses covered with sweat, and their harnesses white with foam, decided that she had just learned something very important. This good mother raced up the stairs. She hurried into the room, fell into her son's arms, and cast on the table the papal letter which secularized Joseph, and the King's order giving him the name of Saint-André de Rosann, the title of count, and the right to succeed M. de Rosann as a peer of France…Joseph fainted from happiness…He woke up and cried: "O mother!…You have given me honor…and I owe you my life two times now…"

"My son, now your marriage is legitimate."

The former priest glowing with hope, joyous

with an indescribable joy, went into Melanie's room, where she was prey to a violent bout of fever. Joseph arrived by his wife's bed, he took her hand, he kissed it with ardor: he wants to speak to her, the bubbling of his heart stops him…

"Joseph…What is it?"

"Melanie, when I married you I was a priest…"

"I knew it!…" she responded growing paler, (Joseph and Madame de Rosann were stupefied) "and," she said, "that is what is killing me. Joseph, maybe I loved you…"

"Who told you?" The vicar interrupted. "Who was the monster?…"

"Argow…Three weeks ago, he came to tell me the fatal secret. Go, he has his vengeance."

"Melanie! Melanie!" cried the vicar, "I am not a priest anymore!…Here is the Pope's letter… which…"

At these words, said without consideration, Melanie…My pen escapes me….

...

...

...

Can you see on the Rue des Amandiers two very simple carts advancing slowly to the last resting place?...

A single man follows the first one...the man is pale, he is dishevelled, he is only looking at the ground...

A woman follows the second one: it is Finette weeping for Madame Hamel...

The weather is gray and the ground dirty with a liquid mud. Joseph and Finette do not see anything. Despite the lack of trappings at this funeral procession, many people stop and consider one of the most touching scenes that pain has ever offered.

Madame de Rosann did not see her son again, even though he had promised to return...

The angels of heaven have taken back the present that they loaned to the earth...

....

Forseeing my own pain, at this moment, I placed the conclusion of this work at the beginning.

Editor's note

Just as I finish this tale, some friends have given me documents which permit me to give a sequel to this story. Then, as soon as the jury of the Court of G..., in the department of Isère, has made its decree, I will give to the public the sequel to the *Vicar*.

It will appear at the start of next December; and this new novel will have for title: *The Criminal*.

H. DE SAINT-AUBIN.

The America Awards

FOR A LIFETIME CONTRIBUTION TO INTERNATIONAL WRITING
Awarded by the Contemporary Arts Educational Project, Inc.
in loving memory of Anna Fahrni

The 2006 Award winner is:

JULIEN GRACQ (LOUIS POIRIER)

[France] 1910

Previous winners:

1994 AIMÉ CESAIRE [Martinique] 1913

1995 HAROLD PINTER [England] 1930

1996 JOSÉ DONOSO [Chile] 1924-1996 (awarded prior to his death)

1997 FRIEDERIKE MAYRÖCKER [Austria] 1924

1998 RAFAEL ALBERTI [Spain] 1902-1998 (awarded prior to his death)

1999 JACQUES ROUBAUD [France] 1932

2000 EUDORA WELTY [USA] 1909-2001

2001 INGER CHRISTENSEN [Denmark] 1935

2002 PETER HANDKE [Austria] 1942

2003 ADONIS [Syria/Lebanon] 1930

2004 JOSÉ SARAMAGO [Portugal] 1922

2005 ANDREA ZANZOTTO [Italy] 1921

The rotating panel for The America Awards currently consists of Douglas Messerli
[chairman], Will Alexander, Luigi Ballerini, Peter Constantine, Peter Glassgold,
Deborah Meadows, Martin Nakell, John O'Brien, Marjorie Perloff, Joe Ross,
Jerome Rothenberg, Paul Vangelisti, and Mac Wellman.